FULL COURT

Stories & Poems for Hoop Fans

Edited by Dennis Trudell

BREAKAWAY BOOKS
Halcottsville, New York
1999

FULL COURT: Stories & Poems for Hoop Fans
Edited by Dennis Trudell
Compilation copyright 1996 by Dennis Trudell

ISBN: 1-891369-12-1
LIBRARY OF CONGRESS CATALOG CARD NUMBER: 99-73051

First paperback edition, October 1999. (Originally published in hardcover, by Breakaway Books, as *Full Court: A Literary Anthology of Basketball*.)

Published by BREAKAWAY BOOKS
P.O. Box 24
Halcottsville, NY 12438
(800) 548-4348
www.breakawaybooks.com

For a list of other sports literature titles published by Breakaway Books, please write to us at the address above, or visit our website.

FIRST PAPERBACK EDITION

CONTENTS

Introduction
Dennis Trudell

I wanted this book to exist because I love to read and I love basketball.

And there was no gathering of strictly "creative" writing about what is surely one of our most spontaneous, creative sports. While many literary baseball anthologies were available, fans of basketball and writing had only collections of journalism, or journalism mixed with an occasional story and novel fragment. Yet basketball is now our nation's most popular sport (fifty-four percent to forty-six percent over baseball, I read in the newspaper—though we're talking about passion, and how does one measure?). Further, it is a sport that our genders and races and classes play, bumping and rubbing in confined spaces, during all seasons throughout the U. S.: from farmyards and suburban driveways to housing-project courts and packed dirt churchyards. From suction-cup hoops in college dorms to milk crates nailed on phone poles. As I write this, a boy somewhere tosses underwear at a basketball laundry hamper; a girl in pigtails shoots alone in a haybarn; a seventeen-year-old slams an imaginary ball through a netless rim above smashed crack vials.

I once scored sixteen points in a grade-school intramural game to lead "Yale" to a championship over "Army." That is not very interesting to anyone else, but is of lasting importance to me. I had only scored six other points all season; and whatever else happened that day in Morris Peabody's gym—he who in 1950 insisted we shoot underhand free throws—I left there in love with a hole ten feet in the air. With a love song and story, I could never quite tell *enough*. One that later years on other courts, in driveways and parks and schools (on auditorium stages or gyms trespassed on weekends), would broaden and deepen. I learned the joy of jump shooting while learning the one of reading— during those indelible, crazed teenage years of learning to hide erections after glimpsing bras across school aisles. Basketball and stories, basketball and desire. . . . The pairing occurred before I knew enough of this world to count my change. Before I knew enough of language to read or write any truth. The pairing has occurred, and occurs, inside countless others. How could at least some writers not try to make literature about it?

How could at least some of that writing *not* hold the intensity and rhythm of the game itself?

Meanwhile, since 1950 the society around our hoops has changed, sharpened alas in many ways; and poets and storytellers have tried to tell us how and why. The best basketball stories and poems are about something other than basketball, something more. Several years ago I started putting writing I liked in a folder, hoping an anthology might appear to show me still others, and now and then I'd write my own. (Still trying to tell you how that magic bubble felt that even Morris Peabody had to acknowledge . . . how that kid from South Chicago grinned in a Wisconsin park after using my ball for his first basket: first song of ball-through-net.) When no anthology appeared with a literary focus, I decided to make my own.

I think one reason for basketball's popularity has to do with time—the amount of drama that can occur (two time-outs, a three-pointer, answering jump shot, missed wild hook and tap-in) with only twelve seconds left on the clock. A TV game fits more snugly into a viewer's evening than an often endless-feeling nine innings. Basketball's fourth quarter seems more elastic than football's because athletes cover its "field" much faster than any kickoff return. But I believe it is *space*, rather than time, that highlights the sport's appeal and its literary possibilities.

Basketball simply requires less of it, which of course is why it is played in inner cities where ballfields are an extravagance we're apparently unwilling to provide. Thirty-odd kids—two pick-up teams and two waiting, plus advisers, scoffers, younger siblings, and maybe some pets

—can be entertained in the space a pitcher, batter, and catcher would occupy. We could fit several hundred kids shooting through dusk in a single foursome's fairway. And within that confined area, the yearning is always for empty space: the yard of it to a defender's left, the bit of it above his or her palm, the sacred circle of it waiting above grunts and sneaker-squeaks We maneuver for *inches* out there; we fill that bright orange (or rusted outdoor) hoop through amazingly precise calibrations of hand and arm and air and ball.

Basketball is also unique, and a ripe source for literature, in being so physically close to worlds around it. Siblings play in a driveway ten yards from parents ending a marriage, or reviving one. Kids play HORSE in a city park watched by homeless people, jogging executives, drug dealers, a wandering poet, an uncertain priest. Baseball and football and soccer fields are often apart, tennis courts fenced in. Basketball players and kibitzers are more likely, like it or not, to be reminded of what surrounds the game.

Often the grace they display is won from realities looming off the courts as well as from hands and taunts and elbows within bounds.

So. I had some stories and poems in a folder, and later I searched the University of Wisconsin-Madison library for more. I found them, a richer batch than I'd expected, through indexes and roaming aisles and interlibrary loans and dumb luck. I spent hours thumbing tables of contents for possible basketball titles (turning needlessly to many a story or poem: does "A Shot in the Dark" refer to late-night hoops or a gun, or a guess?). I no doubt missed many with non-basketball titles I might have preferred over some here. I advertised in *Poets & Writers* for submissions—and received over one hundred responses. They were fun to read; they confirmed my sense that this book should exist. I want to again thank those of you who sent writing. I returned most submissions, since the library turned up such quality that it was hard for "walk-ons" to get in. But some are included here; and I hope all of you who submitted material enjoy the result you're holding.

I *know* there are other basketball stories and poems out there that should be preserved. I wish I'd found more telling about worlds in and around inner-city courts. I want to know more about the worlds of women players. . . . And about how it feels on NBA courts, and on their benches and spouses' and parents' distant sofas, that sports pages don't tell. We need imaginary writing to help us discern hoops from religion, which sportswear and media concerns want confused. No claim is made that this is the ultimate basketball literary gathering. Only that it is a rich one; I hope later others will help correct what I missed or you haven't written yet, or I was too insensitive to value.

Readers will notice these selections are arranged from youthful settings and concerns, through high school and professional, to writing about aging and death and post-game dreaming and silence.

As editor, I get to name some names here. There was a 1950's All-American named Johnny O'Brien who took his 5' 9" into the pivot for Seattle University and scored many points (fed there by his twin brother). I know because I saw his hook shot in a newsreel as an eighth-grader; the next day I was "Johnny O" whanging hook shots off the rim behind the high school—and my nickname stayed "Ob's" until graduation. Meanwhile, Ohio State's Robin Freeman broke scoring records with his behind-the-head jumper, then dropped out for part of a season because of strain from the publicity. Then returned as a senior to score again and be drafted to the NBA, then lost fingers in an accident with an axe. . . . And I was learning how basketball isn't separate from what resonates through literature.

Later I read that Robin Freeman became a dentist—and if that seemed sad to a young Trudell wanting to continue seeing that jumper, it now holds the resonant hopefulness I most deeply value in poems and stories. The best creative writing about basketball or anything else is always about love. If only love's absence, or its memory; and another name I want here is "Ob's" friend and driveway opponent, Ken Stepien, 1938-1990.

There was another Seattle player, "Downtown" Freddie Brown of the NBA, who scored a lot before scoring more crucially off the bench as they won a championship in 1979. Sportscasters would explain his nickname after he'd hit again from "way downtown"—and I'd yell the word to my sons in our parlor. But what I remember more vividly is his grin lighting up the TV, as Magic Johnson's and Isaiah Thomas' soon would: reminding us that if the game is about arcs and angles, coach-diagrams and sneaker prices and TV ads . . . it was and still is mostly about joy. "Downtown!" I yelled when he made a three-pointer in the Old-Timers' game a few years after retiring; and a few minutes later I got to yell it again. And then again, and yet again.

I always like the shooters—gunslingers. I grew up with all those 1950's Westerns. Although I believe that our nation's future won't truly grin until gatherings of "radical" energy somehow triumph, I guess a boy inside me still hopes for Shane. The stories and poems printed here suggest what other literary anthologies do: we fall short of our capacity for love and joy, despite our lovely games. No solitary gunner will clean out the valleys for us; no string of NBA championships will make life hopeful for kids who can't afford tickets, can't afford ball or grin. That will happen only when the grace, the teamwork, on hardwood floors and gritty asphalt is matched off court.

Dennis Trudell
Madison, Wisconsin

Full Court

At Center

Jonathan Penner

"**Y**our father remains a highly sexy man," Bruce's mother said. She meant well, but it was preposterous, and he only stared at her. Like his father, he was fat.

At this point—it was a talk she had with him often—his mother might get crude. "Women like men with some meat on the behind," she would say, curling her fingers.

These reassurances deepened his misery. What did she know about it? On the other hand, Bruce believed that his father, who never said a word on the subject, understood his feelings exactly. Playing basketball on the outdoor court at his junior high school, he had sometimes seen his father's Buick go by slowly and sympathetically.

Still, he was surprised when one Saturday his father came downstairs in a brand-new pair of sneakers and suggested, "Let's go shoot some hoops. Maybe I can show you a few things." He was surprised, and dubious. He certainly couldn't imagine his father leaping and ballhandling like the pros, or even like some of the older kids he played with. They went to a park across town, where there would be nobody Bruce knew. The basketball courts lay baking in the sun. His father peeled off a sweatshirt: his T-shirt was tight and robin's egg blue. His stomach hung. The crests of his nipples protruded shamelessly.

"At center, Big Jack Bienstock," he said, and dribbled up to a basket. His shot bounced high off the backboard. He jogged after the ball with closed fists, his rear end bouncing, and Bruce saw that he had made a bad mistake in agreeing to come.

First, his father said, they would work on foul shots. "You stand so." He planted himself on the foul line, dangling the ball in front of his crotch. Suddenly he squatted. Then he straightened, threw up his arms, and the ball went flying over the backboard.

Bruce chased it. "That's the old-fashioned way," he yelled over his shoulder.

"What?"

But his father must have heard, because when Bruce returned with the ball he was frowning. He told Bruce, "This is the way the big men shoot."

"I'm not a big man."

"You will be."

This would be over soon. In fact, Bruce could pretend that it was over already, that he was smiling at the memory of himself practicing the absurd shot. His father, keeping up a line of encouraging chatter, retrieved the ball with hustle and snapped bounce passes back to him.

But in a few minutes his father sank to the asphalt, winded. "Never smoke," he said. He wiped his forehead and stretched out at full length, like an earthworm after an all-night rain. When his breathing had eased he lit a cigarette.

Bruce practiced layups, starting his dribble from midcourt and driving as hard as he could for the basket to flip the ball gently up against the boards. He was missing more than he made. "Straight in," his father yelled. "Don't use the boards. Up and in."

"You're supposed to," Bruce said, knowing it would do no good.

"Like this." His father ground out his cigarette and slowly got up. Then he grimaced. He grabbed his right calf with both hands, hopping on his left foot.

Bruce came close, frightened. "What is it?"

"Cramp." His father sank back down to the asphalt, massaging his calf, rolling from side to side with his teeth bared.

When he could stand again he said, "That's it," and hobbled to the car. Bruce, anxious to get home and over to the junior high, ran ahead bouncing the ball, suddenly weaving his way to the hoop, grunting as he soared for a two-handed dunk.

But in the car his father said, "It's just as well we stopped. I'm having a little chest pain."

Bruce looked sideways. His father was hunched behind the steering wheel. "Did you have a heart attack?"

"Who knows?"

He hugged the basketball, breathing in its dusty rubbery smell. If his father died, he imagined, he and his mother would get a smaller car. She would call the Salvation Army to take away his father's clothes. His father's packed closet would be empty, dusty, and his mother would sleep alone. He wished he were someplace he could cry.

His mother was surprised to see them back so soon. His father told her, "I had a little chest pain, just a little." She glared at him, smacked Bruce's shoulder, then wheeled around without a word and grabbed the telephone.

Bruce came down from his room after the doctor had gone. His mother had begun to prepare supper. His father was sitting calmly at the kitchen table, a pillow behind the small of his back, reading the newspaper. "Are you okay?" Bruce asked.

"He couldn't tell for sure. He said I should rest, that's all."

"We'll eat early," said Bruce's mother. "Then Dad will lie down, and you can go out and play."

"He didn't think you should go to the hospital?"

"No. Don't worry, now," said his father. "Go wash up."

A half-flour later Bruce was outside again, bouncing his ball the three blocks to the junior high school. It was strange: he wanted to stay home. It would be his fault, he felt, if his father died while he was out playing. But with so little daylight left, and a game probably going on right now, his body took him to the schoolyard no matter what he wanted to do. When he could hear the players, each shout doubled as it rang off the brick building, he held the ball in his arms and ran. "Hey," he yelled, rounding the corner of the school. "Can I get in?"

Nobody answered, and he saw that he couldn't—it was already three against three. He didn't mind much. He often liked watching the good players more than he liked actually playing.

Little Madora was silky and fast. Madora didn't run, he sprang, and at every step his long brown hair flew wild. Then for a second he'd freeze like an animal, except that he'd toss his head once, and his hair would fall perfectly into place.

Paulie Pilner, the tallest, looked clumsy standing still. But he could melt every joint into the curve of his hook shot, as though the ball were a comet and he its tail. His jump shot began with an enormous bound, knees tucked up, so that he hung in mid-air high above the court until gravity pulled down the defender who had jumped with him, and then Paulie would release his high-arching shot.

Dick Brown's deadly jumper was the opposite, a beeline. And where Paulie was slow-motion, Dick was lightning: he was up and his shot was off and he was down again, already starting to follow in, while the man guarding him, seeing his mistake too late, was just beginning to rise in a useless leap. On the drive, Dick could break up his last step into a dozen fake moves, then get off his shot as though he were unguarded.

"Dick's a good guy," Bruce remarked to his friend Charley, who had just arrived and was sitting next to him, waiting for the next game.

"Dick's good," Charley agreed. "He taught me how to ass out."

Bruce was annoyed to hear that Dick had taught Charley. He said, "My father taught me some stuff today. He's not so bad."

"Like hell," Charley said indifferently. "That tub of lard?"

The game ended. Bruce and Charley were let in to play four-on-four, full court. Paulie Pilner's team, the losers, chose Charley, so Bruce got to be on Dick's team.

He had to guard Charley, which was hard. Charley was fast. "Hands up," Dick Brown coached. "Watch your man." Bruce tried, but playing full court he could never keep up. Bodies were flashing all around, and the shouting confused him. He stumbled after Charley, gasping.

Somebody said, "Our ball," and he turned to head the other way. Then everyone leaped together, struggling in the air. He was spun outward from the center, lunged back in and was kicked and elbowed. The ball was free at his feet and he pawed at it but couldn't hold on. Charley slipped by him for an easy basket. "Asshole," someone muttered.

They hardly ever passed him the ball. He got to shoot only twice, two easy bunnies. The first time, Ernie Rich loomed up and blocked the ball, and the other team took it away on a fast break. Madora said, "Fucking kid eats it." The second time he went too far under, and the ball hit the rim on the way up, rebounding into his upturned face. The rest of the game he was snuffling blood, wiping until his forearm was red. "The kid's got guts," Dick Brown said.

To Bruce's surprise, his team won. He licked his lips where the blood had dried, swearing to himself that he would do better in the next game.

But as soon as it started he knew it was going to be even worse. Charley kept getting around him and scoring. Ernie Rich's little brother, Junior, knocked him down, and Bruce was sure it was deliberate. Both times he got hold of the ball he was called for traveling.

They were behind, within one bucket of losing, when Dick Brown called time out. "We need some hoops," he told his team in a huddle. He put his finger on Bruce's chest, which Bruce tried to tighten, hoping Dick wouldn't squeeze one of his plump breasts. "You basket-hang," Dick whispered.

They came out of the huddle and Bruce trotted the length of the court. "Well, well," said Madora, noticing. Then the other team took the ball downcourt, and Bruce was left all alone under the basket.

Squinting, he watched the play at the far end of the court, waiting for a pass to be launched his way. Madora was dribbling back and forth, looking for an opening. Suddenly he flashed by Ernie Rich, making him stumble into Paulie Pilner, and drove for the basket. But Dick leaped and got a fingertip on Madora's shot. He leaped again, beating Paulie for the rebound.

Then from the tangle of bodies Bruce saw the ball rise and loop toward him, like a bomb released by the setting sun, and Dick's voice yelled, "Don't travel!" The pass was perfect. It took one bounce and settled into Bruce's arms. Everyone was running, streaming up the court toward him, Madora practically flying in the lead.

Don't travel, Bruce told himself, and struggled not to lift either foot from the asphalt. He picked out his spot on the backboard and locked his eyes there. But in the corner of his eye flashed Madora bearing down on him like a lynx, he wrenched his head around to look, and when he looked back his spot was gone. His muscles froze. At the last moment he managed, with a little lurch from the waist, to get the ball into the air, and Madora seemed to leap over his shoulder to slap it hard against the backboard, where it bounced off into Paulie Pilner's arms. Paulie flipped it downcourt to Charley, basket-hanging in turn, who banked it in. The game was over.

"Enough of this shit," Ernie Rich said.

Dick Brown looked at Bruce once. "Christ," he said softly.

Bruce tried not to meet anyone's eye. But Junior Rich walked up to him and stood so close their chests were touching. Dick said, "Fuck off, Junie."

"Aw, Dick," Junie said. "It's a fair fight." He bumped Bruce.

But Ernie Rich said, "Shut up, you little shit," and grabbed his brother by the shoulder. "He ain't worth fighting."

Now Paulie had taken out cigarettes, and Dick said, "Gimme." Paulie offered the pack around. "Hey," said Junie, grabbing. His eyes lit. Bruce saw with amazement that Junie had forgotten all about fighting—he hadn't even been mad. "Let's go around back," Junie said. "If my old man drives by he'll cut off my nuts."

Paulie passed a lighter. Then they all walked, Bruce in the rear, around the corner of the school building, out of sight of the road. It was starting to get dark.

Bruce knew he should already be home—for the first time since he had come, he wondered how his father was. But he felt unable to leave while his disgrace was so fresh. They all settled down in the darkness, on the steps to the gym, everyone smoking but Charley and him. The cigarettes' glowing tips moved in arcs, dimmed and brightened. Bruce found a spot near Dick. The air was getting chilly, but the steps were still warm.

"She starts shaking," Paulie was saying.

"I'll give her something to shake," said Madora.

Bruce could tell they were talking about Linda Kent, the sexiest girl in the junior high. He didn't know her, but she was famous—she'd do anything, she couldn't control herself. When you kissed her she began to shake. Bruce had talked about her to younger boys, repeating what he'd heard, and by now she seemed like someone he knew very well.

"She starts shaking," Paulie said. "I haven't even done anything, and she's going ape."

"I'll give her an ape," said Madora.

"I'm kissing her," said Paulie, "and she's shaking and like rubbing her tits against me. Then she takes my hand and sticks it up under her sweater."

"Jesus," said Junie, rubbing his crotch. "What're they like?"

"They're like that." Paulie pantomimed the palming of two basketballs. "I can't hardly get my hands around them." He reached up, groping at the height Linda Kent's breasts would be if she were standing in front of them. Junie rubbed his crotch harder. His brother said, "Junie, don't be so disgusting, you little prick," and grabbed for Junie's hand. "Rape, rape!" Junie squealed.

Listening there in the growing dark, his legs angled so no one could see he had an erection, Bruce felt at the center of the universe. From the nearby woods came the mating song of hundreds of frogs, rebounding off the walls of the school until it came out of the dark from everywhere. Bruce felt as though the only real place in the world was where he was sitting, in a dim cloud of smoke from the glowing cigarettes. He breathed it in until he felt light-headed with serenity. "I slide my hand down," Paulie said, "and she's wet. She's like a furnace. She's creaming for me."

"So?" asked Dick. "You screw her?"

"You know it."

"My ass."

"Go ahead, ask her." Paulie sulked a moment. Then he continued, "She's creaming for me. And she's shaking like all over. And she grabs my leg. And I've got this huge rod on."

"Jesus," said Junie, staring at Paulie's lean crotch.

"I've got this rod on. And she says Oh, Paulie, you're so *hard*. And she starts to rub it. Jesus." Paulie slipped a hand down the front of his pants to ease his position. Junie did the same. His brother raised a fist, and he hurriedly withdrew his hand.

"Then she says, Oh, Paulie, my pants are wet. And she takes them off. So I open her up and slip it in."

"My ass," said Dick.

"What's it like?" asked Junie softly.

Paulie took a long drag at his cigarette. "Nosy little prick, aren't you."

"I'll give her a nosy little prick," said Madora. "Right in the old twateroo."

The cigarettes were burned down, and one by one they ground them out. Paulie handed around the pack again. Madora took one, and Ernie took two for himself and Junie. Even Charley took one. When the pack came to Dick Brown he held onto it for a minute. "Hey Paulie," he said. "How about if this kid gets one?"

"Paulie, no," Junie whined.

"He'll puke his guts out," warned Madora, and then Bruce realized that it was himself they were talking about.

Paulie shrugged. "It don't make any difference to me. But not if the kid's gonna burn it."

"He'll inhale," Dick promised. He turned to Bruce. "You want to try it?" He held up the pack, flipped it from one hand to the other.

Bruce didn't. His father had stained, sick-looking fingers, panted when he climbed stairs, sometimes coughed until he was purple, and said it was smoking that had ruined him. "Sure," he said.

Dick handed him a cigarette. "Put it in your mouth and sort of draw through it," he said. "Easy, or it'll burn." He reached for Paulie's lighter.

Bruce was surprised at how slight the cigarette was. It had no substance at all, he could hardly feel it in his hand. But when he put it in his mouth it seemed huge, and he almost gagged. "You're drowning it," said Dick, and showed him how to hold it between his lips by the very tip. Then he struck the lighter. "Just draw easy." As the flame touched the cigarette, Bruce tightened his lips around its base and breathed in.

What he wasn't prepared for was the heat. He'd thought maybe he wouldn't like the taste, but had never imagined what was happening now: it was as though he'd swallowed flames. He staggered up, unable to breathe, the cigarette dropping from his lips, his eyes watering so he couldn't see. He took a few steps, still couldn't breathe, and sank to the pavement. It felt like a heart attack.

Then the night air was searing his lungs and throat, each breath making him cough as though his organs would come out his mouth. Someone sat him up and held his shoulders—it was Dick—and he heard Charley say, "Bru? Are you okay?"

"Fucking kid drags up half the cigarette," said Madora.

When he could, Bruce got up and walked away. He sat down by himself against the wall of the school, where the others' voices reached him unintelligibly. All he could see was the glow of their cigarettes, which might have been yards or miles in the distance.

The night was getting cold. He held his throat and shivered, waiting until he was well enough to go home without his parents seeing he'd been smoking. The frogs, which had grown silent during his coughing, one by one took up their old song.

He hated himself for having hoped he could ever be like Dick or Paulie. He might never play basketball again, or touch a cigarette as long as he lived. No matter how his mother licked her lips and curled her fingers, no one would tell him, "Bruce, you're so hard," and touch him, any more than that could ever have happened to his father. He could picture his father as a boy, plump and short-winded—his father was what such boys became.

Now the glowing sparks were rising. They started to float away from him. He heard Charley call, "Bru?" He didn't answer. A minute more and the points of light were gone. Bruce sat in the unbroken dark, his back against the school building. A little wind came up, and the night grew colder.

He was still there, hours later, when a new and brighter light appeared. It came around the corner of the school, its beam sweeping from side to side. "Thank God," said his father. "Are you all right?"

"You're supposed to be in bed," said Bruce. "How about your heart?"

"You're freezing, don't you know that?" His father warmed him for a minute against his soft stomach and chest. Then they walked home. His father took it slow and asked him to carry the flashlight. The frogs were trilling, filling the dark with their cry of urgent love.

Backboard and Hoop

Rodney Torreson

Even when it arrives at the driveway,
there's this feeling that
the boy inhabits it, that he's surged
through the long stem
of a basketball pole,
blossoming out—
his back all backboard;
his heart all hoop,
its net willing to stretch for a moment
to hold each idea
which passes through.

This boy who hates
daisies and marigolds
becoming the only flower he would be.

In one afternoon with the
aid of his father
he plants his larger self in the asphalt,
grows right up to the roof
of the garage—content now
to let his backboard shrug off
all pain, never dodge
a thing in his way.

For awhile he stands there trying to believe
what he sees and feels—that he is twelve-feet tall,

his whole body branching
in fiber glass and steel.

All evening he leaps, his hands
raised in glory before himself,
and dribbling out his little dance.

First Cut
Jack Ridl

The night before,
eight of the players
slept. Each of the rest
lay wondering if his name
would not be on the list.
"Tomorrow we'll post
first cuts," Coach said.
"If you're on the list,
you're still on the team.
If not," and he shrugged.
Twenty-two went to look,
hoping to see themselves
among the chosen.
For years these names had been nothing
more than something they had answered to.
But today, hurled back
to the earth's first days,
they could feel the finger
of the first caller point
then choose. God said, "Smith,"
and Smith walked on among the elect.
On the wall, next
to Coach's office door,
the list. Some came
early, stood, stared,
and left. Some waited.
Coach had told them
not to say a word.
Some held out past lunch,

then gave in, went,
and saw. At practice.
Coach called together
the chosen. "All right,"
he said, "you've made it
this far. There will be one more
cut. Twelve of you will make it.
We'll go one more week. OK,
wind sprints." The others
looked for something
else to do, wished
they'd never tried, searched
for a word to use
to cut out their hate,
felt a fire burn around their name.

The Body Politic
Theodore Weesner

Five-five and one-twelve, thirteen years old, out of an obscure elementary school, a complete unknown, Glen Whalen walks into the boys' locker room to spin the dial of his combination lock. Emerson Junior High. It's a school with a double gym with a whiskey-colored floor upon which street shoes are never allowed.

The occasion: seventh-grade basketball tryouts.

Glen removes items from his gym bag and places them on the bench. Two pairs of white wool socks, white hi-top sneakers, gym shorts, T-shirt, jock. All but the T-shirt are new. He has to remove staple and paper label from a pair of socks, the jock from the box. The new sneakers, a once-a-year event, promise speed, new squeak-grips on the polished wooden floor, sudden turns, spring. This pair, he has told himself, he'll keep strictly for indoor use, a promise he made to himself in sixth grade too, only to break it during a sunny February thaw to the more immediate promise of running outdoors with seeming lightning speed.

The gym bag is new too, his first, navy blue with brown leather handles, a spontaneous gift from his father as they shopped on Saturday. Except for the sneakers, P. F. Flyers, and the jock, a Bike—a slight necessity, but his first and thus no slight event after all—the items are free of racing stripes and product names, as apparently uncomplicated as other forces at work in the era in which this otherwise unnoticed chapter in sports history is quietly unfolding.

Glen and his father, Red Whalen—the two live alone together in an apartment on Buick Street, in the obscure elementary school district,

just up the hill from Buick Plant Three where Red works the second
shift—picked out the items at Hubbard's Hardware & Sporting Goods
Store downtown. Glen's list from school did not include a gym bag, and
he imagined carrying everything in a paper bag, much as his father always
had a bottle in a paper bag nearby, in glove box, trunk, under the driver's
seat. But his father had already tipped one of those bags a few times by
midday Saturday, the last a sizable snort as they parked in the alley
behind Hubbard's, and there were the gym bags on a shelf before them.

"How you going to carry all that gear?"

Glen, looking in the same direction, did not say.

"Let's do it right," his father said. "Fight them to the end. On land,
in the air, on the sea." There was that reddish glow in his cheeks, the
film over his eyes, his Mona Lisa grin.

Blue is the wrong color, though, Glen realizes when a string of five
boys—tall, renowned Ray Peaks among them—enters the locker room,
each carrying a kelly green gym bag. The school colors are green and
white, Glen knows, alas, in this moment, even as he knew it all along.
Green and white, fight fight! "Shoot!" he says aloud. "Belly high . . .
without a rubber," one of the five boys sings out as they turn into a
nearby aisle.

Glen's plain white T-shirt also identifies him as an outsider. It's true
that other white T-shirts are present in the gathering of twenty-five or
thirty, but each is worn by a boy who handles a basketball with his
elbows out, or one who cannot get his feet, in concert with his hands,
to comprehend the concept of *steps*. Then two more boys wearing white
T-shirts walk in, but the two—they have to be twins—are blubbery
with jelly rolls around their middles, with near-breasts, and each wears
knee guards, elbow guards, and wire cages over glasses. Otherwise most
of the boys wear kelly green basketball jerseys, although no such item
was included on the mimeographed list. One boy wears a flowered
bathing suit that he had outgrown perhaps a year earlier.

Coach Bass walks into the gym carrying a new ball, blowing his whistle, shouting at them to return the balls to the ball bin, to never take a ball from that bin unless he says to! Appearing then, making a jogging entrance from the tunnel onto the glossy floor, are the boys of the green gym bags. The five, Glen notices, wear uniform gray sweatshirts—over green sleeveless jerseys, it will turn out—above white gym shorts and, laced in a military staircase braid into their white sneakers, matching green shoe laces. They are the ones, everything about them seems to say, who know the score, who already have it made at Emerson Junior High.

Coach Bass, ball under his arm, tweets his whistle, tells them to sit down. He paces to and fro before them, shifts the new ball hand-to-hand as he talks. He introduces the locker-room man, "Slim" who stands at the tunnel entrance watching. The best players and hardest workers will make the traveling squad of ten, he tells them. That's the way it is. This isn't elementary school anymore and that is the black-and-blue reality of competitive sports. A list will be posted on the bulletin board outside his office after practice on Friday. BUT, he adds, raising a finger. That's not all. Any boy—any one of them who has the desire. Who is willing to do the work. Can continue to attend practices. AND—from among THOSE boys—TWO alternates will be selected to dress for each home game.

Glen sits watching and wondering. Two alternates for each home game. It means everyone has a chance. Sort of. But does the Coach mean the same two, or two new ones each time? There are so many students here in junior high—hundreds more than in the small brick elementary school he attended last year.

Building and grounds cover acres. And any number of ninth-grade boys actually have mustaches, are over six feet tall. And some of the girls—wow!

The Coach blows his whistle again. He snaps, "On your feet!" and they jump, almost as one, as if the process of selection is related to how quickly one can get upright. All but Ray Peaks, Glen notices. Ray Peaks—his arms appear to reach his knees—pushes up from one hand

and is the last to stand. Still he is the first to receive a pass, as the Coach snaps the new ball to him and tells him to lead a line along the wall of folding doors.

Glen follows into the line and performs as instructed. He joins rows of five, back-pedals, sidesteps side-to-side, starts and stops. However anxious he feels he does not have the problems of any number of boys who move left when they should move right, cross their feet when they should sidestep, stop when they should start. He dribbles in and around strategically placed folding chairs. He exchanges passes along a line of others and takes his place at the other end. He follows through one line to shoot a lay-up, and another to rebound and pass off. He begins to perspire, to breathe more deeply, to relax a little, and begins to observe the others in their turns as he waits in lines. And, like others, he glances to the Coach now and then, to see if he can see whatever it is the man is taking in.

Junior-high basketball. For home games the panels will be folded away, bleachers will unfold from either side, and the space and glossy floor—the surface is no less than beautiful, precious, an expanse of fixed lacquer upon which to perform—will offer a dimension that is possibly magical. Ray Peaks, Glen hears in one of the moving lines, could play with the senior team if he wanted.

Glen tries harder, tries to concentrate. However new he is to organized drills and dashes, shouts and whistles, it is becoming increasingly apparent that he is far from the worst. For while the gang of five seems to know all of the moves, any number of others, here and there, now and again, continue to reveal various shortcomings. And—that most promising sign—going in on a bounce pass down the middle, to go UP! and lay the ball over the front edge of the rim without crashing into the Coach where he is positioned just under the backboard, Glen hears at his back that phrase which shoots him through with sudden hope. "Nice shot there."

Friday waits before them as the week moves along, but Glen goes about life and school in his usual ways. He has never *made* anything like a team before, and even as he entertains his degree of hope, he hardly takes on any of the anxieties of expectation. Good things come home when you don't stand at the door waiting, his father has told him, and Glen gives little thought to what it will mean if he does or does not make the team. He will probably keep trying, he thinks, on the chance of dressing as an alternate.

He begins to eat lunch with Norman Van Slyke, who sits in front of him in homeroom. Glen's father leaves him a dollar on the kitchen table every morning for lunch and on his own Glen has fallen into a habit of walking three blocks from school to a small corner grocery he spotted sometime previously. Cold weather has yet to arrive and at the store—Sam Jobe's Market—he stands inside near a red pop case to eat, or he sits outside in the sun. Lunch is a packaged pie, usually pineapple but sometimes cherry, a Clark bar or two, and from a glass-bowl machine, five or six pennies' worth of Spanish peanuts to feed into his bottle of Hire's Root Beer, which salty beetles, as he thinks of them—perhaps Japanese, which are popular at the time, although he has never seen one— he pops to oblivion between his teeth as he drinks his root beer.

Norman Van Slyke's looks made Glen smile the first time he saw him in homeroom. Sparse hairs sprout already from the short, thin boy's upper lip, just under his adhesive-tape-ringed glasses, and his extensive nose projects in the midst of this confusion like an animal reaching its head from a hole in the ground. Norman's features twitch; the periscope that is his nose seems to look around at times, to glance up and down and to the side.

Glen calls him Rat Nose at once, and the name brings immediate snickers of pleasure from the other boy. In turn, Rat Nose identifies Glen as Weasel, and they take on the names and wear them along the street as easily as old sweatshirts.

After-school practices continue. Each morning, coming out of Civics and turning right, headed for Geometry, Glen discovers that he passes Ray Peaks going the other way. On Thursday morning, the lanky boy utters, "Say," in passing, and on Friday, when Glen speaks first, says, "Hi," to the school's already-famous athlete, Ray Peaks winks in a natural and friendly way that reminds Glen of his father's winks.

Glen also hears or learns in the days passing that the boys of the kelly green gym bags all attended the elementary school attached to the very end of Emerson Junior High. So it is that they had used the glossy hardwood double gymnasium all those years, stopped by after school to see home games and, as it also comes out, played together for two years as teammates in a Saturday morning league. In practices, when teams are identified, and when they scrimmage, the five boys, Ray Peaks ever the nucleus, move as one.

Glen's basketball experience was different. His elementary school, near Buick Plants Two and Three along a branch of the city river, had neither gymnasium nor coach. A basement classroom served as a gym, under the guidance of the gym teacher, Mrs. Roland. Painted blackish brown, its high windows and ceiling light fixtures caged, the room offered a single netless rim fixed flush to the wall, eight or nine feet from the floor and perhaps eighteen inches from the ceiling. The clearance was enough for either lay-ups or line drives.

No matter, Glen always thought, for in gym class they only played little kid games in circles anyway and only once was basketball ever given a try. Mrs. Roland, whistle around her neck, glasses on a separate lanyard, demonstrated—to introduce that one game—by hoisting the cumbersome ball from her side with both hands, kicking up one ankle as she tossed it at the basket, hitting the *bottom* of the rim. Then she selected teams—which selections for any real sport, indoors or out, were always maddening to Glen, as she chose captains and teams by height rather than ability. And she officiated the year's single basketball game by calling one jump ball after another, the contest lasting three minutes or less, concluding on a score of 2-0.

Tall boys will always be given the breaks, Mrs. Roland seemed to say. And if your last name starts with W, your place will always be at the end of the line.

Glen did play outdoors. At least a year earlier, as an eleven-year-old, he paused on a sidewalk beside a cement driveway at the side of a church along Buick Avenue and discovered not Jesus but basketball. The church was First Nazarene and the boys playing under the outdoor hoop were high-school age. Glen stood and watched, and when a loose ball came his way, he shagged it and walked it back several steps to throw it to the boy walking toward him.

"Wanna play, come on," the boy said.

Glen was too thrilled to be able to say. He did walk toward the action, though, nodding, although he had just a moment ago touched a basketball for the first time in his life. "You're on my side," the boy said. "Gives us three on a side."

Anxious, Glen moved into the area as instructed. The boy who had invited him—who was pointing out the sides, treating him as some actual person he had never known himself to be—turned out to be the seventeen-year-old son of the church's minister. Glen had never encountered a generous teenager before, and his wonder was such that he might have been a possible convert to nearly anything, but no such strings were attached. The seventeen-year-old boy was merely that rarest of individuals in Glen's life, a teenager who wasn't mean.

The game—Twenty-one—progressed, and passes were sent Glen's way as if he knew what to do. He did not. He passed the ball back each time, another time bounced it once and passed it back, and no one said anything critical, nor cast any critical glances, and the minister's son, who was already a memorable figure to Glen, said at last, when Glen single-dribbled again and return-passed the ball, "That's the way."

It would seem that Glen was being indulged, but something in the way the game was managed made it no less real as a contest. The minister's son had Glen put the ball in play each time it was his team's turn to do so, and in time he said to him, "Don't be afraid to take a shot," and when Glen passed off instead, he said, "Go ahead, take a shot or you'll never learn." A chance came again, and even as it may not have been the best opportunity, Glen pushed the ball two-handed toward the basket, only to see it fall short by two or three feet.

His teammates recovered the ball, passed and circled, and the boy said to him, "That's okay, good try, try it again." In time there came another opportunity, closer in, and this time the ball hit on the rim, hesitated, and, alas, dropped through, and the boy said only, "There you go, that's the way," as if it were just another basket among all that might pass through such a metal ring and not Glen Whalen's very first. Glen continued with the game, too, as if nothing out of the ordinary had happened. But by the time evening air was descending he had grown so happy a glow was in his eyes, and for the first time in his life he was falling in love with something.

He had to be told to go home. When the sky was so dark the ball could be spotted only directly overhead, a black moon against the night sky, and three of the other boys had drifted away, the minister's son finally said to him that he had better head on home, it was getting late. As Glen started off, though, the boy called after him, said they played every night at that time, to stop by again, and if he wanted to shoot by himself, the ball would be just inside that side door and he was welcome to use it just so he put it back when he was done.

Glen shot baskets, hours on end, entering into any number of imaginary schemes and games, and that summer and fall alone, until snow and ice covered the driveway, he played away a hundred or more evenings with the older boys, game after game, unto darkness. The games were three-on-three, although there were evenings when enough boys showed up to make three or four teams and to continue to play a threesome had to win or go to the end of the line. Glen loved it; he learned most of the moves and absorbed them into his system as one does. And so it is, on Friday after school, when practice ends and he follows along with the others to the bulletin board between gym and locker room and reads the typed list there between shoulders, reads it from the top—*Raymond Peaks*—down, the tenth name on the list is *Glen Whalen*.

He is invited to lunch. In school on Monday, outside his homeroom, one of the boys of the green gym bags—Keith Klett, also a guard—appears at Glen's side and doesn't ask him but tells him to meet them out front at lunch time. His house is only two blocks away, the boy adds; it's where they go to eat.

Seeing Rat Nose later, Glen mentions that he is going to eat lunch with the basketball team, and he experiences but the slightest twinge of betrayal. When he gathers with the others by the mailbox, though, there are only six of them who cross the street to walk along the residential sidestreet and Glen realizes, for whatever reason, that he is being selected by the five as a sixth man. He is being taken in. And he is not so naive that he doesn't know the reason; basketball is at the heart of it and some one person or another, or the Coach, has to have noted, as the line goes, that he is good.

Four of the five—all but Keith Klett—carry home-packed lunches in paper bags, and Glen is asked about the whereabouts of his own. "You can make a sandwich at my house," Keith Klett says. "No charge."

So Glen does—nutty peanut butter on fluffy Wonder Bread—in a large kitchen and large house which if not elegant are far more middle-class than any house he has ever visited in a similar way. He is impressed by the space; there seem to be so many rooms, rooms of such size, a two-car garage outside, a sun porch, a den; then, up a carpeted turning stairway to a second floor, Keith Klett's bedroom is larger than the living room in the four-room walk-up apartment he and his father have called home for the last couple years.

No less noticeable to Glen's eyes are the possessions, the furnishings and appliances, a boy's bedroom seemingly as filled with sports equipment as Hubbard's Hardware, and, on a counter, a globe that lights and an aquarium with bubbles but no fish—"the dumb jerk peed in the tank and they all croaked," Ray Peaks says—and model planes, ships, tanks, a desk with a lampshade shaped like a basketball, and, in its own bookcase, an *Encyclopaedia Britannica* set just like the set in the junior-high Reference Room. And—the reason they can troop through the house at will, the reason to troop here for lunch in the first place—

Keith Klett's parents are both at work.

Making a sandwich in the kitchen, following each of Keith Klett's steps, including the pouring of a glass of milk, Glen follows into the den where the others sit around eating. Hardly anything has been said about basketball, and some joke seems to be in the air, but Glen has yet to figure out what it is. Sandwich packed away in two or three bites, two-thirds of his glass of milk poured in after, Keith Klett, smiling, is soon on his feet, saying to Glen, "There's something you have to see," slipping away to run upstairs as Ray Peaks calls after him, "Keith, leave that crap alone, it makes me sick."

There is no response.

"What's he doing?" Glen asks.

"You'll see—it'll make you toss your cookies."

Reappearing, a grin on his face, holding something behind his back, Keith Klett moves close before Glen where he sits chewing a mouthful of peanut butter sandwich. The others titter, giggle, offer expressions of sickness, as Keith Klett hangs near Glen's face and sandwich a white rectangle of gauze blotched at its center with a blackish red stain. Even as Glen doesn't know exactly what it is, he has an idea and pulls his neck back enough, turtle-fashion, not to be touched by the daintily held object.

"Get out of here, Keith!" Gene Elliott says, adding to Glen, to them all, "Anybody who gets a charge out of that has to be a pervert."

Not entirely certain of the function of the pad of gauze, Glen decides not to ask. As Keith returns upstairs, white object in a pinch of fingertips, Glen finishes his sandwich, drinks away his milk, and carries the glass to the kitchen sink where he rinses it out, as he does at home. Perhaps it has to do with his father working second shift, leaving him to spend his evenings generally alone, or maybe it has to do with his not having brothers or sisters with whom to trade jokes and stories, but Glen has a sense, realized for probably the first time, as he and the others are walking back to school, that maybe he is shy or maybe he doesn't have much that he wishes to say. It's a disappointing realization in its way, and he is disappointed too, in some attic area of thoughts, with the group of five that has decided to take him in. He had imagined something else. And a twinge continues in him over Rat Nose going off on his own. One thing Glen does seem to see; he is a person. Each of them is a person, and each of them is different, and so is he, which is something he had never thought about before.

The season's first game is away, Friday after school. Lowell Junior High.

Thursday, at the end of practice, they are issued green satin trunks and white jerseys with green satin letters and numbers. Glen will always remember that first digital identity, Number 5, will feel a kinship with all who wear it. Cheerleaders and a busload of students are scheduled to leave at 3 P.M. the next day, the Coach, clipboard in hand, tells them as they check the uniforms for size. Team members are to gather at the rear door at exactly 2:30.

"You have a parent who can drive?" the Coach all at once asks Glen.

"No," Glen says, feeling that old rush of being from the wrong side of something.

"You don't—your mother can't drive?"

"I just live with my father," Glen says.

"He can't drive?"

"Works second shift."

The Coach makes a mark on his clipboard, goes on to question others. In a moment, in the midst of assigning rides, he says, "Keep those uniforms clean now, and be sure to bring clean socks and a towel."

Four cars, including the Coach's own, will be making the drive, he announces at last. "Two-thirty on the button," he adds. "If you're late, you miss the game. And no one will change cars. Everybody will come back in the same car they go in."

The next afternoon, entering the strange school building across town, filing into a strange locker room, they select lockers to use and the Coach comes along, giving each of them a new pair of green shoelaces. Glen—he rode over in the Coach's car with two other silent second-stringers—continued more or less silent now, sitting on the bench, removing his still-clean white laces, placing them in his gym bag, replacing them with the green laces. He also unstaples his second new pair of wool socks, thinking that later he will remove the new green laces and save them and the second pair of socks for games only.

At last, dressed in the school uniform—Number 5; he loves the number already and tries, unsuccessfully, to glimpse it over his shoulder—and new socks and bright shoelaces, he stands up from the bench to shake things out, to see how he feels. Nervous, he realizes. Frightened, although of what exactly, he isn't sure. Goose-bumped in locations—along thighs, under biceps—where he has not known the chilled sensation to visit him before, he notices that one, and then another and another, all of them, have laced in the green laces in the stairway military pattern, while his make their way in X's. He feels himself a fool. Was there time to change? Should he say something?

The Coach holds up both hands. "Now I know you all want to play," he says. "Chances are you won't. Depends on how things go. One thing —I want each and every one of you to understand before we go out that door. You will listen to what I say and you will do as I tell you. There will be no debates. There will be no complaints during or after this game. Anyone who complains, about the game, or about teammates, or about anything, will find himself an ex-member of this team. Nor will there be any arguing with officials. No calls will be disputed. Remember: Losers complain and argue—men get the job done. They stand up to adversity. They win.

"Now, we're going to go out there and have a good warm-up. The starting five will be the starting five from practice and Ray Peaks will be our captain for this game. Now: Let it be said of you that you tried your hardest, that you did your best. Now: Everyone pause, take a deep breath.

"Let's go! Green and white!"

Throughout the warm-up, throughout the entire first half, in a continuing state of awe and shock, Glen's goose bumps maintain their topography in unusual places. It is the first time he has ever performed or even moved before a group of people purposely assembled to watch and judge and count, and even as this occasions excitement in him, a roller-coaster thrill, his greater sense, sitting on the bench in the middle of the second-stringers, is one of highwire anxiety. His eyes feel frog-like, his neck has unforeseen difficulty turning in its socket, chills chase over his arms and legs like agitated sled dogs.

From folded-down bleachers on this side of the gym only—opposite is a wall with high, wire-covered windows—Lowell Junior High students, teachers, and parents clap, cheer, and shout as the game moves along. Glen sits there. He looks around. His neck continues to feel stiff and sluggish. It occurs to him as he glances to the lighted scoreboard at the left end of the gym, that he does not know how long the halves are. Six minutes and departing seconds remain in the first half, then, all at once, five minutes and a new supply of seconds begin to disappear into some tunnel of time gone by.

To Glen's right, before the narrow width of bleachers next to the door that leads to their locker room, the cheerleaders from his school, half a dozen seventh-grade girls in green and white, work, against all odds, it seems, to do their job:

Peaks, Peaks—he's our man!
If he can't do it—nobody can! Yayyy!

Glen does not quite look at the cheerleaders; so carefully dressed, he feels he has gone to a dance of some kind when he has never danced a step in his life and would have declined the invitation if he had known it would lead to this. The seconds on the clock chase each other away; then, again, another fresh supply. Glen looks to the action out on the floor without knowing quite what is happening. Nor can he entirely grasp what it was he is doing sitting there on the bench. Even as he went through the warm-up drills, he did not look at any of the spectators; rather he looked ahead, or at the floor, or kept his eye on the ball as it moved here and there. How has it come to this? Where is he? His team, he realizes, is behind 17-11, and he could not tell anyone how this had come to pass.

No substitutions. As the first half ends and the Coach stands up, Glen moves with the other second-stringers to follow along with the starting five to the locker room. Glen feels no disappointment that he has spent this time sitting and watching, nor any urge to be put into the game. Sitting on the bench in that costume, getting his neck to swivel; it seemed contribution enough. As they pass before the group from their school, however, and names and remarks of encouragement are called out, he hears distinctly, "Go get 'em, Weasel," and looks over to see Rat Nose's face looking at him, smiling, pleased, and a pleasure of friendship leaps up in Glen's chest.

The Coach paces and talks and points. They are behind 19-11. He slaps a fist into an opened palm. Glen continues to feel overwhelmed by all that surrounds him, but on the thought of Rat Nose sitting out there, calling him Weasel, he has to stop himself from tittering and giggling out loud. For one moment, then another, it seems to be the funniest thing that has ever happened to him.

"Now we don't have much time," the Coach is saying. "We have to get the ball in to Ray Peaks. If we're going to pull this out, we have to get the ball in to Ray under the basket! Now let's get out there and do it. Green and white, fight—okay?" he inquires with some uncertainty.

On the floor, going through a confused warm-up, Glen glances back at the group from his school, looks to see Rat Nose there in particular, but the group is too far away and at such an angle that he cannot be sure. Then they're being herded back to their bench; maybe they aren't supposed to warm up for the second half—no one seems to know.

Glen sits in the middle of those on the bench and stares at the game as before. Five-on-five, two officials in black-and-white striped shirts. Whistles. The scrambled movement of basketball at ground level. Hands raised. Shouts from the bleachers. Yet again he has forgotten to check the beginning time. Nine minutes thirty seconds remain as he looks for the first time. The score? His next realization is that he has not been keeping score. He is too nervous for math, he thinks. Home 25 / Visitors 16. The next time he looks, the clock shows eight minutes forty-four seconds. His team, he realizes, has scored but five points so far in the half. The other team's lead is increasing. It looks like his team is going to lose. That's what it looks like. There is Keith Klett snapping a pass to the side to Gene Elliott as they move before the scrambled concentration of players at the far end and Glen experiences a vague sense that they are somehow progressing in the wrong direction, and he experiences a vague sense, too, of hearing his name called out: "Whalen—Whalen!"

It is his name in fact, and there is the Coach's face as he looks, his fingers indicating sharply that he is to move to his side. The next thing Glen seems to know, as if he had received a blast of frozen air, is that he is crouched, one hand on the floor, next to the Coach's knee. In this location the volume of the game, the cheers, and spectators, seems to have increased three times over. "Check in at the table, next whistle, for Klett, get that ball to Ray Peaks!" Glen hears, sees the Coach spit the words at him from the side of his mouth all the time continuing to watch the action at the far end.

Stealing along in the same crouch, Glen reports in over the table top, says, "Whalen for Klett—I mean Number 5 for Number 7."

Taking a duck-step or two to the center line, Glen looks up to the scoreboard. Home 27 / Visitors 16. Seven minutes thirty-one seconds.

A whistle blows out on the floor and at once a horn honks behind him, giving him so sudden a scare, he seems to lose some drops in his pants. "Substitution Emerson," the man calls.

Glen moves onto the floor, into the view of all, seeking Keith Klett; spotting him, he says, "In for you," and believing he is the object of all eyes, moves past him toward the end of the court where the other team is putting the ball in play, not knowing, in the blur of things, if it is the consequence of a basket or not.

Nor does he see Gene Elliott for the moment as, before him, an official hands the ball to a Lowell player. The boy passes it at once to a player who turns to start dribbling downcourt and Glen dashes toward him and the ball, slaps the ball away, chases it, grabs it in both hands, pivots, looks to find his fellow guard, to get rid of the ball, as he is poked in wrist and forearm by someone's fingers and whistle blows sharply, close-by.

"Foul! Lowell! Number 13!" the official snaps. "One shot! Number 5!"

The players return, taking their positions. "That's the way! Way to go!" comes from Glen's teammates.

He stands waiting at the free-throw line. The others settle in, lean, wait. He has done this a thousand times, and never. The ball is handed over. "One shot," the official says. Glen looks to the distant hoop; he finds presence of mind enough to call up something of the endless shots in the church driveway, although the message remains elusive. He shoots, from the chest, as he had in the driveway, although they were taught in practice to shoot from between their legs. Hitting the rim with a thud, the ball holds, rolls, tries to get away to the side, cannot escape, falls through.

"Way to go, Whalen," a teammate remarks, passing him on the way down the floor. "That's the way," comes from another.

Glen moves toward the out-of-bounds line again, toward the other guard, as the ball is about to be put in play. He looks over for Gene Elliott again, but doesn't spot him, as the ball is passed in, and the guard receiving the ball, more alert this time, starts to dribble up court as Glen rushes him, explodes over him, somehow hits the ball as the boy swings it in both hands, knocks it loose, chases it, dribbles it once in the chase, looks again for his teammate as the Lowell player is on him, jumps, shoots—sees the ball hit the backboard, hit the rim, go through—and hears an explosion of applause from the other end of the gym.

At once he moves back in, pursuing the ball, as a teammate slaps his back, says, "Great shot!" and hears his coach call out, "Go ahead with that press, that's the way!" and hears the other team's coach, closeby, snarl to his guards, "Keep it away from that guy will you?" and hears

Gene Elliott, inches away, say, "Coach says to go ahead with the press."

There he is, poised, ready, so thrilled already that his eyes seem aflame, as the Lowell players are all back down-court and are taking more time. He glances to the clock: seven minutes twenty seconds. In about ten seconds, he realizes, he has scored three points, which message keeps coming to him, that he has, in about ten seconds scored three points, that it is true, he has, and it is something, it is all things, and everything he has ever known in his life is different now.

The ball is moved along this time. At the other end, in their zone defense, the other team loses possession near the basket, and players run and lope past Glen as he circles back, and the ball is passed to him, and he dribbles along, eluding a Lowell player, passes off to Gene Elliott, sees Ray Peaks ranging to the right of the basket, and when the ball comes back to him—it will be his most satisfying play, one which is no way accidental, no way lucky—he immediately fires a long one-handed pass, more football than basketball, hard and high, and to his amazement Ray Peaks leaps high, arms extended, whips the ball out of the air with both hands, dribbles at once on a pivot-turn and lays it in neatly off the board, and there comes another explosion from behind them. And there is Ray Peaks seeking him out, grabbing his arm, hissing in a wild, feverish whisper, "That's the way to pass! Keep it up! Keep it up! We're going to beat these guys!"

The game progresses. Glen intercepts a pass and goes two-thirds of the court to put in a lay-up just over the front edge of the rim, as they were instructed, and he scores two more free throws, to go three for three, bringing his point total to seven, but his most satisfying play is the first long, high pass, and the most exciting experience of the game is the fever which infects them all, especially Ray Peaks, who scores any number of added baskets on his high, hard passes, and Gene Elliott, too, who passes harder, as they all become caught up in the fever, including the Coach, who is on his feet shouting, clapping, waving, and the group from their school, whose explosions of applause keep becoming louder and wilder, until, suddenly to Glen, both horn and whistle sound, and there comes another explosion of applause, and the Coach and players from the bench are on the floor, grabbing, slapping, shouting, for the game is over and they have won, and they know things they had not known before, and none can quite get enough, it seems, of what it is they have not known until this very moment.

As they move and are being moved toward the locker room, Ray Peaks is slapped and congratulated, and so is Glen. There is the Coach, arm around Glen's shoulders, voice close, calling to him, "That full-court press was the thing to do! You ignited that comeback! You turned it around!"

The celebration continues in the locker room. The final score: Home 29 / Visitors 33. Locker doors are slammed, towels are thrown around, there is the Coach congratulating Glen again, slapping his shoulder, calling to them all, "That full-court press turned it around!" Glen learns, too, in the melee, that only two players on his team have scored, he and Ray Peaks, seven points and twenty-six, and everything, all of it, keeps occurring over again for him as a surprise, and as a surprise all over again, and he lets it go on as it will, a dozen Christmases and birthdays combined, accepts the compliments, knows in some part of himself already that he is changed by what has happened, has been granted something, knows these things, and does not volunteer in any way that at the time he simply chased the ball because he was so confused by all that was happening around him that he did not know, otherwise, what it was that he was supposed to do.

Monday it is back to school and lunch hour as usual. After school, though, as practice moves along, as they run through drills with the dozen or so alternates, there comes a time for the Coach to name squads of five, and the name, Glen Whalen, is called to run out and join the first team, in place of Keith Klett, who is left to stand with the others. It is not something Glen anticipated—is a small surprise—but as it happens the logic is not unreasonable to him. Nor is anything unreasonable to the other four, who congratulate him in small ways as he takes his place on the floor.

Keith Klett stands among the others, retreats, Glen notices, to the back row. His eyes appear not to focus on anything in particular as he stands looking ahead, glancing around.

They come face-to-face after practice in the locker room. Glen, sitting on the bench to untie his shoes, looks to the end of his aisle and sees Keith Klett staring at him. "You suck-ass," the boy says.

Keith Klett walks on. Glen doesn't say anything. He sits looking that way for a moment and doesn't know what to say or do.

Nor does he see the other boy when, undressed, towel around his waist, he walks along the main aisle to the shower. He wonders if they will fight, there in the locker room or out behind the school, and although the prospect of everyone streaming along uttering "Fight, fight," excites and terrifies him at once—he'll do it, he thinks—nothing of the kind happens. The remark stays within him like a speck; it stays and stays.

At home that night he thinks of resurrecting his friendship with Rat Nose and the thought appeals to him, as if to return home after having been away. Then he wonders if Rat Nose might turn his back on him—who would blame him?—and he worries about it until the next day when he encounters Rat Nose near his locker in the hall.

"Still go to Jobe's Market?" Glen asks.

"Sometimes," Rat Nose says.

"Wanna go?"

"Sure—I don't care—wanna go?"

They walk along the hall toward the door. There is no mention of a change of any kind and they move along as if nothing has happened, as if it is merely another day.

Charge

Christopher Gilbert

Gimme the ball, Willie is saying
throughout this 2-on-2 pick-up game.
Winners are the ones who play, being
at the sidelines is ridiculous.
So what happens here is a history
won not by the measure of points,
but by simply getting into it.
Willie plays like it could all be gone
at once, like his being is at stake.
Gimme the ball, he cusses.
Gwen Brooks' player from the streets.
The game is wherever there's a chance.
It is nothing easy he's after,
but the rapture gained with presence.
His catalogue of moves represents
his life. Recognize its stance.
So alive to be the steps
in whose mind the symbol forms,
miraculous to be the feeling
which threads these steps to dance.
The other side is very serious—
they want to play him 2-on-1.
Messrs. Death and Uniformity.
He's got a move to make them smile.
Gimme the ball, Willie says again
and again, "*Gimme the goddamn ball.*"

Lowell High
Tom Meschery

Our red brick square gymnasium was an anachronism
Among the steel-ribbed, concrete muscled ellipses
And angles of the day; it was full of shadows—
The floor corduroy, the backboards wood
And the rims were bent with age
        (the relentless ricochet of basketballs).
It had none of the embellishments
Found in more modern gyms.
It was simply a no-nonsense structure
Built to house players not spectators.
Surrounded by its gray walls and wrinkled floor
We practiced two-to-six, six days a week.
And throughout that time—four years—
Our coach, who was as old as the building,
Taunted and inspired us, swore and cajoled us.
He taught us to play without frills.
We became red brick and corduroy
And learned to see through shadows.

Familiar Games
Jonathan Baumbach

Every family has its games. Ours were in the service of an ostensibly competitive hierarchy. We had to defeat our mother—the game was basketball in those days—before we got to play our father. Not that we got to play him after that either, but if we were ever to play him, the obstacle of our mother had first to be set aside.

Our mother was usually too busy to play, and sometimes too busy to discuss her busyness, though one suspected that she practiced on the sly. If her form was wanting, or subtly underdeveloped, she had an uncanny knack for putting the ball through the hoop from the oddest angles. She played, whenever she could be enticed into a game, in an apron and slippers, and at times, when coming directly from the kitchen, in rubber gloves.

She gave advice while we played, suggestions for improvement, a woman with a pedagogic bent.

The game I most remember is not one of mine but a game my younger brother played against Mother. Phil had challenged me first, but for some reason—perhaps because I thought he might be able to take me—I declined the contest. Having limited natural ability, Phil practiced at every opportunity, studied self-improvement. One could wake up at two A.M., look out the window, and see him taking shots in the dark. His tenacity awed me.

Our mother was not awed. "This will have to be quick," she said, making the first basket before Phil could ready himself on defense. "There's something in the oven that needs basting."

"Did that count?" Phil asked, withholding strenuous complaint, not wanting to provoke her into resigning from the game, one of the lessons by example she occasionally offered.

"I'll do that over," Mother said. "You weren't ready."

Phil insisted that it was all right, that even had he been fully prepared he couldn't have stopped her shot.

Phil took the ball out at the crest of the driveway, which was approximately thirty-five feet from a basket hung on a wooden backboard from the top of our garage, dribbled to the left, then to the right, then to the left again, proceeding by degrees to an advantageous spot. Our mother waited for him, unmoving, at the foul line, her arms out.

Mother blocked Phil's first shot, knocking it behind him. Phil ran down the ball and resumed his pattern of moving ostentatiously from side to side. He told me later that his idea was to get Mother to commit herself.

It was Mother's policy to treat Phil's feints and flourishes as invisible gestures. The more Phil flashed about, showcasing his skills, the more unblinkingly stationary Mother became. Phil's brilliant maneuvering tended to cancel itself out and he invariably ended up coming right to Mother, shooting the ball despairingly against her outstretched hand.

"That's not getting you anywhere," she told him.

That knowledge had already inescapably reached Phil, and one could tell he was planning new strategy, though at the same time he also wanted to demonstrate that his original plan of attack was not without merit. He was down three baskets to none before he decided to relinquish his exquisite shuffle and shoot from the outside.

Phil sinks his first long shot and Mother's lead falls to two.

I've neglected to mention procedure, assuming mistakenly that we all play this game in the same way. In our rules, the player that has been scored upon gets the ball out, which tends to keep the games closely contested. Not always. If Phil is to catch up, it will be necessary for Mother to miss at least two more opportunities.

It is Phil's strategy to force Mother to shoot her odd shot from just beyond her range. He presses her when she takes the ball out, swiping at it repeatedly, on occasion slapping her hands.

"I don't enjoy that," she complains. "I don't think it's very nice."

Phil apologizes and steps back, giving Mother the breathing room she needs to launch her two-handed shot. One of its peculiarities is that when it leaves her hands it never seems to be moving in the direction of the basket. In its earliest stages, the poorly launched missile seems fated to fall short and to one side, an embarrassing failure. Halfway in its course, the ball seems buoyed by an otherwise unnoticed wind and accrues the remote chance of reaching the front or side of the rim. The shot outlasts expectation, gains momentum in flight, and instead of touching the front of the rim, lifts over it, ticks the back rim, echoes off the front, and drops through. For an opponent to watch the flight of one of Mother's shots is to risk heartbreak.

Phil has seen Mother's game before and is no longer as vulnerable to the disappointment that comes of false expectation.

"That's a terrific shot," says Phil, hitting one of his own as Mother basks in the compliment.

Unharried by Phil, Mother misses high off the backboard, the shot extending itself beyond the call of accuracy. Phil takes the rebound and dribbles into the corner.

"That must be very tiring," says his stationary opponent. "I don't think you ought to waste so much motion."

Phil takes a jump shot from the corner and cuts the deficit to one. It is a shot he has rehearsed, though he shakes his head as if blessed by undeserved fortune.

"That was a beauty," Mother says, pretending as she does disinterest in the outcome. She shuffles into position to launch her shot, Phil crowding her, waving his arms. Suddenly, accelerating the pace of her shuffle, she goes by him, a move neither Phil nor I have witnessed before. She lays the ball in off the backboard, though it characteristically revolves around the rim a few times before dropping.

Phil, one can tell, is dismayed, has his mind on defending against Mother's next shot instead of readying himself for his own. A half-hearted jump shot falls short and rolls out of bounds. Mother's ball.

Leading six baskets to four, Mother refuses her advantage, or gives that appearance, hefting her odd heave with more than usual indifference, the ball missing long and to the left. "What was I thinking of?" she says to herself.

One is never sure whether it is generosity or tactic.

Phil matches Mother's indifference with a shot even further off the mark than its predecessor.

"Are you letting me win?" Mother asks.

It is only after Mother hits her next shot, a casual two-hander that bounds in off the backboard, that Phil is able to regain his touch. "You may have made that one, but you're rushing your shot," Mother tells him.

Phil says it's not so.

"Believe what you like," says Mother. "I'm only telling you what I know to be true."

"Why don't you give me the credit of knowing what I'm doing?" says Phil.

While this argument is going on, Mother sinks another long shot, increasing her lead to three baskets.

Showing off, Phil dribbles under the basket and lays the ball in from behind his ear.

Our mother claps her hands in appreciation. "That maneuver, if maneuver is the word for it, took my breath away," she says.

The score at this point—I am serving as scorekeeper for the match— is eight baskets for Mother, six for Phil. The first player to reach twelve, while being at least two baskets ahead, is the victor.

Although comfortably in the lead, Mother appears disconsolate, nudging the ball in front of her with the toe of her slipper.

"What's the matter?" Phil asks her.

"Who said anything was the matter?"

Phil is momentarily defeated by Mother's question, gives his opponent considerable space for her next shot.

She takes her time, holding the ball out toward Phil, teasing him with its proximity. "Aren't you playing?" she asks him.

"Take your shot, okay?"

"I'm waiting for you, big shot," she says, dandling the ball. "You're not guarding me the right way."

Phil inches closer, waves an arbitrary hand in the direction of the ball.

And still Mother refuses to launch her shot.

"What have I done wrong?" Phil wants to ask. I know the feeling, have been trapped in similar mystifications.

Mother sits on the ground, her arms crossed in front of her. Phil, not to be put in the wrong, follows suit. The progress of the game has been temporarily halted.

Mother gets up after a while and announces that she is willing to continue if Phil is willing to apologize for his misbehavior.

Phil says he's sorry, says it two or three times since, as it appears, he has no idea what for, and gets to his feet.

Mother scores on a long, unlikely shot that angles in off the back-board. Phil shoots before readying himself and misses to the right, rushing to the basket to retrieve his own rebound. Unguarded, he scores on a lay-up and receives some brief applause from his opponent.

"Thank you one and all," he says, mocking himself, flipping the ball behind his back to our mother.

"I hope you're not trying to impress me," she says, nullifying his basket with one of her own.

Phil dribbles behind his back, through his legs, whirling and turning, exhausting his small repertoire of tricks before kicking the ball out of bounds.

When in the course of her deceptively effective performance Mother reaches eleven baskets, needing only one more to claim victory, she hits a cold spell and misses on her next five attempts. Phil, more by attrition than escalation of skill, gradually edges to one basket behind.

The association comes unbidden and without rational cause. I was in the garden with my mother. We were weeding, or she was; I was watching the process or looking for something to do. There were children in the next yard playing. I could see them, just barely, through the spaces between the slats in their high fence. The game they were playing was like no game I had ever seen before.

There were two of them—at first I thought there were four—a boy and a girl, my age or a year or two older. The girl was taller than the boy and more obviously mature, but girls tend to be more advanced at that age. The reason I didn't know them was that they were new to the neighborhood, their parents—I'm assuming they were brother and sister, though perhaps not—had just bought the house next door.

Did they think the high fence of their garden screened them from the eyes of outsiders? I couldn't imagine what they thought. It may have been they were unconcerned with the opinions of others.

The top half of the girl, at least that, was uncovered and one of her budlike breasts available to my limited perspective. The other breast, insofar as I could tell, was covered by the back of the dark blond head of the boy. The girl's long hair, raven black, glistening in the sun like wet tar, covered much of her face. The boy seemed to be pecking at her small breast in imitation of a chicken. The girl was laughing, though without sound—at least I heard no sound—her wide mouth appearing periodically through the waterfall of her hair. The boy danced up and down, moving from one foot to the other.

I felt something stiffening against my leg and turned away, turned in a way that protected my secret from the possibility of Mother raising her eyes. The price of my reticence was to give up my view of the game on the other side of the fence. I sensed that Mother was watching me, that she would look up from time to time to see what I was doing, though I never caught her in the act.

When I cautiously returned to my vigil, the picture had changed, took some moments to assimilate in its new form I blinked my eyes, sucked in my breath.

"What was that?" my mother asked without raising her eyes.

"It wasn't anything," I think I said, not wanting to be heard, not by them, thinking the words rather than saying them.

The first thing I saw was the girl's naked behind thrust out like a thumb, her long hair screening it from full view. She was standing with her legs apart, knees bent, leaning forward. The boy was not where I could see him, not at first. Momentarily, the girl jumped forward, legs askew, as if imitating a frog. Then the boy—he had been somewhere else in the yard—performed a similar jump. I assumed they were playing Follow the Leader or some game of similar principle. It seemed innocent enough except for them both being unclothed and except for the apparent excitement in the air, the sense that they were doing something in violation of the rules. When the girl hopped on her left foot the boy recorded the gesture with his own. Then she hopped on her right foot, as did the boy. Then she did a tumble in the grass, a forward somersault of no special difficulty, though done with exceptional grace. The boy leaned forward to do his, then apparently decided against it. The girl stamped her foot in mock anger, a hand on her hip.

"If you won't do it, you'll have to pay the penalty," I think she said. "And you know what the penalty is, don't you?"

In the next moment she was chasing him around the yard, calling out some threat I couldn't quite hear and was unable to imagine. The word penalty was part of it. I could only make out their relative positions when they crossed my line of vision. The boy kept dodging her, putting himself in peril then slipping away.

I heard my mother groan with exhaustion, an oblique request for aid. I was afraid she would see what I was looking at, so I withdrew my eyes, pretended to study the ground.

I went down to my knees, staying as close to the fence as I could without creating attention, and dislodged a handful of weeds and grass.

I was about to glance through the slats when I saw my mother standing over me, her huge shadow preceding her. "Make sure you get the roots," she said. She was there to offer instruction.

While she was there, more shadow than substance, I didn't dare look through the spaces in the fence, though the temptation was extreme.

What was the penalty the girl whose name I may have known and have now forgotten intended to exact? My life, I thought at the time, depended on such knowledge.

I pulled the weeds as she advised, thinking if I did it right, she would go away, but she continued to watch and to instruct, though there was no longer any point to her instruction, no longer the slightest need.

"You're doing very nicely," she said, "except some of what you pull out aren't weeds."

"It's like having someone read over your shoulder," I said. "You make me self-conscious. I know what to do. You don't have to watch."

"I know I don't have to," she said. "I'm watching because I enjoy watching you weed."

The only way to get her to move away, I thought, was to stop weeding, which I did, announcing I was bored, lying on my back in the grass with my arms out. The sun was hot and I could feel my face burn.

Nothing I did or didn't do would get her to leave. Something astonishing was going on on the other side of the fence, and I was missing it because of Mother's lingering presence. I mentioned that I heard the phone ringing in the house but that didn't move her. I weeded in another part of the garden, thinking she would follow me there to see how I was doing. I was sick with desperation.

She didn't follow, remained standing with her back to the neighbor's high fence, surveying her garden with benign indifference, a permanent obstruction to my hopes.

When Phil tied the game at eleven all, Mother broke her fast and scored on a towering set shot that bounded in off the back rim, the ball in flight for the longest time, seeming to hover over the basket awaiting official clearance to land.

Mother's sudden resurgence of skill seemed to discombobulate Phil who disguised the tension he felt, the sense of impending failure, by becoming silly. He wriggled with mock arrogance as he took out the ball, whistling over and over some mindless jingle from a detergent commercial. You could see he was afraid to let the ball out of his hands. Though our mother gave him ample room, he withheld his shot, edging the ball closer to the basket by degrees. Mother stepped away at his approach, bided her time. I would have called to him to shoot—it was hard to resist—but it wasn't my part. Greedy for better position, Phil forced his way closer, Mother acceding step for step. When he decided he was close enough—he was already under the basket—and sought to reclaim his dribble, the ball glanced off his foot and went out of bounds.

"What bad luck," Mother said.

Phil kicked the ball before turning it over, said he would never play this effing game again, not if his life depended on it.

Mother reprimanded Phil for his poor sportmanship, said it didn't matter who won, it was the fun of the game and what you learned from it that counted.

Phil said if there was any fun in losing, none of it had ever come his way.

Although Phil had in effect conceded defeat, the game had its course to run. Mother had a habit of keeping things going beyond their normal duration.

Clenched with mock determination, Phil crowded Mother as she put the ball in play, waving his arms in her face, goading her with childish taunts. He would not give up the last basket, he was letting us know, without the formality of a struggle. One could see that Mother disapproved of the tactic, thought it excessive or in bad taste. At one point she put down the basketball to shake a finger at him. "Don't make me lose my temper," she warned him.

Phil, his face red, said he was only doing his best and no one could be faulted for that, could they. Could they?

Mother thought this assertion unworthy of a reply.

"Are you ready?" she asked him.

"If you're ready, I am," he said. "I got your number, lady."

In deliberate fashion, Mother feinted to the right and sidestepped to the left, hip to the right, step to the left, shoulder to the left, sidestep to the right.

Phil grudgingly yielded space, side step by side step, the court shrinking on him, his balance confused. Still, he would not let her have her way, not then, not for a moment.

The repetition of her movements would only take her so far and just when we thought she had nowhere to go she surprised us again. In the next moment, or the next, she appeared to take flight, spinning in the direction opposite from the one she had been going, rising from the ground, lifting the ball over her head with two hands as she flew Neither of us believed what we saw, required at the end the corroboration of the other's witness. Mother, in her apron and house slippers, taking flight, rising to the height of the basket, suspended like disbelief in air, slipping the ball through the rim like a gift, like a secret. Phil stood at her feet and waved, a belated farewell, his mouth agape.

In later years, if one of us derogated her ability, the other would bring up the recollection of her glorious moment as reproof. Mostly, it was as if it had never happened.

Mother circled the basket, keeping her observers in momentary suspense, before donating the ball to the charity of her triumph.

When she returned to the ground she apologized for letting herself get carried away.

Phil fought back tears, offered the hand of a graceful loser.

Mother enthused over the improvement in Phil's game, said that in truth she had been lucky, that Phil would surely win the next time. Phil, you could tell, was willing to believe her. He was young enough then to trust forever in illusion.

To Throw Like a Boy
Nancy Boutilier

He whose testicles are crushed or whose male member is cut off
shall not enter the assembly of the Lord. —Deuteronomy 23:1

Despite appropriate estrogen levels,
I learned at an early age
to throw like a boy.

When Billy Lester cried
for being chosen last
the other boys called him a girl.

As we grew older
our language grew richer.
"You woman," hissed Brad Seeley
when David Matsumura walked away from a fight.
I was better versed in cussing
than body parts by the time I was
singing the neighborhood slang.

"You pussy," I screamed at my brother
when he refused to play me one-on-one.
Although he had 6 inches and 40 pounds on me,
he cringed at the insult, accepted my challenge,
and I stood my ground when he drove to the hoop.
I don't remember slamming asphalt,
but I came to hearing the compliment
"Man, your sister sure has balls."

Such flattery ran dry
when I hit the age of Kotex.
Without words for rhythms
my body understood
I had to choose
between exile into womanhood
or their loudest praise of me,
inclusion as one of the guys.

Unsexing myself was easy at fourteen,
but fourteen lasts only one year
and the swelling of breasts
tingling between thighs
put me at war with my body.
Too much ambition, too little food—
going to every extreme to avoid being
without balls, a pussy, a woman.

The Touch
Justin Mitcham

for my mother

You stepped out the back door, drying your hands
on a plain white apron
and watching me slap the new basketball down
on the driveway's nearly flat hardpan,
unable to control it or to stall,
for long, its falling still.

You held out clean, wrinkled hands for the ball,
let it drop and caught the rise
with the fingertips, never with the palm,
allowing no sound but the ball's hollow bounce,
crouching low, either small hand
moving *with* the ball.
            And years later,
when the Newton County Rams came down,
like the cavalry at dawn on a few Cheyenne,
in a hot-breath man-to-man press, the best plan
was to get the ball to me. Even now,
I return to that late fall morning
when you taught me what a softer touch could do,

how to go where I needed to, never looking down.

Horse

Ann Packer

When I entered the ninth grade I had just turned fourteen and I wanted more than anything to be a pompon girl. My desire had formed over the course of the summer: my friends and I customarily ate lunch on the benches near the English office, but during the long idle months I had taken to imagining myself moved as if by magic to the picnic table in front of the snack machines, which was handed down, with all the arrogance and inevitability attached to the turning over of a monarchy, from one pompon squad to the next. Our school colors were red and yellow—crimson and gold, we called them—and by the end of the first day of school the idea of owning one of those short, flip-skirted red and yellow dresses had taken over my mind The football season pompon girls had shown up in their new outfits, and I was enamored even of the spotless white Keds they wore. Tryouts for the basketball pompon squad weren't until the beginning of October, but within days I had cleared out our garage and claimed it as my practice area. I set up my record player on the shelf where my mother kept the tools, and I listened to all of my albums, over and over again, in an effort to find a song that would inspire me to make up a winning routine. The routine, according to the printed rules I got from the girls' P. E. office, would be composed of a series of "steps"—dance steps, I decided—of my devising. The only fundamental thing about pompon was pompon step itself, a kind of miniature running in place that would form the basis of everyone's routine. The rest was up to me.

One Saturday morning, as I passed through the kitchen on my way to the garage, my mother cleared her throat and said she wanted to talk to me. She was sitting at the table, stacks of envelopes and her big, ledger-style checkbook lined up in front of her. She was paying the bills.

She pulled her reading glasses down onto the tip of her nose and looked up at me. "Found a song yet?" she asked evenly.

"Not yet," I said.

She nodded, and I wondered whether she was finally going to condemn my pompon dreams. So far, she hadn't come out against them—she hadn't, for instance, told me that she thought the whole concept was sexist or exploitative or elitist or even just plain silly—and because of her very neutrality I'd been assuming the worst. It wasn't like her not to comment.

"I got a call last night from Jim Baranski," she said, naming our down-the-street neighbor, who coached basketball at the local college. "One of his players needs a place to live and Jim thought we might let him have the guest room."

"Why would we do that?" I said.

"That's what I asked Jim. I'm not looking to be anybody's frat mother."

"So that was that?"

"The poor guy was supposed to have a full scholarship, but it fell through. If he can't find a place to live for free he's going to have to leave school. Jim says he's willing to do yardwork in exchange for a room.

"If we need yardwork done," I said, "maybe we should just get a gardener."

"We're not exactly rich at this point," my mother said, her voice tight and controlled. She cleared her throat and went on in a friendlier tone. "Jim said it might be nice for Danny to have a guy around. You know, an older guy—someone he could do things with. Play basketball and stuff."

Now I understood; and I understood that she wasn't asking my opinion so much as pleading with me not to say no. My father had died a year earlier, a heart attack at forty-five, and my ten-year-old brother Danny had become a big source of worry to her. He spent all his time in his room, reading Planet of the Apes books and drawing highly detailed maps of outer space. The maps were really good: all the lines were meticulously drawn; the planets were colored in to look like real spheres; and everything was carefully labeled in his tiny, scientist's script.

"When's he moving in?" I said.

"Elizabeth."

"Well?"

She began flipping through the bills. "I told Jim we'd try it for a month. And if any of us doesn't like it that'll be that." She looked up at me, a small, desperate smile on her lips. "His name's Bobby. He's going to bring his things over tomorrow."

"OK."

"Really?"

I forced a smile. "Sure," I said. "It'll be good for Danny." But I thought, a basketball player? It seemed like an insult to my father's memory: he had taught philosophy at the college, and his favorite and only sport had been speed-reading paperback mysteries.

The guest room was right next to my room, and I got up early the next morning to take a last look at it. My room had been decorated—very decorated—according to my specifications six or seven years earlier, it was all pink and white, and whenever I felt the girlishness of it too keenly I would go into the guest room and lie on the bed in there. It was a big, square, airy room, full of plain oak furniture. The only adornment was an elaborate cut glass water pitcher on the dresser, anywhere else it might have looked gaudy, but it was the perfect touch in that austere room.

I stood in the doorway and tried to imagine a college basketball player living next door to me. The room was empty except for when my grandmother came to visit, and although I could never really hear her, I always felt aware of her when she was there—of her breathing, of her sighing, of her rolling over in bed in the middle of the night.

I went down to the garage and, as I had every day for the past two weeks, I worked on my pompon step. It wasn't, I had quickly learned, as easy as it looked. You had to jump from foot to foot, pointing first your left toes, then your right toes, then your left toes, then your right toes, and all the while you had to keep your hands at your waist, but not around your waist: they had to be bent at the knuckles so your fingers and thumbs wouldn't show. It was a little boring, but I didn't mind spending so much time on it because the next thing I had to do was settle on a song and start working on my routine. I knew it would have to involve some kicking, some little flips of the shoulder, and, most important, the splits, and although I'd been stretching every day I could only get down to about eight inches off the ground.

Early in the afternoon, a car came up the driveway and stopped just on the other side of the garage. I turned off my music. A couple of doors slammed; then I heard a deep voice.

"Nice deal, Bobby. Maybe they'll go away a lot and you can have some parties."

"Quiet." His voice was clear and rather high for a man's. "They might be able to hear us."

I lowered the arm of the record player back onto the album I was playing, turned the volume up, and sat down on the garage floor, my bare legs touching the cold concrete. I listened to the muffled sounds of people going back and forth, from car to house, for the next five or ten minutes. After a while the commotion stopped, and I knew my mother and Danny were talking to Bobby and his friend. She had probably offered them iced tea, maybe even sandwiches. The only thing I had with me to read was the pompon tryouts instruction sheet, and I read it through several times, trying to concentrate on all the details—what kind of gloves you were supposed to wear, how long your routine should be, when the winners' names would be posted. There was one paragraph that I kept going back to. It said, "The pompon girls represent everyone at Murphy Junior High. They are our ambassadors to schools all over the county. Even when they're not in uniform they feel like pompon girls, and it's important that they look that way, too. This means extra special attention to personal hygiene and grooming. Any girl who doesn't know what this means should speak to Mrs. Donovan in the P.E. office as soon as possible."

I didn't know what it meant—I assumed it had something to do either with shaving under your arms or getting your period—but I wasn't about to ask Mrs. Donovan. With my mother I had only recently managed to shut down communication about such things; as far as I was concerned, we had covered what needed to be covered. The occasional appearance on my desk of pamphlets entitled "Your Changing Body" or "A Single Egg" suggested that she disagreed.

Finally, I heard the car starting up again, and I turned the music off in time to hear the low-voiced guy say, "Later, bro."

"See you at practice," Bobby said.

They said a few more things, but in voices pitched so low I couldn't hear them. I imagined they were talking about me: saying how strange it was my mother hadn't made me say hello, that I must be one of those shy girls who couldn't look anybody in the eye. Either that, or they were wondering what I looked like, what color hair I had. What my body was like.

At six Danny came out to tell me dinner was ready.

"What are we having?" I asked.

"Steak," he said. "Baked potatoes with sour cream. Corn on the cob with butter. Chocolate cream pie."

He was joking. All we ever had now was fish. Sometimes she put a sauce called Mock Hollandaise on our vegetables, but usually it was just lemon juice and pepper. There was no salt in the house anymore, no butter.

I laughed. "What'd you read today?"

"I didn't really read."

I turned from him and began stacking my records together.

"She invited him to eat with us," he said.

I didn't reply.

"That guy. Bobby."

I wheeled around. "I know who you mean. What do you think I am, stupid?"

His face turned a delicate shade of pink, the color he used to get when he had a fever. He was wearing a nerdy little plaid shirt with a too-big collar, and his head looked unbearably small to me.

"I'm sorry, Dan," I said. I took hold of his shoulders and pulled him to me. "You're almost as tall as I am, sonny-boy."

"Won't be long now, moony-girl." He pulled away from me and I followed him into the house.

Bobby Johansen was very tall: six foot four, I later learned. His hair was pale blond, almost colorless. He was leaning against the kitchen counter, wearing shorts, and I thought his legs would probably come up to my chest if we stood close.

My mother was washing lettuce. "*Here* she is," she said, as if my whereabouts had been a mystery. "Elizabeth, this is Bobby Johansen."

"Hi," I said. The table was set for four, and my mother had even used cloth placemats; lately even the usual woven straw ones had gone missing more often than not.

"Hey, Elizabeth," he said. "How's it goin'?"

I looked up at him and shrugged. "OK."

He didn't seem to know what to do with his hands. First they were on the counter behind him, then they were clasped in front of his fly, then crossed tightly over his chest. "What do you go by?" he said. "Liz? I've got a cousin Liz, just about your age."

"Elizabeth," I said.

"We used to call her Bit, though," my mother said. "Didn't we, honey?"

"We?" I said.

She pursed her lips. "Danny did. He couldn't say Elizabeth, he said *Elizabit*. Then it was just Bit. Right, Dan?"

"A few hundred years ago," Danny said.

"Well, anyway," my mother said to me. "We were thinking maybe after dinner the four of us could play a game. Monopoly or something."

"Can't," I said. "Math test tomorrow."

My mother yanked a square of paper towel from the roll and began arranging the wet lettuce leaves on it.

"I used to be pretty good at math," Bobby said. "If you need any help."

"That's OK," I said. It was in my mind to say, I'm pretty good at math, too; but I managed to stifle it. "Thanks, though."

There was a silence. I was still holding my records, so l went upstairs to put them in my room. The guest room door was ajar and I pushed it open. A couple of worn-looking green duffel bags were lying on the bed, with T-shirts and sweat clothes and towels spilling out as if they were someone's cast-offs at a garage sale. I tiptoed across the room and opened the closet door. It was empty except for three pairs of high-topped white leather sneakers arranged in a row on the floor. I bent over and picked up a shoe. It was longer than my forearm and it smelled: of dirty laundry and of sweat, but of something else, too—a sharp, leathery scent. It was, I decided, the smell of arrogance.

The following Friday, at the lunch-time rally that was the official end of the school day—during football season we got out early for away games—I stood by myself and studied the football pompon girls' new routine. They would do it again at half-time later that afternoon, but I wasn't going to the game; none of my friends ever went, and I was too shy to go to an away game alone. If I'd been asked why I wanted to go, I would only have been able to say that it had something to do with my father dying: that it wasn't the game so much as the way everyone looked after the game as they poured onto the field from the bleachers, uniform expressions of joy or despair on their faces.

I rode my bicycle home through the college, thinking that I would have the house to myself for the afternoon. Students were lying on the grass in little groups, and I looked at them more carefully than usual, wondering if Bobby was among them. I hadn't seen him since the day he moved in. He had a meal plan at one of the dorms and he studied at the library, so all I knew of him so far was the sound of his footsteps on the stairs as I was falling asleep. He didn't even leave his toothbrush in the bathroom.

The guest room door was closed. I went into my room, put my books on my desk, and lay down on my bed. I closed my eyes and waited to see what would materialize—the glittering ballroom, the dark restaurant, the umbrella-shaded outdoor cafe: at that time the arena of my fantasy life was limited to places where I would not be alone with the object of my idylls. After a moment, the restaurant hovered into view. The walls were lined with smoky mirrors, the tables covered with pale pink linen and set with gold-rimmed china. I was tall and sleek in a clingy silver gown sewn all over with shimmering little beads. A handsome, square-jawed man—with whom I never, in all the adolescent hours I spent in his company, exchanged a word—met me at the door and guided me to our secluded table, his hand in the small of my back. (I had just learned about the small of your back; it was where you were supposed to aim your tampon, and although that was nearly as unpleasant to think of as it was to do, the idea of that spot had a kind of power over me. It suggested romance—not the candlelight and flowers kind, but something easier, more intimate.)

I heard a noise from Bobby's room. It wasn't much of a noise: low and repetitive and only vaguely vocal. But before I was really even aware of the sound, I'd convinced myself that sex was taking place on the other side of the wall.

I turned my radio on, loud, and sat at my desk looking at my Latin book, my heart pounding. A moment later I got up and clomped past the guest room and down the stairs. I paused in the kitchen, but the idea of the two of them—Bobby in pajama bottoms, a tousle-haired girl in the matching pajama top—coming down in search of something to drink sent me out to the garage.

Leaning against the wall was a brand-new basketball hoop attached to a backboard. I looked it over for a minute or two: the backboard was white with jaunty red trim; the basket itself was a metal circle from which hung a flimsy-looking white net. I bent my knees and tried to lift it, but it was surprisingly heavy.

"Careful with that, it's heavier than it looks."

I turned around and Bobby was standing in the doorway, his long arms dangling by his sides.

"I was going to put that up for Danny this afternoon," he said. He was wearing gym shorts and a grey T-shirt, and there were big dark stains where he'd been sweating. I must have been staring, because he said, "I was doing sit-ups."

"Danny's not much of an athlete," I said.

"Everyone likes to shoot baskets."

"Does my mother know?"

He gave me a funny look. "She bought it."

I turned from him and examined the hoop again. "These strings don't seem too sturdy," I said.

He laughed and came over to where I was standing. "They're not meant to hold any weight. They hug the ball when it goes through so it'll drop down gently instead of flying all over the court. Stick around while I put it up and I'll show you."

"I have homework,. I said.

He nodded "More math?"

"Latin.'

"Can't help you there. The only Latin I know is pig."

I edged toward the door. "Well," I said. "See you later."

"O-say ong-lay," he said with a smile.

A few nights later my mother came into my room on her way to bed. I was rearranging my closet, and she sat at my desk and watched me. "I guess we should get you a new parka this year," she said.

"This one's OK." I hung it on a hook inside the closet door.

"Maybe a down one," she said. "I was thinking we should go up to Tahoe in February. Try again." When I was eight or nine the four of us had spent a miserable weekend trying to learn to ski; we'd never gone back. My father had liked to say that we were the only family in

California who *didn't* love the fact that the mountains were only five hours from the beach.

"Down jackets aren't good for skiing," I said. "Too bulky."

"Elizabeth," she said. "Why do you have to be so difficult?"

I looked at her; her lips were pressed into a narrow line. "I'm not being difficult. I just don't happen to want a down jacket."

"That's not the point," she said. "I mention skiing and you don't react at all. Can't you at least say, 'Yes, Mother dear, a ski trip would be lovely,' or 'No, Mother dear, the idea of trying to ski again makes my legs turn to jelly'?"

I turned back to the closet. Very quietly, I said, "I'll go if you want me to."

"I want you to have an *opinion*."

I shrugged, but suddenly there were tears running down my face. I stared at my clothes.

"Eliz?"

"I can't."

She came over and touched my shoulder and I turned around. "What is it?" she said. She pulled me close and held me, and my shoulders started to shake. "What is it?"

I shook my head.

She ran her hand up and down my back. "Tell me," she said. "Poor baby, to have such a brute of a mother. Tell me."

I pulled away from her, got a Kleenex from my desk, and blew my nose. "Why do you have to get so mad at me?"

"I'm sorry." She sat down on my bed and shook her head. She looked very small, sitting there; small and tired. There were wrinkles around her eyes and mouth, and her hair looked thin and lifeless.

I heard the sound of someone—Bobby—opening and closing the front door and coming up the stairs. A moment later, the guest room door closed.

"I'm sorry," my mother said again. "I'll try to be better."

I held my forefinger up to my lips, then pointed at the wall dividing my room from Bobbie. *He can hear us,* I mouthed.

She smiled at me. "He doesn't care," she whispered.

"Well," I whispered back, "I do."

With the coming of the basketball hoop Bobby was around more, and I had to find a new place to work on my pompon routine. I moved down to the basement, and against the muffled yet insistent sounds of the basketball bouncing on the asphalt and—thud—hitting the backboard, I settled on the Beach Boys' "I Get Around," and began to choreograph my moves.

Late one afternoon, when my routine was going badly and the Beach Boys' falsettos were all but drowned out by the hammer of the basketball, I decided that I'd had enough. I marched up the stairs and out to the driveway, icily polite equivalents to WILL YOU PLEASE SHUT UP running through my mind. But when I saw Danny standing there looking at the ball, which seemed bigger around than he was, I couldn't say anything. I watched.

"OK," Bobby said, glancing at me, "dribble a couple of times and then when you shoot try for some backspin." He held his hand up, palm to the sky, and flicked his wrist a couple of times. "Roll the ball up your fingers."

Danny bounced the ball, then threw it at the basket; it hit the rim with a metallic clang and careened past me. I turned and ran after it, then carried it back and handed it to Bobby. "Want to try?" he said.

I shook my head.

He gave the ball back to Danny. "That was better," he said. "Try again."

On the fifth shot, the ball hit the backboard, rolled around the rim, and went through the net. "Great," Bobby said, giving Danny's shoulder a little shake. "That's the stuff."

He took the ball and without looking at me backed up so that he was standing just a few feet from me. Without seeming to aim, he tossed the ball and it sailed through the air and went cleanly through the basket without touching the backboard or the rim. "Swish," he said.

Danny caught the ball and came running over. "Can we play HORSE?" he said.

Bobby looked at me and smiled. "Only if your sister will try a shot first."

"Blackmailer," I said.

Danny handed me the ball and I moved closer to the basket. I held the ball in front of my face, closed my eyes, and threw.

"Two points," Bobby yelled. "Whoo!"

Danny clapped and called. "Maybe you should try out to play instead."

"Ha ha," I said. I tugged at my shirt, which had ridden up and exposed my stomach when I threw the ball.

"Play HORSE with us," Danny said. "Please?"

"HORSE?" I glanced at Bobby; he stood there with the ball tucked under his arm, looking at me. "I don't think so, Dan."

"You don't even know what it is. Let me at least explain it to you." Danny held out his hands and Bobby threw him the ball. He bounced it and looked up at the basket. "Say I go first. I stand wherever I want and try for a basket. If I make it, the next person has to stand in the same spot and shoot. And if they don't make it they get an H. And you keep moving around and whoever spells out HORSE first loses. Get it? They're a horse. Come on, it's fun."

"Sorry, kid," I said. "Got to practice. I have no time for this 'fun' of which you speak."

"Your graciousness," he said, and bowed to me.

"Your majesty," I said, bowing back.

I turned and headed for the house. "Bye, Elizabeth," Bobby called to me as I reached the kitchen door. "Nice to see you again."

I needed some white gloves. My mother had said not to worry; she had several pairs I could choose from. The Saturday before tryouts I asked her to let me see them.

She led me up to her bedroom and pulled a shoebox from the back of her closet. "I know you can't believe it," she said, "but your mother used to be the picture of elegance."

We both laughed; she was wearing blue jeans and an old checked shirt, her usual weekend attire. Even when she went to work I thought she looked a little mannish—she dressed in somber colors, never wore jewelry.

She slipped the top off the box and pulled away some tissue paper "God," she said.

I looked into the box, and it was a strange sight: over a dozen gloves, some white, some beige, even a single navy blue one, all lying in a tangle. "How orderly," I said.

"Don't give me any lip, kid," she said, smiling. She set the box on the bed and we began sorting through it, putting the gloves in pairs.

"Where's the other blue one?" I said.

"Long gone." A dreamy look came over her face and for a moment I thought she was going to tell me a story. But all she said was "Lost to another era."

There were four pairs of white gloves in all, but none of them seemed right to me.

"What's wrong with these. Elizabeth?"

"The rules didn't say anything about buttons."

"Well, what about these?"

"There's a huge stain on the left one."

"It's on the palm, no one'll see it."

"Mom."

"These?"

"Too long."

Finally she sat on the bed and looked at me, her mouth in a half-frown.

"I'll ride over to the shopping center and buy some," I said. I began piling the gloves back into the box.

She grabbed my wrist. "Elizabeth, for God's sake, you're only going to wear them for ten minutes."

I shook her hand off. "I want to look nice."

She stood up and cut me a disgusted look, then stalked out of the room. I hurried after her and caught up with her on the stairs.

"Why shouldn't I get new gloves?" I said. "What do you care? I'll pay for them."

"I don't care," she snapped.

"Mom," I said.

We reached the bottom of the stairs and she turned to face me. "It's just so silly, Elizabeth," she said quietly. "It's beneath you."

I opened my mouth, but nothing came out.

"Your father would—"

"Well lucky for me he's not here to see it!" I jerked open the front door and hurried out of the house. My bicycle was locked, and I had to twist the dial several times before I got the lock to open.

Twenty minutes later I was at the shopping center—without a cent. I decided to look around anyway; when I found the gloves I wanted I would ask the saleslady to hold them for me, then go back home for my wallet.

I went into Penney's and found the glove department. There was no one behind the counter, so I circled the glass case, looking. There were leather gloves and wool gloves and gloves made of bright red satin, but I couldn't find a single pair of white gloves.

"Can I help you?"

A woman stood behind the counter, blue hair piled on top of her head. I told her what I wanted and she said, "Oh, we haven't carried white gloves in ten years, dear. Is it for Halloween?"

"Um, no."

"Prom?" she asked, cocking her head gaily.

"No, I just need them for school."

She raised her eyebrows. "School play?"

"No, I—thanks anyway." I turned and hurried away.

"You might try Peaches and Cream, dear," she called after me.

I got outside the store and leaned against the wall. My face felt hot. At the other end of the shopping center was Bullock's, where my mother took me twice a year for school clothes. I decided to go there first, even though Peaches and Cream was on the way; Peaches and Cream was a shop full of breakable knickknacks and precious little silk flower arrangements, and although I'd never been in it I had always held it in a kind of contempt: it seemed to have nothing to do with real life.

But Bullock's didn't have white gloves, either. I wandered around the ground floor of the store, and, as if I were languishing in a boat on a hot day and needed the feel of the water, my hand trailed behind me, touching whatever I passed: wool, leather, chrome. In the makeup department I slowed even more, studying the nail polish and lipstick at first one counter, then another. A young woman in a salmon-colored lab coat caught my eye.

"Free makeovers today," she said. "Would you like one?"

"I don't have any money," I said.

"They're *free*."

"But I won't be able to buy anything after."

She patted the seat of a chair set against one of the counters. "You'll feel better."

I glanced around the area; it was nearly empty. I climbed onto the chair.

"I'm Kristen," she said. "Tell me a little about what you usually wear. Makeup-wise, I mean."

"Oh, just a little eyeshadow and lip gloss," I said, although in truth I never wore a stroke of either.

"What's your name, honey?"

"Elizabeth."

"Well, Elizabeth, I'm going to start with a little foundation." She unscrewed the top of a small white bottle, tipped some liquid onto her fingers, and began dabbing the stuff onto my face.

Another salmon-coated woman appeared. "Oh, *fun*," she said. "Wild Sage on her lids, don't you think?"

"I was thinking Midnight Velvet," Kristen said.

They joined forces. They mixed colors. They tried a little of this and a little of that. Half an hour later Kristen offered me a hand mirror.

"You're going to love this, Elizabeth," she said.

I searched the image for signs of myself, but I looked like a stranger —not just someone I didn't recognize, but someone who wasn't quite human. My cheeks had unnatural-looking hollows, and across each cheekbone was a slash of pink. They had used so much mascara it looked as if I were wearing false eyelashes.

"Well?" Kristen said.

"She has to get used to it," the other woman said. "It's a change." I handed Kristen the mirror. "It's a whole new me."

She gave me a wide smile. "I knew you'd like it."

I thanked them and left the store. There were some benches arranged around a fountain and I slumped onto one. I closed my eyes and felt the sun on my hair and skin. My face felt odd, as if I'd washed it and let it dry without rinsing the soap off. I thought about the pompon tryouts instruction sheet, the part about hygiene and grooming. I wondered whether everyone else would be wearing a lot of makeup for the tryouts: I knew that the other girls who were trying out were the kind who *did* wear eyeshadow and lip gloss to school every day. I imagined myself in the girls' gym on the day of the tryouts, standing there in my forest green polyester one-piece gymsuit and my white gloves, waiting for my turn; my stomach did a queasy dance. Then I thought about what my mother had said, and I stood up, ready to try Peaches and Cream.

And there was Bobby.

He was coming toward me, but he hadn't seen me yet. I thought of running, but I knew that would attract more attention than anything. Hoping I would somehow be invisible to him, I sat down on the bench again and stared at the ground.

"Elizabeth?"

I looked up. "Hi."

He did a quick double-take, so subtle that if I hadn't been looking for his reaction I might not have noticed it. "What are you doing? He put his foot up on the bench next to me."

"Shopping."

"What have you bought? I need socks."

"Nothing," I said. "I forgot my wallet."

He laughed. "Window shopping, more like, huh?" He turned and sat on the bench, a few feet away from me.

"I guess so."

We sat there staring straight ahead, not talking. I was certain that he thought I was the most pathetic person on earth, that he felt too sorry for me to make a get-away.

"So," he said.

"So," I said.

"Can I ask you a question?"

I turned to look at him.

"What happened to your face?"

I felt, surprisingly, that I had a choice: I could die of embarrassment or not, it was up to me. I smiled, and a moment later we were both laughing. "I had a makeover," I said.

"In there?"

I nodded. "There were two of them, Kristen and someone else. It took half an hour. It was free."

"What a bargain," he said, and we both laughed. "I don't know, I think Kristen and her friend are in the wrong line of work."

"What?! You don't think they're artists?" I stood up and struck a pose.

"More like morticians."

"So that's why I couldn't recognize myself in the mirror. I look dead."

We both started to laugh again, but a shadow of unhappiness fell over me and although I kept laughing, I was thinking about my father; we'd had an open casket, against my wishes, and when I saw him lying there, a false rosiness on his waxy cheeks, I felt a tiny pinprick of shock, as if I had to learn all over again of his death.

I looked at Bobby and he was biting his lip. He smiled quickly and stood up.

"Maybe I could help you buy your socks," I said. "I mean, I'm sure you don't need help, but maybe I could go with you."

"Actually," he said, "I do need help. I can never decide on colors. Red and yellow or blue and green."

"You wear red socks?"

"No, no," he said, laughing, "the bands on top. I need tube socks. For practice." He dribbled an imaginary basketball, then shot it into the sky.

"Would you like to go to a movie tonight?" my mother said at dinner that evening. I'd been back and forth to the shopping center until the middle of the afternoon—I'd finally found some gloves at Peaches and Cream—and since I'd gotten home she and I had been distant and polite when we'd seen each other, as if we were strangers whose paths kept crossing in some foreign city.

"No, thank you," I said. "I've got to spend some time on things that are beneath me."

She colored, and Danny looked down at his plate. "I'm sorry, honey," she said. "I didn't mean it, it was a dumb thing to say. I just don't want you to be disappointed."

'When I don't make it?" I asked, standing up to clear the table.

Danny all but leapt from his chair and hurried from the room.

"Oh," my mother said quietly, and covered her mouth with her hand. She shook her head, and I could see she was fighting tears. After a moment she turned and faced the door, following Danny's path with her eyes. "Should I—"

I went over to her and held her head to my chest. "He's OK," I said. I think we should just leave him alone."

"The old laissez-faire attitude was never my strong suit," she said. The vibrations her jaw made against my stomach as she spoke felt strange. She sighed and put her hands on my hips and I moved away. She looked up at me. "Show us your dance, honey," she said. "I think it would mean a lot to Danny."

I nodded. *Dance*, I thought.

"And to me, too, of course."

"Tomorrow," I said.

But the next day, a Sunday, Danny had been invited by a friend's family to go to San Francisco, and it wasn't until Monday night, just two days before tryouts, that I allowed my mother and Danny into the basement to watch me run through my routine.

"OK," I said when we got downstairs, "I'm going to pretend you guys are the judges."

Danny had perched on the washing machine. My mother leaned against the dryer. "How many are there?" she said uneasily.

"Six," I said. There would be Mrs. Donovan; Coach Simpson; Sally Chin, the head pompon girl for the football season; two guys from the basketball team; and Miss Rosenthal, a Home Ec teacher—my Home Ec teacher, as it happened, and it was she who worried me most. We had somehow, already, not hit it off; the other girls in the class were already on their A-line skirts, but I just couldn't finish my pot holder. I was afraid she would take it out on me in the judging.

"Six?" my mother said.

"The competition is going to be tough," Danny said. "We've got some very critical judges, ladies and gentlemen, and only five of these fifty beautiful young ladies will be selected. Sam, tell us a little about how the competition works."

"Fifty!" my mother said.

"He's joking, Mom. It's twenty-two."

"Oh, that's not so bad," my mother said. "Five out of twenty-two." But she looked unhappy.

"And now, from our own Manzanita Drive, it's Elizabeth Earle," Danny shouted.

"Quiet," my mother said, elbowing him.

I winked at Danny and turned to start the music. I stood with my back to them, my hands at my waist, my right knee bent. Then, on cue, I whipped around and started the routine.

It was the first time I had done it in front of anyone, and the thing I was most conscious of was the fact that I could not keep a smile on my face: Smile, I would tell myself, and my lips would slide open, and I would think about the kick I was doing (was my knee straight? were my toes pointed?) and I would realize my mouth was twisted into a tight knot again.

I finished with the splits, my arms upstretched in a V for Victory.

"Yes," Danny cried, leaping off the washing machine. He high-fived me and ran up the stairs to the kitchen.

My mother smiled at me. "Very nice," she said.

I sighed and turned around.

"Really, honey," she said. "It's good—you got all the way down on your splits. I'll bet most of the other girls can't do that."

Danny came running back down the stairs, waving a piece of paper on which he'd written "9.9" with a thick pen. "An amazing routine from Elizabeth Earle," he cried.

"Thanks, Dan." I looked at my mother. "Well, it'll all be over in two days."

"Who knows?" she said. "Maybe it'll just be beginning."

They went upstairs while I took the record off the turntable and put it back in its paper sleeve. I wiped my sweaty palms off on my shoes— I'd decided not to wear the gloves for practicing, to keep them clean— then I turned the basement light off and climbed the stairs.

My mother and Bobby were sitting at the kitchen table. When my mother saw me she said, "Elizabeth got her tryouts day after tomorrow."

Bobby looked at me. "Nervous?"

I nodded.

"Twenty-two girls are trying out for five spots," my mother said.

"OK, Mom." I looked at Bobby's feet. "Are you wearing your new socks?"

He pulled up one leg of his jeans to display the bright red and yellow bands around the top of his sock. "Listen," he said, "try not to be too nervous. It'll show, and that'll be the thing that gets you. Know what I mean?" He turned to my mother. "They totally watch for whether the girl has the right look. You know, smiley, bouncy. Believe me, I was once a judge for one of these things."

"Maybe you should do your routine for Bobby," my mother said.

"Absolutely not." His words had sent my heartbeat out of control. Eyeshadow and lip gloss, I thought, like it or not.

"Please?" he said.

I shook my head.

"Well, just remember," he said. "You've got to smile."

I felt my face fill with color.

My mother coughed and said, "You know, honey, you did look a little fierce down there."

I gave them a frozen grin. "Like this?" I said through clenched teeth.

"That's the one," Bobby said. "Glue it on."

"Goodnight," I said. Without looking at either of them, I got myself a glass of water and climbed the stairs.

"Elizabeth?" Danny called from his room.

I stopped in his doorway. He was lying on his bed, our giant world atlas open in front of him. "Planning a trip?" I asked. I sat down next to him and glanced at the atlas; it was open to a page showing the whole of Africa. "They say Morocco is nice this time of year."

"It was good," he said. "I'm sure you'll make it."

I shrugged. "Not according to Mr. Basketball down there."

"What did he say?"

"Nothing. I can just tell. He thinks I'm not pretty enough."

"God," Danny said. "He does not. You are so puerile sometimes."

"Puerile?" I laughed and reached over to tickle his neck. "Little Mr. Vocabulary."

"Don't call me little." He scrambled off the bed and assumed a body-builder's stance. Then he put his hands on his hips and began mimicking my pompon kicks. "Do they have pompon girls in Morocco?"

"Danny!"

He started wiggling around, his arms snaking out from his sides. "I'm a Moroccan pompon girl," he said. "Elizabethahad Earlakim."

"Danny," I said. "Stop, tell me the truth. Did I look fierce?"

Of course I didn't make it. Ten or twelve years later, at parties, I would offer up the comic spectacle of myself standing in the girls' gym, my back to the judges, my eyelids powder blue, my white-gloved hands clenched into fists, my right knee bent: my hopeful, embarrassed self waiting for the music to start. I would say that as I slid down into the splits at the end, my arms in their V, I caught Miss Rosenthal's eye and mistook her horsey grin for congratulations on a job well done, when in fact she was trying to get me to smile. I would perhaps also say—although this wasn't true, I was far too nervous for such fancies—that as I stood in the locker room changing out of my gymsuit, I had a triumphant vision of myself on the floor of the basketball court at half-time, facing the crowded bleachers in my crimson and gold dress, and that I felt a thrill of fear at the idea of doing something so marvelously alien. I would say, in closing, that I was lucky: no one could admit to actually having been a pompon girl. The cachet was in having wanted to, and failed.

Here's what I never said: After the list was posted I telephoned my mother to come pick me up; it was nearly six o'clock and the afternoon light was fading. I was sitting on the curb in the parking lot hoping that Bobby wouldn't be around when I got home, when the memory of my mother's voice came to me. "Your father would—" it said. Your father would, your father would . . . And I was filled with sickness because I realized that she might have been wrong. Wouldn't he, after all, have been on my side? What would he have thought? *Well, lucky for me he isn't here to see it.*

A little while later my mother arrived; neither of us spoke on the way home.

As we turned into our street, I saw that Danny and Bobby were outside the house, shooting baskets. "No," I said, turning to her. "Oh, please.'

"What?" She put her foot on the brake.

"I can't see him right now. Can't we go to the store or something?"

"You look fine, honey."

"Mom," I said. "It's not how I look. He'll think I'm such a loser. He'll try to get me to play basketball. Please."

She steered the car to the curb and cut the engine. She turned to face me. 'You don't get it, do you?" she said. "He doesn't think you're a loser. He's scared of you."

"Bobby?"

"Terrified. You're what's standing between him and a place to live. Next week his month is up, and if we say he can't stay he's in big trouble. He's scared you want him out."

My mouth fell open. "He told you this?"

"Elizabeth," she said. "Believe me. No, he didn't tell me, but I know. You can be—formidable."

I looked out the window at our house. Dusk was coming on quickly now, but still they played. I watched Danny make three baskets in a row. Then Bobby took the ball, backed up to the foot of the driveway, and drove in for a lay-up. "That was a good shot," I said. I turned back to my mother.

She had picked up my gloves, which I'd thrown onto the seat between us, and was pulling them on. She held her hands up in front of her face and looked at them. Then she reached out and ran her finger down my cheek, a soft, velvety touch. "I'm sorry you didn't win," she said.

I sat without speaking for a while. Then I took her hand and pulled at the fingertip of the glove."What am I going to do with these?"

"I know of this shoebox," she said. She smiled at me; then she started the car and drove the last hundred yards to our house.

When they saw us, Danny and Bobby stopped playing. I got out of the car, and for a moment neither of them said anything. Then Bobby said, "I'm sorry, Elizabeth—it's too bad." He brushed the hair off his forehead and I could see he was trying to think of something to add.

"Thanks," I said.

Danny bounced the basketball a couple of times. Without quite looking at me he said, "We could play one game of HORSE before dinner."

"I'm kind of tired, Dan."

He bounced the ball again.

"We could just play GOAT," Bobby said. "That would be quicker."

"Or DOG," Danny said, smiling.

I set my books on the trunk of the car. "Jeez, guys—I'm not in a hurry. Let's play RHINOCEROS."

"All right," Danny said, jumping up and down. "You'll play."

I looked at Bobby and we exchanged an amused smile.

"I know," Danny went on. "I have a great idea. Let's play ANTIDIS-ESTABLISHMENTARIANISM."

"What?" Bobby said.

"Antidisestablishmentarianism," Danny said. "It's the longest word in the English language."

That was something he'd gotten from our father. As a game at dinner we used to have these sort of spelling bees, and Danny always insisted that the longer a word was, the harder it would be to spell; our father gave him "antidisestablishmentarianism" once to show that he was wrong.

"Danny," I said, "spell 'puerile.'"

"Hold on, you two," said Bobby. "I think it has to be an animal."

A Basketball Game at Newburgh Middle School
Aleda Shirley

The cheerleaders limber up; their sneakers,
stiff with white polish, squeak at each step.
The band strikes up the fight song.
Motes swirl around the horns and drums
but it's sawdust I imagine, soft and fragrant,

rising from the planks of the gym floor
as if the floor somehow recalled
the lumberyard, the logging camp,
the forest. A boy dunks the ball and dribbles
back down the court past his parents

in the bleachers. From the windows near the ceiling
January light falls in great sheets over the girls
who wear like bright sweaters the stares
they attract. On the sidelines, two of those
who didn't make the squad move their lips:

they know the words to every cheer.
In fifteen years, these girls will be the mothers.
I'm too far away to make out which of them it is
who stands on a porch in light snow.
Her son in the driveway shoots free throws.

Bouncing off the garage door, the ball lands
on a white boxwood and sends snow like sparks

in every direction. She thinks of air shimmering
like heat as she tumbled through it, backflips and aerials.
It's cold. Her son bags three in a row. Should she call

him in? What was his name, the boy who first kissed her?
Trembling, she's afraid no touch will ever
thrill her as much as that of her own hair
falling across the bones of her face,
one afternoon when all eyes were on her.

Slam, Dunk, & Hook
Yusef Komunyakaa

Fast breaks. Lay ups. With Mercury's
Insignia on our sneakers,
We outmaneuvered the footwork
Of bad angels. Nothing but a hot
Swish of strings like silk
Ten feet out. In the roundhouse
Labyrinth our bodies
Created, we could almost
Last forever, poised in midair
Like storybook sea monsters.
A high note hung there
A long second. Off
The rim. We'd corkscrew
Up & dunk balls that exploded
The skullcap of hope & good
Intention. Bug-eyed, lanky,
All hands & feet . . . sprung rhythm.
We were metaphysical when girls
Cheered on the sidelines.
Tangled up in a falling,
Muscles were a bright motor
Double-flashing to the metal hoop
Nailed to our oak.
When Sonny Boy's mama died
He played nonstop all day, so hard
Our backboard splintered.
Glistening with sweat, we jibed
& rolled the ball off our
Fingertips. Trouble

Was there slapping a blackjack
Against an open palm.
Dribble, drive to the inside, feint,
& glide like a sparrow hawk.
Lay ups. Fast breaks.
We had moves we didn't know
We had. Our bodies spun
On swivels of bone & faith,
Through a lyric slipknot
Of joy, & we knew we were
Beautiful & dangerous.

El Diablo de la Cienega

Geoffrey Becker

The black sports car that pulled up in a puff of dust alongside the La Cienega Community Center looked like a big hand, placed palm down in the red dirt. Ignoring it, Victor kept his feet in front of the chalked line on the cracked concrete. The door clicked open and a very tanned man with straw-colored hair got out, stuck his hands into the pockets of his chinos, and leaned back to watch. No time left on the clock, Spurs down by one. As always, the game had come down to this one deciding moment. Victor made the first shot, then lobbed up the second for the win. There had never really been any doubt. Just for the hell of it, he made them again.

The late afternoon sun glinted off the broken windshields of a half-dozen wrecked and rusting cars across the road. Beyond them sat nine mobile homes, all in poor repair, set at odd angles to each other. The community center, a square building with flaking yellow stucco and one intact window, sported a tiny sign indicating that it had also once served as the La Cienega Volunteer Fire Department. From the south wall, a faded outline of a mural of the Virgin someone had begun long ago and never finished gazed out, faceless. The building was abandoned but, with the exception of a few weedy cracks in its surface, the basketball court alongside it was still in good shape.

Victor looked over briefly at the man, then continued shooting. He tossed in seven consecutive baskets before one finally circled the rim and hopped back out.

"Hope I didn't make you nervous," called the man.

Victor, twelve, had recently experienced a growth spurt that had turned him into a gangly, stretched-out cartoon of what he'd looked like the year before. He was particularly sensitive to criticism. Catching the ball, he responded by spinning around and executing a perfect hook shot that touched nothing but net. He turned and faced the man.

"Victor Garcia?"

"Sure," said Victor.

"I've heard about you." The man got up from where he was leaning and walked onto the court. He wore a pink LaCoste shirt and Top-Siders. The license plate on his car said Texas. "I like to shoot a little hoop myself now and then. Usually, when I go someplace new, I ask around to find out who's good."

Victor eyed him with suspicion, but also a certain amount of pride. It was, after all, about time he got some attention.

"Fact."

"Who'd you ask?"

He waved his hand in the general direction from which he'd come. "Guy up the road."

"Lopez?"

"I think he said his name was Lopez. What's the difference? He was right. You've got the touch. Not everybody does, you know. Just the right balance of things—you concentrate well, but you're relaxed, too."

Victor glanced across the street, where a tiny dust devil spun in the yard in front of Rodriguez's place. "What are you, CIA?" he asked.

The man shook his head and chuckled. "Close, though. FOA. Ferrari Owners of America."

"Ferrari? That's what this is?"

The man smiled, his lips drawing back to reveal a set of china-white teeth, and waved toward his car. "You have to pass a stupidity test to qualify for one. Getting parts is murder. On my fourth clutch. I'm up here for a convention. Southwest chapter—we're meeting in Santa Fe this year. I always try to drive around and see the country a little. It's beautiful out here—all these extinct volcanoes. Kind of violent, if you know what I mean. You're lucky to live where you do."

"I guess," Victor said, dubiously. He didn't feel particularly lucky.

"I mean it. Look around. It's true what they say about northern New Mexico. There's a quality to the light. Sky's as blue as a polished gemstone. What do you all say? 'The Land of Enchantment?'" He raised his hands as if demonstrating a magic trick, then smiled and indicated that Victor should give him the ball, which he did. He bounced it once, then took a shot—a perfect swish. The hairs on his muscled arms stood high off the skin, making him appear to have a kind of golden aura. Victor retrieved the ball.

"Nice," he said, passing it back. Phony as blue macaroni, he thought to himself, which was something Rodriguez liked to say. A hunk of old metal tubing lay on the ground a few feet away, and Victor figured if he needed, he could probably get to it quick enough to inflict some damage.

The stranger eyed the basket and did it again.

"Victor Garcia," he said, walking over to get the ball from the pile of rubble where it had rolled. "Are you a betting man?"

"I got nothing to bet," Victor said.

"That's OK. We can negotiate. I just think it might be fun to have a little competition—you and me. Friendly."

He decided the stranger was harmless. "Free throws?"

"Maybe. Maybe something a little more challenging."

A car came up the road, its muffler dragging noisily on the dirt and gravel. Victor's mother was returning home from the motel where she changed sheets.

"I got to go," Victor said, taking back his ball, though reluctantly. He would have liked to show this man what he could do.

From his pocket, the man withdrew a black leather wallet, and out of that he took a business card which he handed to Victor. It read: E. Crispin Light, Import/Export.

"Most of my friends just call me Money," he said. "It's my basketball name."

"Money?"

"You know—money in the bank. Kind of like Bill Bradley was

'Dollar Bill.' "

Victor looked again at the card. The printing on it was in gold. "What does the *E* stand for?"

"Good, good," said Money, grinning. "Most people don't even ask. The fact is, it doesn't stand for anything. I put it on there because I think it looks classy. What do you think?"

Victor shrugged. Across the road, he could see his mom struggling with groceries. "You coming back?"

"You bet." Money looked at his watch. "Tomorrow evening. Will you be here?"

"I'm always here," said Victor, coolly.

"All right. You go on home now and look after your mom."

Victor shielded his eyes against a sudden gust of wind that threw a curtain of dust up around them. "What do you know about my mom?"

"Did I say I knew anything?" He smiled. "I'll see you tomorrow, Victor." He shook the boy's hand. His was hard and calloused as if, even though he appeared to be rich, he still did a fair amount of manual labor. Gardening, maybe, Victor thought. The man got back into his car and drove off in the direction of the setting sun.

The understanding came to him clearly, in the middle of the night, when he awoke to the sound of his mother's coughing. This was a nightly occurrence—the luminous readout on his alarm clock said 3:06, and as he lay waiting for the sounds to subside, he was filled with a mixture of fear and pride. He really was good. Not just good the way anyone who practices enough can become good, but special.

He got up and went into the kitchen to make himself a cocktail, his name for the milk, Nestle's Quik and raw egg drink he'd invented as part of his personal training regimen. From her bedroom, his mother continued to cough, a deep, body-racking sound that seemed to originate in her stomach and work its way up.

Taking his drink, he unlocked the door and stepped outside. There were stars everywhere, more than he'd ever seen. In the darkness, the shapes of the wrecked cars were ominous, lurking monsters. Victor walked toward them, if only to prove to himself he wasn't scared. Something moved on one of the hoods and he halted. Gradually, his eyes became more accustomed to the light and he saw a small lizard. It was watching him.

"It's you, isn't it?" he said.

The lizard did not move. Even out here, the sound of his mother's hacking was clearly audible, the only disturbance in the night's solemn quiet.

"I'm ready to deal," said Victor. "I know who you are. I know what you want. I'm not afraid. If I lose, you can have my soul, to be damned to eternal hellfire. But if I win, I want you to make my mom OK again." He paused for a moment, considering whether to throw in something else, too, like a million dollars, or a starting position with the San Antonio Spurs, but it seemed to him that if he were fighting the forces of darkness, it would be best to keep his own motives as pure and true as possible. "Tomorrow," he said. "Sundown. "

The lizard continued to look at him. Then, to Victor's astonishment, it nodded its head once and scurried away.

As he passed his mother's door on his way back to bed, Victor stopped and whispered, "It's all right. I'm taking care of everything. "

But E. Crispin Light did not appear the next evening. Victor spent over two hours on the basketball court, dribbling, shooting, working on the basics, keeping his eye out for the black sports car. It was too bad, because his shooting was dead accurate—he hit nineteen out of twenty from the free throw line. He felt certain he could have beaten all comers, even an emissary from the Prince of Darkness. Eventually, as the light began to fade, he put his ball under one arm and walked home.

His mother was watching *Wheel of Fortune*.

"If only I could spell a little better," she lamented. "I'd go to Hollywood and clean up on this game." She held a small clay pot in one hand, a paintbrush in the other. She picked up extra money painting Anasazi designs onto local pottery for sale to tourists. She was very pale. Victor's father had been Mexican, but his mother was from California, a thin woman of Irish extraction, with large, sad eyes. Though she'd been sick now on and off for the better part of a year, she refused to go to a doctor. They had no insurance. Her one gesture toward her health had been to quit smoking, but it had only seemed to make the coughing worse. She held out a pot. "Want to try one?"

Victor shook his head. "I'm thinking," he said.

"What you need is some friends," she said. "You spend too much time alone."

"I don't need no friends," he said.

"Any. 'I don't need any friends.'" She raised her eyebrows, then drew a line around the lip of the vase. "Alabaster caught a lizard this morning. Tore the poor thing to bits."

Victor swallowed hard. "A lizard?"

"You know. One of those grayish ones."

Alabaster, who was part Persian, lay in the windowsill, cleaning her paws. Victor stared at her, trying to see if she looked any different. After all, he reasoned, it might have been any lizard.

"Are you all right?" asked his mother. "You look a little pale."

"I'm fine," he said. "How are you?"

"Oh, on a scale of one to ten, today was about a four, I'd say."

"It's going to get better," he told her. Then he excused himself and went to his room.

The plaza in Santa Fe was filled with Ferraris, all of them polished to a radiance, reflecting sunlight, smelling richly of gasoline and leather. They were arranged by year and model—scores of them parked side to side, their owners hovering about, keeping a wary eye out for people who might ignore the DO NOT TOUCH signs in their windshields. Victor locked his bicycle and wandered among the automobiles, looking for one in particular. After making almost a complete circuit of the plaza, he found it, wedged in among six others of exactly the same style, but the only black one with Texas plates. He looked around for Money, but he was not in the immediate area. Victor peered in, cupping his hands to the tinted glass, half-expecting to see a dance of writhing, tortured souls. The inside did look like another world, but only a wealthy one. The control panel was polished walnut, the seats a deep, red leather. There was a Willie Nelson cassette in the tape deck, a New Mexico highway map on the dashboard. A little disappointed, he stuck his hands in his pockets and turned.

"Hello, Victor." For a Texan, Money had almost no accent at all. He wore sunglasses and a maroon golf shirt.

"What happened?" said Victor. "You didn't come."

"Yeah, sorry about that. We had a big dinner at the hotel and it got late. I'll make it up to you."

Victor tried to seem as though he didn't care. "You're the one wanted to come and shoot."

"I realize that, and I feel badly about it. If I'd had your number, I would have called."

Victor didn't mention that for the past two months, as a part of an economizing measure, they'd been doing without a phone. He thought again of the lizard. "You were where?"

"At a dinner. That's what we do at these conventions. We drive our cars to some central location, then hang around eating and drinking. It's pretty boring, really, but it gets me out of the office. Buy you an ice cream?"

Victor accepted, and the two of them took their cones to a bench.

Money took off his glasses. "Have you decided what you want to play for?"

Victor met his eyes, which seemed to him like cold, blue stones. He thought of the devil movies he'd seen. It seemed a peculiar question. "Do I have a choice?"

"There's always a choice. Only remember, never get into a bet you're not prepared to lose."

"I'm not going to lose. And you're going to help my mother."

"What are you suggesting, Victor?"

"She can't sleep, and she's got trouble with her breathing."

"Then she ought to see a doctor."

"Give her back her health," said Victor. "If I win, that's what I want."

He took out a set of black driving gloves and swatted a fly that had landed on his knee. "And if I win?"

"You can have my soul."

Money arched an eyebrow. "Your soul?"

Victor nodded. "You heard me."

"Big stakes."

"Yes."

Money thought this over for a moment. He bit into the cone part of his ice cream and chewed noisily, then swallowed. "I think you may have mistaken me for someone else. I'm only a businessman who likes to play a little ball. But all right, you're on."

Just then, a man with a bullhorn made an announcement.

"That's my category," said Money. "Let's go see if I won anything."

Victor followed him to where a man in a plaid jacket stood next to a blonde lady in a white jumpsuit, carrying a clipboard. She took the bullhorn and announced the winner's name, and a fat man in a brown cowboy hat jumped up to accept the plaque.

Victor watched Money's reaction, expecting to see anger, possibly rage. The potential seemed there—behind Money's cool, sculpted face, there was a hint of something smoldering, competitive and mean. But he just shook his head.

"These things are all fixed," he said. "I don't even know why I bother."

The evening was a hot one, with only the vaguest hint of a breeze from the southwest. Victor was out on the court early, dribbling around, working on his bank shot. True to his word, Money appeared a little after seven, his black car still shiny as glass in spite of the dust its tires kicked up. The engine roared and was silent.

He was dressed in worn blue gym shorts and a red tank top, and his sneakers were red canvas high-tops from another era. He was muscled and trim, but he looked very human, and for a minute, Victor wondered if he might be wrong about him. Maybe he really was what he claimed, just a rich guy who liked to play basketball. But the devil could be a trickster—he knew that from Rodriguez's woman, Opal, whose entire life seemed to be made up of encounters with him. The Evil One took a special interest, she said, in tormenting her. Just last week, a mysterious wind had taken a sheet off her clothesline and hung it from the branches of a nearby cottonwood, where it flapped like a sail for two days because Opal refused to have anything to do with it. She'd finally given Victor fifty cents to climb up and get it.

Money tossed a basketball to Victor, who caught it and examined its material and make. Leather, with no visible trademark—good grain, easy to grip. He bounced it and took a set shot which fell two feet short of the basket. He adjusted and proceeded to put the next five into the net. "I'm ready," he said.

"We'll play Death," said Money. "A game of accuracy. Shoot to go first."

"Don't you want to warm up?"

"I'm always warm. Go ahead."

Victor took a foul shot and sank it. Then Money went to the line, crouched with the ball under his chin, eyed the basket and shot. The ball bounced off the rim.

Victor grinned. "Maybe you should have warmed up."

"Your shot," said Money.

Victor figured he'd go for it, right from the start. He walked off the court, over to where the Ferrari was parked, and from there put up a long, high, arching shot. It looped three times around the rim and flew out.

"Don't be too cocky," said Money. "Rule number one." He collected the ball, dribbled out to a crack in the pavement where the top of the key would have been and executed a turnaround jumper that fell perfectly through the hole.

Victor took the ball and repeated the shot. Still, he was furious with himself for giving up the advantage. Now, he was on the defensive, forced to wait for his opponent to miss.

Shot for shot, they were both perfect. Money did a backward lay-up, but Victor easily made one too. Fall-away jumpers, hook shots, they each sank everything they put up. Finally, after nearly five minutes, a sloppy jump shot gave the advantage back to Victor. He put in a twenty-foot banker. Money whistled, walked to the spot and did the same. Rather than try something else, Victor took the shot again—he had a sense that he'd make it, and he figured he'd keep going from the same place until Money missed. He didn't have to wait. Money's attempt went off the backboard, missing the rim entirely.

"You've got *D*," said Victor, a little louder than he'd intended.

"Just shoot the ball," said Money.

It went on, a slow game, a game of nerves and of strategy. Money kept trying to distract him.

"Are you worried? I know I would be. You've got a lot at stake here."

"I'm not scared," said Victor. In fact, he was getting a little nervous. He'd never thought the contest would last this long.

"But your soul. That's a big wager. Maybe you're betting over your head."

"You don't scare me."

"I'm not trying to scare you. I'm trying to let you know that I appreciate the seriousness of your convictions. For me, basketball has always just been a game. I don't let it obsess me the way you do. That's why I'm going to win, because I have less at stake. I'm more relaxed."

"If it was just a game to you, how come you came out here to find me?" Victor went to the foul line, stood with his back to the basket, and put the ball in backward, over his head.

"Well," said Money, "isn't that special?" He tried the shot and missed.

"*D-E* for you," said Victor.

Within a few minutes, Victor started missing shots, ones he should have been making. Money played with an icy calm, calculating his shots like geometry problems. It was as if, Victor thought, unseen forces were acting upon him, making him miss. To make matters worse, each time he did, Money smiled at him and said "thunk." Pretty soon, Victor was behind, with three letters. Glancing over at the Ferrari, he saw that Alabaster was curled up on the hood, sunning herself. It was, he thought, a very bad sign.

"We can quit now," said Money. "I don't mind."

"No way."

"Don't kid yourself, Victor. You're going to lose, in spite of that name of yours. But it doesn't matter. There's nothing magical about being a good basketball player. It won't do anything for you down the road, other than make you wish you spent your time on something more useful. You'll never be a great—you've got no killer instinct. And you're too short."

"Stop talking," said Victor.

"Just trying to get you to be realistic."

Just then, one of Rodriguez's dogs got loose, ran across the street, and began barking at the stranger. Money froze in the middle of the court as the black-and-white mongrel bared her teeth and snarled, tail flat down as if she expected at any moment to be kicked. Rodriguez himself appeared after about a minute, a beer in his hand, to grab the dog by the collar.

"Who's winning?" he asked.

"That's one fierce hound," said Money, nervously keeping his distance. "Hunter?"

"No hunter," said Rodriguez. "She's a lover. Just had her third litter this year." He pursed his lips, eyeing this stranger with the nice car. "You want some puppies?"

"No, thanks," said Money.

"Ten bucks," said Rodriguez. He was a squat, muscular man, with a hank of hair that dangled loosely over his forehead.

"I don't much like dogs."

"No, man. Ten bucks the kid beats you."

"Well. Ten bucks it is," said Money. "Where were we?"

"My shot," said Victor. Think no bad thoughts, he told himself. Keep your heart pure. He put in a running hook.

Money made his hook, picked up his own rebound, and bounced the ball back to Victor.

"I need another beer," announced Rodriguez, and dragged the dog back across the street. He returned moments later with a six-pack and settled in the dirt by the side of the court to watch. After a little while, he was joined by Opal, her heavyset, Navajo features almost making it seem as if she were wearing a mask. She broke open one of the beers and tipped her head back to receive the contents.

Over by the trailers, the competition across the road was attracting attention. Many of the residents began to emerge to see what was going on. The two long-hair drunks whom everyone called Manny and Moe, and who worked as part-time construction workers when they weren't sleeping off the booze, walked slow circles around Money's car, nodding their heads and making approving comments. Distracted by them, or maybe just growing tired, Money bounced one off the rim.

"That's D-E-A," said Rodriguez, who had appointed himself referee.

"I know what it is," said Money. "Please, don't touch the car."

There was now a small crowd gathered—nearly fifteen people. Somebody brought out potato chips and passed them around. Victor felt as if he were in a spotlight. These were people who generally ignored each other, except for a nod in passing, but there was a real sense of community as they watched the contest. Last to come out was Victor's mother. Shielding her eyes against the slanted light, she looked pale and ghostlike. The wind, which was beginning to pick up as it always did at this time of day, tossed her housedress around her knees.

Victor did a reverse lay-up. There was a smattering of applause.

The sweat stood out on Money's face as he bounced the ball in preparation. Then he moved under the basket and flipped the ball backward over his head. As he did so, one ankle buckled and he went tumbling forward onto the pavement.

"Damn," he said, holding the ankle in front of him like a foreign object. He kneaded it for a few moments, then hobbled to his feet.

"D-E-A-T" sang Rodriguez. "Uh-oh."

Victor considered. Repeating the lay-up would finish Money off easily —with his twisted ankle, he wouldn't have a chance. But it seemed like a cheap ending, and Victor had an audience. He wanted to do something spectacular.

"Everything on this shot," he heard himself say.

"Everything?" Money said, cautiously. "Are you sure?"

"Everything. "

"Done," said Money.

"What are you guys playing for, anyway?" asked Rodriguez. When there was no answer, he shrugged and opened another beer.

Victor walked the ball right off the court, out into the dirt lot beyond it, a few feet from a particularly nasty-looking cholla. The crowd let out a cheerful noise, encouraging, but with laughter mixed in—no one believed for a moment that the wiry, sad-faced twelve year old could possibly hurl a ball that far, let alone make it go through a hoop. Money hobbled around in obvious pain, but the look of amusement on his face was unmistakable.

Victor knew the moment he looked at the basket and saw how far he was away, that this was impossible. He'd overdone it—he was way beyond his range. But he couldn't see any way out now without losing face. In his hands the ball seemed to gain weight, as if it were filling internally with liquid. Money was still smiling at him. His neighbors watched in anticipation. His mother stood among them, her hands clenched in fists at her sides. He'd blown it, he told himself. He'd failed to stay pure. Pride was one of the seven deadly sins (he was pretty sure about this), and his own had brought him to the brink of the abyss.

Holding the ball to his chest, he gauged the distance to the net and prayed for a miracle. He did not want to die. He tried to imagine what it would be like to spend eternity soulless, in a box, no air, no light, the rough wood pressed up against his face. For a moment, he felt as if his feet had grown roots and that his bones extended deep down into the earth, into places damp, fungal, and cool. Then he put the ball as high into the air as he could possibly throw it.

Moving in what seemed like slow motion, the ball described an orange-brown arc, at the very top of which it hung for a moment, certain to fall short. Then, out of the south, a powerful wind kicked up, and for a moment, the whole world seemed to shake. Tumbleweed rolled around the court, and the rim of Rodriguez's beer can was coated with red-brown dust. Descending on the shoulders of the wind, the ball actually cleared the basket, arriving first at the backboard, then glancing smoothly down through the net.

Victor screamed at the top of his lungs, and his voice was joined by a chorus of others from across the road.

"Never happen again in a million years," said Rodriguez, walking onto the court.

"Lucky," said Money, shaking his head.

"Hey, man," said Rodriguez. "He beat you square and fair. Pay up."

Money hobbled over to his car and brought back a wallet. He took out a ten and gave it to Rodriguez.

"You don't owe the kid no cash?" asked Rodriguez.

"No," said Money. "I don't."

"So, what then?"

Money shrugged and shook Victor's hand, then went back to his car and got in.

"What about our deal?" said Victor. He felt suddenly anxious, more so than he had during the game.

Money leaned his head out the window and looked at him long and hard. "I never expected to lose," he said at last. His tinted window hummed and closed, leaving Victor staring at his own reflection. Then the Ferrari's engine fired, coughing dust out around the back tires. Spewing gravel behind him, Money pulled out onto the street and headed in the direction of the county road.

"Fucking Texans," said Rodriguez. "Think they own the world." He spat into the dirt. "You shoot pretty good basketball, my friend. But you don't know the first thing about gambling." He turned and headed back, Opal following at his heels. Across the street, most of the onlookers had already returned to their trailers.

Victor's mother put a hand on his head. "Did you bet with that man?" she asked.

Victor said nothing.

"What did you bet?"

He didn't answer. The wind that had come and carried his shot home was gone, and in its place, the evening crept in, cool and still.

She shook her head in frustration. "I don't know what it is with you these days," she said. "I don't know what you're thinking." She put her forehead up against his and stared directly into his eyes, but he was silent. "Don't stay out too long," she told him finally. She walked back across the street.

Alone now on the court, Victor saw that Money had left his ball. It sat in the dirt, near where his car had been parked. He picked it up and bounced it a few times, the smack it made against the concrete seeming to echo off the surrounding hills, a lonely, casual sound. He felt cheated. Still, something had happened—he knew that. He would not allow himself the easy luxury of disappointment. For a brief moment, the powers of the universe had convened in his fingertips. He watched the lights come on in the different trailers, listened to the sounds of Opal and Rodriguez starting up one of their nightly arguments. He bounced the ball a few more times in the dimming light, watching his shadow move against the pavement, taller than any man's and growing longer with each passing minute.

Basketball
Louis Jenkins

A huge summer afternoon with no sign of rain . . . elm trees in the farmyard bend and creak in the wind. The leaves are dry and gray. In the driveway a boy shoots a basketball at a goal above the garage door. Wind makes shooting difficult and time after time he chases the loose ball. He shoots, rebounds, turns, shoots . . . on into the afternoon. In the silence between the gusts of wind the only sounds are the thump of the ball on the ground and the rattle of the bare steel rim of the goal. The gate bangs in the wind, the dog in the yard yawns, stretches and goes back to sleep. A film of dust covers the water in the trough. Great clouds of dust rise from open fields that stretch a thousand miles beyond the horizon.

Dushay's Friend
Dennis Trudell

Dushay knifed between two punks, double-
pumped going up—and died; his friend
froze in the gunshots' echo as 'Shay
bounced off the post and left it smeared.
And left it smeared. The basketball rolled

west across State . . . and Dushay's friend
walked after it, and kept walking. Later
cops asked his name and nobody knew.
"Dushay's friend," " 'Shay's man, man," they
heard with shrugs. And shrugged. Never

found him or Little Truck's basketball
again. Dushay's friend walked due west
that day for six hours; then he dribbled
two hours more and slept in a field.
Next morning the basketball glowed so

orange the smeared post in Dushay's
friend's mind was dulled—and he dribbled
the ball through a town. That night
it glowed the moon two towns away.
And a post there glowed. And Dushay's

friend's tears as he made 'Shay's shot.

State Champions
Bobbie Ann Mason

In 1952, when I was in the seventh grade, the Cuba Cubs were the state champions in high-school basketball. When the Cubs returned from the tournament in Lexington, a crowd greeted them at Eggner's Ferry bridge over Kentucky Lake, and a convoy fourteen miles long escorted them to the county seat. It was a cold day in March as twelve thousand people watched the Cubs ride around the courthouse square in convertibles. The mayor and other dignitaries made speeches. Willie Foster, the president of the Merit Clothing Company, gave the players and Coach Jack Story free suits from his factory. The coach, a chunky guy in a trench coat like a character in a forties movie, told the crowd, "I'm mighty glad we could bring back the big trophy." And All-Stater Howie Crittenden, the razzle-dazzle dribbler, said, "There are two things I'm proud of today. First, we won the tournament, and second, Mr. Story said we made him feel like a young mule."

The cheerleaders then climbed up onto the concrete seat sections of the Confederate monument and led a final fight yell.

Chick-a-lacka, chick-a-lacka chow, chow, chow
Boom-a-lacka, boom-a-lacka bow, wow, wow
Chick-a-lacka, boom-a-lacka, who are we?
Cuba High School, can't you see?

The next day the Cubs took off in the convertibles again, leading a motorcade around western Kentucky, visiting the schools in Sedalia, Mayfield, Farmington, Murray, Hardin, Benton, Sharpe, Reidland, Paducah, Kevil, La Center, Barlow, Wickliffe, Bardwell, Arlington, Clinton, Fulton, and Pilot Oak.

I remember the hoopla at the square that day, but at the time I felt a strange sort of distance, knowing that in another year another community would have its champions. I was twelve years old and going through a crisis, so I thought I had a wise understanding of the evanescence of victory.

But years later, in the seventies, in upstate New York, I met a man who surprised me by actually remembering the Cuba Cubs' championship. He was a Kentuckian, and although he was from the other side of the state, he had lasting memories of Howie Crittenden and Doodle Floyd. Howie was a great dribbler, he said. And Doodle had a windmill hook shot that had to be seen to be believed. The Cubs were inspired by the Harlem Globetrotters—Marques Haynes's ball-handling influenced Howie and Goose Tatum was Doodle's model. The Cuba Cubs, I was told, were, in fact, the most incredible success story in the history of Kentucky high-school basketball, and the reason was that they were such unlikely champions.

"Why, they were just a handful of country boys who could barely afford basketball shoes," the man told me in upstate New York.

"They were?" This was news to me.

"Yes. They were known as the Cinderella Cubs. One afternoon during the tournament, they were at Memorial Coliseum watching the Kentucky Wildcats practice. The Cubs weren't in uniform, but one of them called for a ball and dribbled it a few times and then canned a two-hand set shot from midcourt. Adolph Rupp happened to be watching. He's another Kentucky basketball legend—don't you know anything about Kentucky basketball? He rushed to the player at midcourt and demanded, 'How did you do that?' The boy just smiled. 'It was easy, Mr. Rupp,' he said. 'Ain't no wind in here.'"

Of course, that was not my image of the Cuba Cubs at all. I hadn't realized they were just a bunch of farm boys who got together behind the barn after school and shot baskets in the dirt, while the farmers around complained that the boys would never amount to anything. I hadn't known how Coach Jack Story had started them off in the sev-

enth grade, coaching the daylights out of those kids until he made
them believe they could be champions. To me, just entering junior high
the year they won the tournament, the Cuba Cubs were the essence of
glamour. Seeing them in the gym—standing tall in those glossy green
satin uniforms, or racing down the court, leaping like deer—took my
breath away. They had crew cuts and wore real basketball shoes. And the
cheerleaders dressed smartly in Crayola-green corduroy circle skirts,
saddle oxfords, and rolled-down socks. They had green corduroy jackets
as well as green sweaters, with a C cutting through the symbol of a
megaphone. They clapped their hands in rhythm and orchestrated their
elbows in a little dance that in some way mimicked the Cubs as they herded the ball down the court. "Go, Cubs, Go!" "Fight, Cubs, Fight!" They
did "Locomotive, locomotive, steam, steam, steam," and "Strawberry
shortcake, huckleberry pie." We had pep rallies that were like revival ser-
vices in tone and intent. The cheerleaders pirouetted and zoomed skyward
in unison, their leaps straight and clean like jump shots. They whirled in
their circle skirts, showing off their green tights underneath.

I never questioned the words of the yells, any more than I questioned the name Cuba Cubs. I didn't know what kind of cubs they were
supposed to be—bear cubs or wildcats or foxes—but I never thought
about it. I doubt if anyone did. It was the sound of the words that mattered, not the meaning. They were the Cubs. And that was it. Cuba was
a tiny community with a couple of general stores, and its name is of
doubtful origin, but local historians say that when the Cuba post office
opened, in the late 1850s, the Ostend Manifesto had been in the news.
This was a plan the United States had for getting control of the island
of Cuba in order to expand the slave trade. The United States demanded that Spain either sell us Cuba at a fair price or surrender it outright.
Perhaps the founding fathers of Cuba, Kentucky (old-time pronuncia-
tion: Cubie), were swayed by the fuss with Spain. Or maybe they just
had romantic imaginations. In the Jackson Purchase, the western region
of Kentucky and Tennessee that Andrew Jackson purchased from the
Chickasaw Indians in 1818, there are other towns with faraway names:

Moscow, Dublin, Kansas, Cadiz, Beulah, Paris, and Dresden.

The gymnasium where the Cuba Cubs practiced was the hub of the school. Their trophies gleamed in a glass display case near the entrance, between the principal's office and the gymnasium, and the enormous coal furnace that heated the gym hunched in a corner next to the bleachers. Several classrooms opened onto the gym floor, with the study hall at one end. The lower grades occupied a separate building, and in those grades we used an outhouse. But in junior high we had the privilege of using the indoor rest rooms, which also opened onto the gym. (The boys' room included a locker room for the team, but like the outhouses, the girls' room didn't even have private compartments.) The route from the study hall to the girls' room was dangerous. We had to walk through the gym, along the sidelines, under some basketball hoops. There were several baskets, so many players could practice their shots simultaneously. At recess and lunch, in addition to the Cuba Cubs, all the junior high boys used the gym, too, in frantic emulation of their heroes. On the way to the rest room you had to calculate quickly and carefully when you could run beneath a basket. The players pretended that they were oblivious of you, but just when you thought you were safe and could dash under the basket, they would hurl a ball out of nowhere, and the ball would fall on your head as you streaked by. Even though I was sort of a tomboy and liked to run—back in the fifth grade I could run as fast as most of the boys—I had no desire to play basketball. It was too violent.

Doodle Floyd himself bopped me on the head once, but I doubt if he remembers it.

The year of the championship was the year I got in trouble for running in the study hall. At lunch hour one day, Judy Howell and I decided to run the length of the gym as fast as we could, daring ourselves to run through the hailstorm of basketballs flying at us. We raced through the gym and kept on running, unable to slow down, finally skidding to a stop in the study hall. We were giggling because we had caught a glimpse of what one of the senior players was wearing under his green practice shorts (different from the satin show shorts they wore at the games), when Mr. Gilhorn, the history teacher, big as a buffalo, appeared before us and growled, "What do you young ladies think you're doing?"

I had on the tightest Levi's I owned. When they were newly washed and ironed, they fit snug. My mother had ironed a crease in them. I had on a cowboy shirt and a bandanna.

Mr. Gilhorn went on, "Now, girls, do we run in our own living rooms? Peggy, does your mama let you run in the house?"

"Yes," I said, staring at him confidently. "My mama always lets me run in the house." It was a lie, of course, but it was my habit to contradict whatever anybody assumed. If I was supposed to be a lady, then I would be a cowboy. The truth in this instance was that it had never occurred to me to run in our house. It was too small, and the floorboards were shaky. Therefore, I reasoned, my mother had never laid down the law about not running in the house.

Judy said, "We won't do it again." But I wouldn't promise.

"I know what would be good for you girls," said Mr. Gilhorn in a kindly, thoughtful tone, as if he had just had a great idea.

That meant the duckwalk. As punishment, Judy and I had to squat, grabbing our ankles, and duckwalk around the gym. We waddled, humiliated, with the basketballs beating on our heads and the players following our progress with loud quacks of derision.

"This was your fault," Judy claimed. She stopped speaking to me, which disappointed me because we had been playmates since the second grade. I admired her short blond curls and color-coordinated outfits. She had been to Detroit one summer.

During study-hall periods, we could hear the basketballs pounding the floor. We could tell when a player made a basket—that pause after the ball hit the backboard and sank luxuriously into the net before hitting the floor. I visited the library more often than necessary just to get a glimpse of the Cubs practicing as I passed the door to the gym. The library was a shelf at one end of the study hall, and it had a couple of hundred old books—mostly hand-me-downs from the Graves County Library, including outdated textbooks and even annuals from Kentucky colleges. That year I read some old American histories, and a biography of Benjamin Franklin, and the "Junior Miss" books. On the wainscoted walls of the study hall were gigantic framed pictures, four feet high, each composed of inset portraits of all the faculty members and the seniors of a specific year. They gazed down at us like kings and queens on playing cards. There was a year for each frame, and they dated all the way back to the early forties.

In junior high, we shared the study hall with the high-school students. The big room was drafty, and in the winter it was very cold. The boys were responsible for keeping the potbelly stove filled with coal from the coal pile outside, near where the school buses were parked. In grade school during the winter, I had worn long pants under my dresses—little starched print dresses with gathered skirts and puffed sleeves. But in junior high, the girls wore blue jeans, like the boys, except that we rolled them up almost to our knees. The Cuba Cubs wore Levi's and green basketball jackets, and the other high-school boys—the Future Farmers of America—wore bright-blue FFA jackets. Although the FFA jackets didn't have the status of the basketball jackets, they were beautiful. They were royal-blue corduroy, and on the back was an enormous gold eagle.

I had a crush on a freshman named Glenn in an FFA jacket. He helped manage the coal bucket in the study hall. Glenn didn't ride my bus. He lived in Dukedom, down across the Tennessee line. Glenn was one of the Cuba Cubs, but he wasn't one of the major Cubs—he was on the B team and didn't yet have a green jacket. But I admired his dribble, and his long legs could travel that floor like a bicycle. When I waited at the edge of the gym for my chance to bolt to the girls' room, I sometimes stood and watched him dribble. Then one day as I ran pell-mell to the rest room, his basketball hit me on the head and he called to me flirtatiously. "I got a claim on her," he yelled out to the world. If a boy had a claim on a girl, it meant she was his girlfriend. The next day in study hall he showed me an "eight-page novel." It was a Li'l Abner comic strip. In the eight-page novel, Li'l Abner peed on Daisy Mae. It was disgusting, but I was thrilled that he showed me the booklet.

"Hey, let me show you these hand signals," Glenn said a couple of days later, out on the playground. "In case you ever need them." He stuck his middle finger straight up and folded the others down. "That's single F," he said. Then he turned down his two middle fingers, leaving the forefinger and the little finger upright, like horns. "That's double F," he said confidently.

"Oh," I said. At first I thought he meant hand signals used in driving. Cars didn't have automatic turn signals then.

There were other hand signals. In basketball, the coach and the players exchanged finger gestures. The cheerleaders clapped us on to victory. And with lovers, lightly scraping the index finger on the other's palm meant "Do you want to?" and responding the same way meant "Yes." If you didn't know this and you held hands with a boy, you might inadvertently agree to do something that you had no intention of doing.

Seventh grade was the year we had a different teacher for each subject. Arithmetic became mathematics. The English teacher paddled Frances High and me for stealing Jack Reed's Milky Way from his desk. Jack Reed had even told us he didn't mind that we stole it, that he wanted us to have it. "The paddling didn't hurt," I said to him proudly. He was cute, but not as cute as Glenn, who had a crooked grin I thought was fascinating and later found reincarnated in Elvis. In the study hall I stood in front of the stove until my backside was soaked with heat. I slid my hands down the back of my legs and felt the sharp crease of my Levi's. I was in a perpetual state of excitement. It was 1952 and the Cuba Cubs were on their way to the championship.

Judy was still mad at me, but Glenn's sister Willowdean was in my class, and I contrived to go home with her one evening, riding her unfamiliar school bus along gravel roads far back into the country. Country kids didn't socialize much. To go home with someone and spend the night was a big event, strange and unpredictable. Glenn and Willowdean lived with three brothers and sisters in a small house surrounded by bare, stubbled tobacco fields. It was a wintry day, but Willowdean and I played outdoors, and I watched for Glenn to arrive.

He had stayed late at school, practicing ball, and the coach brought him home. Then he had his chores to do. At suppertime, when he came in with his father from milking, his mother handed him a tray of food. "Come on and go with me," he said to me. His Levi's were smudged with cow manure.

His mother said, "Make sure she's got her teeth."

"Have you got your teeth, Peggy?" Glenn asked me with a grin.

His mother swatted at him crossly. "I meant Bluma. You know who I meant."

Glenn motioned with a nod of his head for me to follow him, and we went to a tiny back room, where Glenn's grandmother sat in a wheelchair in a corner with a heater at her feet. She had dark hair and lips painted bright orange and a growth on her neck.

"She don't talk," Glenn said. "But she can hear."

The strange woman jerked her body in a spasm of acknowledgment as Glenn set the supper tray in her lap. He fished her teeth out of a glass of water and poked them in her mouth. She squeaked like a mouse.

"Are you hungry?" Glenn asked me as we left the room. "We've got chicken and dumplings tonight. That's my favorite."

That night I slept with Willowdean on a fold-out couch in the living room, with newspaper-wrapped hot bricks at our feet. We huddled under four quilts and whispered. I worked the conversation around to Glenn.

"He told me he liked you," Willowdean said.

I could feel myself blush. At supper, Glenn had tickled me under the table.

"I'll tell you a secret if you promise not to tell," she said.

"What?" I loved secrets and usually didn't tell them.

"Betty Jean's going to have a baby."

Willowdean's sister Betty Jean was a sophomore. On the school bus her boyfriend, Roy Matthews, had kept his arm around her during the whole journey, while she cracked gum and looked pleased with herself.

That evening at the supper table, Glenn and his brothers had teased her
about Roy's big feet.

Willowdean whispered now, "Did you see the way she ate supper? Like a
pig. That's because she has to eat for two. She's got a baby in her stomach."

"What will she do?" I asked, scared. The warmth of the bricks was
fading, and I knew it would be a freezing night.

"Her and Roy will live with us," said Willowdean. "That's what my sister Mary Lou did at first. But then she got mad and took the baby off and
went to live with her husband's folks. She said they treated her better."

The high-school classes were small because kids dropped out, to
have babies and farm. They seemed to disappear, like our calves going
off to the slaughterhouse in the fall, and it was creepy.

"I don't want to have a baby and have to quit school," I said.

"You don't?" Willowdean was surprised. "What do you want to go to
school for?"

I didn't answer. I didn't have the words handy. But she didn't seem to
notice. She turned over and pulled the quilts with her. In the darkness,
I could hear a mouse squeaking. But it wasn't a mouse. It was
Willowdean's grandmother, in her cold room at the back of the house.

That winter, while basketball fever raged, a student teacher from
Murray State College taught Kentucky history. She was very pretty and
resembled a picture of Pocahontas in one of the library books. One
time when she sat down, flipping her large gathered skirt up, I saw her
panties. They were pink. She was so soft-spoken she didn't know how
to make us behave well enough to accomplish any classwork. Daniel
Boone's exploits were nothing, compared to Doodle Floyd's. During
the week the Cubs were at the tournament, Pocahontas couldn't keep us
quiet. The school was raising money for next year's basketball uniforms, and each class sold candy and cookies our mothers had made.
Frequently there was a knock at the door, and some kids from another
grade would be there selling Rice Krispies squares wrapped in waxed
paper, or brownies, or sometimes divinity fudge. One day, while

Pocahontas was reading to us about Daniel Boone and the Indians, and we were throwing paper wads, there was a sudden pounding on the door. I was hoping for divinity, and I had a nickel with me, but the door burst open and Judy Howell's sister Georgia was there, crying, "Judy Bee! Mama's had a wreck and Linda Faye's killed."

Judy flew out of the room. For one moment the class was quiet, and then it went into an uproar. Pocahontas didn't know what to do, so she gave us a pop quiz. The next day we learned that Judy's little sister Linda Faye, who was three years old, had been thrown into a ditch when her mother slammed into a truck that had pulled out in front of her. The seventh-grade class took up a collection for flowers. I was stunned by the news of death, for I had never known a child to die. I couldn't sleep, and my mind went over and over the accident, imagining the truck plowing into the car and Linda Faye pitching out the door or through the window. I created various scenes, ways it might have happened. I kept seeing her stretched out stiff on her side, like the dead animals I had seen on our farm. At school I was sleepy, and I escaped into daydreams about Glenn, imagining that I had gone to Lexington, too, to watch him in triumph as he was called in from the sidelines to replace Doodle Floyd, who had turned his ankle.

It was a sober, long walk from the study hall to the rest room. The gymnasium seemed desolate, without the Cubs practicing. I walked safely down the gym, remembering the time in the fourth grade when I was a flower girl in the court of the basketball queen. I had carried an Easter basket filled with flower petals down the center of the gym, scattering rose petals so the queen could step on them as she minced slowly toward her throne.

I was too scared to go to the funeral, and my parents didn't want me to go. My father had been traumatized by funerals in his childhood, and he didn't think they were a good idea. "The Howells live so far away," Mama said. "And it looks like snow."

That weekend, the tournament was on the radio, and I listened carefully, hoping to hear Glenn's name. The final game was crazy. In the background, the cheerleaders chanted:

> *Warren, Warren, he's our man*
> *If he can't do it*
> *Floyd can—*
> *Floyd, Floyd, he's our man*
> *If he can't do it*
> *Crittenden can—*

The announcer was saying, "Crittenden's dribbling has the crowd on its feet. It's a thrilling game! The Cubs were beaten twice by this same Louisville Manual squad during the season, but now they've just inched ahead. The Cubs pulled even at 39-39 when Floyd converted a charity flip, and then Warren sent them ahead for the first time with a short one-harder on Crittenden's pass. The crowd is going wild!"

Toward the end of the game, the whole Coliseum—except for a small Manual cheering section—was yelling, "Hey, hey, what do you say? It looks like Cuba all the way!"

As I listened to the excited announcer chatter about huddles and time-outs and driving jumps and hook shots, I forgot about Judy, but then on Sunday, when I went to the courthouse square to welcome the Cubs home, her sister's death struck me again like fresh news. Seeing so many people celebrating made me feel uncomfortable, as if the death of a child always went unnoticed, like a dead dog by the side of the road. It was a cold day, and I had to wear a dress because it was Sunday. I wanted to see Glenn. I had an audacious plan. I had been thinking about it all night. I wanted to give him a hug of congratulations. I would plant a big wet kiss on his cheek. I had seen a cheerleader do this to one of the players once after he made an unusual number of free throws. It was at a home game, one of the few I attended. I wanted to hug Glenn because it would be my answer to his announcement that he had a claim on me. It would be silent, without explanation, but he would know what it meant.

I managed to lose my parents in the throng and I headed for the east side of the square, where the dime store was. Suddenly I saw Judy, with her mother, in front of a shoe store. I knew the funeral had been the day before, but here they were at the square, in the middle of a celebration. Judy and her mother were still in their Sunday church clothes. Judy saw me. She looked straight at me, then turned away. I pretended I hadn't seen her, and I hurried to the center of the square, looking for Glenn.

But when I finally saw him up ahead, I stopped. He looked different. The Cubs, I learned later, had all gone to an Army surplus store and bought themselves pairs of Army fatigue pants and porkpie hats. Glenn looked unfamiliar in his basketball jacket—now he had one—and the baggy Army fatigues instead of his Levi's. The hat looked silly. I thought about Judy, and how her sister's death had occurred while Glenn was away playing basketball and buying new clothes. I wanted to tell him what it was like to be at home when such a terrible thing happened, but I couldn't, even though I saw him not thirty feet from me. As I hesitated, I saw his parents and Willowdean and one of his brothers crowd around him. Playfully, Willowdean knocked his hat off.

The tournament was over, but we were still wild with our victory. Senior play practice started then, and we never had classes in the afternoon because all the teachers were busy coaching the seniors on their lines in the play. Maybe they had dreams of Broadway. If the Cubs could go to the tournament, anything was possible. Judy returned to school, but everyone was afraid to speak to her. They whispered behind her back. And Judy began acting aloof, as though she had some secret knowledge that lifted her above us.

On one last cool day in early spring we had cleanup day, and there were no classes all day. Everyone was supposed to help clean the school grounds, picking up all the discarded candy wrappers and drink bottles. There was a bonfire, and instead of a plate lunch in the lunchroom— too much like the plain farm food we had to eat at home—we had hot dogs, boiled outside in a kettle over the fire. The fat hot dogs in the cold air tasted heavenly. They steamed like breath.

Just as I finished my hot dog and drank the last of my RC (we had a choice between RC Cola and Orange Crush, and I liked to notice which people chose which—it seemed to divide people into categories), Judy came up behind me and whispered, "Come out there with me." She pointed toward the graveyard across the road.

I followed her, and as we walked between solemn rows of Wilcoxes and Ingrahams and Morrisons and Crittendens, the noise of the playground receded. Judy located a spot of earth, a little brown heap that was not grassed over, even though the dandelions had already come up and turned to fluff. She knelt beside the dirt pile, like a child in a sandbox, and fussed with a pot of artificial flowers. She straightened them and poked them down into the pot, as if they were real. As she worked tenderly but firmly with the flowers, she said, "Mama says Linda Faye will be waiting for us in heaven. That's her true home. The preacher said we should feel special, to think we have a member of our family all the way up in heaven."

That was sort of how I had felt about Glenn, going to Lexington to the basketball tournament, and I didn't know what to say. I couldn't say anything, for we weren't raised to say things that were heartfelt and gracious. Country kids didn't learn manners. Manners were too embarrassing. Learning not to run in the house was about the extent of what we knew about how to act. We didn't learn to congratulate people; we didn't wish people happy birthday. We didn't even address each other by name. And we didn't jump up and spontaneously hug someone for joy. Only cheerleaders claimed that talent. We didn't say we were sorry. We hid from view, in case we might be called on to make appropriate remarks, the way certain old folks in church were sometimes called on to pray. At Cuba School, there was one teacher who, for punishment, made her students write "I love you" five hundred times on the blackboard. "Love" was a dirty word, and I had seen it on the walls of the girls' rest room—blazing there in ugly red lipstick. In the eight-page novel Glenn had showed me, Li'l Abner said "I love you" to Daisy Mae.

Basketball Player
Leonard Michaels

I was the most dedicated basketball player. I don't say the best. In my mind I was terrifically good. In fact I was simply the most dedicated basketball player in the world. I say this because I played continuously, from the time I discovered the meaning of the game at the age of ten, until my mid-twenties. I played outdoors on cement, indoors on wood. I played in heat, wind, and rain. I played in chilly gymnasiums. Walking home, I played some more. I played during dinner, in my sleep, in movies, in automobiles and buses, and at school. I played for over a decade, taking every conceivable shot, with either hand, from every direction. Masses cheered my performance. No intermission, no food, no other human concern, year after year they cheered me on. In living rooms, subways, movies, and schoolyards I heard them. During actual basketball games I also played basketball. I played games within games. When I lost my virginity I eluded my opponent and sank a running hook. Masses saw it happen. I lost my virginity and my girl lost hers. The game had been won. I pulled up my trousers. She snapped her garter belt. I took a jump shot from the corner and another game was underway. I scored in a blind drive from the foul line. We kissed good night. The effect was epileptic. Masses thrashed in their seats, loud holes in their faces. I acknowledged with an automatic nod and hurried down the street, dribbling. A fall-away jumper from the top of the key. It hung in the air. Then, as if sucked down suddenly, it zipped through the hoop. Despite the speed and angle of my shots, I never missed.

Beyond The Chain-Link Fence
Sean Thomas Dougherty

Something bad's beginning. Cops
Pause at the corner light
And then the red & blues
Flare after some kid cutting
Down an alley, he's gone—
They'll never catch him! Alex nodding,
"It was Road Runner come to life."
And Wally counters, "No.
Just Breeze—*turned to animation.*"
Now Lowell's here, eyeing the court,
Noticing something's different,
The pure paint. Between his Nikes
And an ancient gob of gum,
The foul line, freshly sprayed.
"Someone must've came
In the middle of the night,
Because the Parks Department
Never does nothing around here."
Paul & Shane show up
With tall faces, pointing & saying,
"Doesn't it look beautiful?"
Polyester nets bought from saved
Purse snatching money, we laugh.
And the ball they've brought
Is new, too! . . . Some days,
The sun feels warmer on your head,
And the little leaves
Of autumn all fall friendly,
As if they're reaching
To slap five with your hand.

The Blood Blister
Willie Morris

"**M**en is motivated by two things," Asphalt Thomas was wont to say—"reward and fear." Late afternoons were for basketball practice, and two nights a week for the games.

He harangued us unmercifully in the practices. "You're the puniest excuse I ever *seen* for ballplayers," he would shout, after some special miscue. "Start hustlin' or I'll put somethin' on you Moses couldn't get off. You couldn't whup the little girls' team at the Ursiline Convent. Keep your eyes open, dammit. A man can observe a whole lot by just watchin'." Then, a little further into the scrimmage, morose and growling, his whistle hanging disconsolately from his bullish neck, he would say, "Noggin, what the hell's wrong with your scrawny ass? I don't appreciate them black circles under your eyes. What time you get in last night?"

" 'Bout eleven, I think."

"Yeah? Hong Kong time? Get your pitiful tail off the court. I'm gonna play a little with these other turds." Using his long thorny elbows as he played, he would smack skulls, noses, ears, midriffs, making buffoons of his sullen charges with his deft Southeastern Conference moves and fakes and shots, leaving us prone on the floor in his imperious wake. After his fifth straight basket he would say, "I'm hotter than a depot stove," and then he would have us circle the arena twenty-five times around with his sadistic windsprints, and order Leon the manager to guard the water fountain in the locker room afterwards.

During the games I sat at the end of the bench and, like a neglected and forgotten sophomore gosling, more or less languished there. Because of the injuries there were only nine boys on the team, almost all of them seniors, but Asphalt Thomas would sometimes look down my way where I crouched numb and fetuslike to avoid his attention. One was not at all unproud in those days of the crimson knee-guards and the heavy crimson warm-up suits with "F. L." in white over the Number 18 on the back, but what in the world was I doing there? Why did I love the game so much?

Soon in high school there would also be some football and baseball, but there was something about this game that especially attracted and excited me, some soaring sense of beauty and accomplishment and adventure and even mischief to it, that when you wanted to you could play it all by yourself, and use your imagination on your own private fantasies. I was forever whipping the loathsome, arrogant Kentucky Wildcats on twenty-footers at the buzzer. And it was *fun*, putting the ball into the hoop, and then the melodic whish of the net strings when it was true—it was the sound of the *whish* above all that mattered so much. Not long before he died my father had put up a goal for me in our backyard when I was hardly tall enough to get the ball to the rim, but over the years my solitary practices in all climates and seasons, once or twice even in the snow when the net itself was frozen solid, had earned me my place on the varsity. It seemed a long time ago that I first started coming out here in the yard, alone, shooting the ball through the lonesome moments until it was too dark to see the hoop or the ball against the sky, succumbing to the lazy thoughts and daydreams, a formless rite of solitude, trying to figure things out a little, about try-ing to grow up, I guess, and over time the bouncing ball and my own footfalls had worn away the grass, so that the ground around the goal was spare and hard and useful.

Travelling to our away games on the feeble crimson-and-white sports bus with "The Choctaw" emblazoned on its sides, we would watch the nocturnal prospects drift past, the dark expansive flatland with its row after row of seared cotton, and the precipitous piney woods ensnarled in the sleeping kudzu, and the little secluded hamlets of the black prairies with their weak and trembling lights and worn facades and bereft thoroughfares. Asphalt Thomas would be at the wheel, and dead leaves swirled on the highway and insects splattered against the windows in the departing counterfeit spring, and the older players in their mad and boisterous horseplay, which by his bemused demeanor the coach himself seemed vaguely to elicit after a victory:

"Hey, Coach, can't we go no *faster?*"

From behind the steering wheel, looking straight ahead: "You don't deserve to go no faster. We only beat them fairies ten points."

"Hey, Coach, let's stop for some *beer!*"

"The way *you* played, you'd vomit up Pet milk."

Their names were Clarence, Thomas, Jerry, Calvin, John Ed, Percy, Verner Ray, their nicknames being "Bouncer," "Noggin," "Steak Lips" (for reasons obvious to all), "Termite" (shortened to the more manageable "Term"), "White Boy" (his full name being Clarence White), "Muttonhead" (because his head was shaped like a sheep), and "Blue" (because he was Syrian, and the others claimed he *looked* blue). Who would forget the crackerbox gymnasia of these poor little towns—the old hissing radiators, the narrow erstwhile locker rooms crawling with water bugs and roaches, the pony-tailed cheerleaders in saddle oxfords and pleated mid-calf skirts, the white wooden backboards and cheap tacky panelling, the abandoned elevated stages where a few dozen spectators sat on portable green bleachers—the benches and scorers' table right up to the out-of-bounds lines, the ancient round clocks with the swooping second hands, better than the digital ones later, tying you more truly to *time* because not so stark and precise—a little like life itself in its passing? When Term or Blue churlishly complained of the conditions, Asphalt would rejoin: "Fancier than what *I* played on at your age. You're spoiled as a shithouse rat." The walls stood so close to the floor that White Boy made a basket while running fast and sprinted right through a door into an empty classroom and knocked over several chairs and desks.

If Asphalt Thomas vilified *us* during practices, imagine his conduct with the referees. "They don't know whether I'm gonna kiss 'em on the mouth or kick their ass," he would say of his own shifting cajoleries and rages, his sly supplications and venomous ill tempers. Once during a time out he accosted one of them and whispered: "Ain't it about time you get your damned *cataracts* took out, Randy?" and withdrew his big grey pocketknife, and on another tense occasion said to a hairless and vociferous Italian among their number, "You screamin' dago! You're bald as a gorilla's nuts," which earned him not one but *two* technical fouls, Asphalt later philosophically explaining: "That's because a gorilla's got two nuts, like everybody else." The partisans in these tough little towns, adults and students in equal fervor, cursed and defiled our team, considering us metropolitans, and an angry echelon in one of them threw rocks and empty bottles at us as we rushed from the gymnasium to the bus, and Asphalt Thomas herded us aboard and then stood briefly at the driver's door and shook his fist at them and shouted: "You scraggly-ass pointy-head peckerwoods! You don't know basketball from cuckoo squat!" but even he would wisely drive us out of there in a hurry.

My girlfriend Georgia merely tolerated the sport of basketball. She would go to the home games, usually sitting alone, or sometimes with Mrs. Idella King, the English teacher, who was scarcely aware of the rules and regulations but attended out of fealty to her unlikely protege, Asphalt Thomas. The team roster was now depleted to eight, and one day after practice Asphalt Thomas pulled me aside. "I gotta use you a little tomorrow night. Don't drink no milk or Cokes or water. Don't drink nuthin'. Get a good night's rest. Pray to the Lord. My boys are droppin' like flies." I tossed and turned in my sleep, and all the next day my stomach churned with a million wavy butterflies. Sure enough, with four minutes to go and a nine-point lead Asphalt Thomas looked down my way. "Get in there for Blue. He looks like he's ready to throw up." I felt naked as I entered my first varsity game, and glacial and cold in my joints. It turned out all right. "You just lost your cherry," the coach said to me afterwards. "Didn't do much harm at all." In the next game three nights later I played a few minutes and was as self-satisfied as I had ever been in making six points against the lumbering and unfortunate team from Tuckaho. An *athlete?* Hardly yet. Moody and distracted as ever, my mother was frantic on the subject. "It's *dangerous,*" she said. "You're going to get hurt, I know it. They're better than you. Wait and see. *You're going to get hurt!*"

That year was Fisk's Landing's turn to have the conference high school basketball tournament. These were flatland boroughs more or less the size of our own, summoned from the anxiety and ambiguity of the flat-land of those times to our place (a funny league, to tell the truth, and not especially good in basketball, stepchild as this was to the football grid-iron, but who would volunteer to admit it?) and the town had sought to embellish itself for its incipient visitors. Why did little American towns come so alive then for outsiders? Was it from fear of seeming paltry before their own eyes? Of assuaging their own day-to-day isolation? Or in this instance had death's specter itself, the returning Korean dead, spurred the urge of release? There were directional posters on the light-posts—self-flattery indeed to think someone might get lost here—his-torical signs in front of the old houses, crimson-and-white bunting on the storefronts, and an enormous multi-colored streamer on the court-house: "Welcome, King Cotton Conference!" The yellow out-of-town school buses were everywhere, and dozens of cars with the license plates bearing the alien county names, and in the afternoons the cheerleaders from the other towns strutted the narrow streets around the school. Asphalt Thomas was in his utmost element, and ubiquitous, offering directions to all comers, talking basketball in agitated little clusters with the rival coaches, one of whom had been his teammate on the land-grant university team, exchanging high-flown felicities with the visiting princi-pals and superintendents—"I'm gonna be one of them *principals* when I hang up the jock," he said to me of them—"just as well get used to my future *colleagues.*" The gymnasium was packed for the competition: Thursday and Friday matches, both boys and girls, then the semi-finals and finals all Saturday, and the festive containment of organized celebra-tion reminded one a little of Fisk's Landing Christmas.

Early in our first game, Blue sprained his ankle and had to leave for
the season. Then, toward the end of the third quarter it finally happened, as I knew with dire inevitability that it would and must—White
Boy crashed mightily to the floor near our bench with two adversaries
asprawl him, and his wail of distress rose up and filled the noisome and
crowded assembly, suddenly mute now as he grimaced in honest pain,
heaving and sputtering on the hardwood like a fallen sparrow, his whole
left arm protruding outward from his torso at a grotesque, unholy angle.

Asphalt Thomas chewed his gum as he bent before the stricken warrior. "Can you fix him?" he asked the manager-trainer Leon, who was
examining the injury.

"Nossir, Coach. This thing's broke."

"Hurts like shit," Blue said. "Gimme a shot, Leon."

"I'm jinxed," the coach said after he comforted the contorted victim
as he was led away to the hospital. "What the devil did I do to deserve
this?" Then he dubiously turned to me. "Well . . ."

This was the big time. I was consumed with the same dry-mouthed
giddiness the first day I kissed Georgia. Please, I silently beseeched the
entire Anglican hierarchy: No mistakes. The prayer was in its fashion
answered. Playing the entire final quarter I committed no blunders, but
for that matter did not make a single contribution that to this day I can
recall—an invisible entity, more or less, if ever there was one. Luckily our
squad was leading by several points when the quarter began. The opponents were big and aggressive but slow and cumbersome, and we won.

But the next morning, Friday, when my dog Dusty woke me with a
copious lick or two to the nose as usual, my whole lower right foot was
a terrible blood blister. From my toes down to the arch was a pool of
blood, covered with bursting membrane. I had had two or three before,
but nothing ever like this one. I have an almost Quaker distaste of
blood, so one can imagine the horror with which I greeted this sight; to
my surprise, however, I did not faint, or even retch. I must have hurt it
the night before, somewhere late in the game, but I had thought it only
a bruise. Now, on this morning as I got out of bed, I could barely walk,

the massive blister mocking one's efforts, indeed as I see now perhaps even one's very youth itself. I stripped off my pajamas and looked myself over. From a blow I remembered to the thigh, I perceived I even had a charley horse. Asphalt Thomas once told the team charley horses were inevitable for ball players, as if ordained by the Old Testament, and he also often surmised that blood blisters were the price one paid for being fast and a little bow-legged, as I was and am—not fast now, but still a little bow-legged. Nonetheless it was humiliating to discover one had *both*, and this after a scant and obscure and lusterless quarter.

I knew I had to get out of the house quickly, before my mother found me in harm's way, for her reaction would have been little shy of epileptic in its magnitude. Happily she and her dance students were leaving that afternoon for a two-day recital in the capital city and would not return until Sunday. Now I put my ear to the door, and was for the first time grateful for the sounds of the tap dancing in front. I was tempted to telephone Georgia to come get me in her car, but decided to make my own way. Ordering Dusty to stay, I limped out the back porch and detoured through Mrs. Griffin's yard to the boulevard, hitchhiking a ride with a schoolmate's father to the schoolhouse. I hobbled toward Mrs. Idella King's homeroom. Great stabs of pain were shooting around my foot, and then the charley horse started to throb too; my whole lower body was insufferable, and this made me feel both angry and vulnerable, especially angry. I had never really been hurt before, and this was a new moment in life. My thoughts went out to the official military escorts accompanying the hometown dead from Korea who had converged on Fisk's Landing with missing ears, fingers, and toes.

Georgia was tarrying inside the main entrance under the Plato statue just before the bell. "I waited for you. Are you hurt?"

In time's perspective I probably should have been proud of my wounds in front of Georgia, an honorable gladiator representing his school no matter how ineffectually, as in the Baptist preachers' oft-mentioned tale of the poor crippled lad who ran in the race because he was all his town had. But the thought of the pool of blood in the blister left no room for heroic pretensions.

"Good game," Mrs. King said. After roll call she took me to the back of the classroom and got me to take off my shoe and sock. Georgia and three or four others came over to watch. The sight of Mrs. King bending down in her black dress with the Phi Beta Kappa key dangling from her necklace to examine one's own blood blister was unflattering, and the way the other students stared down at me as if I were little more than an experimental cadaver in a windowless morgue was discomfiting. "Asphalt should see this," Mrs. King said.

She wrote me out a hall pass. I went down the corridor to the coach's office under the gymnasium, but he was not there. "He's teachin' driver's ed first period," Leon told me as he tossed last night's uniforms into the washing machine. "You hurt, ain't you? You sure *look* hurt." I attended the first class, then went to the gym again. Asphalt Thomas was sitting in the little cubbyhole adjoining our locker room, a dip of snuff lodged in his nether lip. "Let's see." Again I removed the shoe and sock.

"*Whew!* Worst I ever saw," he said, spitting all the while into a paper cup and gazing philosophically at the foot. "We'll handle it. We don't play again til tomorrow anyhow. Besides, we're down to the bottom of the barrel." He reached in a drawer of a battered oak desk, rummaged around, and brought out a long needle. He also withdrew a box of Diamond matches and began to heat the end of the needle.

Do we have to do this? I remember asking.

"Turn your head, then," he said. "Prop up the foot."

I closed my eyes. There was a quick, sharp pain, accompanied by an audible *swoosh*. When I opened my eyes again, there were splashes of blood on the dingy walls.

"Have to wash that damned stuff off," he said. "Now *that* was a blood blister. Where's Leon? *Leon!*" Leon came in with a wet rag and cleaned up the mess.

"It's okay now," Asphalt said. "Don't even need wrappin'. I got twenty against Vandy on the road after a blood blister bad as that." The blister was indeed subsiding, like a derelict hose after the water had gone through, and it felt better already, the lifting of a weight. From a bottle Asphalt now applied a generous amount of tough-skin, the cure-all of the era. He used half a bottle, and the smell was piquant.

"Got a little charley, Leon said? How come you so beat up? You only played a *quarter*. Got to protect yourself better. Use the elbows when the zebras ain't lookin'. And I don't mean chicken wings, I mean real *elbows*." Now he examined my thigh. Then he handed me a tube of analgesic, the hot kind—"Red Hot Kramer" on the tube itself, or known to us colloquially as "Atomic Balm." I rubbed most of it into the skin. "Just go ahead and empty the fucker," he suggested. "We got a year's supply." After that he and Leon wrapped the thigh in an Ace bandage, then put about five yards of adhesive around it. "Don't take this off til after the finals," he said, "if we get to the finals. You can take showers in it. It's waterproof. Just shake your leg and limber up every little while. Can't let it get stiff, like a click. Maybe run some in the back this afternoon. Idella might let you out of class to run some. You're a rookie and damaged goods, but all I got. Got to play with pain. Pain never hurt a real player. The Lord's testin' you. Keep your brain off the foot and on the game. I always played best hurtin'. Sank twenty-four against Auburn with a busted-up nose with blood for snot."

His admonition rang hollow in my head when that afternoon during study hall I went out in a sweatsuit behind the gymnasium to loosen up my leg. It was cold and clear, not a cloud in a matchless azure sky, and a flock of wood ducks flew in pristine V-formation overhead. There was a girls' game in the gym, and the noises of the crowd drifted out that way. Four or five of the cheerleaders from Monroe City, planters' daughters, were resting on the lawn; I recognized them from the school dances in the flatland. "What's wrong with *you*?" one of them inquired. "You smell like a drug store." They drew back in mock sympathy, slouching as they had learned from their mothers in the plutocratic flatland manner, hips arched high, hands angular on each side of them. "How's that Georgia?" And they laughed inanely and chattered in the timeless flatland persiflage like a skittish cluster of parakeets as I circled the field again.

The omniscient Asphalt Thomas had observed this tableau from the back door of the locker room. I knew he had been there because of the sound of his jangling keys, his keys to every room and closet and alcove and recess in the entire school building. "Showin' off to the little gals," he said as I came in, "them silly little spoiled rich gals that giggle all the time. Better go home and soak the leg and don't drink the water and sleep twelve hours."

The team went into the semi-finals the next afternoon, Saturday, against Monroe City, people overflowing into the balcony and hallways, some propped on boxes and ladders and watching through the high windows outside, and there was a good flavor of bourbon everywhere.

Merely adequate as I was, playing most of the game and scoring a paltry four points, the remaining seniors, Muttonhead, Term, Noggin, Bouncer, performed with such deft and unexpected nobility that Asphalt Thomas called it the best-played game of the season. In the closing minutes one of the opposition's Notreangelo boys (they had three) whacked me across the back of my neck with his clenched fist when the referees were somewhere else. *"Kick the bastard out!"* I heard the shout from the grandstand. It was unmistakably Georgia, and I learned later that several of the surrounding onlookers stared at her coldly for long moments, and a pastor's wife complained to Idella King, who replied in words that ring down to me now: "Well, they *should* have kicked him out." Fisk's Landing prevailed by six points and would play in that night's championship.

Dizzied, throbbing, I soaked myself under the water spout of the shower. My thigh under the elastic bandage was burning hot, my foot an enormous palpitation. I asked Asphalt Thomas for a bandage on the foot. Once more he looked it over. It was crimson at the bottom now, with shrivelled skin at the edges, but yellow too from the plentitude of medicine. It looked awful. "Naw," he said. "The blood has to circulate. It's healing real nice." Leon gave me three aspirin, then applied more tough-skin, so that I looked like a leper there.

Having defeated Monroe City and the Notreangelos, we would play the last match for the trophy, which Fisk's Landing had not won in ten years, at nine that evening, four hours away. Our adversary would be the only accomplished team in the conference, Lutherville, with the best and most adept player in that league, the all-state Number 8, averaging twenty points a game. Our game would follow the girls' finals.

All high school locker rooms have likely smelled the same since time began. The mingling scents of ammonia, analgesic, tough-skin, iodine, and the Chlorox bleach of Leon doing the washing as we waited for Asphalt Thomas on that distant afternoon linger with me now, so that the assembled odor of it is still as real to me as any I have ever known.

When everyone was ready Asphalt Thomas got us together there for a talk. Unlike at school, he dressed up for the games, as if paying a kind of pious sartorial obeisance to the sport itself, and on this day he wore a sleeveless half-buttoned wool sweater over a shirt and tie, the tie so short that it did not even reach to his midriff. "You men sucked it up out there today. I'm proud of you. See what you can do when your mind's off the snatch?" He told us to go home and relax and not eat too much. "Don't even *think* about losin', for Chrissake. Tell your mommas to cook you a small hamburger steak or somethin' like that, but no *grease*." He wanted us back an hour and a half before the game, he added, because he was working on a special defense against Lutherville. "We once tried this against LSU," he said, "when they had a big ol' center and damned tricky guard. We got to hold down Number 8 and Number 20. But don't worry your heads til you get back. Then we'll worry. Let's whip their maggot-ridden asses. What are we—men or mice?" As the others filed out, he took me aside. "You're on Number 8. I ain't got no choice." Number 8!

Georgia drove me around town for a while. Fisk's Landing was striking in this dying afternoon. The out-of-towners were milling about the courthouse and the main street, spilling in and out of the restaurants, cruising the boulevard in their cars admiring the houses. The green-and-white crepe of Lutherville abounded, and near the Elk's Club the impromptu cheers of their assembled students filled the brisk twilight. On the next corner I even sighted the Notreangelo who had whacked me in the neck only two hours before. He was standing there with his tough upper-flatland chums, including his snarling, swarthy siblings, and when he saw me he stared in haughty and immured disdain.

We went to Georgia's parents, who had promised something to eat. Then she and I sat on the front porch. The air felt good. It was getting on to dark now and the blow on the neck was beginning to hurt for the first time since the game; little shooting stars would appear before my eyes when I turned my head, and the blistered foot was all but numb. I wondered why I had ever voluntarily gotten into this, for in that moment it really did not make good sense. Was there an Anglican prayer against Number 8?

"I've thought of you all day. You look funny." Kneeling before me she took off my shoe—everyone seemed to want to take off my shoe—and gently massaged my foot.

From the school across the street the crowds were congregating for the girls' game. Georgia's mother and father came out the door on the way to the gym. At Georgia's caressing touch I had felt a surprising swell at my thighs, and I hid them quickly with my hands. "Kick a little tail, boy," her father said. Her mother tentatively assessed us as Georgia rubbed the foot. "Are you going to the midnight show after the game?" she asked. "Yes'm." Georgia said, and we all departed toward the school.

In the locker room toward the end of the girls' game, Asphalt Thomas had the big portable blackboard with his X's and O's, and he went over them meticulously—a floating zone around the basket against the tall Number 20, man-to-man on Number 8. Then he just stood there for a second summoning his words. He often dropped scriptural references into his terse pre-game speeches, sometimes claiming a large regard for religion, although I suspected he did not believe any of it to be true—had he lost it on Okinawa? "Get out there and *fight*, men! Run out on that friggin' court with your hand in the hand of the greatest coach of all times—not me, but the head coach from

Nazareth." Just before we went out he approached me again. His eyes were glistening as he sat on his haunches and whispered, "If Number 8 bends down to tie his damned shoelace, you bend down and untie it. If he goes to the commode to take a crap, you follow him and lock him in. If he spits, you spit." I sat there before him on the locker room bench. "You scared? Nervous? When I was eighteen years old," he said, "I crawled halfway across every damn island the Pacific had, on my belly, scared shitless. Think about that when you get out there." We put tough-skin on our hands before leaving. As the home team, Asphalt said, we would start off with a fairly old ball. If the zebras brought in a new, slick ball, we had more tough-skin on the bench. In the warm-ups, the tough-skin with the old balls made the shooting easy, as all basketball boys of that time with tough-skin on their hands and old balls to shoot know and remember.

Number 8 was the swiftest I had seen, and smart, and also a gentleman. His fakes left you breathless. "Keep away, keep away!" he would shout nervously as he moved, but he would never have whacked one across the neck with the referees not watching as the Monroe City Notreangelo had done. He was only an inch or so taller than I, but heavier, and two years older, and I was no match for him; nothing I had ever learned had prepared me for this public humiliation. Why had Asphalt Thomas allowed me to play the entire game? Our team was beaten badly.

Right at the final buzzer I ran into the wall after a loose ball and was sitting against it on the floor. The game was done, and the Lutherville people were rushing onto the court to cut down the nets, their cheerleaders performing one somersault after another on the hardwood. Blood was oozing a little from my shoe and my mouth felt full of cotton. Number 8 came over and sat down next to me. "Damn, I'm tired," he said, and extended his hand. Three years later he would be all-Southeastern Conference at the state university, and honorable mention All-America. And here, too, is the yellowed clipping from the Sentinel in front of me now:

Kent "Lightnin" Boult, all-state standout of Lutherville, scored 28

*points Saturday night and wrecked Fisk's Landing's defenses as the
Bobcats defeated the valiant but injury-riddled Choctaws. 56-33, for the
conference crown.*

As a man Asphalt Thomas was streaked with raw violence, yet he had
a curious begrudging tenderness in him which always surprised me at
age sixteen, the ferocity and the care existing there in odd and unexpected tandem. In the locker room after the game he cuffed me gently
on the head. "Don't worry, kid," he said. "You're young. You *learned*. Put
on some weight. Use the elbows more. Work on the jumper."

Almost everyone was gone. I was the last to leave, except of course for
Leon. Georgia was waiting under a young oak on the campus. In the pungent shadows was the promise of early spring. Across the street from
where we met were the two Negro shacks, hushed now except for the
woman on the front stoop of one of them tending to a bawling infant.

"Are you all right?"

I was okay.

"You played good."

"Oh, come on."

"Well, you did. *I* think you did."

For years, I had an ugly burn on my thigh from the analgesic under
the bandage. There is still to this day, as I age, a slight remnant of the
burn there, and sometimes I look at it and remember those days. But
mostly, really, as the years pass, I do not think much about losing to
Lutherville, or the ingenious Number 8, before the packed house at
home. I merely recall how I was hurting after that game, and Georgia
there, and in the parked sedan how gentle she was with my wounds, her
tender touch, and the mingling pleasure and pain.

At the High School Basketball Championship Game
Barbara Murphy

The game is clumsy. Both teams look
as though they have played better.
These are other people's children playing
for the highest stakes they know.
Watching the star player I know only from his number,
I see how he looks like his mother, tosses
his head the way she does, passes his hand
through his hair as she might, making
her point in a long meeting.

When the game is over and our team has won,
a basketball bronzed like a baby's shoe
is wheeled out on the floor and the crowd's
whoops become background music. The players
are in love with themselves and leave
the gym wrapped in each others' arms.

This has nothing to do with you,
I want to tell my friend from work.
But she knows this already, her face
full of relief, not victory.
She will go home, drink wine, take a nap;
her son will talk to a local reporter,
take a long, noisy shower, go to parties
with friends she barely knows.

Did I think it would be forever:
the mothers arriving at nursery school,

the children happy, but ready to leave
their plastic boats and cups
in the deep, sloppy sink, run to us
with their wet fingers and sneakers.
Or was it never really like that?
Were we always narrow in doorways,
watching them intent in their circle,
not breathing as they passed
the beanbag quickly, so that
when it slipped or landed
in the wrong hands, it would
not be our fault.

For Brothers Everywhere
Tim Seibles

There is a schoolyard that runs
from here to the dark's fence
where brothers keep goin to the hoop, keep
risin up with baske'balls ripe as pumpkins
toward rims hung like piñatas, pinned
like thunderclouds to the sky's wide chest
an' everybody is spinnin an' bankin
off the glass, finger-rollin off the boards
with the same soft touch
you'd give the head of a child, a child
witta big-ass pumpkin head, who stands
in the schoolyard lit by brothers givin and
goin, flashin off the pivit, dealin
behind their backs, between their legs,
cockin the rock an' glidin like mad hawks—
swoopin black, with arms for wings—
palmin the sun an' throwin it down,
an' even with the day gone, without even
a crumb of light from the city, brothers
keep runnin-gunnin, fallin away takin
fall-away jumpers from the corner,
their bodies like muscular saxophones
body-boppin better than jazz, beyond
summer, beyond weather, beyond
everything that moves, an' with one shake
they're pullin-up from the perimeter,
shakin-bakin brothers be sweet
pullin-up from the edge of the world,
hangin like air itself hangs in the air,

an' gravidy gotta giv'em up:
the ball burning like a fruit with a soul
in the velvet hands while the wrists whisper
"back-spin" an' the fingers comb the rock
once—lettin go, lettin it go like good news—
'cuz the hoop is a well, *Shwip!* a well
with no bottom, *Shwick!*
an' they're fillin that sucker up.

Posting-Up
Stephanie Grant

My senior year fourteen girls showed up to our first practice. The year before the team had been only half as strong: not enough bodies to scrimmage even. Which didn't bother our coach, Sr. Agnes, who had spent thirty of her seventy-odd years as a cloistered nun and who confused basketball with dodgeball. Sr. Agnes had retired at the end of last season. My dad said it was A Blessing In Disguise. Rumor was that our new coach, Sr. Bernadette, had gone to college on basketball scholarship. She was late getting to the first practice though, so we all stood around shooting baskets and checking each other out. I counted four, maybe five, point guards.

Every player in the city knew Kate Malone, if not by sight—she was six feet tall, with a mass of bright red hair—then by reputation. She led the Catholic league in total points scored for both boys and girls, and she had been kicked out of five Catholic schools in three years. Whatever school she ended up with, she took to the Catholic League Tourney; I'd watched her win with a different team all three years. Kate was the only new student at Immaculatta in 1973 who wasn't fleeing a court order: Immaculatta was her last hope for a parochial school education. The school before us—Sacred Heart—was in Dorchester, but not the Irish part. Kate had been the only white starter for Sacred Heart, which seemed more incomprehensible than her eighteen or nineteen points per game.

She stood at one end of the gym, shooting. Two other new girls waited beneath the basket for her to miss. Basketball etiquette required them to pass back the ball whenever she sank it. They looked pretty bored.

At the opposite hoop, Irene Fahey was practicing lay-ups. The rest of us stood in a rough semicircle around the basket, taking turns with the remaining ball. Irene wove in and out of us, charging from the left, then right, retrieving her own rebounds—whether or not she scored—dribbling out and flying back in, all the while asking questions about Immaculatta and the team.

"What was your record last year; I mean are you guys the losingest team in history; Who's your new coach? Is she a million and one years old like your last coach? I can't imagine losing all the time. I mean did you guys like to lose, or what?"

Irene was the second best basketball player and biggest mouth in the Catholic league. The year before she took Perpetual Faith to the play-offs with a 13-and-2 record. They lost to Kate's team in the next-to-last round by three points.

"You got a team this year, that's for sure. I've never seen so many freaking guards in one place before. I wonder who she's gonna start?"

Irene left Perpetual Faith, she confided in us at the top of her lungs, because her mother felt "the quality of education was deteriorating." Eventually I learned what that meant: Irene left because Perpetual Faith was one of the few Catholic schools in Boston that had black students, and it had accepted more blacks since the busing crisis began. Not only white parents took their children out of public school after the court order became final. Most of the black families removed their kids because they were concerned for their safety, which was exactly what the white parents said. Even I knew that the black people had real reason to worry. The first day of school a busload of black second-graders got stoned by white parents in Southie. We watched it on the news. My mom and dad were so disturbed they shut off the TV.

"Couldn't wait to get outta Perpetual Faith, that's for sure. Goin' downhill, you know what I'm saying?" Irene stomped on my toes on her way to the hoop.

Her lay-ups became so disruptive to our shooting that we were forced to join her. The girls who had been shooting with Kate (or hoping to shoot with Kate) left her to practice with us. Kate didn't budge, and Irene didn't ask.

Irene made me anxious. She sighed loudly at each of our mistakes, like somehow we were personally disappointing her. I missed every lay-up because I knew she was watching. We kept quiet during the drill and grew bored, but we were afraid to say anything. A tiny, dark-haired girl suggested we scrimmage. She was very serious looking. I had never seen her before, which was weird because I went to all the league games, Catholic and city, and I knew all the ball players. Irene was irritated.

"Ya, and who are you? Where'd you play? Not in this league, I don't think. Not too many guineas in this league. Not that I have anything against Italians. Don't get me wrong. Just never seen them play any kinda b-ball."

"Assumption," the girl replied, unflinching. I stared at the gym floor, nauseated; we didn't use words like guinea in my house.

"Assumption?" Irene looked puzzled. "Never heard of it. Where's Assumption?"

"Springfield," she responded, still indifferent. Her voice was low and steady.

"Ya, then how come I never heard of it? I got relatives in Springfield, and I've never heard of Assumption. You wouldn't be lying to me, would you; I hope not, lying is a cardinal sin, you know; it'll put a black mark on your soul, and guineas start out with half-black souls because of the Mafia. You can't afford too many cardinal sins."

"No, I wouldn't lie to you. You haven't heard of Assumption because it's not a high school. Assumption College." Ice edged the dark girl's words.

"I don't get it. What's your name?" Irene lost some of the color in her face.

Bernadette. Sr. Bernadette. And you're Irene Fahey. That right?"

Irene nodded, ash-grey. All of us looked a little ill, except Kate who was still shooting baskets. The bounce bounce of her ball kept time.

"Why didn't you tell us who you were?" Irene choked. "And how the hell old are you, anyway?"

Sr. Bernadette shrugged. "I just wanted to see you play relaxed, without knowing the coach was watching. And it's none of your business how old I am. Just graduated from Assumption last spring and took my vows at the same time. Any more questions?"

Silence. Then Irene "Don't they have a height requirement for nuns, for Christ's sake?"

There was a collective gasp. Everything I'd ever heard about Irene Fahey was true.

"No, but there are requirements for being on this team." Sr. Bernadette took a step toward Irene. "One of them is respect. If I get any more lip from you, your behind is going to be warming the bench all season. I don't care who you are or how good you play. Got that?"

"Got it," Irene smiled a big, fake smile. "Got it, got it. I mean you're the boss, right? You're about as big as my kid sister, but you're the coach and whatever the coach says, goes."

I was sweating. Irene lived by the axiom that the best defense is a good offense.

Sr. Bernadette fixed Irene with a glare so cold that every girl within ten feet hugged her arms to her body. I remembered what I had heard in school about Italians and the evil eye and was instantly ashamed.

"Kate, come down here, will you? We're gonna scrimmage. I'd like everyone to introduce herself first. Tell us your name, what school you played for last year, and what position."

There did seem to be something sort of otherworldly about Sr. Bernadette, I had to admit. Like how come she already knew our names?

Everyone shifted her weight from leg to leg as we went around the circle. There were six new girls.

"Maura Duggan, Dorchester High, point guard."

"Frances Fitzgerald, Southie, point guard."

"Peggy Gallagher, Charlestown High, forward."

"Pat Gallagher, Charlestown High, forward."

"Irene Fahey, Perpetual Faith, point guard."

"Kate Malone, Sacred Heart, point guard."

Point guard is like quarterback, only for basketball. She's your best player. She controls the ball. My dad says point guards are born, not made, that it's their disposition more than their skill that a coach looks for. I had never seen so many in one room.

Sr. Bernadette bounced up and down on the balls of her feet. All the guards stared at their hightops only one of them would get to play point. Kate and Irene never looked at each other.

I started playing basketball because my dad wanted me to. He used to coach boys basketball at Most Precious Blood and coached my brother Tim when he went there. It was sort of like a dynasty, Dad and Tim together for four years. *The Meagher Dynasty* people called it. Dad insisted I play because of my height. I'm 5-foot, 11 1/2 inches tall, and have been since eighth grade. My brother is 5-foot-7. Tim played guard at Most Precious Blood, but was too short for college ball. I think it made him crazy that I got the right body for basketball but didn't know how to use it. Of course if Dad had given me one-fifth the attention he gave Tim growing up, I'm sure I'd have been a lot better. For a while I was hoping Tim and I were going to be the dynasty—*The Tim and Theresa Meagher Dynasty*. But it never worked out.

When I enrolled at Immaculatta in 1969, it was a small, eggheady parochial school for girls who would rather read than do just about anything else. Our basketball team had had thirty-seven consecutive losing seasons. My senior year, everything changed. Busing doubled the enrollments of Boston's Catholic schools. Even though we were technically outside the neighborhoods designated for desegregation, we were close enough to absorb the shock of white students leaving the public schools. Not counting the incoming class, seventy-one new students matriculated in 1973. Six of them were basketball stars. The Sisters said it was God's will.

The whole first week of practice was like tryouts. Sr. Bernadette tried every possible combination of players. She ran very serious practices. The first hour we did drills, ball handling, lay-ups, shooting, and passing. The second hour we broke into teams and scrimmaged ourselves. When boys did this the two teams were called shirts and skins, because one team played bare-chested. When we scrimmaged, one team had to put on these horrible green smocks called pinneys. Everyone complained when they had to wear them. Irene said they looked queer. Sr. Bernadette called the team wearing pinneys "green" and the team without "white." Kate was always on the white team.

Tall people like Kate usually don't play point guard because more often than not they're lousy dribblers. The ball has so far to travel to get to the ground that it's easy to steal from them. Taller girls like me play underneath the basket, as forwards or centers. We spend most of our time fighting for good position and pulling down rebounds, so we don't get a lot of experience dribbling, faking people out, or setting up plays, which is what guards do. We mostly get a lot of experience hitting people. The few tall players who dribble are often so awkward that you don't have to guard against them very closely. Their Own Worst Enemy, as my dad would say. But Kate was not like that. She had a very low dribble for someone her height, and it was almost impossible to steal from her. She never seemed to crouch or bend over when dribbling, which left me with the impression that her arms were abnormally long. In fact, I would have sworn that her hands hung down past her knees. Though, when I saw her off the basketball court, her arms were normal long, but in proportion with the rest of her.

Irene was built a lot more like your average high school point guard than Kate: short and skinny. Really skinny. No hips and breasts that were all nipple. (A terrific advantage on the basketball court, as in life.) In fact, if it weren't for her long, Farrah Fawcett hair and accompanying makeup, Irene could easily have been taken for a boy.

There were two schools of thought on eye shadow when I was in high school: some girls meticulously matched it to their outfits, being sure that their highlights—above the lid and below the eyebrow—corresponded to the contrasting color in their clothes. Others matched make-up with eye color, varying only the intensity of the shade. Irene was a renegade, defying both traditions, insisting on sky blue—despite her brown hair and eyes and rainbow assortment of J Crew polos. Irene's rebellion stopped here, in all else she was the standard bearer and enforcer of the status quo.

Irene also played more like your average high school point guard than Kate did. She was completely self-absorbed and unconscious of the rest of us. Irene shot whenever she had the ball. She dribbled too much (even if well) and she wouldn't pass. She tried endlessly to go in for lay-ups. She didn't think. Irene played like a one-person team, dribbling and shooting, dribbling and shooting.

Of course she got good at both because she had so much practice, but she was lousy to play with.

Friday afternoon after our first week of practice, Sr. Bernadette told us who would play where. We sat, as we had all week, far apart from each other on the bleachers of the gym listening to her comments about our play. She read without looking up from the notes she had taken on her coach's clipboard. We each had a towel and were conscientiously wiping away the day's sweat. Only Kate was still. She sat with her endless legs apart, one planted—knee bent—on the bleacher on which she sat, the other stretched out in front of her, ankle resting on the next, lower tier. Her freckled arms wrapped around the near leg, securing it to the seat. Sr. Bernadette looked up when she got to the end of her notes.

"Starting lineup will be as follows: Pat Gallagher, forward; Peggy Gallagher, forward; Theresa Meagher, center; Irene Fahey, off guard; Kate Malone, point guard. These are not lifetime memberships. If you play well, you keep your spot; if you don't, you rest a while. It goes without saying that everyone will play."

Before St. Bernadette finished her last sentence, Irene was in the showers. Her little body was rigid as she hightailed it across the gym but her large mouth was open and slack, mumbling things we all tried not to hear.

Sr. Bernadette was the best coach I'd ever had. And the coolest teacher. Unlike most of the other nuns at Immaculatta, she was post-Vatican II, which meant she didn't wear a habit and she smiled at you when she spoke. But Sr. Bernadette was the most post-Vatican II nun I ever knew. She wore her hair short, but not severe. It was thick and black, stylishly cut in a shag. She had bright black eyes and smooth, almost-brown skin. During the day she wore jeans, and at practice she wore shorts and a tee shirt. Hers are the only nun's knees I've ever seen. She talked nonstop about basketball, and she shouted when she was angry or excited. She said "pissed off." She ran. Her last name was Romanelli, which was a big deal at the time because Irish people dominated the Catholic league then, and because what you were, like which Church you belonged to, mattered.

Her office was at the far end of the girls' locker room, next to the exit doors. Its walls were half wood, half glass, and you could see her working away at her desk as we got dressed to leave. The glass was opaque, with a bubbly texture, so you could see her outline. Sometimes girls went in to talk with her after practice if they were having trouble, or if Irene had said something particularly mean to them. I liked to take my time getting dressed so I could watch her move around her office.

There was a lot of talk about Kate's past. Particularly from Irene. Of special interest was why she had been bounced from five Catholic schools. Kate always left practice immediately, without showering; as soon as the door shut behind her, the discussion began. Irene would parade around the dressing room still pink-faced from practice, wet from the shower, and wrapped in a thick white towel. She would stop at practically every stall, grab onto the chrome curtain rod overhead and swing into our rooms unannounced as we changed.

"My cousin Mary Louise was at Our Lady of Mercy with Kate two years ago and she says Kate was expelled for refusing to go to religion class and disrespecting the nuns. She wouldn't even go to Mass."

Irene would pause, release one hand from the chrome bar to readjust the tuck and tightness of her towel, which was arranged to give the appearance of a bust, and continue talking and swinging one-armed.

"But my mother says her mother's just too cheap to pay tuition. Each year they pay half in September and promise to pay the rest by Christmas vacation. But never do. Can you imagine that, your mother lying to the nuns? Jesus Fucking Christ that's gross."

The first time Irene popped uninvited into my dressing room, I was mis-stepping into my underwear, damp from a hurried toweling-off. She stared at my body as I fumbled with leg holes.

"What do you think, Saint Theresa?" Irene always called me that. "I heard that our star player did it with black boys when she was at Sacred Heart."

Irene's mouth stayed open in a question mark as she surveyed my nakedness. I pulled on my jeans before answering. Somehow Irene always asked you questions that made you a jerk for just thinking about answering them. Her eyes traveled from my (now covered) thighs to my bare breasts. The stall was too small for me to go anyplace, so I stood there growing red, trying to come up with an answer I could live with. Irene was discovering that I had the biggest breasts on the team.

"Jesus Fucking Christ you've got big tits," Irene said. "Hey, Frances! Maura! Did you realize what big fucking tits Saint Theresa has?" A small crowd gathered. My dad says that people like Irene are a form of penance.

Our first game was against Irene's alma mater, Perpetual Faith. We all were quiet on the bus ride over except Irene; she gave us a pregame scouting report on her old teammates. We learned what everyone's shooting percentage was and who shaved her armpits.

When we climbed down off the bus at Perpetual Faith we could see the other team watching us, but we pretended not to. They were peering out of the small rectangular windows set high in the walls of the gym We knew that they had to be on tiptoe, standing on top of the bleachers; we knew because we did the same thing when the teams came to play us at Immaculatta. I could picture their stretched arches as they leaned against the glass. They were sizing us up, gauging their strength, laughing at the shrimpy girls, worrying about the tall ones.

Sr. Bernadette had told us to look at the back of the head of the girl in front of us as we filed into the gym. Kate led the processional, followed immediately by Irene. Perpetual Faith's players were shooting when we entered, spread out in a fan underneath the basket. Most of them knew Kate by sight, having lost to her in the past. You could see them pulling aside the new players to explain.

"No, no, the tallest girl's the point guard. The other one, the next-to-tallest, she plays center. Watch out for the guard, that's Kate Malone."

I was self-conscious, not being the tallest and playing center. I knew I got the job because I was tall enough and because busing had brought us only forwards and guards. I would have been happier hiding out as a forward; I would have felt less responsible. One of the Gallagher twins could have played center, they were good enough, they were better than me. But Peggy and Pat had played as forwards together all their lives. Choosing one as center over the other would have disturbed their equilibrium.

I wished I was a star center, the way Kate would have been. Lots of people thought that using her as a guard was a waste. But Sr. Bernadette knew that if Kate played center, Irene would be point guard, which meant that nobody but Irene (least of all Kate) would touch the ball.

My biggest shortcoming was that I wasn't aggressive enough, wasn't mean. I was taller than most of the centers I played, and I regularly got good position. I was a decent rebounder, although I've never been a great jumper, and frequently got outjumped by some little, but elastic girls. Offensively I was a nightmare. No guts. Most of my opportunities to score came from one-on-one matchups: me versus the other center in the middle of the key smack underneath the basket. I was easily intimidated. If a girl played me close, if she bumped me or perhaps pushed me a little just to let me know she was there, I would back right off. I would pass back out of the key, move the ball farther away from the basket. I was exasperating, really. Irene said so, right to my face at practice. I guess I sabotaged a lot of good plays that way by panicking.

I got constant advice from my teammates and Sr. Bernadette about posting-up, which is hoopster language for these one-on-one battles I kept avoiding. I got advice about staying firm, and wanting it bad enough, and going straight up or going up strong and even, mixing it up with the big girls. But it was useless, the language alone confused me. Mixing what up? With whom? People assumed I couldn't post-up because I was afraid of the other girl, afraid she would hurt or humiliate me. But it wasn't true.

I played the entire first quarter on the verge of puking, praying no one would pass me the ball. Defensively, I was solid enough: mostly I just stood there and let girls run into me. Irene and Kate shot from everywhere. Swish, swish, swish, went the ball through the hoop. I didn't come close to scoring until the second half when they substituted in a new center.

Kate and Irene had brought the ball up, and were weaving in and out of the key. I was directly underneath the basket, hands up, my back to the other center. She looked familiar, but I couldn't quite place her. I heard nothing but the sound of my own heartbeat and breathing. Sr. Bernadette waved wildly from the sidelines and I could see her mouth-ing directions. A play and then several plays unfolded around me. I tried to stay focused on the ball. My opponent and I do-si-doed for position. Finally, I heard a sound that didn't belong to me: the chink chink of Mary Jude McGlaughlin's cross and Virgin medallion hitting against each other.

Mary Jude was a friend of my cousin Anne, and from what Anne used to tell me, she was shy, devout, not overly intellectual, extremely sweet, and oppressively pretty. She had been warming the bench for Perpetual Faith for three years, and had scored twice during brief cameos, once for the opposing team. Mary Jude touched my soaked back lightly, just above my hip, with the tips of three fingers on her right hand. Her breathing was soft and even, and although I couldn't see her face, I knew she was smiling. Mary Jude never didn't smile.

I sighed. Here it was again. How could I possibiy compete against such goodness? How could I fake left, all the while knowing that I would be moving to my right, digging my shoulder into Mary Jude as I pivoted, and lightly pushing the ball into the basket? How could I leave her standing there, as people had so often left me, mouth agape, embarrassed, wondering what had just happened, How could I press my advantage knowing the punishment she would take from her teammates, punishment I knew only too well? Worst of all, Mary Jude would smile through it all. This registered as sin to me. Something I would have to purge from my soul in order to receive communion next Sunday. Something, if left unattended, I would burn in hell for. So I didn't.

When the ball finally came to me, I was a knot of anxiety. I turned and faced Mary Jude. I held the ball high, above her head, and discovered I was right about her smile. She beamed at me. I smiled back. She had huge brown eyes. In the half second before I was going to pass the ball back to Kate, one of Mary Jude's teammates whacked the ball out of my hands and into the hands of their point guard. They scored before I turned around.

Irene was all over me.

"Jesus Fucking Christ, what was that? You plan to just give them the ball all day? Whose side are you on anyway?"

I blanched. The one legitimate basket Mary Jude had scored in the last three years was against me. I let her. It was as if I had no choice: it meant so much to her. I was terrified that Irene had figured it out; that she would tell about Mary Jude and the others like her. And there were others. Lots of others. I guess I knew the other centers wanted to win as much as I did, and I couldn't stand the thought of taking that away from them. It wasn't that I liked to lose; I hated to lose. But I guess I hated making other people lose worse. And besides, I was used to it.

I knew that this weakness was ten times worse than plain cowardice. I was My Own Worst enemy. And now, potentially, the team's.

We won anyway. The first in an endless season of wins. We beat Perpetual Faith 59 to 36. Kate scored 23 points, Irene hit for 19. The team was ecstatic. Sr. Bernadette lectured us on the bus on the way home. I sat as far away from Irene as possible. Sr. Bernadette crouched in the aisle between the seats, pivoting left and right, facing each of us directly as she spoke. Sr. Bernadette had a custom of grabbing your shoulder or your knee or whatever was handy when she talked to you, so she was impossible to ignore. That day on the bus she got so close to me I could feel her breath on my face. I didn't hear a word she said, but I remember how she looked up close. Her hair was damp and limp from all the perspiring she had done during our game, her face glistened and the muscles on her neck stood out. Her black eyes were as black as her missing habit, and luminous.

Usually I hated the bus rides. If I could have, I would have sat right by Kate, who took the seat directly behind the bus driver and across the aisle from Sr. Bernadette. I was dying to be included in their conversations, to listen to Kate talk basketball, and to be on the receiving end of Sr. Bernadette's intensity. They sat at a slight angle to each other so that

their knees touched, and Kate held the playbook on her lap. Sr. Bernadette gestured from the book to the air in front of them, with one hand
going back periodically to Kate's shoulder to confirm her understanding. Kate stared closely at the invisible drawings in the air between them.

Irene occupied the very last bus seat by the emergency exit; the rest
of us were staggered in the seats just before her. The cooler you were
the farther back you sat and the closer to Irene you positioned yourself.
I sat alone, as far away from Irene as I could get without leaving the
group entirely. She talked nonstop about Kate. My ears burned red as I
slumped forward in my seat pretending not to hear her, pretending to
read the book in my lap, stealing glances at the front of the bus.

But I was, I knew, as guilty as Irene. Like her, I was obsessed with
Kate I wanted to know everything: what her family was like, why she
kept changing schools, where she learned to play so well, whether she
liked us, whether she liked me. In retrospect, I was infatuated with her,
and it was my first big, stomach-wrenching infatuation. But I didn't
know to call it that. I didn't even know enough to be embarrassed.
Although, thank God, I knew enough to keep it from Irene.

I listened very closely to the horrible things Irene said. Each day she
had a new story explaining Kate. Kate was on drugs; she was a klepto-
maniac; her mother was a prostitute; her family was on welfare; they
were really Protestant Irish; her father was a Jew; Kate was on the Pill;
and, the worst possible slander for our immaculate ears, she had had
two abortions. Everyone knew that Kate lived alone with her mother,
and this in itself was extremely suspect. Some kids at Immaculatta had
as many as ten brothers and sisters; most of us had at least four. I had
never met an only child. Sr. Agnes said they were sins. And Catholic
families were not families without fathers.

If Kate knew about the rumors Irene spread, she never let on. Kate
rarely spoke. She had no friends on the team, or at Immaculatta, as far as I
could tell. When Kate spoke it was b-ball talk. At practice she doubled as
Sr. Bernadette's assistant coach, showing us moves and illustrating plays.
One week Kate was assigned to demonstrate posting-up to the centers

and forwards. That Monday we gathered around her underneath one basket, while Sr. Bernadette hollered at the guards at the opposite end of the court.

"First you have to find out where you are. Establish some territory. Take up some space. Back your butt into the other girl. See how much room she'll give you. Once you know where she is and how much she'll take, then you're ready. The first rule in posting-up is wanting it. Even if your hands are up like this for the ball, no guard's gonna pass it unless your face says you want it. The second rule is not thinking about it too much. Get ready and go. The longer you wait, the more likely it'll be taken away."

Was she talking just to me? Did she know? Had Irene told her something, or was I that transparent?

"Get out of your head, Theresa," Kate said on Tuesday. "I can see you thinking. Get out of your head."

"How?" I asked. "How can you see me thinking?" And to myself: *What can you see me thinking?*

"I just can," she shrugged. "And if I can, so can they. So lose it, whatever it is."

I struggled to empty my face. I struggled to eliminate Mary Jude and the others from my consciousness.

"Well you don't have to look like an idiot." Kate smiled at my vacant expression. The other girls laughed, and I was giddy with the attention. Emboldened, I asked her how come she knew so much about basketball.

"I don't really know," she said, completely serious. "It's like I was born knowing."

"Did your father teach you?" I ventured. "Or your brothers?" Heads turned; ears pricked expectantly.

She shook her head, No. Now her face emptied. End of conversation.

But I couldn't let it go. After practice, I followed her to her locker. She hadn't heard my footsteps over the noise of the girls taking showers, so she jumped when I said loudly into her left ear, "Uncles or cousins?"

"Uncles or cousins, what?" She looked angry.

I had never been this close to Kate, and now I saw the details of her face for the first time. Her skin was pale—red-head pale—and a pattern of soft brown freckles ran across the bridge of her nose and splashed onto her cheeks. Her eyes were clear blue. They widened with shock and anger as I persisted.

"Did your uncles or cousins teach you to play?"

"Why are you so anxious to know who taught me what? Maybe I taught myself. Maybe, like I said, I was born knowing. Maybe I couldn't help but learn. What's it to you?" She crossed her long arms in front of her chest and grew two inches. Her thin Irish lips pursed.

"I was just curious. Thought maybe if I knew what you did to get so good, I could learn a little faster. You know." Sweat collected on my eyelids.

"Look, lemme give you a tip, save you some time. The thing you need to do more than anything else is be in your body. I've seen it before. Lots of girls play in their heads. Get back here," one of her extraordinary arms flashed out and smacked me in the roundest part of my belly. The spot she touched burned, and I could feel little waves of heat fan out until my fingertips were warm. I knew the color was draining from my face. I nodded and bent forward a little, in an unintentional bow, and got stuck there. I tried to smile my thanks, but I couldn't move my muscles the way I wanted. Finally, I just backed away. We didn't speak again until Friday.

"Terry, come here."

Terry? No one called me Terry. It was always Theresa. I looked behind me; perhaps there was a new girl I didn't know.

"Yes, you, Terry. Come here. Come guard me."

We had had a week of posting-up lessons—we had practiced both offensive and defensive positions—and it was time to show Sr. Bernadette what we had learned. I couldn't move.

"Quit stalling, Terry. Get over here."

Terry. I said it over to myself. Kate had a name for me.

Slowly, anxiously, I got in position behind her. She grew taller and wider until I could see nothing but her muscled back and clump of braided hair. All week I had practiced against the Gallaghers and lost. How could I possibly defend against Kate?

She inched me back toward the basket with her butt. Her shoulders twisted left, then right, then left again. Finally Kate stepped away from me, turned, and shot. When I could at last see the ball. I started moving toward it, straight up into the air. My shoulder left its socket, released my arm, which floated up to touch the hall, and returned. Before I knew it, we were all three back on the ground.

"Not bad, Terry. Not bad at all." Kate looked surprised, but not displeased. "Now just stay there." She slapped one arm onto my shoulder, retrieved the ball with her free hand, and pumped it into my stomach. "Don't think about what you did, just stay here. In your body."

But I was already out, thinking about my new name, afraid of what I'd just done.

As we won more and more, I grew increasingly frustrated with my inability to score. I wanted to be part of the team in a way that I wasn't. I wanted to slap hands with everyone, triumphant, after an especially tough basket. Or, more truthfully, I wanted everyone to slap my hand, the way they slapped Kate's and Irene's. I wanted to be sought after. I wanted Kate to congratulate me in the same expressionless, monotone manner in which she congratulated Irene. I wanted the cool indifference of excellence.

So at the halfway point in the season, after we'd won twelve straight games, and we were looking like we couldn't lose, I began practicing on my own, mornings, before school. An hour and a half of shooting and dribbling (I set up those fluorescent orange cones and did figure eights around them) every day. I got a little better and a lot bored. Playing alone had its limitations; it's one thing to shoot from eight feet out, it's another thing to shoot from anywhere with someone's hand in your face. And I had no one to post-up against. So I started looking for a morning pickup game.

All the league stars played mornings. Many of them played nights, too, after regular practice or games, after dinner, under streetlights that had been rigged with hoops. I knew that Irene played early mornings in the school playground with a bunch of girls from Perpetual Faith. Girls-room girls. Smokers. They all wore eye shadow that matched their sweatpants and tons of St. Christopher medals and gold crosses that were constantly being tucked into ironed, white tee shirts. Irene was the best athlete there, and she tenaciously maintained possession of the ball, so after a few wasted efforts I decided to try a boys' game. I went to several boys' Catholic school playgrounds and found as many games. It didn't work. I realized that a girl's ability was always a problem for boys. If I wasn't as good as they were, they humiliated me by never passing me the ball; if I was as good, they humiliated me by never passing me the ball. Only girls who were as talented as Kate could play with boys without humiliation. Finally, I got up the courage to ask Sr. Bernadette. I tapped on the bubble glass of her office door one day after practice, after everyone had gone.

"Come in," she hollered, and swiveled in her chair. The office was warm and smelled of leather from balls and gloves and cleats.

I stood with my hands behind my back, one hand still on the doorknob.

"What's up, Theresa?" She smiled. She looked even smaller sitting down; her feet swung an inch above the ground.

"I, umm, I was wondering if you, umm, knew of a game I could play in mornings. Other than Irene's game." I turned the knob in my hand. It was slippery.

"What about my game?" she offered immediately.

"What about your game?" I was confused.

"My game." Sr. Bernadette stood up and jammed her hands in her sweatpants pocket.

"You coach a game? I'm looking for a pickup game, not another team." I leaned back into the door.

"No, I play in a game. A pickup game." She was still smiling.

"You play in a pickup game?" I didn't know nuns could do that. After all she had played in college before she took her vows.

"Theresa, what's the problem? Am I not being clear? I can't imagine being any more clear, really." Sr. Bernadette's smile waned and she seemed a little exasperated.

"No. It's just that, what do you mean, a game?"

"Jesus. I mean I play in a morning pickup game and would you like to play with us?"

For Christ's sake, I had made a nun swear. I opened the office door and took a half step out. "Well, yes, I mean, are you sure it's OK?"

"It's OK," Sr. Bernadette sighed. "Where are you going?"

"Then OK. All right. See you there. Where is it?" I was outside her office now. Only my head stuck into the warmth.

"Dorchester." Sr. Bernadette stepped toward me.

"Dorchester. OK. No problem. See you then. Tomorrow OK?" I closed the door. Then opened it. "How do I get there?"

Sr. Bernadette laughed and sat back down. "You can catch the bus on Randolph Avenue, right in front of Immaculatta."

"No problem," I lied and shut her door for good. I couldn't believe it! Sr. Bernadette invited me to her personal game. Her very own private game. I floated home. Maybe now I could sit in the school bus with her and Kate. Maybe now I would be protected from Irene.

The next morning I had to take two different buses to get there, and I had to lie to my parents about where I was going. Dorchester was off-limits.

I jumped off the bus three blocks too soon. My stomach knotted. It was a big, public school playground with several hoops. A handful of men played at the near corner. I stood by the fence in front of them, hidden by their moving bodies. I could see Sr. Bernadette and her friends warming up at the far end of the concrete park. I had imagined the way they might look several times last night I dreamed that they played in full habits. My mind pictured every possible combination of athlete and cleric on the court. But I never guessed they would be a mixed group, even in Dorchester. I didn't know any black people, none of my friends knew any black people, so I hadn't imagined them in Sr. Bernadette's basketball game. I waited for everyone to start playing before I walked over.

Kate was there! I gasped at the sight of her, exhilarated and disappointed. Sr. Bernadette had invited another person from our team to share in her private life. I was not so special after all. I wondered how long they had been playing together, and if they had become friends.

The knot in my stomach tightened.

There were ten women playing hall, including Kate and Bernie—which is what they called Sr. Bernadette. Two more women sat next to me on a green wooden bench that was rooted into the cement a few feet behind one of the hoops. I was sweating so much that my thighs slid off the bench and little pieces of green paint stuck to me when I stood up. The women at my side watched the game closely, calling out encouragements.

The first play I witnessed was a court-length pass to Kate, who was waiting underneath the basket. It took three seconds. They tried the exact same thing next possession but someone on the other team leapt into the air and stole away the play. I was out of breath just watching them.

They fought hard for rebounds and loose balls, and sometimes knocked each other down. One woman got roughed up three times in three consecutive plays. She was a forward and a very aggressive rebound-er. She had the same coloring as Sr. Bernadette; another Italian I guessed. Her dark hair stood out every which way. Each time she hit the cement, whoever knocked her down helped her up. By the third fall everyone was laughing. She even smiled, although you could see she was hurt. Someone said it was a good thing she had so much padding, and they all laughed louder. The well-padded woman walked stiffly around the court, rubbing her behind. The others stopped to catch their breath, bending completely over, resting their hands on their knees so that their elbows jutted out and made shelves of their arms. Everyone's tee shirt was stuck to them.

After a minute or two, one of the point guards approached the injured forward and spoke to her. She massaged the woman's butt like it was her shoulder or something. They walked slowly over to the bench. We all stood up.

"Sub," said the guard, looking at me. "We need a forward."

The injured player lay out flat on the ground in front of the bench. She brought one knee up to her chest and held it there tightly. Her sore cheek lifted off the ground. One of the women who had been calling encouragements hustled onto the court.

"You sure look like a forward," the guard shrugged, letting her eyes travel up and down my full length. I felt that same funny heat wave I felt when Kate touched my stomach that time after practice.

"Center," I whispered.

"No kidding?" She smiled. "You're gonna play against Katie?" She shook her head. "Aren't you the brave one. I'd be whispering that too, if I were you." She sped back to the game.

I hadn't even noticed that Kate was playing center. I wondered if it was because they needed a center, or because there were guards who played better than Kate. I had never seen a guard better than Kate, so I watched the friendly woman play.

She reminded me of Irene—except that she was more friendly and she was black—they had the same build and the same jauntiness. She was everywhere at once. It was the kind of attitude you hate in people you don't like. It didn't bother me so much in her. She stole the ball five times in about eight tries.

I was used to seeing people steal a lot. Kate and Irene did it all the time, but against lesser players. This guard was something else again. The women she stole from were no pushovers; they could handle the ball, every single one of them. Where she edged them out was in speed and desire. Just a millisecond faster: she would attack the ball the instant after it was released from her opponent's hand, but before it touched the ground. She didn't grab the ball with both hands: that would have been too awkward, and too easy to defend against. She just tapped it lightly to one side and was gone. Like that. Desire so overwhelming you couldn't see it happening.

My dad had a drill test for desire. He said that desire was the most important thing in an athlete. Only he called it playing with heart. That's how he picked his starters: the five guys with the most heart played. At home, he would roll a basketball on the ground away from me and Tim. When it was a few feet out, he'd blow his coach's whistle and we'd lunge for it. On the cement driveway. We'd dive and grovel and kick for the ball. That was what I thought desire looked like. Desperation and skinned knees. I had trouble recognizing the smiling guard's desire, desire that left no room for alternatives. Desire that brought pleasure.

She was having a great time. Everyone was.

They were a strange-looking bunch. All different sizes and colors and abilities. I had expected them all to be the same. They were not. The guard who reminded me of Irene was 5-foot, 4 inches tall. The other point guard was equally as small, but had legs the thickness of fire hydrants. She could touch the rim of the basket; she could alley-oop.

There was something peculiar about them. Something I couldn't quite name. They were women, not girls. For the first time I saw the difference. I realized that this was what made Kate stand out so at Immaculatta; and that this, somehow, was why she had been thrown out of five Catholic schools. There was a sturdiness about them, a sense of commitment to life, like at one point they each had made a conscious decision to stay alive. They had made choices.

The longer I watched them play, the more inexplicable they seemed. I had never met women like them before. My mother, none of my friends' mothers, were like these women. Yet deep in my stomach they were familiar. I began to suspect I'd met them before and searched my brain for a memory. Nothing.

Kate was playing against a tall light-skinned black woman named Toni, who was as skinny as she was long. Kate seemed thickset by comparison. They spent most of their time about a hair's width apart, exchanging bruises. Fifteen minutes into the game, Kate elbowed her in the head, accidentally, while pulling down a rebound. It smarted. Toni staggered toward the bench, holding her head in her hands. "Sub," she hollered. Everyone else stopped moving.

"Toni, Toni, you okay? Talk to me, Toni." Kate's face was a mask of concern.

Toni turned to them, fingering the growing lump on her head. "You playing football out there, Malone, or what? No finesse, I tell you, Irish girls got no finesse."

Everyone smiled; a few giggles escaped. Kate tried not to laugh.

"Your concern is underwhelming, Malone, underwhelming" Toni resumed her stagger toward the bench and plowed directly into me.

"Who are you? More Irish, I see. I need a sub. Go play against your cousin, will ye. You can beat up each other for a while." She shoved me onto the court.

Irene's look-alike came immediately to my rescue. She grabbed me by the shoulder.

"No problem, no problem. Maureen's here, and she's gonna take care of you. Mo's gonna help you out. What's your name, sweetheart? If you're gonna play with us, we need to know your name."

"Theres—Terry," I said, looking away from Kate "Terry Meagher."

"Okay, Terry Meagher, it's two-one-two zone." She dragged me over to my new teammates. "You just stand in the middle with your arms up like this, okay?" Mo threw both of her arms into the air, her little body making a giant X. "Me and Bernie are your guards, Merril and Sam are behind you Got that?" She stood frozen in a half-jumping jack. I nodded.

Everyone grunted hello, and Bernie—Sr. Bernadette—winked at me. Mo flung one arm over my shoulder and pulled me to her. She covered her mouth with her free hand and whispered loud enough for everyone to hear "Don't let Katie get inside, okay? You're finished if she gets inside. Foul her if you have to."

I looked into Mo's eyes. Dark brown eyes in a dark brown face. Irene came to mind: how like Mo she was. How she would hate that. I thought about Mom and Dad. How grateful they were to have sent me to Catholic school, years ago, before it all started, before yellow school buses meant anything more than transportation. I pictured the busload of black second-graders that got stoned. I remembered the TV news clip my parents had kept me from watching; before they shut it off, I had recognized an Irish flag waving behind the mob of white parents.

Mo's left hand hung pink and brown over my shoulder, an inch from my face. I reached up and pressed it with both of my sweaty hands. "Cold hands," I smiled at Mo.

"They're always that way, even when I play." Mo looked directly at me.

"Cold hands, warm heart," I offered, and was instantly embarrassed. "It's an old Irish saying," I backtracked. What was I doing?

But Mo seemed charmed. "I like that. Cold hands, warm heart. Good for you. I like that. You're gonna do just fine. Well, let's go, Terry Meagher. And watch out for these cold-hearted women with hot shots." She laughed and shook her head.

The rest of the game seemed to go in slow motion. I knew it was faster than any other game I'd ever played in, but I could see every detail like it wasn't, like I was watching it under a magnifying glass.

I kept one eye on Kate, one eye on the ball, and one eye on Mo, who was never far from the ball. Then it happened. I was in the middle of the key, with Kate at my back. Mo brought the ball up and charged around me, into the key, making like she was going in for a lay-up. But instead of shooting, she dropped the ball back for me. Her move drew everyone with her, over to the right side of the key. Well, almost everyone. I was just left of center, with Kate between me and the basket.

So I did what Kate taught me. Fake right-left-right, turn, and up into the air. Kate was there, matching everything. A long, strong arm shot into the air and slapped the ball a second after it left my fingertips. We three thudded to the ground. The ball bounced hard, back into my hands. I held my breath. Kate was huge in front of me. Left-right-left, this time and up again, knees bent, arms stretched. Kate's arm grew longer than mine. She slammed the ball. We crashed down. People began murmuring encouragements. I heard my name. This time the ball dropped to Mo. She fired it back to me. I was shocked. She was closer to the basket than either Kate or me. Mo smiled and rolled her eyes up to the clouds. So I went up again no fakes, just straight up into the air, Kate following.

She would beat me like this every time, I knew, so without ever having done it before, and a little off-balance, I hooked the ball. I had seen people do it before, mostly smaller players who were trying to get over big girls. Irene could hook, Sr. Bernadette could hook, and I had seen Mo do it once early that morning. But I myself had never tried it, not even in practice. It wasn't really a conscious decision, my right elbow just bent, all by itself, and let the ball go. It cleared Kate's fingers, smacked the backboard a little too hard, and fell into the hoop. This time we both landed on our butts.

From the ground, everything finally made sense. I knew what Kate meant by being in one's body: I was in mine. I looked up at the calves and thighs surrounding me. These women were in every inch of theirs. They seemed completely without fear of their bodies, of each other, of their desires. I could see that they even liked their bodies, which is what at first seemed so peculiar. I had never met a woman who liked her own body.

I stayed on the ground, not wanting to get up. I knew that being in my body meant choosing myself. And choosing desire. So few women I knew had chosen themselves: Sr. Bernadette, Kate, and in her own evil way, Irene.

Sr. Bernadette walked over to Kate, who was still flat on her hack, and extended both her hands. Kate grabbed hold and Sr. Bernadette yanked her to her feet. Kate seemed about eight feet tall standing so close to Sr. Bernadette. They just looked at each other, and I could tell that they were, indeed, friends. But somehow it didn't bother me so much now.

Kate let go of Sr. Bernadette's hands and stepped over to me. She reached out one hand and pulled me up. She dusted my behind and shrugged, indifferent "Nice move . . . Who taught you that?"

"No one," I said. "No one taught me that." And she nodded.

Rebounding
Ronald Wallace

All thumbs, clown
of the key and back court, king
of the limp pass and spastic dribble,
I knew I was no
Alcindor. Still,
one season, I remember,
everything I threw up to the rim
went in:
the defense doing double takes
at the net's appreciative swish
as I forced the foolish ball up
from anywhere on the court.
Who could explain it?
The ball had eyes, they said.
My fumble fingers grown
a logic all their own.

Until the last game
of the playoffs,
standing under the basket
all alone,
one free throw down
and five seconds to go,
shouting at the desperate guard,
the shot already
lifting from my fingers
as the ball came rolling
toward me, slow, too slow
me, up there in the air

empty-handed, the ball slowly
rolling out the door
and down these many years,
rolling still,
careening off the fingertips
of every dumb mistake
I'd ever make.

And so, poised here, midair,
shouting for attention
to anyone who'll hear,
my hands above the rim,
I'm dreaming these words up
from nothing. Rebounding.
Stuffing them in.

The Leap
Cliff Dweller

Shooting hoops,

you realize that

the spirit of the universe

swirls around you

like a gentle

blue light

The lowering sun beckons

your eyes and nothing else

This is all you need

This is your life,

that hunk of

one city street,

and you become

a thing of beauty

jumping through

the evening's stillness

with this pumpkin

in your hand

You choose

to be outside

playing basketball

because you have

a small hole to fill

A net of darkness

that you love

more than a best friend

Street lights are shining again

in the shadow of the city

You're in the middle,
catching the ball

before you leap

as high as Olympus

And suddenly you see

your fingertips

on the ball
growing older,

growing darker,

the very last drop

of immortality

Hoop

John Sayles

"**R**ule Number One," Jockey would only have to bend a little to line up his shots, "Never Show Your Speed." Five-seven-two, corner pocket. Jockey liked to punctuate his lectures with combination shots. Anybody at the Hibernian could tell you Jockey Conn would pass up a half-dozen straight chippies for a three-ball combination.

"You show your speed and they got you pegged. They know just what you can do and what you can't do. They know where to hurt you, Sport. Am I right?"

Brian liked the way Jockey would always call him Sport. The old man always called him "boy," or, if he was really gassed, "sonny."

"You pay attention to the Jockey now, boy," the old man would call from the bar. "There's many a thing worth learning they don't teach at that school." And Slim Teeter would say A-men. The old man and Slim would be trying to get in as many cold ones as possible before five o'clock when the prices went up. The bartender would usually be Sweeny, sitting over a racing form circling his picks. Sweeny never played, he just picked and followed the results.

"I've saved a fortune in my time," he'd say when the regulars prodded him. "If I was a gamblin man I'd been a pauper years ago." Sometimes Sweeny would help Brian remind the old man that supper was ready. "The boy's been here a half-hour, McNeil," he would say, "and Hell hath no fury like a woman with a cold pot roast on her hands."

On game days, days when there wasn't practice. Brian's mother would send him over. She started sending him after the time the old man got pinched for taking a leak in public. She never started dinner till five. When the old man got up to leave Slim would wink and toast him with a beer glass.

"Until tomorrow, Hugh."

"Until tomorrow."

The men who sat at tables still told stories about the old man. Stories about the fights he'd won, the tricks he'd played, the witty things he'd said at just the right time. About the devil he was as a young man. They still told stories about the old man and dragged him over to verify that the truth had been told and bought him a drink and then tucked him back into his slot at the bar.

"You see that shot I just made, Sport? What would you say the odds against were? Hundred to one? Am I right? But when she fell in the pocket, did you see me whoop an holler? When I missed that gimme, that five in the side, did you see me piss an moan? Nosir, you did not." The felt was always covered with smudges from the Jockey's cigar drop-pings. The light was off center so that when your back was to the bar you threw shadows on the table. The cue sticks on the wall rack were all crooked. Jockey said you'd be better off using a baseball bat. Jockey packed his own stick, three sections that screwed together.

"Nosir, I didn't bat an eyelash either time. The less you let them know about you, the better off you are. Keep em guessing and you're one step ahead of the game." Seven-five combination, opposite corner. Jockey would have the stogie in his mouth and he never blinked. Brian had never seen Jockey blink.

The old man's eyes ran, he blinked all the time. Slim Teeter played hide-and-seek, avoiding his own eyes in the mirror behind the bar.

"The best face, Sport, is no face at all."

"A-men."

"He burned your ass, man. Burned your *ass*! And you *had* the turkey, had him nailed to the floor."

Brian sat in front of his locker and almost smiled at the sound of Lucius Foster ragging Preston in the next row.

"Where's yours?" said Preston. Too tired to yell.

"My what?"

"Your money. We went halfs, remember? Win or lose. That's two-fifty."

"Shit, man."

"You're the one upped it to five dollars. Don't you go tellin me 'shit.'"
Preston and Lucius both came out of the Children's Home and went for
brothers. Scratch one and the other would bleed.

"Here."

"All you got is change?"

Brian considered yelling over the locker that they could pay him
tomorrow but he decided not to. One of Jockey's rules, Never Rub It In.

"Man think I'm made of money."

"Forget it. Pay me when we get back."

Brian waited till he saw Preston's feet before he looked up. Preston had
red-and-white checkered laces which Coach let him wear for practice. For
games he had to use plain white like everybody else. Coach said appearance was important for the proper mental attitude. Coach wouldn't let
you wear a kneepad unless you could show him the bruise.

Preston laid five dollars next to Brian on the wooden bench. "There you go."

"Right. Nice game."

"Yuh."

Preston was a light-colored one, the kind the others called Chinaman.
The kind the old man said made the best pimps. Preston wore a religious
medal that sometimes hopped up and stung you when you played him.

"You almost took me," said Brian, but Preston was already gone
around the corner. Five bucks was no little thing at the Children's Home.

"Not only do they ask for it, they beg for it." Three-seven-eleven, off
the cushion and in. "And who are you to disappoint them?"

The word had gotten out about Brian and Condredge Holloway, the
one from 13th Street Park that everybody called Boots. The word of how
he had bet Boots on a one-on-one game and Boots had swallowed it.

Everybody knew Boots was crazy, the white boy was on the varsity at school and, blood or not, Boots didn't even start for the Boys' Club. But Boots only lost it by three, he was close all the way and the white boy only came back to take it at the end. The word got out that maybe McNeil was only good as a team player, a pass-an-pick dude. One of Coach's boys.

"Hey! McNeil! Brian!" Practice had just broken up and he was heading down to the showers. Lucius pulled at his jersey from behind. "I hear you a gamblin man."

"Huh?"

"You an ole Boots. One-on-one game."

"Oh. Yuh. I almost blew it." He'd really have to work hard to make it look good with Lucius. Lucius gave away four or five inches and had almost missed the last cut.

"You want to try your luck again?"

"Against you?"

"Naw! Think I'm crazy like Boots?" Lucius had a chipped tooth up front that made him look like he was smiling more than he was. "You an my man Preston."

He could see Preston waiting beneath the far basket, dribbling a ball idly. "Preston's pretty good."

"You're a starter. He's only sixth man."

"He's taller than me."

"By a hair."

Brian sighed. It was a pretty fair nibble. "Okay. Fifty cents." Back into it easy, Jockey would say. never let them know you smell blood.

"Aw, man, make it a dollar. I mean Coach must think you better. He got you startin."

He sighed again and frowned. "Okay. A dollar."

Lucius smiled and gave a little laugh. Preston nodded to Brian and they started. Game to twenty-one, winner's outs.

Brian drove past but blew his first two shots. Just barely blew them. He only drove to the right. He got himself behind by four and settled there, matching points with Preston. There was only the three of them left in the gym, squeaking soles amplified, ball thumping back hollow from the empty bleachers. Echoes. It was nice, Brian calmed and played with Preston. He was down 16-12 when Lucius started laughing out loud.

"You are *done*, McNeil, kiss it good-bye."

Brian was on the outside, dribbling. "Game's not over yet."

"It is for you, man. Aint no way you win this one. No *way*. You *done* for, Jim."

Brian backed away from Preston a little, still bouncing the ball, and looked over to Lucius. "Done my ass."

"Oh-ho! Listen to him! Care to put some more coin on it?"

Brian made an elaborate thinking frown. "Yeah. Okay."

Preston waited with his hands on his hips, looking from Lucius to the white boy and back.

"Five dollars, Brian. Make it five. See what kind of balls you got."

He sighed and said okay and saw Preston cross himself. Preston had his right knee taped.

Lucius cracked up and did a little dance. "McNeil, buddy, your mouth just sign a check your ass can't cash." Lucius already had his money spent.

Brian shot from where he stood, shot easily as if throwing the ball away, and didn't blink when it swished.

"Sport, if God didn't want them gaffed, he wouldn't of made them fish. You don't take it, somebody else will." Jockey always ignored the sign on the wall and tried masse shots that barely missed. "Five hundred to one against. Anyhow, what I mean is, if you're gonna play for keeps you use everything you've got. An the most important thing you got is a sense of timing. Got to know when to coast and when to turn it on. Am I right? Got to hear Opportunity when she knocks."

"You listen to the Jockey," the old man would say, "that's very sound advice he's giving you. Opportunity will rise up but you have to take advantage of it. I missed my main chance and I'll regret it as long as I live." The old man would have his work jacket on, the one he had worn when he ran the day crew at the switching yard. He still wore it to keep the night watch over the deserted tracks.

"Op-por-tunity," Slim Teeter would declare from the pinball machine. "A-men." The pinball machine in the Hibernian was called the Riverboat Minstrel. Blackfaced jigdancers goggled and grinned pink smiles full of watermelon seeds. Slim was a terrible machine player but liked the lights and the balls and the exercise. Slim said a man could drink all day as long as he got his exercise.

"You keep your eyes open, boy, opportunity is everywhere. Everywhere." The old man never turned, but talked to Brian by way of the mirror over the bar. "Twenty years on the railroad and never once did I ask myself where those loads, those trains, were heading. That's where it was, and I never went after it. Right under my nose and there I was, too blind to smell it."

"What your father means, Sport, is you go where the action is. You settle for what you got and life passes you by." Seven-ten combination, side pocket. "Right under your nose."

"Wasted my youth on a dead-end job. And youth, youth you never get back. Never."

"You were never wrong, McNeil," Slim would say, opening his eyes wide to signal a joke, "you were born with one foot on that rail and a beer bottle in your chubby little hand."

The old man would nod. "There's truth in that," he would say, and motion Sweeny for another cold one.

Brian shot from where he stood, shot easily as if throwing the ball away, and didn't blink when it swished.

Time was when he'd have called out "Goodwood!" or "Doosh!" or slapped himself five. Asphalt and chain-net days, pre-Coach days, when Hoop was the language you spoke, the language you thought in. When if you popped the chain it was a word on your tongue and you gave it voice.

Brian shot from where he stood and his tongue ached to call the swish in midair, ached for the days of Rudy and Fatback and Waterbug, for the games they put on. Rudy got rabbit legs, it would start. From his balls up he's all Rudy, but those pins got to come off some bunny. Brian would start it, Hoop-talking, Hoop-thinking, all of them would start it, playing their stories on tongue and asphalt. Rudy got rabbit legs, all thick an bulgy above the knee and stringy-like below it. And he pump the mothers mile-a-minute, hippity-hop, zippin round you ankles (Rudy short) and pushin that roundball up front, ball's a rabbit too. Rudy hop after it, fastest thing going cept maybe Humminbird White from down 13th Street Park and of course Waterbug. I mean Waterbug is *Waterbug*, you don't get faster. Rudy come bumpin and slidin up the middle, then jump out from the brier patch an lay it over the edge. Rudy go *up*. Little bit of a thing, no biggern a minute, up pawin round the rim. It was Rit, Big Wop, that got burned so he got to get back when his side gots the ball. Rudy start it back of the line and flip to Ernie. Ernie turns ass to the board and throw up that worthless hook he does, ball get lucky an hit high off the board stead of clearing the fence and go rolling down the street. Preston bring it down, throwin out his skinny arms and butt like somethin big gonna fall on him. Gets it back to Waterbug and we into it. Bug begins to work his show, hundred moves a second, talking to the asphalt with the ball, playin sounds down there and dancing to em. Brian flash open for a second but Waterbug busy, still working, he pass off when he get good an ready. Sees you when even you don't know you're open, got to be ready. The Bug he got eyes in his ears, back his head, man see you when you sleepin an know when you awake. Bug come down the right side till he throw one on a bounce to Rit, Big Wop put his underhand shitshot in. Ghinny is all ass and a yard wide, don't nobody get front of him when he's cuttin hard.

Screamin Winnie Wills starts in, his old high voice is always being coach and spectators, "Move the baw, move the baw, move the baw!" he go on like some old farm bird. Just a thing he does, like Preston wear that cross. Waterbug throw it to Winnie, shut him up for a second. Man can't talk with his mouth an the ball at the same time, he dribble hisself caught in the corner an heave it back out to Brian. Brian go left on Fatback, Back gives him that first step (Back like to rest on defense). B. push hard down the left baseline, slow a bit where it's sandy so he don't slide out, go up switch it to the right an let it go—ching! "Goodwood!" Old rusty-red net singin his song. Preston got it now, start in with his old back-up basketball, closin in slow, lookin back over his shoulder at the rim nown then, oh them nuns is done a number on this child's *style*. There's FUCK YOU in blue spray paint on the backboard from last Halloween, you puts the ball gainst the Y for a right-hand hook and gainst the C for lefty. Press put a right-harder smack on that Y but too hard, bound gets kicked out to Ernie at his spot, left corner the foul circle and it's in. Can't let the fat boy shoot from his spot, turn into a machine there. Rudy get halfway through the middle but Bug is tight with him so he dump it back to Fatback coolin his heels at the center line (Back like to get his rest on offense, too). That round middle-age gut bouncin once every two dribbles, he commence to workin on Brian. Stares at the ground under the man's feet, plays by the landmarks the ants leaves him. Halfway through a dribble he throw it up, straight up. Back's shot always got to make its mind whether to come down or go into orbit. Falls through the net without a sound. Shit a pickle. "Nice," he says. Back always say that when he hits one, nice. Ernie dribble in slow, the only speed he got, when Waterbug cop it right from under his legs. Man steal the pennies off a dead man's eyes he needed two cents. Bug zigs and zags till he got Rudy goin one way an hisself goin the other to ram in a jumper. But Winnie Wills fall down and cut hisself on the bottle glass, ain't no big thing and he want to run home for surgery or somethin, can't but touch the dude an he fall apart. So Dukey Holcolmb come over from where he been foolin by the eight-foot basket an it starts up again, playin our show—

Rudy—Hoppin to the ball, rock forward then back then forward then ba—then shoot forward pickin Bug off to lay up a scoop but—

Rit—"Voit!!" say the Big Wop, waitin all along to cram that Wilson sandwich down the man's throat—

Bug—Work a lightnin show past three men, offer Preston a stuff but dump it back to Rit on a lay-up, good.

Rudy—Swipe the inbound pass, sees Ernie where Ernie should be—

Ernie—Spotshot, good.

Back—No move, no dribble, just look at Brian's laces for a second then let loose a skyball, freezes with his arm pointin up—

Ball—Check out the stratosphere, gets lonely an come down like a
mortar shell off the rim, climb again, come down to Brian—

Brian—Got the floor now, dribble an look around for where to put
in his two points' worth, walkin, talkie, signifying in Hoop—

Brian shot and didn't blink when it swished. "Thirteen-sixteen, my
ball." He could see every step to his winning. Businesslike, just push where
Preston was weak and execute. *Execution*, that was Coach's favorite word.

"Five of us there were, and only my poor brokenhearted mother to take
charge." The old man would be on his fifth or sixth beer. It was usually
somewhere in there that he'd get sentimental and start being Irish.

"We were so poor I had to wear my brother's shoes for a year when
they were a full size too big for me. Stuffed with newspaper."

Slim would wait a moment for the bells to quiet, for the steel ball to
run off the table. "We were so poor we had to patch the soles of our
shoes with cardboard."

"Shoes," Jockey Conn would say, squinting over the cue bridge.
"Who had shoes?"

Brian peeled his practice uniform off and tucked the money in his
Converse. Coach had given everybody who made the team a free pair.
They were always called Converse instead of sneaker, the same way
Theopolis Ruffin always said his father would pick him up in the
Cadillac instead of the car. If you weren't on the team you wore Keds or
Red Balls or the kind that were two bucks a pair mix'n'match from a
bin in the supermarket. But if you made Coach's team you wore
Converse All-Stars and nobody would steal them even if you didn't
Magic Marker your name on the insteps. They were that easy to trace.

The others were already done with their showers and getting dressed.
Brian listened to them yelling and snapping towels and shouting the
dozens at each other over the locker rows. Trench warfare.

"Hey Dukey! Du-key!"

"Hey what?"

"Is it true what they say bout your mama?"

"Aw shit, man, don't start."

"It true she got some new furniture? Three beds and a cash register?" Laughter was invisible, scattered through the locker room.

"Man, you mama like a birthday cake. Everybody gets a piece."

"Yeah? You mama an me got one thing in common."

"What's that?"

"You!"

"Shit, Gregory's mama got the only pussy in town that makes change."

"So who wants change for a nickel?"

Brian ducked as somebody's jockstrap flew over the locker top. Wire-stiff with old sweat, it skittered along the floor like an elastic tarantula.

"You mama like a cup of coffee, man. Hot, black, an waitin for the cream."

"Black? Who you callin black? Listen to the shit call the dog smelly. Your mama so black she got to drink buttermilk so she don't pee ink."

"Yeah, you mama, she lays for 'fays an screws with Jews."

"Ha. Hey Preston! Press-*tone*, you there?"

Preston usually played. Preston could cut with the best of them.

"Yeah. I'm here."

"Why ain't we heard from you?"

"I don't have a mama. Remember?"

"A wasted youth. Only got as far as the tenth grade at St. Paddy's."

"A-men. St. Paddy's."

"It was a shame to see it fold."

"A-men."

"True, it was going down when the Eye-talians started moving in, but where else in fifty miles was there a high school half as good? And now that it's gone where can you send your boy for a Catholic education?" The old man would address the bar as if it was full, though there was only Teeter beside him, Sweeny at his horses, Jockey and Brian.

"Where, I ask you? Couldn't raise the money, they said. The people

of the diocese just couldn't dig deep enough. But they'll pay for it in
the end, they will. They'll pay through their teeth."

"Public school is free."

"Sweeny, you pay nothin, you get nothin. Public school! My boy
here is at public school. A basketball player. Tell him, boy, on the starting five. How many white?" The old man's finger would jab at him
from the mirror.

"Just me."

"There's your public school! Only one white boy on the floor. Oh,
they'll pray they had St. Paddy's back, now that it's too late."

"You'll always have your coons in basketball." The eight ball would roll
ever so slowly to thunk in the corner pocket. "Basketball is the coons' game."

The score reached 19-18, Preston's lead, Preston's ball. Lucius had gotten quiet. Preston drove and stopped to put up a short jumper. Brian had
watched the same shot pass under his nose unmolested the whole game,
but this time he slapped it from the air and recovered it back behind the
line. When Preston came out to guard him he went left for the first time,
hard and straight and fast. Preston could only turn to watch. 19 all.

The move was a drawn-out version of The Rocker, Waterbug's
favorite. Waterbug had played ahead of Brian on the varsity for a while.
Bug was Coach's playmaker, his hand on the floor. Bring the ball down
the court, glance to the bench, raise his hand in fingers or call out a color
to set the pattern. Coach had them playing the post-and-pick pattern
basketball he had played when he was a student at the high school, back
when there was no three-second rule and you had a center jump after each
score. "The year they cut the bottom out the peach-basket" was the way
Bug put it whenever they'd pass the trophy-case picture of Coach and his
beefy Irish teammates. "Man was a star the year they made the ball
round." It was a drag-ass, ham-and-eggs kind of basketball but if you
wanted to play for Coach that's what you played. And playing for Coach
was the price for all the other things, for the names in the paper and the
girls jumping round cheering your name, for satiny uniforms and Cons on

your feet. For a chance to show your game off to the college recruiters. So Waterbug set up Coach's patterns, called Number Two or Green Play and watched the team be run ragged by the run-and-gun pro style everyone else was using. Waterbug played ahead of Brian on the varsity, shooting four or five times a game and never from more than fifteen feet. For a while.

They'd lost the first three games of the year and were well on the way to losing the fourth. Brian had only seen action late in lost causes. Though he sat next to Coach, there was little chance he'd be called in before the outcome was decided. A minute man.

The other team knew all Coach's patterns by heart, Waterbug would get the first pass off and it would bog down. Late in the first half he called Number Four. But somewhere between the calling and the pass-off Bug saw an opening, the kind of half-step you thought about twice unless you were very fast. A risk. He faked and drove through for a lay-up. The next time down he interrupted the flow of the Green Play to throw in a thirty-footer. Coach wouldn't even allow them beyond twenty feet in practice. The others smelled it, felt something was up with Bug and took it off his hands. Theopolis Ruffin peeled back to steal the inbound pass, Perry Blaydes put a move on his man and threw in a double-pump hook shot. Waterbug led an improvised full-court press, zipping all over the floor giving instructions, pushing them on. "Stop an pop!" he yelled, "Run an gun! Shake your tailfeathers, children, let's get on the *case* here!" They were running loose and grinning, grinning on the basketball floor as it they were playing a game. They went into the locker room at halftime with a two-point lead.

Coach kicked chairs over. Coach threw chalk. Coach told them they weren't a bunch of sandlot kids anymore, they were a disciplined team and should act it. He told them not to let a few lucky buckets go to their heads, if he had to make substitutions he wouldn't hesitate. Waterbug sat through it all without speaking or looking up, sat and rubbed his legs with the baby oil they used so their legs wouldn't look all smoky. Jumpin Juice they called it.

"You've got to keep them under control," Coach said to Brian as they walked out for the second half. "They've got no self-discipline. That's why they're the sprinters and never the long-distance runners. Get yourself good and ready, son."

Waterbug went back to the patterns and tried to stick with them. He was poker-faced down the floor, raising fingers and passing off, dropping back to face the inevitable fast break from the other team. The game slowed, the crowd grew quiet. They went down by six points. It was Lucius who started.

"Hey Bug," he called out from the end of the bench, "lemme ast you a question. What ever happen to run an gun?"

"That's right, that's right." Dukey Holcolmb picked it up. "What ever became of stop an pop?"

"Scoot an shoot?"

"Jump an pump? Shake an bake?"

Most of the bench had picked it up, calling out as Waterbug dribbled the ball down the floor.

"Hey Bug," they called, "what ever become of slip an slide?"

"Float and flutter?"

"Style and pride?"

Waterbug stopped a good thirty-five feet out and picked up the ball. The crowded gym was still as everyone waited for him to raise a finger or call out a color. "Say now," one of them yelled into the silence, "what ever happened to *Water*bug?"

They hardly saw the shot. That's how it was when he had a notion and he took it—like a snakebite. The ball swished and Brian felt Coach's hand on his neck.

"You go in there, son," he said, "and settle the boys down. Show me what you can do."

Brian crouched by the scorer's table, waiting for a whistle that would allow his substitution, and for a moment caught Waterbug's eye. Bug smiled and shook his head slowly.

Bug took the ball down the court and felt the ball alive in his hands. Felt the eyes of all the players and all the spectators oh that ball and knew for now he had control of the game. He took the game and ran with it, feeling the pressure of Coach, the pressure of Brian, the pressure of all his careful, defensive games driving him forward through the snatching hands, felt it chasing him desperately around the floor. Bug listened hard for the rhythm of it, listened to the hard rubber kissing of sneaker soles on the floor, saw everything clearly written in feet, the distribution of weight, the leanings and balances, feints and retreats, and he was a half-step ahead of them all. He snaked through the other nine bodies to the basket, then left the crowd-roar hanging and dribbled past it and on out to open floor again. He teased the players with his ball, played the growing cheers and whoops of his audience in and out, in and out, handling the ball with breathless speed, offering it out for a dozen near-steals and snapping it back from the brink. He heard the crowd-sound building to a payoff and the tension for release building inside him and cut hard for the far corner, whipping away, back to the basket using up every bit of old asphalt flash-and-dazzle left to him, then jumping, turning, lofted a soft, slow, impudent shot as he flew out of bounds, a shot that said there's nothing you can do, there's nothing any of you can do about the Bug but watch and wait as it floated to be swallowed by the hoop.

People were laughing and clapping and slapping five in the stands and at first when he heard the buzzer Brian didn't want to move. But he trotted on and tapped Waterbug on the shoulder. "Have fun," said the Bug, "it's all yours."

Waterbug lasted another two weeks on the bench before he quit. He sat at the very far end, beyond Lucius. Brian saw him sometimes on the street in his P.F. Flyers and they would nod. Word was that Bug had picked up as a ringer for the local ICC team.

Brian took the ball back and went hard left again on Preston, then switched right for another lay-up. Preston's bandaged leg didn't plant when he had to change directions. 20-19. Brian faked right, went two long strides and stopped dead. Preston tried to dig in but the knee buckled. He knelt on the floor and saw the last point go in. 21, game.

"They'll always figure that it was luck, or cheating, or anything but the

simple fact that you're better than they are and always will be." Thirteen-
two-nine, off the cushion to kiss the five ball in. "Let em. Let em believe
anything their hearts desire if it makes em feel better and keep coming
back for more. But you've won, Sport, and that's the name of the game.

Brian was alone in the showers until Lucius and Preston came in and
walked past him to the far end. Preston wore his medal in the shower.
Preston had won the medal for getting a hundred on a test in Confirm-
ation class. Brian and Preston and Lucius had played wall-ball against the
chapel at St. Thomas after class every Wednesday, played until the nun
from the Children's Home came and honked.

There wasn't much warm water left but Brian stayed under till the two
had finished and walked past again. When he heard their locker doors
slam he turned the shower off. He liked to be alone in the locker room
sometimes, he liked the echoes he made. Like being in a church after
everybody had gone. Brian dried himself on the way back to his locker.
The five dollars were crumpled and sitting on his pants. His Converse
All-Stars were gone. No idea who it could be, he would say. What can you
expect from them, Coach would say, and order him a new pair.

"That's the way it is, Sport. The way to be a winner. You and me both
know there's only one place that matters, and that's First Place. Am I right?"

At about quarter to five Sweeny would start clearing his throat and
looking over to the pool table and making little dusting motions on the
bar-top. Jockey would pay no attention. But at exactly five, without
looking up at the clock, Jockey would sweep the balls into the pockets
with his hand. He'd unscrew his cue into sections and put them in their
leather sheath. He'd pull the green cap with the Hibernian insignia from
his back pocket and jam it on his head. Sweeny would pass the push
broom and the dustpan over the bar to him.

"Another day," Jockey would sigh, "another dollar."

Anthem

Stephen Vincent

America, if you were a basketball court,
I'd double dribble down
all your edges. America, if you were a
basketball court, I'd take my shots
in every State. I'd begin with a foul
in Chicago, a set shot in Florida, a hook
in Alabama, and a jump shot in Washington.
O, America, I'd put hoops on all your edges,
backboards against every border and sea.
America I would elbow across country kicking
my feet up and over every player in sight. America,
I'd give you naked cheer leaders, electric bands
and Referees guided by the strings
that hang down from the Justice of Heaven. America,
I'd name everybody as my players. The teams
would be bi-sexual and place women in the spring
of every step. We'd move so fast you wouldn't be able
to count the colors of our players. There would be such rhythm
that the governor of every State would have to hide
in his box seat. The rafters would be loaded with lightning,
magnifying and giving life to each move, each pleasure.
We'd make this country move like a cyclone in heaven,
the star white twirl of our ankles
would crack and clear
the trance of Death. Nevada and Virginia would be the locker rooms
out of which we would come storming with our underground passions.
We'd have the tip-off in Kansas while the rooters swayed
to the rhythm of the Wizard of Oz, the fingers of the centers touching
and turning the ball like the small eye

of the Gulf's tornado. On defense, we'd move from State to State,
keeping our hands moving like quick birds
or breezes that tickle the slim stalks of wheat. On offense,
our bodies would move like ploughs insistent on breaking
the hard, spring ground. A chest pass over Nebraska,
fast breaks that we could steer through either Texas or Montana,
quick little lay-ups through Oregon and Idaho, or little Vermont
and Maine. A bounce pass through Oklahoma and Tennessee. Faking,
moving, stopping, elbowing, quick as possible, deft as
both the sparrow and the hawk, pressing our feet against the floor,
bringing our arms up, springing as high as we can, letting the ball leave
our finger tips in a high, slim arch, watching it slip through a dark rim
into the white strings
and out of the new net. It would be a great game. Children would be born
from the depths of our springs. A fall away jump shot would yield
to the embrace of mothers. The long overhead pass from one end
of the court to the other would provoke
a family reunion. O, America, the land of the living,
the land of the dead, the land of our yet unknown gods
would be revealed through the terrible precision
of each of our moves. America, our heels charged with lightning,
our toes with sparks, we'd get all your States to nourish
each and every rooter. Loaves of bread and fish
would be on every corner. Your tired brown bleachers would be turned
into all colors of the rainbow. America, America,
if you were a basketball court and this brought us so close
to Heaven, when the Game was over, the sweat glimmering down
our silver spun bodies, America, we'd all slow down
and, as a finish to our efforts
we'd bring Mick Jagger in,

and watch him dance, move and sing,
and, as the white lights
went out, putting our arms
around each other, we'd watch him
take a fine, straw broom
and begin to gracefully sweep
the whale hearts
off the whole length of the floor.

The Man with the Perfect Jump Shot

Corey Mesler

How he leaves the ground
from the balls of his feet;
how his hands carve a slow
unfolding as the ball leaves
them; how his eye follows
the arc through the cotton
net (what we call string
music) even back to earth.
The man with the perfect jump shot
is playing his game.
Everybody picks him first;
he is constantly surrounded.
He is like the groom at
the reception. He is like
the poet only in heaven.
His is a grace born like Mozart
was born and a rhythm timed
to the planet's rotation
which is not unlike the
spin of the basketball on its
absolute flight. The crowd
holds its collective breath when
he releases. The air fairly
hums with expectancy. But there
is no tension present: the man
with the perfect jump shot
never misses. Rainbow after rainbow
as natural as light. A divine

trajectory. And tonight the man
with the perfect jump shot is
in our gymnasium; he is on our
team. Tomorrow he may be elsewhere.
Tomorrow he may be against us.
But tonight, here in our tiny
world, tonight, thanks be to God
in his wisdom, we are playing
with the man with the perfect jump
shot. We say it to ourselves
to be reassured: the man with the
perfect jump shot is on our team.
The man with the perfect jump shot
loves us. He would do anything for
us, even die. The man. The man
with the perfect jump shot.

The Only Traffic Signal on the Reservation Doesn't Flash Red Anymore

Sherman Alexie

"Go ahead," Adrian said. "Pull the trigger."

I held a pistol to my temple. I was sober but wished I was drunk enough to pull the trigger.

"Go for it," Adrian said. "You chickenshit."

While I still held that pistol to my temple, I used my other hand to flip Adrian off. Then I made a fist with my third hand to gather a little bit of courage or stupidity, and wiped sweat from my forehead with my fourth hand.

"Here," Adrian said. "Give me the damn thing."

Adrian took the pistol, put the barrel in his mouth, smiled around the metal, and pulled the trigger. Then he cussed wildly, laughed, and spit out the BB.

"Are you dead yet?" I asked.

"Nope," he said. "Not yet. Give me another beer."

"Hey, we don't drink no more, remember? How about a Diet Pepsi?"

"That's right, enit? I forgot. Give me a Pepsi."

Adrian and I sat on the porch and watched the reservation. Nothing happened. From our chairs made rockers by unsteady legs, we could see that the only traffic signal on the reservation had stopped working.

"Hey, Victor," Adrian asked. "Now when did that thing quit flashing?"

"Don't know," I said.

It was summer. Hot. But we kept our shirts on to hide our beer bellies and chicken-pox scars. At least, I wanted to hide my beer belly. I was a former basketball star fallen out of shape. It's always kind of sad when that happens. There's nothing more unattractive than a vain man, and that goes double for an Indian man.

"So," Adrian asked. "What you want to do today?"

"Don't know."

We watched a group of Indian boys walk by. I'd like to think there were ten of them. But there were actually only four or five. They were skinny, darkened by sun, their hair long and wild. None of them looked like they had showered for a week.

Their smell made me jealous.

They were off to cause trouble somewhere, I'm sure. Little warriors looking for honor in some twentieth century vandalism. Throw a few rocks through windows, kick a dog, slash a tire. Run like hell when the tribal cops drove slowly by the scene of the crime.

"Hey," Adrian asked. "Isn't that the Windmaker boy?"

"Yeah," I said and watched Adrian lean forward to study Julius Windmaker, the best basketball player on the reservation, even though he was only fifteen years old.

"He looks good," Adrian said.

"Yeah, he must not be drinking."

"Yet."

"Yeah, yet."

Julius Windmaker was the latest in a long line of reservation basketball heroes, going all the way back to Aristotle Polatkin, who was shooting jumpshots exactly one year before James Naismith supposedly invented basketball.

I'd only seen Julius play a few times, but he had that gift, that grace, those fingers like a goddamn medicine man. One time, when the tribal school traveled to Spokane to play this white high school team, Julius scored sixty-seven points and the Indians won by forty.

"I didn't know they'd be riding horses," I heard the coach of the white team say when I was leaving.

I mean, Julius was an artist, moody. A couple times he walked right off the court during the middle of a game because there wasn't enough competition. That's how he was. Julius could throw a crazy pass, surprise us all, and send it out of bounds. But nobody called it a turnover because we all knew that one of his teammates should've been there to catch the pass. We loved him.

"Hey, Julius," Adrian yelled from the porch. "You ain't shit."

Julius and his friends laughed, flipped us off, and shook their tail feathers a little as they kept walking down the road. They all knew Julius was the best ballplayer on the reservation these days, maybe the best ever, and they knew Adrian was just confirming that fact.

It was easier for Adrian to tease Julius because he never really played basketball. He was more detached about the whole thing. But I used to be quite a ballplayer. Maybe not as good as some, certainly not as good as Julius, but I still felt that ache in my bones, that need to be better than everyone else. It's that need to be the best, that feeling of immortality, that drives a ballplayer. And when it disappears, for whatever reason, that ballplayer is never the same person, on or off the court.

I know when I lost it, that edge. During my senior year in high school we made it to the state finals. I'd been playing like crazy, hitting everything. It was like throwing rocks into the ocean from a little rowboat. I couldn't miss. Then, right before the championship game, we had our pregame meeting in the first-aid room of the college where the tournament was held every year.

It took a while for our coach to show up so we spent the time looking at these first-aid manuals. These books had all kinds of horrible injuries. Hands and feet smashed flat in printing presses, torn apart by lawnmowers, burned and dismembered. Faces that had gone through windshields, dragged over gravel, split open by garden tools. The stuff was disgusting, but we kept looking, flipping through photograph after photograph, trading books, until we all wanted to throw up.

While I looked at those close-ups of death and destruction, I lost it. I think everybody in that room, everybody on the team, lost that feeling of immortality. We went out and lost the championship game by twenty points. I missed every shot I took. I missed everything.

"So," I asked Adrian. "You think Julius will make it all the way?"

"Maybe, maybe."

There's a definite history of reservation heroes who never finish high school, who never finish basketball seasons. Hell, there's been one or two guys who played just a few minutes of one game, just enough to show what they could have been. And there's the famous case of Silas Sirius, who made one move and scored one basket in his entire basketball career. People still talk about it.

"Hey," I asked Adrian. "Remember Silas Sirius?"

"Hell," Adrian said. "Do I remember? I was there when he grabbed that defensive rebound, took a step, and flew the length of the court, did a full spin in midair, and then dunked that fucking ball. And I don't mean it looked like he flew, or it was so beautiful it was almost like he flew. I mean, he flew, period."

I laughed, slapped my legs, and knew that I believed Adrian's story more as it sounded less true.

"Shit," he continued. "And he didn't grow no wings. He just kicked his legs a little. Held that ball like a baby in his hand. And he was smiling. Really. Smiling when he flew. Smiling when he dunked it, smiling when he walked off the court and never came back. Hell, he was still smiling ten years after that."

I laughed some more, quit for a second, then laughed a little longer because it was the right thing to do.

"Yeah." I said. "Silas was a ballplayer."

"Real ballplayer," Adrian agreed.

In the outside world, a person can be a hero one second and a nobody the next. Think about it. Do white people remember the names of those guys who dove into that icy river to rescue passengers from that plane wreck a few years back? Hell, white people don't even remember the names of the dogs who save entire families from burning up in house hres by barking. And, to be honest, I don't remember none of those names either, but a reservation hero is remembered. A reservation hero is a hero forever. In fact, their status grows over the years as the stories are told and retold.

"Yeah," Adrian said. "It's too bad that damn diabetes got him. Silas was always talking about a comeback."

"Too bad, too bad."

We both leaned further back into our chairs. Silence. We watched the grass grow, the rivers flow, the winds blow.

"Damn," Adrian asked. "When did that fucking traffic signal quit working?"

"Don't know."

"Shit, they better fix it. Might cause an accident."

We both looked at each other, looked at the traffic signal, knew that about only one car an hour passed by, and laughed our asses off. Laughed so hard that when we tried to rearrange ourselves, Adrian ended up with my ass and I ended up with his. That looked so funny that we laughed them off again and it took us most of an hour to get them back right again.

Then we heard glass breaking in the distance.

"Sounds like beer bottles," Adrian said.

"Yeah, Coors Light, I think."

"Bottled 1988."

We started to laugh, but a tribal cop drove by and cruised down the road where Julius and his friends had walked earlier.

"Think they'll catch them?" I asked Adrian.

"Always do."

After a few minutes, the tribal cop drove by again, with Julius in the backseat and his friends running behind.

"Hey," Adrian asked. "What did he do?"

"Threw a brick through a BIA pickup's windshield," one of the Indian boys yelled back.

"Told you it sounded like a pickup window," I said.

"Yeah, yeah, a 1982 Chevy."

"With red paint."

"No, blue."

We laughed for just a second. Then Adrian sighed long and deep. He rubbed his head, ran his fingers through his hair, scratched his scalp hard

"I think Julius is going to go bad," he said.

"No way," I said. "He's just horsing around."

"Maybe, maybe."

It's hard to be optimistic on the reservation. When a glass sits on a table here, people don't wonder if it's half filled or half empty. They just hope it's good beer. Still, Indians have a way of surviving. But it's almost like Indians can easily survive the big stuff. Mass murder, loss of language and land rights. It's the small things that hurt the most. The white waitress who wouldn't take an order, Tonto, the Washington Redskins.

And, just like everybody else, Indians need heroes to help them learn how to survive. But what happens when our heroes don't even know how to pay their bills?

"Shit, Adrian," I said. "He's just a kid."

"Ain't no children on a reservation."

"Yeah, yeah, I've heard that before. Well," I said. "I guess that Julius is pretty good in school, too."

"And?"

"And he wants to maybe go to college."

"Really?"

"Really," I said and laughed. And I laughed because half of me was happy and half of me wasn't sure what else to do.

A year later, Adrian and I sat on the same porch in the same chairs. We'd done things in between, like ate and slept and read the newspaper. It was another hot summer. Then again, summer is supposed to be hot.

"I'm thirsty," Adrian said. "Give me a beer."

"How many times do I have to tell you? We don't drink anymore."

"Shit," Adrian said. "I keep forgetting. Give me a goddamn Pepsi."

"That's a whole case for you today already."

"Yeah, yeah, fuck these substitute addictions."

We sat there for a few minutes, hours, and then Julius Windmaker staggered down the road.

"Oh, look at that," Adrian said. "Not even two in the afternoon and he's drunk as a skunk."

"Don't he have a game tonight?"

"Yeah, he does."

"Well. I hope he sobers up in time."

"Me, too."

I'd only played one game drunk and it was in an all-Indian basketball tournament after I got out of high school. I'd been drinking the night before and woke up feeling kind of sick, so I got drunk again. Then I went out and played a game. I felt disconnected the whole time. Nothing seemed to fit right. Even my shoes, which had fit perfectly before, felt too big for my feet. I couldn't even see the basketball or basket clearly. They were more like ideas. I mean, I knew where they were generally supposed to be, so I guessed at where I should be. Somehow or another, I scored ten points.

"He's been drinking quite a bit, enit?" Adrian asked.

"Yeah, I hear he's even been drinking Sterno."

"Shit, that'll kill his brain quicker than shit."

Adrian and I left the porch that night and went to the tribal school to watch Julius play. He still looked good in his uniform, although he was a little puffy around the edges. But he just wasn't the ballplayer we all remembered or expected. He missed shots, traveled, threw dumb passes that we all knew were dumb passes. By the fourth quarter, Julius sat at the end of the bench, hanging his head, and the crowd filed out, all talking about which of the younger players looked good. We talked about some kid named Lucy in the third grade who already had a nice move or two.

Everybody told their favorite Julius Windmaker stories, too. Times like that, on a reservation, a basketball game felt like a funeral and wake all rolled up together.

Back at home, on the porch, Adrian and I sat wrapped in shawls because the evening was kind of cold.

"It's too bad, too bad," I said. "I thought Julius might be the one to make it all the way."

"I told you he wouldn't. I told you so."

"Yeah, yeah. Don't rub it in."

We sat there in silence and remembered all of our heroes, ballplayers from seven generations, all the way back. It hurts to lose any of them because Indians kind of see ballplayers as saviors. I mean, if basketball would have been around, I'm sure Jesus Christ would've been the best point guard in Nazareth. Probably the best player in the entire world. And in the beyond. I just can't explain how much losing Julius Windmaker hurt us all.

"Well," Adrian asked. "What do you want to do tomorrow?"

"Don't know."

"Shit, that damn traffic signal is still broken. Look."

Adrian pointed down the road and he was right. But what's the point of fixing it in a place where the STOP signs are just suggestions?

"What time is it?" Adrian asked.

"I don't know. Ten, I think."

"Let's go somewhere."

"Where?"

"I don't know, Spokane, anywhere. Let's just go."

"Okay," I said, and we both walked inside the house, shut the door, and locked it tight. No. We left it open just a little bit in case some crazy Indian needed a place to sleep. And in the morning we found crazy Julius passed out on the living room carpet.

"Hey, you bum," Adrian yelled. "Get off my floor."

"This is my house, Adrian," I said.

"That's right. I forgot. Hey, you bum, get your ass off Victor's floor."

Julius groaned and farted but he didn't wake up. It really didn't bother Adrian that Julius was on the floor, so he threw an old blanket on top of him. Adrian and I grabbed our morning coffee and went back out to sit on the porch. We had both just about finished our cups when a group of Indian kids walked by, all holding basketballs of various shapes and conditions.

"Hey, look," Adrian said. "Ain't that the Lucy girl?"

I saw that it was, a little brown girl with scarred knees, wearing her daddy's shirt.

"Yeah, that's her," I said.

"I heard she's so good that she plays for the sixth grade boys team."

"Really? She's only in third grade herself, isn't she?"

"Yeah, yeah, she's a little warrior."

Adrian and I watched those Indian children walk down the road, walking toward another basketball game.

"God, I hope she makes it all the way," I said.

"Yeah, yeah," Adrian said, stared into the bottom of his cup, and then threw it across the yard. And we both watched it with all of our eyes, while the sun rose straight up above us and settled down behind the house, watched that cup revolve, revolve, until it came down whole to the ground.

The Only Game
Carl Lindner

Look at it this way—
all of a sudden
you find yourself
near a schoolyard
and you can't tell
just how good
is the guy out there,
shooting and dribbling;
before you know it
you're in a game
of one-on-one
and it's his ball out
and the rules
keep changing
and he won't let on
when or how
and every time
you ask the score
there's that grin.
You'd feel better
if you could see
his eyes, but sun-
light keeps
shining behind his head
no matter where you go
and all you see are teeth.

Fast Break

Edward Hirsch

In Memory of Dennis Turner, 1946-1984

A hook shot kisses the rim and
hangs there, helplessly, but doesn't drop,

and for once our gangly starting center
boxes out his man and times his jump

perfectly, gathering the orange leather
from the air like a cherished possession

and spinning around to throw a strike
to the outlet who is already shoveling

an underhand pass toward the other guard
scissoring past a flat-footed defender

who looks stunned and nailed to the floor
in the wrong direction, trying to catch sight

of a high, gliding dribble and a man
letting the play develop in front of him

in slow motion, almost exactly
like a coach's drawing on the blackboard,

both forwards racing down the court
the way that forwards should, fanning out

and filling the lanes in tandem, moving
together as brothers passing the ball

between them without a dribble, without
a single bounce hitting the hardwood

until the guard finally lunges out
and commits to the wrong man

while the power-forward explodes past them
in a fury, taking the ball into the air

by himself now and laying it gently
against the glass for a lay-up,

but losing his balance in the process,
inexplicably falling, hitting the floor

with a wild, headlong motion
for the game he loved like a country

and swiveling back to see an orange blur
floating perfectly through the net.

The Ultimatum of Hattie Tatum
Dick Wimmer

Hattie Tatum stood 6'2 in sneakers. She'd been the center for the girls basketball team of her all-black high school in Spartanburg, South Carolina, had twice won all-State honors, and was generally considered an exceptional athlete. Following graduation, however, her mother had died, and, being poor, she and her older sister Cora decided to move north to find employment. Cora had a classmate working in Great Neck, so they headed there, registered with the Ring-a-Maid agency, and a week later, both had jobs: Cora in Harbor Hills and Hattie with the Levitases of Steven Lane. After a month, though, Cora, fed up, was fired and went home, leaving Hattie alone in Kings Point.

The house, a sprawling split-level ranch with Grecian columns, had recently been bought by Shelly with the windfall from his in-laws' estate, but was mortgaged up to the hilt—as his wife kept constantly reminding him. Yet to him it was a dream come true, finally living in the town's most exclusive section, and didn't Ro now have her best friend, Carole Friske, around the corner and, of course, Marcia Levy always at hand. Vance, their oldest child, was ten, and Lisa, seven and a half. Both were tall for their age, Vance extremely bright and taken with sports, and Lisa, a tomboy, detesting frillies or dress-up clothes. Just last week, Shelly had installed a basket at the far corner of his driveway and directly facing his garage, thus leaving thirty feet for playing space. The masonite basket was low, only eight feet high, had an orange rim, blue and white net, and cost him $9.95 at Korvettes. On a Saturday afternoon, he and Vance had crowded into Sporting Goods and Shelly'd picked the next-to-cheapest, a moderate choice, it looked good enough.

When Hattie arrived, the children hardly noticed. They'd had maids in the past; why should this one be any different? Only she was as big as their father and skinny as a pole. Hattie was friendly but reserved, and the children found they could do pretty much what they liked with her; she was no disciplinarian. But the housework was another matter. She never seemed able to please Mrs. Levitas, and it took two weeks before she could fully adjust to her "system." Rochelle, a management major while at Simmons, stressed that word, everything had to be done with a system, otherwise nothing was accomplished at all.

Under Rochelle's guidance, Hattie began to settle into the family routine. She had her own room, a small, narrow cubicle off the laundry room, an old RCA ten-inch TV, and a chest of drawers. It was removed from the rest of the house, so she had relative privacy, except when Shelly washed his softball uniform or the children raced past in games of tag. Hattie, though, was constantly at Rochelle's beck and call.

Any time was acceptable for her directions or orders of the day. "I'm going out now, Hattie, and I'll be back at three. If anyone calls, I'm at the hairdresser's. And if it's Mrs. Friske, tell her I'll see her at the game." Hattie often as not forgot these messages, and, under Rochelle's continued guidance, began yet another system, namely, jotting them down— Rochelle purchasing a pad and magnetic gold pencil for notetaking.

Meals, too, were a problem. She was constantly forgetting the A-1 sauce or ketchup for Mr. Levitas, and Lisa usually wanted cola instead of 7-Up or 7-Up instead of root beer. Hattie, of course, ate after, but it was lamb and pork chops like she'd never tasted and occasionally even leftover steak, always more than enough; and though she was never inclined to gain weight, she'd added six pounds after a month.

School would be over soon, the summer soon beginning, and when told she was to take the children outdoors during the afternoon and watch them, Hattie was delighted. They had a large backyard, but as the sun continued to shine, Vance decided he'd rather be playing basketball. So Hattie would stand behind him while he pushed or threw up his shots, hard flings that Hattie retrieved: the feel of the ball again, its smooth, grainy texture, so fine in her hands. But she never shot, just watched—while Lisa was given her one chance in five—or retrieved the ball for Vance.

After a week of this, as her ache to play kept growing, an opportunity finally arose. Vance had flung a wild hook down the drive, Hattie off in pursuit of the ball. But when she returned, the children had moved to the back lawn and were involved with their toy soldiers, leaving Hattie, ball in hand, alone on the court. She looked around. Mrs. Levitas was still at her husband's game, no cars passed, the children were sprawled now on the warm grass, and Hattie held the ball. She looked around again, walking down the drive to check if any maids were out or other children coming—no, not a soul. She couldn't stand it much longer. Every day the feel and bounce of the ball and never being able to shoot. It was overwhelming. Just last week on her day off, she'd gone into Corona to meet Cora's friend, who took her to a nearby Y. But it had been a tiring trip and she'd arrived home later than usual, when the children were asleep. So the chances seemed remote of doing that again. But now she held the ball in her palm and the court was clear. She bounced it twice—the children hadn't noticed—then cut toward the basket, dribbling behind her back and on out to the foul line, a faint chalk scrawl, stepped forward and tossed up her favorite shot, a long, looping one-harder that went swishing cleanly through, gathered in the ball and moved to the corner, along the rock border of the drive, for a sweeping right-hand hook. By this time, Vance had turned and, seeing Hattie gracefully glide over the asphalt, was transfixed. On and on she played, the children abandoning their toy soldiers and sitting against the garage door to watch Hattie spin down the center lane and bank the ball in—and whirling round, coming face-to-face with the two of them.

She was embarrassed, offering the ball to Vance, who shook his head. "I didn't know you played, Hattie. Why didn't you tell us?"

"Here, come on, you shoot."

"No, we wanna watch *you*.

"Please, don't stop!"

So Hattie played on, pausing every once in a while to show Vance how to hold the ball, to shoot a long, looping one—harder, to balance it on the palm, then arch it softly; and with Lisa, teaching her how to dribble, to watch the ball and not just slap at it. The afternoon was growing late, it was now nearly five, and as the mothers and deliverymen drove by, many paused at the sight of this tall black girl dribbling between two small children who giggled and grasped to snare the elusive ball that flickered past on its ultimate way through the hoop. Till Hattie saw them too, and stopped, telling the children they had to go in.

"*NO, NO!* Just one more shot, Hattie, just one more!"

"All right, just one more."

"Bet you can't dunk it," challenged Vance.

"Well lemme see, 'cause at this height, I guess I might," and down the center lane she drove, soared high into the air and slammed the ball through the cords, the children crying, shrieking with delight, and embracing Hattie as they moved indoors.

Rochelle knew nothing of what had occurred; it was their own special secret. But as the weeks passed and school drew to a close, basketball was to become their daily play, hurrying home for a game of Horse or more often watch as Hattie revealed her talent. For talent it was—it had never left her—and Hattie was overjoyed. She would race through her housework, doing it now in half the time. Her weight soon back to normal, she could feel the spring returning to her legs, the touch to her fingertips with each passing day. By now Vance had developed a pretty good one-hander and Lisa at least could dribble in a straight line, but it still was Hattie's show. And show she did, performing acrobatic leaps and jumps, spinning the ball off her index finger, and always finishing with her resounding dunk. So absorbed were they that none of them had noticed the neighbors' blinds bending back, the drapes opening a wee bit, and the cars slowly pausing; for Hattie was becoming known throughout the neighborhood and Great Neck at large. But Shelly and Rochelle knew nothing, only that their children were happier than they had ever seen them with any previous maid, far better behaved, ate all their food at dinnertime, cleaned up afterward—and so, except for Hattie forgetting as usual, had very few complaints.

The following Tuesday, though, Rochelle nearly caught them. Hattie was throwing up a long one-hander as she approached the drive. "Hattie, how come you were shooting and the children were just sitting around?" Vance had interrupted to say that she was just showing them how it should be done when the phone rang, and Rochelle forgot completely about it as Carole chattered on.

But a week later, under the hair dryer at Andre's, she overheard two women discussing this *schvartze* who played basketball in Kings Point. "A maid, too—gets away with murder. You should hear what they say. . . ."

And the following day, when Colandro, her dry-cleaning man, asked how "Goose" Tatum was doing, Rochelle asked who "Goose" Tatum was. "A basketball player, Mrs. Levitas, used to be with the Harlem Globetrotters, almost as good as your maid."

That Friday, she told Hattie she was going to the city with Carole and would be back no later than five. However, she returned at four, the sun of June still shining, and passed slowly by. O my God! There she was *again*. Shooting! And the kids just standing around! Neighbors' eyes were peering out through their blinds, the next-door maid, hand on hip, mop in hand, was brazenly watching, and across the street, Denise Wanderstock, whose husband was head of the School Board, was laughing in her flower bed, obviously delighting in the spectacle. Rochelle sped down Steven Lane, nearly knocking over someone's black footman statue with her U-turn, and roared back up her driveway, screeching to a halt not three feet from Hattie and the kids!

After the irate lecture, Hattie stopped for a week, but at the kids' insistence sneaked out the following Saturday and shot for two hours, with Vance, Lisa, and Colandro keeping watch.

But the reports kept flowing in. Some no doubt malicious, from other maids jealous of Hattie's situation, though she had never worked harder, even learning to serve now with a sense of quiet style. Rochelle warned her again, saying it was the children's court, and she couldn't let this continue. A maid's job was not to play basketball. "No other maid does it.

You don't have to. There's no need."

Hattie tried to explain how much the children enjoyed it, how much she needed it, how it improved her work—"Yes, but it doesn't look good for the maid to be playing and the children just sitting around. It isn't right. And all the neighbors watching."

"Well, we just play for a few hours—"

"No, you just *watch* the children, that's your job, I don't wanna discuss it anymore!"

That night, as *The Late Late Show* came on above Shelly's snuffling snore, Rochelle, nervously puffing on a Tareyton, thought about her neighbors, her husband's mounting debts (if only they knew!), and his wheeling and dealing, from shoes to fabrics to the used carpet business, staying in Great Neck at all costs—and yet even she had to admit how happy she was here in their luxurious Kings Point home. How much had they paid—what, 168? Yes, but that was last winter. Now it was easily worth another 50-60 grand. Lou's father, Sollie Grossbard just two houses down and without a finished basement, sold hers three years back for 143.5—and that after only a month on the market, straight cash! And she has her own room with a TV yet and the run of the house besides! Who's ever home? *Miss* Tatum, the Grand *Dame*! Give them a little freedom and they think they own the world! What more do they want? She makes more than all her relatives put together down in South Carolina or wherever the hell she comes from! All of them now talking back, big mouth she has on her, telling me what she wants! Who does she think she is? Like we haven't treated her nice. What more could we do? Gave her a house, food, clothes, buy her gifts on her birthday—a cake for $6.50 from Benkert's—and how much work does it take to clean this house? I used to do it in two hours, and her it takes all afternoon! And it still isn't clean, always dust under everything, no system. And a few meals a week to prepare? We usually eat out twice a week anyway after the games. And the kids, both at school till three, go to sleep at nine. And what's more, Thursday she's off, one day a week, the same as the rest of them. Gets home at God knows when, sometimes even Friday morning, and we never say anything. Shelly never even *talks* to her, who *bothers* her? She can do what she likes, whatever she wants. She has this whole $200,000 house to herself and she wants to play basketball. Basketball! Who ever heard of such a thing? You never even *see* the other maids, they're all busy working—just my *schvartze*! I have to get one from Spartanburg, South Carolina, who thinks she's a performer. Telling you, the trouble with help today!

But Hattie persisted. What else did she have? Cora wouldn't be back now till late September. Maybe when she'd put enough money away, she could enroll at a community college, but for now her only pleasure, besides the children, was basketball, those odd hours when she could sneak in a few shots and, best of all, replay those high school games of her past.

Shelly couldn't care less. He wanted a maid, a clean house, dinner served on time and generally well prepared—he'd add his own spice—and more important, harmony at home, so Ro would stop nagging him and let him have some peace. But now even *he* had begun to hear little stories about his basketball-playing maid. She was becoming well known, a snide joke at Glen Oaks and among nearly everyone at the games. Who else had a maid jumping around, throwing in baskets? It was ridiculous. People gossiping, it didn't look good, soon that'd be all they'd talk about! But what really bothered him was that this was his *home* and this scrawny, gawky *schvoog* (he always liked that better than *nigger*, that was crass, but *schvoogiedoogie* had a certain flair) was running around outside in full view of the neighbors! Like (God forbid!) she was his kid! Who knows what they might think, his lovely neighbors, four-flushers all! Some distant relative, niece or what, his own illegitimate daughter? The kid from some Negro show doll he'd been *shtooping*, like Leslie Uggams? He and Bucky'd put money in that *facoctah shvoog* review, *Hallelujah, Baby*, lost his shirt! Who knew what they were thinking? This on top of the rest of his worries, debts mounting, Ro and her nagging, his prostate acting up, hemorrhoids, too!

So, Sunday night before *Bonanza* (Shelly's favorite show) came on, Hattie was summarily told. She was called into the den, Rochelle asked to leave, no interruptions, and he snapped off the set.

"How-why-ya, Hattie—listen, there's been a lot of stories—it doesn't look good—the kids just sit around—and I know you get along well with Vance—but the neighbors—I mean the basket is his." Concluding, he lit up a Tiparillo, smoothing down his ringleted hair, and gave her Monday off, he'd make his own breakfast—and settle the housework chores with his wife.

Hattie was cowed. She said she'd try.

And for two weeks she did try. But after a daily diet of quiz shows and cooking shows, soap operas and vintage movies, cards, crosswords, and solitaire, of sheer boredom and repeated cleanings, she asked Mrs. Levitas again. Rochelle's reaction was silence. She had thought the matter closed. She called Shelly's office. He couldn't be bothered now, the rug merchants were driving him crazy, he'd call her back. But she had to wait two hours, and during that time she called Carole, Marcia (who, as usual, wasn't home), and the local agency, found a girl was available on Monday—this was Friday—and told Hattie, upon the advice of friends and family, she was letting her go.

Hattie, though aware of the possibility, still was shocked. She had grown to like Great Neck, the quiet, clean, treeshaded streets, and especially the kids. But she couldn't just sit around like the rest of the maids and housewives. If she worked here, she had to have use of the basket.

So Hattie left. Vance wasn't home at the time. But when he returned and Hattie was nowhere in sight, he asked his mother if Thursday wasn't her day off. Was Hattie sick? "No, dear, she's no longer with us."

"Why?"

"Because—well, because there are certain things we just didn't see eye-to-eye on. I know you liked her very much, but don't worry, there'll be another girl here Monday and things will be just the same as—"

"I want *Hattie!*"

"Look, dear, I know—"

"*No!* Nobody else!"

"Vance, listen—"

"It's not *fair!*" And Vance stormed off into his room and slammed the door. Rochelle started after him when the phone rang. It was Shelly to say he'd be home late tonight, had a meeting with Justin Friske, a possible deal cooking. She told him what had happened, Vance's reaction, and he told her to forget about it. "Hattie, Schmattie, we'll have a thousand maids, tomorrow he won't even remember who she was!"

But the next day Vance shot baskets by himself. Long, looping one-handers indifferently thrown toward the hoop, head down, his eyes rimmed with tears. That night at dinner, he wouldn't eat, and when Lisa started kidding him, calling him a crybaby, he fired a baked potato at her—and was told to go to his room. He wouldn't talk to the new maid, an older woman with a ducal bosom who rolled her r's as in New York and was all for segregation. By this time, Lisa had joined Vance in refusing to talk to the new maid, who told Rochelle she'd run up against this before with children and to just let them brood it out, ignore them, and they'd eventually come around. But three days passed, as Vance and Lisa remained disconsolate, barely touching their food, and Rochelle was now at her wits' end.

"Shelly, we can't live like this. Vance has lost five pounds already, he doesn't talk to me, or to the new maid, just stays in his room, won't even *play* basketball anymore, and Lisa is the same way! What're we going to *do*?"

Shelly, who still had carpets and debts but most of all softball on his mind and couldn't stand any more domestic upheavals, said he'd talk to the kids tomorrow.

But when tomorrow came, Vance and Lisa were gone. They'd slipped out during the early morning hours and by noon had reached the train station, where Dennis Hickey, on duty in his cab, turned them over to a cop, who drove them home. Shelly and Rochelle were beside themselves. They had awakened to a childless house and a carefully scrawled note: IF HATTIE GOES WE GO TOO.

Shelly thanked the officer, offering him a tip, which was refused, then took his children into the den. "Look, this's gotta stop right now. Hattie is only a *maid*, you have your own lives to live. I know how much you liked her, but you still have each other, your mother and me." Vance and Lisa just stared down at the floor. "I don't even know where Hattie is now, she could be anywhere, probably back in South Carolina for all I know—Vance, are you *listening* to me?" Vance glanced up, then his eyes shifted away, as Shelly continued to boil. "From now on, you will eat when we eat and play with your own friends. I'm not gonna be aggravated by your foolishness, young man, is that clear? All right, go kiss your mother."

But though the children made half-hearted attempts to seem happy, their feelings remained unchanged. Vance had lost nine pounds, Lisa'd caught a cold, and the new maid was becoming lackadaisical in her cleaning and was constantly overcooking the meals. Finally, Rochelle couldn't take it anymore. Because of this *schvartze* and her basketball, her home was falling apart. Shelly was more irritable, she was now smoking nearly three packs a day, the house was a mess, and the kids were as thin as toothpicks. Something had to be done! She called the agency, but they wouldn't have another maid till the middle of next week. Carole Friske offered to lend her hers, though only for a few days, any longer was out of the question. "These kids and their maids. Mine was the same way, but they usually get over it—this I never heard of!"

There was only one thing to do: get Hattie back at all costs. She told Shelly. "Now you *want* her back? What the hell's with you? This day, this, next day, that. Ro, make up your mind already!"

"My mind is made up, Hattie has to come back, otherwise we'll both be nervous wrecks!"

"And what about the basketball?"

"We'll discuss it."

Rochelle still had that number in Corona, some friend of Cora's where she could be reached, but Hattie was out, down at the school-yard. "Then please, have her call this number immediately! It's Mrs. Levitas—Levitas with an L—from Great Neck!"

"Yes, ma'am."

A half hour later, Hattie, still out of breath, called. "Hattie, listen, can you come back?"

"Come back?"

"Yes, we've changed our minds, can even give you a raise."

"How are Vance and Lisa?"

"Fine, fine. Listen, do you want to come back or not?"

"Well, I don't know—"

"You don't know, whatta you mean you don't know?"

"Well I may've another job."

"Another job? Where? What kinda other job? Here, in Great Neck, what part?"

"The junior high school . . ."

"*Junior high school*? Our junior high school? Doing what?" (Janitor? Custodian? Dishwasher?)

"Girls basketball coach."

"*Coach*? But how'd you get—?"

"Mrs. Wanderstock got me an interview, this afternoon at three."

"But don't you need a degree, credentials?"

"No, guess nobody else applied, so they decided to—"

"OK, OK, but you'll still need a place to stay, so take the next train out, I'll pay for it, pick you up, and we'll discuss all the details when you arrive."

Rochelle picked her up, discussing the details along the way. "But couldn't you still be a *part-time* maid?"

"And play basketball outside with the children?"

"Well . . ." and they swung into the drive just as Vance and Lisa came home, saw Hattie, and went shrieking into her arms.

It was decided, terms were agreed upon, with Hattie rehired immediately part-time at twice her former wage. The sun kept shining as Vance and Hattie passed the ball back and forth while Lisa watched. Lisa went dribbling through Hattie's legs while Vance watched. Then it was Hattie's turn. The curtains of the neighbors edged back; she was about to perform. Holding the ball in one hand, Hattie spun it up to her index finger and let it whirl. Vance cheered, the ball spun on, Lisa giggled with glee. And then Hattie dribbled back of the key, drove hard to her right and tossed up her long, looping one-harder—Swish!

Cries of joy. On she played as more blinds were bent and cars paused, a dazzling array of shot-making: hooks, behind-the-back lay-ups, banked-in jumpers, two-hand bombs from thirty feet, and, at this low height, a final, soaring, rim-rattling dunk, *whomp*, through the blue and white cords!

In Memory of the Utah Stars
William Matthews

Each of them must have terrified
his parents by being so big, obsessive
and exact so young, already gone
and leaving, like a big tipper,
that huge changeling's body in his place.
The prince of bone spurs and bad knees.

The year I first saw them play
Malone was a high school freshman,
already too big for any bed,
14, a natural resource.
You have to learn not to
apologize, a form of vanity.
You flare up in the lane, exotic
anywhere else. You roll the ball
off fingers twice as long as your
girlfriend's. Great touch for a big man,
says some jerk. Now they're defunct
and Moses Malone, boy wonder at 19,
rises at 20 from the St. Louis bench,
his pet of a body grown sullen
as fast as it grew up.

Something in you remembers every
time the ball left your fingertips
wrong and nothing the ball
can do in the air will change that.
You watch it set, stupid moon,
the way you watch yourself

in a recurring dream.
You never lose your touch
or forget how taxed bodies
go at the same pace they owe,
how brutally well the universe
works to be beautiful,
how we metabolize loss
as fast as we have to.

Cheap Seats in the Kingdome

Sharon Bryan

1

There should be switchbacks,
the climb's so steep up the inside
of this man-made rock. No scenery
but the stenciled altimeter numbers:
37. 38. 39. I follow the others
into our row and lean far back
before I can even imagine turning
my eyes to the floor. The players
look like tiddlywinks. There are ten
empty rows, flimsy tin guardrails,
between us and the next people down.
A few fathers and sons sit at the very top,
as if they could pry up the roof
and get out in a hurry if they had to.
I don't want to complain about tickets
I didn't pay for, so I complain
about the man who sold them. You explain
why it wasn't malicious.

2

Then, just as I'm resting my eyes
on the foreground, an angel passes,
right to left, and sits down four
rows in front of us. She has impossibly
beautiful light blond curls, a tan
jacket, jeans, looks about twenty-
five. Her cherubic, straight-haired son
sits happily next to her, her hair

shining over his shoulder. And then,
dear reader, a rat-faced man comes climbing up,
slopping beer from two paper cups
on his shoes, not caring, and hands one
to the angel, who scoots the boy's ass
over, and then her own, but not much.
I could see what they saw in each other,
endless days of saving and being saved,
their thin bones crackling like cellophane.
She never looked at the boy again,
though he bounced and smiled and was
infinitely good. She told him once
to keep it down, but over her shoulder.

   3
Fourth quarter an old usher puffs
slowly up in full-dress brown and orange,
hands on his knees every few steps,
scanning all our faces for something
No one looks guilty, so he crosses
on an empty row, as if that's what he meant
to do all along, just go for a walk,
listen to his lungs fill up, but not
with air, wonder what it would be like
to pitch forward from here, nothing
in his path, to make one last arc
before he lands, white-gloved but
hatless, at the laced feet of the players
and confounded referees.

4
The Sonics are a point behind
with two seconds to go. The in-bounds pass
goes to Thompson, Skywalker, who lifts himself
straight up, pauses, and shoots
from twenty-eight feet out. Three points,
when we only needed two. Our spirits
rise to the roof. Maybe the boy's her
brother, I think. Maybe there's still hope.

Rookie
Robert T. Sorrells

The sub-assistant coach tootled his whistle twice. Quickly. The Kid snatched one last time at the loose tops of his socks before he began to lean into the man next to him on the circle. The coach set one foot into the small inner ring and smartly tossed the ball high. Four hundred and fifty or sixty pounds of muscle and nerve ends smashed together at the thigh. The tips of three fingers slapped the ball back. High in the air the forward Coco pulled it in over the out-jumped hand of his blue-shirted opponent, spotted the Kid flying down court toward the goal, faked once, then hooked hard over his head. The Kid took the pass over his shoulder in stride, bounced it once, twice, dragged his foot on the third dribble, and twisted as Bonelli shot past—totally faked out. He leaped, turning in midair, and in the old familiar motion laid the ball up and off the backboard.

The hoop trembled as the ball batted about just inside the rim. Then it spun out, and Jasmo, still pushing hard in his eighth year for a real All-Pro slot instead of his annual Honorable Mention, had the rebound down court before the Kid could quit looking at the hoop.

WHAT THE HELL YA WAITIN FOR? the head coach hollered into his bullhorn from the desk on the side of the court. YOU BLOW THOSE EASY ONES AND L. A.'LL HAVE IT CINCHED IN THE FIRST QUARTER. His voice echoed through the empty auditorium at the Armory.

By then the Kid was down on defense trying to keep his teammate-adversary—who *was* All Pro—from driving straight past him. He tried hard to force him into the center where he might be intimidated by

Orville who'd often spin out from behind his own man to raise the longest, widest, thickest hand in pro basketball over his head and start it downward right at the face of any guard stupid enough to drive the center lane on him.

But the Kid wasn't quick enough. Bonelli twitched his right shoulder, lowered it, and drove the line.

The Kid did what he could, but the coach-referee's whistle screamed in his ear.

Number forty-one you're on the HIP! and he made an exaggerated copy of the Kid's last-ditch attempt to save the basket. *Two shots. In the act of shooting.*

YOU WERE SNATCHIN YOUR GODDAM SOCKS AGAIN, FOR CHRISSAKES. The bullhorn's echo rocked across the empty seats.

The Kid strode away hands on hips to take up his position near the backcourt line.

I TOLE YOU AND TOLE YOU, the bullhorn sounded again. *NEVER NEVER NEVER* TURN YOUR GODDAM BACK ON A PLAY EVEN IF IT'S JUST FREE THROWS.

The Kid blushed.

DO THAT AGAINST WEST AND HE'LL *KILL* YA. WE OPEN IN *THREE* DAYS! OR DON'T YOU REMEMBER? He was on his feet now and out from behind the desk.

Bonelli plopped the first one in. Automatic. The Kid wiped his face on his red jersey.

Bonelli plopped the second one in. Automatic. The Kid flipped his mop of hair out of his eyes and stepped up to take the pass from his guard Brown.

Brown was holding up three fingers to signal the pattern he wanted as he whipped the ball over to the Kid who took it easily, whipped it behind his back in a beautiful look-away pass to Coco who had come way up from his usual deep position. Coco whipped it into Orville who shot it quickly back out to the Kid who had dashed in to get his pick. All he had to do was leap and pop it home—the shot was made for him. In college he'd averaged forty points a game on this play for three years.

But Bonelli had hooked a finger ever so lightly into the Kid's waistband. Not much. Just enough to break the rhythm of his reflexes. He could feel the shot sliding just out of control the second it started to leave his hands. When he came down he rushed in to scramble for the rebound, but Jasmo had it: in one hand, then out the other, and Bonelli was laying it up at the far end of the court before the Kid ever got near the basket.

FOR GOD'S SAKE, KID, came the bullhorn at him again. WHEN YOU GOT A JASMO IN THE CENTER, LEAVE HIM TO COCO AND ORVILLE, FOR CHRISSAKE. YOU THINK CHAMBERLAIN'S GONNA GIVE YOU THE BALL? THAT AIN'T KENTUCKY OR VANDERBILT OUT THERE NEXT TUESDAY, SONNY. IT'S THE BY-GOD LOS ANGELES LAKERS.

But the Kid was back-pedaling defensively as fast as he could—and in good position, too—but only because the pass to him from the fast break in-bounds play had been intercepted. He'd missed the signal for it, and was heading back up the court in the wrong direction when the ball was chunked the length of the floor to him.

Bonelli started driving on him again, but the Kid faked with his left hand and Bonelli drove to the outside where the Kid suddenly had him blocked out. And in trouble, too, because the Red team's other forward—Matson—finally decided he'd help out a rookie in a game scrimmage. Bonelli tried to pass the ball out, but the Kid stuck so close to him he couldn't get it away. The Kid finally reached under and between Bonelli's legs and batted the ball loose. It spun away just out of Bonelli's reach. Matson reached down nonchalantly and passed it quickly to Coco who shoveled it to Orville who stuffed it through at the other end.

GOOD PLAY, MATSON, the bullhorn bellowed. THAT'S THE WAY TO LOOK ALIVE.

At the end of the first quarter the score was 13-14, Blueshirts.

During the break, the assistant coaches in charge of the two squads amended game plans they wanted for the second period and started outlining patterns, while the Head Coach—now up in the stands with his bullhorn—kept up a constant commentary.

DISGUSTING. THAT'S WHAT. FOURTEEN GODDAM POINTS, REDS. FOURTEEN. BONELLI, YOU SHOULD HAVE HAD THAT MANY YOURSELF. YOU AND COCO. EACH. HEAR? DO YOU HEAR?

Coco looked up in the stands toward the Head Coach. Bonelli, on the other side of the court, was massaging his right hand. It hurt where the Kid had stepped on him after knocking him down on a charge Jasmo, at six feet eleven and three-quarters inches, stood slouching above the bald, sweating head of his coach. He was looking out at the seats, his jaws slack, the sensitive finger tips of one hand playing slowly off his lower lip so that a series of *plup plup plup plup*'s kept coming from him.

HE'S BEING NICE TO YOU, KID. YOU HEAR, BONELLI? STOP BEING NICE TO HIM. YOU HEAR? KID?

The Kid stepped out from the huddle to acknowledge that he'd heard.

"Whyncha lay off him, Boney?" Andrews, one of the Blue forwards said.

Plup plup plup.

YOU HEAR?

"Screw him," Bonelli said. He flexed his hand.

Plup plup.

His coach went through the defense once again.

"He's after my job."

Plup.

YOU HEAR? AND ANOTHER THING, KID . . .

The assistant coach in charge of the Redshirts looked up at the Kid who was looking up in the seats trying to hear the Head's instructions over the echoing of the bullhorn.

"Hey, Kid. You want to play ball?" the Assistant asked.

"Huh?"

"Then would you please mind listening to what I'm trying to instruct. . ."

YOU HEAR, KID? A QUARTER MILLION DOLLARS GETS SIX POINTS A QUARTER? YOU THINK THE OWNERS GOT NOTHING BETTER TO DO WITH A QUARTER MILLION?

Plup-plup-plup-plup-plup-plup.

"Screw him."

"Does it matter if your pecker drips?" Andrews asked no one in particular.

"All black peckers drip," Bonelli answered.

The Assistant's head bounced and jabbed, red and shiny.

Plup pl . . . "Look out, Wop."

"Up yours, Spook."

Tootle tootle went the whistle, and the Redshirts and the Blueshirts set themselves up in position for the second quarter.

The Kid and Bonelli leaned into each other hip to hip, thigh to thigh. The ball went up: smash, tip. Coco got it again, shot it quickly to the Kid who wheeled to fly down court. Only he ended up on the floor next to Bonelli, both of them clutching their foreheads.

GREAT, KID. THAT'S JUST ABSOLUTELY PLUPERFECTLY *GREAT!* YOU SNATCH THOSE SOCKS AGAIN AND I'LL KILL YOU. I'LL FEED YOU TO JASMO. JASMO, YOU WANT SOME FRESH MEAT?

Plup plup.

CLEAN THAT MESS UP OFF THE FLOOR, FOR CHRISSAKE.

The two men were up and seemed to be all right. All of the Blueshirts and most of the Redshirts were gathered around Bonelli, looking at his forehead for any tragic evidence of fracture or brain damage.

Coco lumbered over to the Kid who was trying to break into the circle around Bonelli to see if he was all right.

"Stick your head in a All Pro's face again and you're in *bad* trouble, boy. *Real* bad trouble." And he stalked off, legs stiff and menacing.

QUARTER OF A MILLION BUCKS AND YOU JUST BLOW IT LIKE THAT, SONNY. NOT TO MENTION AN ALL PRO. CAN *YOU* TAKE HIS PLACE THIS YEAR, SONNY? CAN *YOU* AVERAGE TWENTY-SIX A GAME THIS YEAR, FELLAH?

"Fellah . . . fellah . . ." the words ricocheted and echoed through the Armory gym.

"You all right, Bonelli?"

"Screw him. He wants my job."

The Blues took it in from out of bounds, and they tried the second quarter again.

Midway through, the Head smashed the seventh bullhorn of the practice session. Bonelli heard and called a timeout.

"You ain't passin off, Wop," the other guard, Smith, said.

"Screw it."

"You tryin to play a one-man game, Peckerhead."

"Up yours, Spook."

Plup. "Watch it, Guinea-Wop."

"Up yours, too, Spade."

Plupplupplupplupplup.

"You ain't drivin," Coco yelled at the Kid, and jabbed him hard in the sternum for emphasis. "You not *help*in' " (jab jab *jab*jab) "anybody at all." Jab jab.

"I'm trying, Coco. Christ! What's everybody so badassed for today?"

"I've fed you ten times more than I *ever* feed Bonelli, and you haven't done a damned thing."

"They're not falling, Coco. What can I do?"

"Hey, man," Orville put in over the coach's head. "You're taking shots when there aren't any. I set you picks and screens till I'm about white and you don't use them. You pass off when you got a good shot, and shoot whenever that dumb, olive-brained foreign Italian Wop bastard yells 'shoot' at you."

"Why's everybody so tight-assed today?"

WE PLAY L.A. TUESDAY, LADIES. TODAY'S SATURDAY, GIRLS.

"Hell, it's just an exhibition, Orville."

"*Just*," screamed the Assistant. He stopped in the middle of a complex explanation of a one/three/one offense he had been working on just for today's scrimmage. "*Just*? Jussst? Keee *Rist*, Fellah."

Both teams seemed to settle down a little until halftime. Then: Blues, forty; Reds, thirty-six.

THAT'S A SWEET HIGH SCHOOL SCORE, the Head spoke gently through the eighth bullhorn of the season. VERY NICE AND SWEET.

During the half each squad went through the entire rigamarole of leaving the floor, going down to the dressing rooms, sucking oranges and oxygen, changing socks, rubbing linament into cramping calves, and listening to the coaches analyze the first half of play.

The Kid felt as though he had breathed deeply only about three times before they were up and back out on court. During the warm-up, he got a ball, shot, reached for another one coming toward him. But Coco intercepted it. And the next. Then he chased after another one, but Matson snatched it away. Thud. Thud-thud. Thudthudthud. The balls bounced all over the floor. The Kid, hands up and out a bit in front of his face, kept waiting for one of the balls to bounce his way so he could take some more practice shots, but none managed to get past his teammates.

Tootle went the whistle. Brown bumped into the Kid hard as he trotted to the bench.

During the third quarter, the Redshirts caught up with the Blues in a ragged, free-lancing, shoot-and-run twelve minutes with lots of body contact and bumping and pushing off out front as well as under the basket. Orville, at seven feet one-quarter inch, was starting to push Jasmo and out-rebound him by that extra inch and a quarter. Jasmo kept thinking about Chamberlain and Russell. Year after year it was Chamberlain and Russell. And Honorable Mention for him. He scored over Russell and held Chamberlain below his average practically every time. But it was always Honorable Mention for ole Jasmo. Even after an article in *Sports Illustrated* about him entitled, "Mr. Consistent." After Russell quit, he thought for a season there would be a chance for him, but then there was young Alcindor jack-rabbiting all over the court. And Chamberlain going on it looked like forever. And even now this second-year bull Orville hawking all over him. Russell gone and ole Jasmo getting too old to cut it. When you got to be canny because you can't be quick . . .

. . . and Bonelli. Never got to play against Cousey. Never got to play against the best guard ever in the whole world history of basketball. Cousey, who was so goddam good he even faked his own teammates out of their jocks. Cousey who could fake three times from when he left the ground to when he dropped the ball in the bucket. Cousey who was so goddam good he could pass off a hundred times more than he ever shot, because he could always get a shot. Always. Cousey could get shots because Cousey always knew where the basket was. And if he had the ball, he could keep it away from anybody. *Anybody.* And he could fake three men out so fast and have a shot away if he wanted, he could just pass off all day long and make a great scoring guard out of his own grandmother. Cousey who had more moves and body English than Elgin Baylor, even—which is saying plenty, because he scores more than Cousey ever did—but wasn't Cousey no matter what. Bonelli, three years All Pro, but never got to play against Cousey and show him how good he was, too. Bonelli, who never got to play *with* Cousey, either for that matter. If he'd played with Cousey, those Jones boys for the Celtics would have warmed the benches till they rotted out from under them, because he and ole Cous . . . Why, he'd have scored forty points a game with ole Cous, because he's about the only guard he'd ever known who could even begin to keep up—really and truly keep up—with Cousey. . . .

MOO-WONK, the buzzer sounded, and there were just twelve minutes left.

Bonelli and Smith were the first-string guards.

Jasmo was the first-string center.

Coco and Matson were the first-string forwards.

. . . last season

Now there was the $250,000 bonus-baby rookie who averaged forty points a game for three varsity seasons in what had to be the best, take it all in all, the best basketball conference in the country. The Kid wasn't going to put Bonelli out of a job, but there were Brown and Smith. And Jasmo had had problems feeding him in time for him to get his best jump shots off. And even if the Kid had had problems with totally different styles of play when he was *with* Bonelli in a scrimmage . . . Bonelli could shoot, drive, and pass. But the Kid! The Kid could do all

that and *handle* the ball, too. Really handle it. At night Bonelli had started having dreams, in which he gnashed his pretty, white teeth because
the Kid reminded him of Cousey. A little. But the Kid was six feet four
inches and could leap very high in the air.

    . . . and he'd put more pressure on Coco and Matson, too, because he
would crawl around in the center and bother Jasmo. Throw him off his
stride just enough, just enough to give Orville the quarter second he
needed to take rebounds from Jasmo. Lots of guards were swapping as
forwards now. You could never be sure.

    Jasmo never got any quarter-million-dollar-bonus, either. Plupplupplup.
"Screw him."

    Score: Blues 86, Reds 87. Bonelli had twenty (but only three in the third
quarter); the Kid had twenty-four (with fourteen in the third quarter.)

    THAT'S A LITTLE BETTER, BOYS BUT YOU'RE PLAYING
FOR JOBS, NOW.

    Jasmo cast a baleful look across the floor at the Kid who had been
helping Orville get all those rebounds. And the man up there yelling at
him to keep his scrawny little ass out of the center. Plup.

    Bonelli flexed his hand.

    Andrews and the other forward, Kelly, a second-year comer, looked
across the court at Matson and Coco who were looking hard back at
them. Everybody breathed heavily as the whistle for the last scrimmage
quarter sounded.

    FOR JOBS, NOW.

    Tootle!

    It was good, hard, but more or less slightly roughneck basketball for
eight minutes. Everybody was very careful to get his good shots, to
work his best defense, to stay clear of fouls.

    Then the Kid, crouching in youthful exuberance, watched a shot by
Matson from deep in the corner bounce high off the rim. It seemed to
go up and up forever, then come straight down very slowly. He plotted
its angle of ascent, gauged its angle of descent, computed the degree of
spin it was collecting, and accurately concluded where he should put

himself to get the rebound. Coco—and Matson himself—were out of it, just about: Coco was screened by Kelly, and Matson was still out on the edge, apparently confused because the shot hadn't dropped for him. Orville was shut out by Jasmo. The time was propitious, the calculations precise. The ball finally hit, skittered, and the Kid was there reaching up with everything figured.

Except Jasmo.

Jasmo was there, too. And though not first, he came with more guns. The Kid had one hand on the ball, but Jasmo swept it away from him. The Kid twisted to avoid that awful forearm and hip as the Jas curled his body down in a short, tight, controlled arc. The Kid was quick. He made no contact. But he hadn't noticed that Jasmo had noticed him. He wasn't prepared for Jasmo's clear-out move. With the ball safely in the vise of his hands, Jasmo straightened and swung his body from the hips up, his elbows out like scythes looking for a field to clear. He got the Kid on his first sweep to the right, but missed Orville—who knew what was bound to come—by a good three inches on the sweep to the left. Even as Orville was blocking Jasmo's clear-out pass, the Kid was crumpling to the deck like the Big Max the second time Mr. Louis met him in the ring. Down and out. Coocooville.

Tootle.

Jasmo's elbow was as big as a child's head.

Tootletootle!

CHRIST.

Slowly the Kid rolled over on his face. Then he stopped moving. Then he rolled over on his back and stooped moving again. His nose probably was not broken, his teeth most likely not cracked off. But his lips were shredded and his teeth were loosened plenty and bleeding at the gumline, and his nose looked like a mushy beet.

IS HE ALIVE?

Coco peered down at him.

Jesus, Jas," he said.

"Your elbow okay?" the Blueshirt's coach asked.

Jasmo screwed up his mouth in pain.

"Take a few shots, Jas, and make sure that elbow's okay."

A QUARTER A MILLION dollars

". . . dollars." The Head Coach was down on the floor by the time the Kid managed to push himself up to a sitting position. The trainer took the smelling salts away and covered the Kid's face with an ice bag.

Jasmo muttered that the Kid had the hardest face he'd ever knocked into. "You sure it wasn't his head?"

"Nah," Bonelli answered. They passed a ball back and forth to each other. "He'd be dead now if it was his head."

The Kid got up in stages: first to his knees for a while, then finally to his feet. The head kept pawing in the ice bag trying to get it down from his face, but the Kid and the trainer kept pulling it back up.

"I wanna *talk* to him," the Head fussed.

The trainer nodded to the side of the Kid's head. "He's got a ear over there," he reminded.

"I tole you and *tole* you," the Head screamed in one of the ears. "When you got a Jasmo in the center, leave him to Coco and Orville. Right?"

The Kid nodded.

"If it's Alcindor, you leave him to Jasmo and Coco. Right?"

The Kid nodded.

"If it's Chamberlain, you leave him to Jasmo and Coco. Right?"

"Yah, yah," the Kid said. He took the ice bag off for a second. "Yah. All right. All right!"

"Well don't you go getting prima donna with me," the Head screamed at the Kid who had covered his face with the ice pack again.

"Murmwrmur," the Kid said.

"What?"

He took the ice bag from his face again.

"I said I'm just trying to play this damn game, is all," the Kid snapped. Still, there was more confusion and hurt in his voice than violence.

AWRIGHT, THEN. THEN PLAY!

They played another two minutes. Ragged. Very ragged. The bullhorn never once stopped. The assistant coaches from the sidelines never let up. The players were punishing each other mercilessly. The body contact for a minute and a half was brutal. Smith held on to Brown who was trying to dribble. Then Coco had the ball. Trying for a hook shot with his right hand, he shoved off with his left by sticking his fist in Kelly's throat. And Jasmo finally pinned one of Orville's arms to his side while Orville whammed and whammed with his other elbow trying to find the Jas's head.

The Head was back down from the stands bullhorning every step of the way to the scorer's bench where three sub-assistants had finally quit trying to keep stat sheets on the players.

"Screw him," Bonelli kept muttering when he could draw the breath. His legs stayed under him only because he refused to collapse on them. You don't run All Pro's off the floor, his training and his pride kept telling his legs. "Screw the son of a bitch."

"Screwhimscrewhimscrewhimscrewhim*screw*him," he shrieked as the Kid finally drove past him. Hard. And leaped fourteen feet from the basket, heading to it like an electronic homing rocket after a bomber.

Bonelli reached out and grabbed at the Kid and got a death grip on his shorts. The Kid was driving so hard he literally pulled himself out of the pants as he leaped, legs still pumping, knees flailing as he soared first through Kelly who hit the deck to get out of the way, and then through Jasmo who tried to, but wasn't quick enough and was knocked, finally, clean off the apron and into the seats where he looked like the come-back Louis after Marciano was through with him.

JEE SUS GOOD GODDAM CHRIST . . .

. . . and the Head was on the floor storming toward the Kid through the carnage: Bonelli—stretched out face down with a pair of men's shorts in his hand; Kelly—lying very quietly on his back, breathing very hard, and looking whiter than ever; Jasmo—managing to right himself, his eyes wide, his mouth hanging slack as he crawled slowly on his hands and knees back to the playing floor. And the Kid himself had miraculously landed on his feet, sunk down to his ankles, and sprung back up.

"You by-God . . . ," the Head stormed. His eyes bulged, the veins in his neck and at his temples looked as though they would explode in a paroxysm of . . .

"Can't you do anything right? Look at *that*: All Pro. And *that*: Honorable Mention for eight years in a row. And *that* . . ."

But the Kid had reached down and taken off his athletic supporter, so he was clad only in sneakers covered by his fallen socks, and his red jersey. He held his jock strap under the Head's nose.

"You want that, too?" he screamed. "You want this, too?" he repeated half a dozen times. Suddenly he wheeled and flung the strap toward the basket. It sailed awkwardly in a none-the-less neat arc and fell on the rim, then nicely through the net. Everyone saw it. Then everyone looked at the Kid, and even though they saw tears pouring from his eyes, they heard something else: a giggle. He choked on it slightly and half-coughed it out, but it was clearly a giggle.

He giggled again. Jasmo had finally gotten his breath and his footing in time to see the young man—looking terribly vulnerable and young—standing in the middle of the basketball court with his prick hanging long and limp. And it occurred to him that the Kid's cock looked a bit like he felt. He giggled at that, pulled his jersey off, and threw it at the basket too. But missed. Then Coco had a sneaker off. He charged at a hobble and dunked it with a great whoop of joy.

The next thing anyone knew, there were shirts and jocks, socks and sneakers, bandages, tape, wrist and forehead sweatbands flying through the air. And there on the basketball court of the Armory were thirteen grown men, buck naked, playing with basketballs. It was much like the warm-up periods before games and second halfs. Except there were great grins and smiles now. The air was swept with the bodies of men: black thighs, brown butts, white calves, arms, backs, bull-like necks. Sweeping, pirouetting, cavorting: a veritable ballet of motion and grace, of preen and—once again—real style, of cock-a-doodle-do and cakewalk and Delta Shuffle on the bounce and pass rhythm of the game with the solid thump-a-thump beat of the balls on the floor. No one played against the other. It was pass and feed, hand off and assist, jump and shoot, drive and dunk. It was approval in dozens of smiles and nods and loving pats of flesh on flesh . . .

At the other end of the court, lined across it like football referees at the ready for the pre-game-toss-of-the-coin-introductions, were the coaches and assistants and trainers. They stared. In the doorway behind them was the assistant equipment manager, toothpick rocking slowly in the wet corner of his mouth. He also stared.

. . . and as suddenly as it had started, it stopped. It was as though a *tootle* had sounded in their heads all at once. They left the floor, quietly joshing, gently chatting with each other, a calmness of civility permeating every sure step of their feet. In the locker room they showered, shaved, dressed, combed their hair neatly, pulled their ties into place deftly, and left.

Back on the court, the coaches broke rank slightly to stand, hands still behind their backs, to mill about aimlessly while the Head, one hand covering his face at the scorer's desk, shook from the sobs no one was blaming him for. The sub-assistant equipment manager quietly make the rounds to pick up the spent uniforms—the odd sneaker in the stands, the blood-flecked elbow pad under a bench. The Head sat at the scorer's table a very long time. Very long.

Tuesday they opened their exhibition season against the Lakers in L.A. The Kid scored twenty-two. Not bad, as they say, for openers. And they hung in to take Los Angeles by three in the last two minutes. The Los Angeles sports writers, looking a bit stunned and confused, kept shaking their heads after the game was over and the out-of-town writers were filing their stories.

"They looked psyched," one of the locals braved. "All night long they looked psyched," as he riffled back through his game notes with awe.

Fingers
Gary Gildner

When Ronald, Mr. Lacey's son, came home from the war, he showered, put on a pair of new jeans and a new T-shirt, found his old high-school baseball cap and pulled it down snug over his forehead, then went outside and shot baskets. He shot baskets for about two weeks. One day Mr. Lacey said, "What about that money you saved up? What are you going to do with it?" Ronald shot baskets for a while longer, then went downtown and bought an old Hudson Hornet. He spent five days driving the Hudson back and forth through town, stopping for a root beer when he got thirsty. On the sixth day, when a tire went flat, Ronald locked the car and put his thumb in the air. The next day in the Atkins Museum in Kansas City, he bought a dozen picture postcards of Houdon's bust of Benjamin Franklin, because with that bald top and that long hair in back that fell to his shoulders, Franklin looked like the queerest duck he'd ever seen. Also, Franklin seemed peeved about something. Then Ronald took a bus to New York City. The ride was nothing to crow about—and for maybe three hundred miles a man next to him wanted to describe losing his prostate gland. In New York Ronald found a room a stone's throw from Yankee Stadium. He sent one of the Franklin cards to his father, saying only, "Love, Ronald." Then he sat looking out the window. On the fire escape was a piece of red balloon that the wind was trying to blow away. Finally the wind succeeded and Ronald was tired. He took off his clothes, climbed into bed, and began to count the fingers on his shooting hand.

One on One
Tony Gloeggler

glance at her packing   say nothing   find the hi-tops hiding
under the bed   lace up tight   tie a double knot   grab the ball
from the closet   squeeze it with both hands   cradle it on your hip
unlock the dead bolt   turn the knob   slam the door   skip
down stairs two at a time   dribble against cracked concrete   sprint
across Spring Street   bend and fit through the hole in the fence

trot across the empty courts   lift the ball in your right hand   kiss
it off the backboard   watch it spill in   find the faded pink line
see Stanley's Moving Van rumble down the block   sink ten foul shots
drift to the corner   swish a couple   tap back rebounds   take pull-up
jump shots   watch a black guy slip through the fence   nod   pass
him the ball   shoot a bit longer   say wanna play some one on one

hit or miss for the ball   fifteen wins   trade outside jumpers
six all   get on your toes   crouch low   get inside his shirt
stick to his skin   bump him with your thighs   hand check   go up
with him   turn and grind your ass in his gut   snatch the rebound
dribble past the foul line   back in   inch closer   pivot   pump
fake   duck under   bank the ball in   grunt and bang until fifteen

play it back   another   again   one more   shake hands   say good game
my man catch you later   drag your ass back home   walk up stairs
slip in the key   open the door   swallow a cold beer   peel off
shirt socks shorts   turn on the shower   step under the spray   burn
your skin with scalding water   get on your knees   hold your head
in your hands   curl into a ball and crawl down the fucking drain

Open Man
Bob Levin

My basketball was riding shotgun and I took it along while I stretched my legs. The attendant checked under the hood and I did my drill. Twenty-five with the right hand, behind the back and twenty-five with the left; then behind the back and over again. My head was up. My body was on guard. My eyes were looking out for hands. The dribble pounded on the concrete like a hammer trying hard to build something that would last.

"Everything's fine," the attendant said. He was thin, in his sixties, grey hair, short and soft like a cat's, half of it burnt off fairly recent. He had a giant diseased mole on his neck and a pair of sharp blue eyes. "Billy" the patch on his jacket said. Billy topped off the gas. "Six-eight oh," he said. "Ten point-three."

He came back with my change. The blue eyes were on me hard. They made me feel every inch of my 6'4" and every pound of my 210. They made me feel my beard and my shades and my shaved head. They made me feel my orange suede low cuts and my cut-offs and my black game shirt with the shoulder stripes. "Ridley Gap," the black shirt said in red. "Ghosts," it said. "13."

"How's a big guy like you fit in a little job like that?" Billy said, patting my "C"'s flank near the painted rose.

"It's OK," I said. "There's like a tunnel where you can stick your legs out straight."

"Oh yeah." He looked inside and then he looked at me again. "You some kind of ballplayer?"

"That's right. Some kind." I took my shades off and rubbed my nose. It was after ten and I'd been on the road since before dinner. The gas fumes hung in the November air. Trucks roared by on the Black Horse Pike. It was cold and the moon was clouded in.

Billy took his time looking at me. He saw a newspaper story. Maybe he saw a face. He put two together with the two he had. "You Manny Baer's boy?"

"Jake."

"Sam," Billy said, sticking out his hand. "I felt real bad hearing 'bout your old man."

I didn't say anything.

"That was sure a screwy way to do it. Manny being such a steady guy and all."

"I don't know," I said.

He thought for a minute. "Maybe you're right. Maybe it just depends on how you look at it if you know what I mean."

"Yeah."

"Still, no offense, it seems kinda goofy to me." A double rigged diesel slowed and turned into the station. "I played against your old man a couple times," Billy said. "Not that I was in his league. Just pick up. You ever get to see him play?"

"I guess I remember some smelly gyms and drinking Birely's afterwards and how his face was flushed." I looked at the road and the truck lights disappearing at the fork. "I don't remember much."

"Well you had to be kind of young."

"Yeah."

He looked at me once more as he headed for the diesel. "He was smart and steady and he didn't make mistakes. A student of the game they called him." He looked at me again. "Bet you're better 'n he ever was, huh? Count of you got all that size."

I shrugged. "Well, it's a different game now."

Billy waved and disappeared on the truck's far side like he was swallowed. The truck was black and caked with mud and steamy and it shook and rocked like a great beast.

My dad had sold the place in Philly and moved out to Sea Bottom after my mom died. I was away at school and didn't come down much. When I did, it seemed to suit him fine. He was just one block from the ocean and one block from the bay. Every morning he'd take out an outboard or else he'd fish off the pier. He put a basket up in back and got all the kids in the neighborhood shooting fouls underhand and throwing passes on the bounce. He had a garden with tomatoes and cucumbers and radishes and one corner that he called his Free Zone where every summer he tried something strange. One summer it was honeydews and another it was wheat. Nothing ever grew that was good in that corner but he didn't seem to mind. Something always might catch, and otherwise it was a good joke. He was smart and steady Manny Baer, a student of the game.

The last time I had seen my father it had been like always. It was before work-outs had started, and I'd come down for a couple days. He asked me how the club looked. He asked me how my roomie Jojo was and if I still thought Walton would make it big. He told me about his fishing and his garden and one or two of his kids. We walked along the beach and at night he did his crosswords while I read. I watched the tube. The crickets chirped; the moths pressed against the screen; and if he didn't know an answer he would ask me. "What the hell's a South American bat?" "Jake, goddammit, you ever eat a six-letter Assyrian fruit?" If I knew the answer I would tell him, but it seemed every time he didn't know one it had me baffled too. If an easy one stumped him, he never let me know.

Even when we said goodbye it was like always. "See you soon," I said and hugged him.

"You look great, Jake. Hit the open man."

"Box out the big guys, star."

He didn't say one thing about the cancer or being seventy or what it was really like being alone at night in the shadows where he was. If I had known what he was planning, you bet to Christ I would have asked.

The letter came about a week later. I think now it was because he'd seen me and wanted it over before my season began. He knew I expected a big one. The letter came special delivery but there was nothing I could do.

Jake:
I am sticking this in the box and then I am heading down to Capt. Nick's and signing out a dinghy for a week. Then I am heading off The Point where the Bay and Ocean meet. When I hit the Ocean I am heading out some more.
Not to worry, star. Nothing you can do. It is done before you get this. I am all packed. I've got the black sweater that your mother knit. The thermos is full of brandy and I'm shipping all the Seconal the Doc would write me up. I've thought it over and it's fine. There is nothing else I want except a good sunset for the ride.

Love,
D

I called the police and I called the Coast Guard too. They never even found the dinghy. The Coast Guard found an empty thermos washed ashore at Saganoock. I took it when they offered, but it could have been anybody's like they said.

I drove through the stinking tidelands past the peeling billboards advertising $4.00 lobster dinners and Bobby Vee concerts. I drove past the burned out shell of the Toujours L'Amour and the hamburger stands that had gone bust waiting for Sea Bottom to become Atlantic City or Wildwood. I crossed the 12th Street bridge and turned right for the end of the island and the house. A For Sale sign was out front and there was dog crap on the lawn. Otherwise it looked like when I'd said goodbye. Someone was keeping the garden up and helping themselves to what was ripe.

With some cardboard from my trunk I shoveled the crap into the street. Then I stood and looked at the house. It was a one-story four room brick house with white shutters and a screened porch and it looked neat and trim and like as nice a place to live as you could want. I didn't go inside. All I wanted to do was look at it again. I knew I could stand seeing it. I knew that would be all right. Inside, though, would be the smells of a closed off place you used to know and I did not want them alive inside my lungs.

I carried my ball around the house with me. The basket still stood above the driveway and the net still waved. I did my drill: twenty-five with the right hand and twenty-five with the left. The tatoo of the ball on the macadam temporarily blocked the dull roar of the ocean at the block's end. I switched on the spotlight my father had put up for the basket he had built. Small brown moths danced in its flame and in the weeds the crickets chirped.

I took a few jump shots. I took a few more. The basket had settled a couple inches and leaned to the right, but I didn't miss. I went into the left corner and began moving in an arc toward the right, staying 15 feet from the basket and shooting as I went. When I hit one corner I started back to the other.

I had been shooting fifteen minutes when this kid arrived. He was nine or ten. He was walking his bike down the alley and watching me all the way. When he got to where I was, he stopped and set the kick stand. "Hi," I said.

"Hi," he said. "Do you live here now?"

"No," I said. "Do you?"

"No. I live over there." He pointed down the alley into the dark. "The man who lived here died."

"Is that right." I dribbled the ball a while. "You figure that it's haunted then?"

"No. That stuff isn't real."

"You're a smart kid." I hit a thirty-footer off the board. The kid ran the ball down and threw it back. "Want to play?" I asked him.

He nodded and came onto the court. "Are you a real ball player?"

"Uh huh."

"I played with some kids in the high school once and they were good. What's your name?"

"Grizzly."

He smiled. "C'mon. What's your real name?"

"That's it."

"Oh," He was not impressed. He was disappointed a little. "Where do you play if you're a ballplayer?"

I pointed at my shirt.

He shook his head and screwed up his nose.

"It's kind of a minor league."

"You ever play with Dave Cowens or Rick Barry?"

"They from that high school?"

"C'mon. You must of *heard* of them."

"Dick Barry?"

"Rick!"

"Oh, Rick Barry. No, I never played with him."

"They don't play where you do?"

"Them and a lot of people besides." We were alternating shots now. You got to shoot until you missed. The kid shot everything two hands. Hold it, feel it, study it, and let it go soft and safe. He was one of my father's boys all right. He had the same wrist release from behind the ears. "You know the guy lived here?"

"He was neat. We used to come over and play with him. All the guys did."

"His basket's crooked."

"No, it's not," the kid said.

I faked firing a pass at him and bounced it off a bicep like the Globies do. "Keep it warm," I told him. "I'll see you in a little bit."

I walked down to the beach. I am going for a walk on the beach, I thought. I laughed at that. One thing burns my ass is all those copout art films ending with a walk along the beach. "I don't know what it means, Frederico. I don't know how it ends." "Just walk him on the beach, Francois. Show the suckers sands and waves." Well that was what I showed me. That was where I walked.

I walked along the beach at the high tide's mark. Under the moon the sea's debris stretched out in a wavering line as far as I could see. I followed the line of debris down the beach. I followed the torn seaweed and the smashed shells, the slices of jellyfish and the legs torn off the crabs, the spider and the blue. The pieces of the dead ran straight down the beach. They ran down all the beaches of the world. I saw nothing that was special. I saw one dead gull that was pretty eaten up.

All the houses along the beach were quiet. All except one. A big one—grey as slate. The lights were on in that one and I could hear a party's songs. I could see the people moving like shadows behind the shades. While I watched, a window opened on the second floor and a man crawled out. He walked slowly and carefully along the roof to the far edge. The man was carrying a drink, but when he got to the edge he set it down. Then he stood and stared at the moon and waved his arms like he was trying to fly.

When I got back to the house the kid was still working on his set shot. His face was sweaty and his shirt was wet. I watched him score. I watched him miss.

"How'm I doing?" he asked, shoving the ball up there.

I didn't answer.

"How'm I doing?"

"Sorry, shot, I was somewhere else. It looks. . . Yeah, it looks OK."

"OK? OK? I'm a lot better than OK." When he shot, he staggered after the ball a step or two. "The man used to say I was as good as anybody he had ever seen."

"Tell you what," I said. I stepped into the light. "I'll bet you a dime you can't make a shot. Any shot you want. I'll bet you a dime you can't put it in."

"Any shot?"

I nodded.

"OK." Real quick, he ran up under the basket. He looked back over his shoulder at me standing on the foul line and smiled like he was ready for me to concede.

"You're a smart kid," I said.

The kid put his hands at the ball's poles and hefted it behind his ears. He bent his knees and sighted at the board. He felt it, he weighed it, he judged the angle and the feet. When his hands started forward with the ball I took one step, pushed off, and swatted it away into the night.

"Heyyy," he wailed.

"It's no good, shot. In fact it shits."

"Heyyy. You cheated. I don't owe you nothing."

"It's slow and it's obvious and it's the dumbest thing I ever saw. They'll knock it down your throat any time they want."

He stared at me. I guess I was yelling a little.

I picked up the ball. "Quick." I hit a jump shot. "Fast." I hit another. I dribbled and I jumped. "Go crazy or they'll knock it down your throat."

"I'm not as big as you. I got to hold it, don't I?"

"Practice, man. Grow up." I turned it off. I was calm. "You don't want them knocking it down your throat, do you?"

"No."

"Damn right. The bastards got enough of an edge as it is. And you can forget that dime."

The ball had rolled into the Free Zone. It lay among some spindly vines. Grapes, I think. An arbor, he had joked. I picked up the ball and stuck it under an arm. I drove the six hours back up to the Gap. We opened at Statetown that Friday. We beat them by eleven and won our first tour. It was the best start in the nine years that I been there.

The Poet Tries to Turn in His Jock
David Hilton

Going up for the jump shot,
Giving the kid the head-fakes and all
'Til he's jocked right out the door of the gym
And I'm free at the top with the ball and my touch,
Lofting the arc off my fingertips,
I feel my left calf turn to stone
And my ankle warp inward to form when I land
A neat right angle with my leg,
And I'm on the floor,
A pile of sweat and sick muscles,
Saying,
Hilton,
You're 29, getting fat,
Can't drive to your right anymore,
You can think of better things to do
On Saturday afternoons than be a chump
For a bunch of sophomore third-stringers;
Join the Y, steam and martinis and muscletone.
But, shit,
The shot goes in.

The Poet's Dream the Night After His Son Scores 36 in a Little Dribbler's Game

Richard Blessing

When I shoot, the glass board bends triple like a tailor's mirror,
and the ball splits like a bullish stock, vanishes
down a tunnel of refractions.

Someone keeps doubling up
on me. He is short when I dribble, tall when I jump.
He shadows me in corners like quick death.

I am home,
but my shirt says "Visitors." It is July in Bradford, Pennsylvania.

I know everything before it happens.

Soon an old man will come through a grove of slack-leaved trees.
He will move down the dusty path that leads to this park
as if he would die if both feet did not always touch the ground.
He will sit on the low stone wall beside the asphalt court.

It is all as I say.

Under the shade of his old man's hat
his eyes are cheering my name as a boy. They are screaming
I must win this one time for him. Everything depends on it.

I am confused. I call time-out, but the clock still runs.

The shadow who guards me has stolen the old man's hat.
I'm quick as a sneeze, he whispers, *tough as week-old cake.*
I'm faster than you will be again in your life.

I throw an elbow and he starts to cry. I stoop to comfort him,
but he is gone with the ball. His sweet base-line jumper
swells the net, swells my heart.

                              Time's running out.
We've lost for good, I tell the old man. Together we sit
on the low stone wall, loving him, hating him, rooting him home.

Whistle and the Heroes
Herbert Wilner

It is only basketball, yet twice a week, in the early night, Marvin Wessel lives the life of a man. He doesn't play before the Garden crowds, and even the time of club ball is far behind, yet Wednesdays and Fridays are the best days of his week. The community center is open on Monday evenings too, but on that night he drives his mother for her injection. It's a sacrifice for Marvin, and they both know it. She might change the day of her appointment, but he never presses her to. Next to the nights that he plays basketball, giving it up on Monday is the other big thing in his week.

His mother alludes often to a devil, and when the doctor first explained her child's cleft palate, she always spoke of it as more of Satan in her life. As a boy, he knew what she said had something to do with him, and he understood no more of it than that. But now he no longer thinks of it. He tries to think of little that is in the past: basketball on the two nights and his job satisfy his idea of time.

Whistle—as his friends have always called him—works as a packer in one of the city's largest department stores. Before that, four years ago, he worked for a button company, but his present job is better. The building is huge and he is shifted among departments often enough to overcome the monotony of his work. The frequent changes make it unnecessary to get too friendly with anyone, and this, also, satisfies Whistle. He feels no need for new friends, and his speech makes it difficult to talk to people he doesn't already know. When the work gets too dull, he thinks ahead to his two big nights.

On a Wednesday or Friday, Whistle is always nervous. This happens as early as breakfast. He fries an extra egg and has milk instead of the usual coffee. He is grateful at these times that his mother always sleeps late and he can manage the mornings for himself. On the subway, he pushes back against the jostling with a little more force, although he is careful to avoid argument. If he is close to a window, he peers at his face, which is trapped in the window against the darkness of the tunnel. He thinks he hardly looks the part he will play that night, and the deception gives him some kind of advantage over the others in the car. At work, when he walks from the packing table for empty cartons, he pushes hard against the balls of his feet. He can feel his calves tighten, and he has to fight the impulse to run a few steps. Even when he packs, the work is not enough to wear away the energy that builds inside him. He is almost pained by the sense of his body, and he is able to isolate parts of it: the weight of an arm, the tension in a leg, the bunching behind a shoulder. This impatience for violent movement compels his mind to wander as he packs, and he lapses into a familiar image of himself. They are jumping under the backboard for a loose ball, and he suddenly angles in from the corner of the court and finds an opening. He cuts in cleanly and leaps with the power of his run to snatch the ball out of the air and come down without contact some fifteen feet away toward the other corner, already dribbling quickly downcourt. The picture excites him, and he works with more conviction at the carton on his packing table.

At lunch, he runs the short distance to the cafeteria, finding little spaces in the hurrying noon crowds. He runs with his feet wide apart and his legs bent slightly at the knees so that he might veer sharply through any sudden opening. Though he can tell himself he runs to get a window seat he doesn't care to understand why this seat isn't so important on other days. He eats quickly, again having milk instead of coffee, and spends the rest of the hour smoking cigarettes and staring out the window. He can usually guess which of the girls that pass are models, and he can even decide between those who work in the high-price houses and the cheaper ones. He has heard enough stories to know they are all tramps, and he has seen it himself when he worked at a dress house. But when one walks by who is beautiful, yet clean—like the fragile girl in a perfume ad—he finds the stories and what he knows hard to believe.

In the afternoon his mind wanders again, and the time passes quickly. If he grows too conscious of his straying thoughts, he works at the packing with a renewed vigor. When it gets toward quitting time, he is pleased by the energy that is still in him. At five o'clock he turns in his slips, knowing that he has packed more than he does on the ordinary days. Men in the same department mutter goodbye to him, and he nods his head and smiles in return. Three middle-aged women work there, but they say nothing to him, though they joke with the other men. In the crowded street he runs again to the subway—the feet wide apart, the knees slightly bent.

When he gets home on Wednesdays or Fridays, he takes the stairs to their first floor Bay Ridge flat two at a time. His mother knows the community center opens at seven, and supper is always ready for him. She finds it a nuisance to have her time fixed this way twice a week, and she complains bitterly about it. She often tells him he must stop playing ball, that he is no longer a boy, that were his father alive he would have to toe the line. But she never forces an argument because she has come herself to depend on these two nights. When he hurries out the door with his gym clothes in a traveling bag, she begins to mutter about her devil as she rubs a hand across her chest.

On the gym floor, Whistle moves with a bird's grace. He uses the game as a gull does the wind, tacking toward the basket in what is almost flight. He is slender and not more than five-ten, and though all the fellows he plays with are much younger than he, many of them are taller and stronger. Some of them, swelling in their late teens, strip to their shorts so that the sweat will shadow the contours of their bodies. But Whistle wears a grey fleece-lined sweater and track pants.

They play on only one basket, yet Whistle rarely stops moving. If there is a loose ball—no matter how far away—he chases for it. If someone is about to shoot, he is already moving toward the backboard for the rebound. Even when he crouches to jump for a ball that has not yet begun to drop, there is so much tension in his poise that there is no apparent halting of motion between the wait and the leap. Yet with all his running, there is a great economy to Whistle's movement. He possesses a flawless instinct for knowing where to be. Despite the smallness of the court, he never collides with the other five who play. There are many such collisions in this unrefereed game, but Whistle is seldom involved in the tangle. The kids, often desperate with his near perfection, claim that his one shortcoming is a fear of the rough stuff, and they try to provoke him. But Whistle knows this is not a part of his game, and he is able, by the certainty of his movements, to avoid it.

It does not matter to him that he is twenty-eight and most of the boys he plays with are still in their teens. Nor does it matter that there is no great audience and the game is only a pick-up affair. It is enough that he performs well and the sweat is on his body. But more than other things, there is that fine chemical change as he plays. Sometimes he will put a hand to his abdomen, as though to feel it. Things inside of him—hard things he is unaware of during the day, but feels now he should be able to touch—loosen as though parts of his body had begun to dissolve. After a few minutes on the gym floor, he can almost hear himself unwinding, as though there were some connection between running and health. When he leaps in from the corner of the court to steal a ball from the taller fellows under the backboard, he may—as he begins to dribble away—raise his head slightly and look back toward the players with a curiously defiant stare in his eyes, a thinning of the lines in his already taut face. Aside from this one lapse, he is all but oblivious to place and time. He does not think once while he plays how much better it all is than his work as a packer, or his life at home. He runs with pursed lips and never speaks, but neither is he aware that he has not spoken.

Yet in his mind there are the impressions of a long time ago. There are many people and various days, but if he were to remember well there would be only one night, there would be the girl and Bernstein. It was eight years ago and a good time in Whistle's life.

It was a winter evening that came with a heavy snow. He would remember that because the girl sat on his lap and he wouldn't help when the car settled on the ice and the fellows got out to push. It was winter, too, because the last he'd ever seen of Bernstein was after the game when the kid had thrown a snowball at the lamppost outside the school, threw it so well that he hit not the post but the lamp fixture, and when it came down it made a splattering thud in the soft snow. Then Bernstein and his gang ran off around the corner, shouting, and Whistle stood there. He looked into the darkness where the lamp had been, looked up at the falling snow, and listened to the echoes of Bernstein's laughter.

It was the winter of the year. Even with the car as crowded as it was, they made vapor funnels with their breathing, and they passed the bottle around often. She swallowed from it along with the other girls, and when she finished and gave the bottle to Whistle, he saw her shoulders shudder and felt her squirm on his lap. She was broad and thin, and her name was Alice. When she turned her face to hand him the bottle, the edge of her profile was rimmed in a soft light. Whistle thought she was very pretty.

It had been Dox's idea that they take the girls to the game. Whistle worked with Dox in the dress house, and Alice worked there too. Dox's date was a model in the place, but Alice worked in the office. Dox insisted she was too thin to be a model, but Whistle thought she was clean and would not be one. He had never spoken to her, and it was Dox who had arranged the date. That made Whistle angry, but he could not understand why. For weeks he had wanted her to see him play. At nights, the desire had made him restless with a new excitement.

After work they went to the New Yorker for dinner. Flip and Artie met them there with their girls, and it was almost a party. They had drinks before dinner, but Artie kept insisting about the game, and so none of the fellows had more than two. Whistle wanted to drink more, but he felt himself tighten when Artie mentioned the game, and he held back.

But in the car when the bottle Dox had bought went around and she would swallow from it and then turn to hand it to him, Whistle was afraid she would hear the beating in his chest. There was the soft light on her face, and she said, "Here, Whistle," without even a smile. But there was an edge to her voice that startled him. He did not think from seeing

her at work that she would drink the way she did, and he believed she was
doing it because the other girls were. But she didn't say anything or even
change the expression on her face when Dox's girl started to curse, and
Whistle felt the blood inside him to the ends of his fingers. He wanted
to take a long swallow when she said, "Here, Whistle," but Artie still kept
on about the game, so he ran a little of it over his lip and passed it on.
She sat well back in his lap, and he had a hand on her shoulder. He
thought ahead to when he would be running on the gym floor and she
would be watching him. Thinking of that relieved the sense of his awk-
wardness. It would be much easier for him after the game. He could look
forward to the party in Dox's basement. He was almost not afraid to
think of taking her home by himself afterwards.

But suddenly, even the thought of the game was strangely frighten-
ing. She might not know anything about basketball. She might not care
at all about how he played. He remembered he had not spoken a full
sentence to her since the evening started. That terrified him now. The
others were all making noise in the car. When he listened, he could hear
Dox's girl laugh loudly. But Alice was quiet. Maybe Dox had spoken to
her before the date. Quickly, without thinking, his fingers—as though
they were apart from the anguish inside him—tightened about her
shoulder. He waited for her to protest, wanting now to be out of the
car, not caring anymore about the game. But she didn't speak. She did-
n't even move. She just sat there on his lap looking out through the
opposite window, the light shading the edge of her fine profile. He felt
his fingers loosen on her shoulder.

Then Flip, sitting in front with his girl on his lap, twisted his head
toward the corner where Whistle sat in the back. Looking past Alice,
Whistle could see Flip's thick neck wrinkle in two ugly folds.

"It's awful quiet back there," Flip said. "They must be having fun.
Whistle didn't even get out to push." Dox's girl laughed. Whistle
thought hard for something to say, but Alice was quiet too. Then
Artie's girl, sitting next to Whistle, spoke.

"Nothing's going on. You take care of your own troubles."

"What did I say?" Flip called back. "I thought I was being nice. I was looking out for Alice."

"I'm fine, thank you," Alice said without moving. Her voice, clear, brittle, sounded in Whistle's ear like the tapping of metal. It came upon him quietly—as though the thought had been in his mind for years—that he was going to love her. They were on the bridge now, and the water below them was dark in the twilight. Looking out between the massive, bolted girders at the river, at the boats, at the snow, and at the lights that beamed their narrow yellow tracks across the water, Whistle lost himself for a moment in a surprising calm. It was as though he had done all this—Alice on his lap and his hand on her shoulder—many times before. He thought he would ask her, after the party, when they stood before her door, to go on a boat ride with him when the warmer weather came. When he turned away from the window, he saw that she had raised a hand to her face to touch precisely with a finger near the corner of her eye. The nail was long and polished lightly, in pink.

"There won't be much for us to do at the game, just watching you guys run around," Dox's girl suddenly said.

"Anxious to get to the party?" Dox asked. Whistle knew Dox had smiled.

"It'll be better than the game," she said.

"I suppose it will," Dox said.

"You girls can bet on that," Flip said.

"There he goes again," Artie's girl said.

"For Christ's sake, what the hell's eating you ?" Flip answered.

"Oh, can it all already, will you," Dox said. It grew quiet and Whistle wondered why Alice hadn't said anything when they spoke about the game. Then Dox looked quickly at his girl.

"You watch Whistle during the game. That'll give you enough to do."

"Why? Is he something special?" She turned a little to look toward Whistle. He bit his lip to stop the childish grin.

"The best basketball player you ever saw," Flip said.

"So what ?" she laughed.

"This one's got the giggles," Flip said. "Listen kid, if girls were basketballs, Whistle would have you all screwed by tomorrow." Flip laughed, and Dox's girl laughed. A small knot of breath caught in Whistle's throat. Then Alice laughed, louder than the others, filling the car with the sound of it, tilting her head back so that her hair fell against his face. She jerked on his lap as she laughed, and then began to cough and laugh at the same time. Whistle heard himself mumble, "Take it easy. Take it easy." When she stopped at last, they were all quiet again. Whistle listened to the continuous grinding of the snow beneath the tires.

"It's going to be a rough game," Artie said, breaking the silence.

"Quit worrying," Dox said.

"Is this a very special game?" Alice asked. Whistle shrugged, then nodded toward Artie. "He thinks so," he heard himself say.

"They're only kids," Artie said, "but they play high school ball together. They got this guy Bernstein on the team. He's got offers from colleges already."

"Oh, is that the kid who plays for Madison?" Alice asked. Whistle looked up eagerly at her. Her mouth was half-parted in surprise. It was small, pretty. He turned his head away.

"How did you know ?" Flip asked.

"He lives on my block. I used to date his brother."

"No shit ?" Flip said.

"Bernstein's a nice kid," Alice said. "I've seen him play."

"You watch Whistle tonight," Dox said.

"Are you really that good, Whistle?" she asked, turning her face down to him. He could not see her face for the shadows, but he thought surely she must hear the beating of his heart. He wanted to be out of the car and on the gym floor. He wanted that very much. He opened his mouth to say something, not knowing what he would say. But then Dox began.

"He ought to be that good. Hell, even I might be if I worked at it like him. Hey Artie, you remember when we were kids and it was ass-cold outside. Below zero, remember? We were going to a movie—*Captain Blood*, wasn't it? You nearly lost an ear on the way. And when we passed the schoolyard, there was Whistle running around in a sweater and steaming like the Fourth of July. He even shoveled the snow away from the backboard, remember ?"

"I ought to," Artie said. "I had to go to the doctor account of my frozen ear. Whistle, you were a crazy kid."

Whistle smiled.

Flip began to sing a song, and his girl joined in. Then Dox and Artie sang, and Alice hummed. Whistle thought confidently of the game. He had hardly spoken to her, had not really touched her. It would be different afterwards. He would sing with them on the way to Dox's place. The words were almost in his mouth now. He liked the light weight of her on his lap, but he wanted to be in the game already. He thought of it longingly, saw himself angling in from the corner for that free ball. But it was hard for him to think only of the game. He got it mixed with the metallic ring of her voice: "Here, Whistle. Here, Whistle."

When the car pulled up before the community center, Whistle thought he should help Alice out, but she was on his lap and had to leave first. Inside the building, they all lingered for a while at the steps to the locker room.

"You girls keep together," Flip said. "We'll see you after the game." Then, looking at Alice as the fellows started down the stairs, Flip added "Having fun ?"

"Terrific," she said flatly. Whistle, already hurrying down the steps, did not look back. The word, the sound of it, terrified him. He'd been a fool with her. He should've said more in the car. He should've maybe touched her arm now before leaving her. He should've held her hand when they were going through the snow. The steps had been icy too.

"You got a big mouth, Flip," Dox said, as he pushed open the door to the locker room.

"Say, what the hell is all this?" Flip complained. "I ain't said one word tonight when everybody didn't come jumping on me."

"Then shut up!" Dox said.

"Cut it, will you guys. Think about the game a little," Artie said. "It ain't going to be a breeze with that Bernstein kid."

They met the rest of the team in the locker room, and as they dressed Whistle outlined the way they'd play. But even as he spoke, he heard the single sound of her sweet voice. He urged them all to hurry.

When they were finally on the gym floor for the pre-game practice, Whistle moved like a diving gull, as though an idea of his body had become dependent upon it. His teammates sensed the urgency of Whistle's motion, and believing he was being driven only by the thought of Bernstein, their own movements became gracelessly self-conscious. The kids and girls and men of the neighborhood who had come to watch talked in low voices, looking from one end of the court to the other, from Bernstein to Whistle But Whistle, even up to the moment when the ball was about to go into the air between the two centers, and Bernstein crouched beside him, thought only that she was watching, that her eyes—with the brows arched curiously—were on him. And a second later, when he moved quickly and the ball was in his hands, he thought of nothing when the ball went through the basket. He indistinctly heard the clamor that rose up from the shot he had made, feeling now only the tremendous uncoiling inside him, as though a wall of air had finally burst from his throat. A moment later when he was under and then past the basket and had scored again, his temples beat with the image of his body that had twisted itself between two men, had gone beneath an outstretched hand and angled the ball against the backboard, all in the motion of an instant. He had no thought that he had twice within a minute's time outmaneuvered Bernstein.

So lost was he in the sensation of his running that he could not say when Bernstein first moved in on him, to be no more than six inches away, no matter where Whistle turned or how fast he ran, to stay there continuously as long as Whistle or his team had the ball, hawking him that way with his adolescent face, his eyes bulging, his mouth open, but with no sweat on his body. He did not even know at first that it was Bernstein who had begun to cling to him, and did not know until he had spent the deliberate effort of minutes in trying to shake him off—who would not be shaken—that the stalking figure always inches away was the Bernstein who'd been spoken of so much, who was the high school star, who had the pop-eyes and open mouth and no sweat and who was to be the way of measuring him. It was against this recognition that Whistle made—when he next got his hands on the ball—his first desperate effort to overcome the kid who was taking him. With a violent wrench of his body that feigned movement in a direction he did not go, Whistle got a foot ahead of Bernstein and drove toward the basket. He left his feet, raising the ball for the shot, and then saw, too late, the blur of the hand that came over his shoulder without touching him to hit the ball cleanly from his grasp. Whistle knew without turning it had been Bernstein's hand. He ran wildly to retrieve the ball he had lost, his body colliding against others. When the foul was called against him, and Bernstein, unperturbed, went to the line and quickly made his throw, Whistle began, for the first time, to think not in the images he always made, but of himself against Bernstein; began to think in advance even of what movements he might make with the other hounding him so. With his mind working feverishly as he ran, Whistle lost possession of his game. When he began himself to sense the loss, his thoughts went past Bernstein, went to Alice who was watching him from somewhere in the crowd. Then Bernstein, almost from the center of the court, soon after the foul, lofted a long set-shot that he turned his back on even before he could see it drop cleanly through the basket. Whistle felt an unfamiliar panic as he ran. He even looked for a second toward the crowd, trying to find Alice where he could not see one face in the blur that was before his eyes.

During the time-out that Artie called, Whistle could hear the words, but he did not listen to what the others said to him. He stared across the floor to where Bernstein stood among his teammates, nonchalant, unsweating, listening and talking. Whistle could see now that Bernstein was not even tall, that he was comically thin, with a sunken chest and no spread at all to his shoulders. Bernstein put a finger to his side and scratched slowly, and Whistle—his eyes hot with anger—thought he would like to drive his fist through the ribs where Bernstein's fingers picked indifferently. When they began to play again, Bernstein started to move as he had not before. Something close to fright tore at Whistle as he tried to keep up with him, to try sometimes even to find him. And always, when Whistle had the ball himself, Bernstein was on him, never touching him, but never more than six inches away, his face thrust out to Whistle's so that Whistle saw, whenever he turned, the popped eyes, the open mouth, the dry skin. Whenever he could get close enough to raise his hands for the shot, there was the other hand raised to the same height, blocking or worrying the ball. Whistle swore at himself for his clumsiness, angry with the body that would not move as he wanted it.

At half-time, on the way to the lockers, moving through the crowd, he passed next to Alice, suddenly, unexpectedly. He lowered his head. He was grateful she had not seen him, that she was talking with Sonny who kept score for them and did not play. But when he moved on and heard the brittle pitch of her laughter come after him, he felt anew the weight that had fallen on his heart since the first moment after work.

In the locker room, Whistle sulked and the others left him to himself. He ran his hands nervously over his knees, and the legs felt insensitive to the touch. He began to think then that he was ill, or having a bad night, and then began to believe that, and believed too—as he remembered the two quick baskets he'd made at the beginning of the game—that it might be only a bad stretch. The name Bernstein came to him from all parts of the room, the words "great" and "what a ballplayer" and "what can you do with him," so that Whistle blurted out, "I'm on to the sonofabitch now. I'll get him this half." He spoke so hurriedly and with so little expectation from the others, that they could not understand the words. But they took from the tone what he had meant, and when they ran from the locker room to the gym, they called encouragements to each other.

A minute after play had started again, Whistle was in the corner of the court, and there was a ball loose in the air under the backboard. He angled in quickly toward the ball, feeling the oppressive weight fall out of him as his feet came off the ground with his leap, his hand outstretched under the ball he was about to seize. And then it was not there and his fingers clutched against the empty space. When he turned his head the thin, no-shouldered, unsweating Bernstein was dribbling quickly downcourt. Whistle felt the air go out of him—as though from a blow—then ran wildly after Bernstein, finally leaving his feet in a desperate lunge for the ball. He came down with a thud against the hard floor. He could feel his fingers claw against the smooth, hot wood. Even in the sudden darkness before his eyes, he knew that he was rolling, felt the joints of his knee and elbow grate against the hardness. Then he knew he was on his feet again and trying to run, but Dox had him by the arms, shouting, "Take it easy, Whistle. Take it easy." They called a foul and Whistle watched Bernstein calmly make it good, watched him while he felt his legs trembling and the blood running from his knee. But he would not leave the game and he was glad about the blood. He began looking once more to the sidelines. He ran wildly after that, not even knowing that Bernstein had begun to ease off, and he fouled freely. He could not hear Dox telling him during the time-outs that it was only a game, that he would be in no shape for the party afterwards, that Alice would get sore.

When they were undressing after the game, Whistle did not know by what score they had lost, nor did he try to think of how many points Bernstein scored and how many he made himself. He started to complain about his knee, and Dox said he would drive him home. But Whistle said no and Dox assumed he would go to the party and went with Flip to find the girls. But Whistle got out of the room later and left the building. He stood for a moment on the corner in the snow that was still falling and saw Bernstein throw the snowball and heard the laughter as they ran away. He started to walk home, not knowing now why he had left. He knew he must have played better than any of the others. Certainly better than Flip. The crowd had clapped when he stayed in the game with the bloody knee. It hurt him now. It hurt a lot. He should get home and clean it out. He wondered if the blood might be staining the snow, but he did not look to see.

He did not go to work the next day, or the day after, then finally quit, telling Dox to say he'd torn the ligament in his knee and the doctor had said to lay off. He learned that Sonny had taken Alice to the party. He could not believe and tried not to care when they told him Sonny had made out.

It was hard to be with the fellows afterwards. No one spoke of Alice to him. He did not want them to talk of her, though it made him uncomfortable to have them say nothing. But they all talked to him of Bernstein. He'd gone on to college and was the leading scorer on the freshman team. He had scored less against Whistle than he did against some college players. They told Whistle this often, but they could not make him care. He tried never to think again of Bernstein. He tried not to think at all about that night. And sometimes, most often at night, late and in bed, he'd shut his eyes tight when he heard the brittle, metallic, "Here, Whistle. Here, Whistle." He continued to play at the community center, but the club team had broken up and none of the fellows was there. Flip had bought a car and Artie had married. They had parties almost every Saturday night in Dox's basement.

When Whistle's mother some months later insisted they move closer to her relatives, she had—against Whistle's indifference—to abandon unused the many arguments she had prepared.

The three hours are over quickly for Whistle, and only while he takes off the sweated suit in the locker room does he begin to feel the punishment of his body. But under the needling spray of the shower, the fatigue leaves him, and he knows only the pleasant splash of the cool water. He thinks of nothing as the shower breaks against the nape of his neck and, clinging, wets the length of his back. He takes no part in the horseplay, but the others are not angry at his aloofness. They think of Whistle as older and funny, but they never accuse him of playing hero.

Always, after the shower, the close night air of the city lingers on his face with a fragrance it does not really own. When a high breeze slants occasionally from the bay through the rows of houses, Whistle is glad he does not bring the car on the nights he plays. He walks the half mile to home in a measured, predictable stride, and there is an inexpressible assertion for him in the small weight of the traveling bag he carries. He has a choice of streets, but he walks along the busiest one, though he pays no heed to the night-noises. The exhaust from a bus, the shouting from a window, a distant, muffled knock are provoking sounds, but Whistle is not trapped in their loneliness. He is conscious only of a fine freedom released inside him, of a restored balance in his body. Occasionally a group gathered idly on a corner will begin to suggest things, but only vaguely, and the impressions are already abandoned by the time he crosses the street. Even on other days, it is hard for Whistle to think back in any specific way. The few fellows that haven't married go their ways, and months pass before Whistle will bother to look up any of them. Even on the Mondays that he drives his mother to the doctor, he prefers to sit in the car and wait for her, looking absently out the window, stirred only by the annoyance of having the night at the gym taken away from him.

When Whistle gets home his mother is already asleep. He takes one of the picture magazines that always lie about the kitchen and goes into his room. Undressed, in bed, by the dim light that hangs from the ceiling, he scans the pages, unmindful really of what he sees. When he puts the magazine away and flicks the light switch, he smokes a cigarette. The taste of it sharpens his ease. In the bright glow of the cigarette's end, there is a hypnotic focus for his sleep. Whistle's mind begins to make pictures. He thinks ahead to the weekend and the possibility of driving to Scranton once more, or maybe this time to Fall River. Since he has bought the car, he toys frequently with these trips, but he does not often go. For he always, afterwards, hates the clumsy, unuseable violence he feels toward the women.

When he feels the heat of the cigarette on his fingers, he drops it, still lit, into the ash-tray on the night table. His mind lingers on the impressions of shots he has made that night, of rebounds he has grabbed by angling in that way from the corner of the court. He thinks of Scranton again, and then of the next night that he will play. The poise—so fine before in his enervated body—begins now to crack. Whistle feels once more the dangerous soaring of his anticipations as he waits for sleep.

Last Shot

Jon Veinberg

Before the game
Farnsworth had said
his heart felt on fire
and inside the heart
was trapped a small dark
horse kicking out
at the bolted door
of his body. Whether
he scored 33 or 34
no one seems to remember
but as for me there's
not enough beer and bean dip
in this county to save me
should the world erase
that clean pick and roll
in double-overtime and how
that orange globe of sun
rose from his fingers that night
to mount its peak three rims
above a landscape of smoke
and balded heads, swayed
and suspended itself
for what seemed a comet's lifetime,
until it finally left its arc
and descended as a ball on fire
travelling through a serene
and perfect net.
It was the first
and only time some of us

cried out in joy so openly
and in public and he pumped
his fists toward and through
the rafters so grandly
that with my own eyes I saw
the glow his body took
until it too ignited into flame
and out of his chest exploded
a herd of wild dark horses
galloping so fast
they left permanent shadows
on the blurred faces
of all those who applauded him.

A Poem for "Magic"

Quincy Troupe

for Earvin "Magic" Johnson, Donnell Reid,
& Richard Franklin

take it to the hoop, "magic" johnson
take the ball dazzling down the open lane
herk & jerk & raise your six foot nine inch
frame into air sweating screams of your neon name
"magic" johnson, nicknamed "windex" way back in high school
'cause you wiped glass backboards so clean
where you first juked & shook
& wiled your way to glory
a new styled fusion of shake & bake energy
using everything possible you created your own space
to fly through—any moment now we expect your wings
to spread feathers for that spooky take-off of yours
then shake & glide till you hammer home
a clotheslining deuce off glass
now, come back down in a reverse hoodoo gem
off the spin, & stick it in sweet popping nets
clean from twenty feet right side

put the ball on the floor, "magic"
slide the dribble behind your back, ease it deftly
between your bony stork legs, head bobbing everwhichaway
up & down, you see everything on the court, off the high
yoyo patter, stop & go dribble, you shoot
a threading needle rope pass sweet home to kareem
cutting through the lane, his skyhook pops the cords
now lead the fastbreak, hit jamaal on the fly
now blindside a behind the back pinpointpass for two more

off the fake, looking the other way
you raise off balance into tense space
sweating chants of your name, turn 360 degrees
on the move your legs scissoring space like a swimmer's
yoyoing motion in deep water, stretching out now
towards free flight, you double pump through human trees
hang in place, slip the ball into your left hand
then deal it like a las vegas card dealer off squared glass
into nets living up to your singular nickname, so 'bad'
you cartwheel the crowd towards frenzy
wearing now your electric smile, neon as your name

in victory we suddenly sense your glorious uplift
your urgent need to be champion
& so we cheer, rejoicing with you for this quicksilver, quicksilver,
    quicksilver
moment of fame, so put the ball on the floor again, "magic"
juke & dazzle, shaking & baking down the lane
take the sucker to the hoop, "magic" johnson
recreate reverse hoodoo gems off the spin
deal alley-oop-dunk-a-thon-magician passes, now
double-pump, scissor, vamp through space, hang in place
& put it all in the sucker's face, "magic" johnson
& deal the roundball like the juju man that you am
like the sho-nuff shaman man that you am
"magic," like the shonuff spaceman you am

From Downtown at the Buzzer
George Alec Effinger

There are a couple of things my mother will never get to experience.

I mean, there are more than a couple, of course, but there are two things that I think of immediately. First off, my mother won't ever know what it's like to see twelve space creatures in blue suits and masks staring at you while you eat breakfast and wash walls and go to the bathroom. That I know. That I can talk about. My mother can't, and just as well, I guess. But believe me, I can.

The other thing is, my mother will never, *ever* know the incredible joy you get, this feeling of complete, instant gratification, when you jump into the air, twist around, and send a basketball in an absolutely perfect arc into the net maybe twenty-three feet sway. You have somebody from the other team leaping up with you, his hand right in your face, but sometimes you have God on your side and nothing in the universe can keep that ball from going through that hoop. You sense it sometimes, you can feel it even before you let go of the ball, while you're still floating. Then it's just the smallest flick of the wrist, your fingertips just brushing the ball away, perfect, perfect, perfect, you don't even have to look. You land on the hardwood floor with this terrific smile on your face, and the guy who had his hand up to block you is muttering to himself, and you're talking to yourself, too, as you run downcourt to the other end. You're happy. My mother will never know that kind of happy.

Not that I do, either, very often.

Now, this newspaper is paying me a lot of money for this exclusive story, so I figure I ought to give them what they paid for. But other magazines have paid others for their exclusive stories, and they might tell stories a little different from mine. That's because no one else in the security installation knew the Cobae so well as I did.

I'll start about a year ago, about a month before I saw my first Coba. I was a captain then, attached to Colonel James McNeill. Colonel McNeill was the commanding officer of the entire compound, and because of that I was given access to a lot of things that I really shouldn't have seen. But I saw those things, and I read the Colonel's reports, and, well, I guess that I can put two and two together as well as anybody. So from all of that, there wasn't much happening around the compound that I didn't know about.

The installation was in the middle of an awful lot of nothing, in one of the smaller parishes in southwestern Louisiana. St. Didier Parish. There was one town kind of large, Linhart, with maybe six thousand people, three movie theaters, a lot of bars. That was it for the whole parish, just about. South of us were towns full of Cajuns who trapped muskrat and nutria, or worked in the cane fields, or worked in the rice fields, or on shrimp boats or offshore oil rigs, or netted crabs. They spoke a kind of strange mixture of English and a French no Parisian ever heard. All around us, and farther north, there were only farms. We were tucked away in an isolated part of the parish, with only a small dirt road leading to the one main north-south route. No one on the base had anything to do with the Cajuns; come furlough time or weekend passes, it made more sense to go to New Orleans, an hour and a half, maybe two hours east of us.

We didn't have a lot to look at except fields on the other side of the wire fence. It was summer nine months of the year. The base was landscaped with a large variety of local plants, some of which I don't even know the names of. Everything flowered, and there was something blooming almost every month of the year. It was kind of nice. I liked the job.

I liked it a lot, until the Cobae showed up.

Before that, though, I wasn't exactly sure why we were there. We were a top-security installation, doing just about nothing. I was kept busy enough with day-to-day maintenance and routines. I had been trans-

ferred down from Dayton, Ohio, and it never occurred to me to ask
Colonel McNeill what the hell we were supposed to be doing, surrounded by a lot of yam fields, between the marshes on the west and
the swamps on the east. I mean, it just never came up. I had learned a
long time ago that if I did just what I was told to do, and did it right,
then everything, absolutely everything, would be fine. That kind of life
was very pleasant and satisfying. Everything was laid out for me, and I
just took it all in order, doing task one, doing task two, doing task
three. The day ended, I had free time, at regular intervals I was paid.
The base had plenty of leisure facilities. It was all just great for me.

Of course, I was a captain.

My main outlet during my leisure was playing basketball. There were
very good gym facilities on the base, and I've always been the competitive type, at least in situations where winning and losing didn't have
much of a permanent effect on my life. I enjoy target shooting, for
example, because there is no element of luck involved. It's just you, the
rifle, and the target. But if you put me down in a hot spot, with people
shooting back, I do believe all the fun would go right out of it.

Forget it. There were always a few other people on the base, not
always male, who liked to get into the pick-up games. Every once in a
while someone would show up, someone I hadn't seen on the court for
weeks. Mostly, however, there were the same regulars. Tuesday and
Thursday evenings, those were the big basketball games. Those were the
games that even I couldn't get into, on occasion. They were what you'd
call blood games. I enjoyed watching them almost as much as I liked
playing in them. Maybe I should have been watching a little closer.

All right, it was in the middle of August, and the temperature outside
was in the low nineties, all the time. Every day. *All* the time. And the
humidity matched the temperature, figure for figure. So we just stayed in
the air-conditioned buildings and sent the enlisted men outside to take
care of running errands. It takes a while to get adjusted, you know, from
mild Ohio weather to high summer in subtropical Louisiana. I wasn't

altogether adjusted to it. I liked my office, and I liked my air-conditioned car, and I liked my air-conditioned quarters. But there were little bits of not-air-conditioned in among those things that got to me and made me struggle to breathe. I didn't think I could hack it as an African explorer, if they still have them, or as visitor to other equatorial places where the only comforts are a hand-held fan and an occasional cool drink.

Terrific. You've got the background. That's the way things were and, like I say, I was all in favor of them just going on like that until I felt like dropping dead or something. But things didn't go on like that.

At the end of August a general showed up, trailing two colonels. They were in one long black car. In three long black cars behind the brass were the Cobae. I think it would be a good idea if I kind of went into detail about the Cobae and how we happened to get them dumped in our laps.

As I learned shortly after their arrival, the Cobae had appeared on Earth sometime in July. I forget the exact date. They were very cautious. Apparently they had remained in their ship in space, monitoring things, picking and choosing, making their inscrutable minds up about God only knows what. A paper that crossed Colonel McNeill's desk, a paper that I shouldn't have seen, said that one Coba appeared in the private apartment of the President. How he got there is still a mystery. An awful lot about the Coba is still a mystery. Anyway, I suppose the President and his wife were a little startled. Ha. Sometimes on silent nights I like to imagine that scene. Depending on my mood, the scene can be very comic or very dramatic. Depending on my mood of the moment, and also what the President and his wife were doing, and how genuinely diplomatic and resilient the President was.

After all, remember that the President is just a guy, too, and he's probably not crazy about strangers materializing in his bedroom. He's probably even less crazy about short, squat, really ugly creatures in his bedroom. Picture the scene for yourself. Take a few seconds, I'll wait. See?

Well, the President called for whomever he usually calls for, and there was a very frantic meeting in which nothing intelligent at all was said. There weren't contingency plans for this sort of thing. It's not often that the President of the United States has to wing it in a crisis situation. And this *was* a crisis situation, even though the Coba hadn't said a word, moved a muscle, or even blinked, so far as anyone could determine.

Okay, imagine everyone dressed and formal and a little calmed down now, thanks to things like Valium and Librium and Jack Daniel's. Now we have a President and his advisors. *They* have a creature in a blue, shiny uniform and a mask over his face. It wasn't exactly a helmet. It covered what we call the Coba's nose and mouth, by liberal interpretation. There was a flexible hose from the mask to a small box on the chest. The President doesn't have the faintest idea what to do. Neither does the Secretary of State, who gets the job tossed to him because it seems like his department. The potato gets tossed back and around for a while. The Coba still hasn't done a doggone thing. As a matter of fact, no one yet has gotten around to addressing the creature (I think here I will stop calling them creatures).

Fifteen minutes after our world's first contact with intelligent life beyond our planet, someone has the bright idea to bring a scientist in.

"Who?" asked the President.

"I don't know," said the Secretary of State.

"What kind of scientist?" asked one of the advisors. "An astronomer? An ethnologist? A linguist? A sociologist? An anthropologist?"

"Call 'em all," said the President, with the kind of quick thinking that has endeared him to some of us.

"Call who all?" asked the advisor.

The President, by this time, was getting a little edgy. He was ready to start raising his voice, a sure sign that he was frustrated and angry. Before that, however, he chose to ask one final, well-modulated question. "There must be one person out of the millions of people in this damn country to call," he said. "Someone best suited to handling this. Who is it?"

There was only silence.

After a while, as the President's face fumed a little redder, one of the advisors coughed a little and spoke up. "Uh," he said, "why don't we hide this joker away somewhere. You know, somewhere really secure. Then we assemble a high-power team of specialists, and they can go on from there. How's that?"

"Wonderful," said the President, with the kind of irony that has endeared him to a few of us. "What do you think the joker will do when we try to hide him away somewhere?"

"Ask him," said the Secretary of State.

Again there was silence. This time, though, everyone looked toward the President. It was a head of state meeting an important emissary kind of thing, so it was his potato after all. You can bet he didn't like it.

Finally the President said, "He speaks English?" No one answered. After a while the Secretary of State spoke up again.

"Ask him," said the S. of S.

"An historic occasion," murmured the President. He faced the Coba. He took a closer look and shuddered. That was the reaction we all had until we got used to their appearance. After all, the President is just a guy, too. But a well-trained guy.

"Do you speak English?" asked the President.

"Yes," said the Coba. That brought another round of silence.

After a time the Secretary of State said, "You've heard this discussion, then. Have you understood it?"

"Yes," said the Coba.

"Would you object to the plan, then?" asked the Secretary. "Would you agree to being questioned by a team of our scientists, in a confidential manner?"

"No," said the Coba, in answer to the Secretary's first question, and "Yes," to the Secretary's second.

The President took a deep breath. "Thank you," he said. "You can understand our perplexity here, and our need for discretion in the whole matter. May I ask where you are from?"

"Yes," said the Coba.

Silence.

"Where are you from?" asked the Secretary of State.

Silence.

"Are you from our, uh, what you call, our solar system?" asked the

President.

"No," said the Coba.

"From some other star, then?" asked an emboldened advisor.

"Yes," said the Coba.

"Which star?" asked the advisor.

Silence.

It was several minutes later that the assembled group began to realize that the Coba was only going to answer yes-no questions. "Great," said the President. "It'll only take years to get any information that way."

"Don't worry," said an advisor. "If we pick the right people, they'll have the right questions,"

"Pick them, then," said the President.

"We'll get to work on it," said another advisor.

"Right now," said the President.

"Check."

"What do we do with it in the meantime?" asked the Secretary of Defense.

"I don't know," said the President, throwing up his hands. "Put him or her or it in the Lincoln Bedroom. Make sure there are towels. Now get out of here and let me go to sleep."

"Thank you, Mr. President," said an advisor. The President just shook his head wearily.

I learned all of this from one of the advisors present at the time. This guy is now appealing a court decision that could send him to prison for five years, because of some minor thing he had done a long time ago, and which none of us understand. He's also writing a book about the Cobae affair.

I wonder how well the President slept that night.

The next morning when they came to get the Coba, someone knocked on the door (come to think of it, what made them think that a Coba would know what knocking on a door meant?). There was no response. The aide, one of the more courageous people in the history of our nation, sweated a little, fiddled around a little, knocked again, sweated some more, and opened the door.

Twelve Cobae stood like statues in the room. The aide shut the door and went screaming through the halls of the Executive Mansion.

Later, when the advisors questioned the twelve Cobae, they discovered that only one would reply, and only with yes or no answers. It was assumed that this Coba was the original Coba who had appeared in the President's bedroom the evening before. There really was no logical basis on which to make this assumption, but it was made nevertheless. No one ever got around to asking the simple question that would have decided the matter; no one thought the matter was important enough to decide.

You know what the strange thing about the twelve Cobae was? You probably do. The strange thing about them was that they all looked the same. I mean, *identical*. Not the way that you say all of some ethnic group look the same. I mean that if you photographed the twelve Cobae individually, you could superimpose the pictures by projecting them on a screen, and there wouldn't be the smallest difference among them.

"Clones," said one knowledgeable man. "All grown from the same original donor."

"No," said another expert. "Even if that were the case, they would have developed differently after the cloning. There would be some minor differences."

"A very recent cloning," insisted the first.

"You don't know what you're talking about," said the second. "You're crazy." This typified the kind of discussion that the Cobae instigated among our best minds at the time.

When the Cobae had been around for a day or two, the President signed the orders creating the top-security base in St. Didier Parish, Louisiana. I was shipped down, everyone else on the base was brought in, and for a little while we worked in relative comfort and ignorance. Then the day came when the general and his colonels arrived, with the twelve Cobae right behind. The four black cars drove straight to a barracks that had been in disuse since the installation was opened. The Cobae were put in there, each in its (I get confused about the pronouns) own room. Colonel McNeill was present, and so was I. I thought I was going to throw up. That passed, but not quickly enough. Not nearly.

The general spoke with Colonel McNeill. I couldn't understand their conversation, because it was mostly whispers and nods. One of the colonels asked me if the Cobae would be comfortable in their quarters. I said, "How should I know? Sir."

The general overheard us. He looked at the Cobae. "Will you be comfortable here?" he asked.

"Yes," said the Coba who did all the answering.

"Is there anything you'd like now?" asked the general.

"No," said the Coba.

"If at any time you wish anything, anything at all," said the general, "just pick up this telephone." The general demonstrated by picking up the receiver. He neglected to consider that the Cobae would have a difficult time making their wants known, limited to two words, yes and no.

A tough guard was put on the building. The general and the two colonels beat it back to their car and disappeared from the base. I looked at Colonel McNeill, and he looked at me. Neither of us had anything to say. None of this had been discussed with us beforehand, because the matter was so secret it couldn't be trusted either on paper or over normal communications channels. No codes, no scrambling, nothing could be trusted. So the general plopped the twelve Cobae on our doorstep, told us to hang tight, that scientists would arrive shortly to study the beings, and that we were doing a wonderful job.

It was a Thursday, I recall. After we left the building housing the Cobae, I went to the gym building and changed clothes. It was basketball night, Cobae or no Cobae.

I remember once, not long after the Cobae came to Louisiana, when Colonel McNeill asked me to show the aliens around. I said all right. I had gotten over my initial reaction to the Cobae. So had the men on the base. They were used to seeing the Cobae all over the installation. As a matter of fact, we became *too* used to seeing them. I'd be doing something like picking a red Jell-O over a green in the mess line, and there would be a Coba looking over my shoulder. I'd take a shower after a basketball game, and when I walked out of the shower room a Coba would be standing there, watching silently while I dried myself off with a towel. We didn't like it exactly, but we got used to it. Still, it was spooky the way they appeared and disappeared. I never saw one pop in or pop out, yet they did it, I guess.

From the arrival of the Cobae, our base became really supersecure. No passes, no furloughs, no letters out, no telephones. I suppose we all understand, but none of us like it, from Colonel McNeill down to the lower enlisted men. We were told that the country and the world were slowly being prepared to accept the news of a visitation by aliens from space. I followed the careful, steady progression of media releases, prepared in Washington. It was a fairly good job, I suppose, because when the first pictures and television news films of the Cobae were made available, there was little uproar and no general panic. There was a great deal of curiosity, some of it still unsatisfied.

I was starting to tell about this particular time when I was giving a guided tour to the Cobae. I showed them all the wonderful and impressive things about the base, like the high chain link fence with electrified barbed wire on top, and the tall sentry towers with their machine gun emplacements, and the guards at the main gate and their armaments, and the enlisted men going about their duties, cleaning weapons, drilling in the heat, double-timing from place to place. If I had been a Coba, I think I might have written off Earth right then and there. Back to the ship or whatever, back into the sky, back to the home world.

The twelve Cobae, however, showed no sign of interest or emotion. They showed nothing. You've never seen such nothing. And all the time only the one Coba would speak, and then only when asked a question to which he could reply with either of his two words. He understood everything, of course, but for some reason, for some crazy Coba reason, he wouldn't use the words he understood in his answers.

I took the aliens through the gym building. I got one of the more startling surprises of my life. A game was going on; ten men were playing basketball, full court. It wasn't as rough as a Tuesday/Thursday game, but it was still plenty physical under the boards. I mentioned casually that this was one of the favorite ways of spending off-duty time. The Cobae stood, immobile, and watched. I began to move ahead, ushering them along. They would not move. I had to stay with the Cobae. I didn't see what interested them so much. I sighed. At that time, no one had any idea what a Coba wanted or thought. I say that as if we do now. That just isn't so, even today, though we're closer to an understanding. I had no way of knowing then that the basketball game would be the link between us and these travelers through space.

Anyhow, I was stuck with the Cobae until the game ended. After that, when the players had gone to the showers, I asked if the Cobae wished to see more of the compound. The answerer said, "Yes." I showed them around some more. Nothing else was interesting to them, I guess, because they just passed in front of everything, their expression blank behind their masks. They never stopped again like they had at the basketball court.

Something about the game fascinated the Cobae. Of course, we've all tried to understand just what. People who in saner days wouldn't be caught dead inside a fieldhouse spent months analyzing basketball like it was a lost ancient art form. The rules of the game have changed a little since its beginning almost a hundred years ago, but the style of play has altered more considerably.

There are different sets of rules, though. You have professional basketball, college ball, high school ball. Minor variations among the different kinds of basketball exist to suit the game to the various levels of competition. Professional, college, high school.

And then you have playground basketball. When basketball was first invented, and during its first few decades of existence, all the players were white. In the professional leagues, this continued longer than on the lower levels. Why? Because of the same reasons that everything else remained white until the black athlete shouldered his way into a kind of competitive position.

For basketball, it was one of the greatest things to happen to the sport.

The great pro players were white in the early years. Once blacks were allowed to play against them, the blacks began dominating the game. Bill Russell, Wilt Chamberlain, Kareem Abdul-Jabbar, Julius Erving, and plenty of others have caused a reappraisal of the old strategies.

Why have blacks taken over professional basketball almost entirely? I have a theory. Sure. But it's full of generalizations, and they're as valid as most generalizations. Sort of, you know. Pretty valid, kind of.

Where do these black ballplayers come from? From ghetto neighborhoods, from poor urban and rural communities. Not without exception, of course, but it's a good enough answer. In a ghetto neighborhood, say in New York, there just isn't physical space for baseball diamonds and football fields. There are basketball courts all over, though. They can fit into a smaller space. You can see a basketball rim attached to the side of a building, with groups of kids stuffing the ball into it, again and again.

Take white players. A lot of them come from better backgrounds. A white kid growing up in a town or suburb has a basketball hoop mounted on the garage. He plays by himself, or with a couple of friends.

On the ghetto playgrounds, basketball can be a vicious demonstration of one's identity. Six, eight black guys beneath a basketball backboard can turn the game into something almost indistinguishable from a gang war. Meanwhile the white kids are tossing the ball and catching the rebounds and tossing the ball. The black kids are using every move, every clever head fake, every deceiving twist of the body to show off their superiority. It's the only way many black youths have of asserting themselves.

One good way out of the slums is through sports. Mostly, that means basketball. The kind of basketball you learn on a ghetto court is unlike any other variety of the sport. It's the kind of ball we played on the base. I was out of my class, and I knew it. But I could play well enough so that I wasn't laughed off the floor.

The Tuesday/Thursday games were playground games, played under playground rules. There were no referees to call fouls; there *were* no fouls. It used to be said that basketball was not a contact sport, like football. Yeah. Try playing an hour with guys who came out of Harlem in New

York, or Hough, in Cleveland, or Watts in Los Angeles. Those guys know just how much punishment they can deliver without being too obvious. Elbows and knees fly. You spend more time lying painfully on the floor than you do in the game. Playground moves, playground rules. Hard basketball. *Mean* basketball.

I played with black enlisted men, mostly. Teams were chosen the same way as on ghetto courts. The people who show up for the game take turns shooting the ball from the free throw line. The first five to put the ball into the net are one team. The next five are the second team. Everyone else watches. Afterward the watchers could go back to their quarters without limping. Few of the players could.

I played often because I practiced my free throws. In off-duty hours I sometimes went to the gym alone and shot free throws for a while. I was good at it. I could sink maybe eight out of ten shots, most of them swishes—when the basketball went cleanly through the hoop without hitting the backboard, without touching the metal rim. All that you would hear was a gentle snick as the net below the rim moved.

I was a good shooter. By myself, that is, without another player guarding me, waving his arms, pressing close, without the other players shouting and running. You don't get such an open shot very often during a game. Without fouls, there are no free throws. During a game I was lucky to score ten points.

The games were an hour long, no breaks. That's a lot of running up and down the court. Even the pros only play forty-eight minutes, resting some of those minutes on the bench, with plenty of time-outs called by the coaches, with breaks for halftime and fouls and free throws and television commercials. We played harder. We felt it. But on those rare occasions when I did something right, it was worth everything I had to take. It was worth it just to hear that *snick*.

There was an unwritten law; we left our ranks in the locker room. I wasn't a captain on the basketball floor. I was a white guy who wanted to play with the black enlisted men. Sometimes I did. After a while, when I showed that I could pretty well hold my own, they grudgingly accepted me, sort of, in a limited way, almost. They gave me a nick-name. They called me "the short honkey."

About September the group of scientists had arrived and began their work. It went slowly because only one of the Cobae could be inter-viewed, and he still said only yes or no.

"Do you come from this part of the galaxy?" asked one man.

"No," said the Coba.

"Do you come from this galaxy at all?"

"No."

The scientist was left speechless. Two thoughts struck him immedi-ately. The Cobae had come a very long way somehow; and it would be very difficult to learn where their home was. All the scientist could do was to run through a list of the identified galaxies until the Coba said yes. And the knowledge would be almost meaningless, because within that galaxy would be millions of stars, none of which could be pin-pointed from Earth. The interviewer gave up the attempt. To this day, we don't know exactly where the Cobae came from.

I had, of course, made a report about the reactions of the Cobae to my guided tour, several weeks earlier. One of the demographers thought that the interest the Cobae had shown in the basketball game was wor-thy of exploration. He proposed that the Cobae be allowed to watch another game.

The game the scientists chose was a Tuesday night bell-ringer. "Bell-ringer" because if you tried to grab the ball away from the strong, agile enlisted men, you got your bell rung. The Cobae were seated in an area out of bounds, along with a team of specialists watching their reactions. Of course, there weren't many reactions. There weren't any at all, while the enlisted men and I shot free throws for teams. I ended up on a pretty good team. I was set for a hard game. The first team, mine, had the ball at the start. I took the ball out of bounds and tossed it to Willy Watkins. He dribbled downcourt and passed the ball to Hilton Foster. Foster was tall and quick. His opponent stretched out both arms, but Foster slithered beneath one arm, got around his opponent, jumped, and shot. The ball banked off the backboard and into the net. We were ahead, two to nothing.

The other team in-bounded and started to take the ball downcourt. I was running to cover my defensive territory, as loose and flexible as it was. We weren't pros. We just chose a man to cover and tried to keep him from scoring. There are lots of interesting ways of doing that, some of them even sanctioned by the rules.

Anyway, as the other team brought the ball down I saw an odd sight. Five of the Cobae had stood up and were walking out onto the basketball court. The scientists had risen out of their chairs. One man turned to the remaining seven Cobae and asked if the five wanted to play. There was silence. The speaker for the group was among the five.

"Do you want to join the game?" I asked the five. I couldn't tell which among them was the speaker.

"Yes," said one Coba. Behind the masks they all looked the same. I couldn't tell which Coba had answered.

"What do I do?" I asked one of the scientists.

"Ask them if they know the rules," said one.

"Do you know and understand how this game is played?" I asked.

"Yes," said the speaker.

I stood there for a while, bewildered.

"Aw, come on," said one of the black men. "Don't let those mothers screw up the game."

"They play," said one of the scientists. The blacks were obviously angry.

"All right," I said. assuming my captain's rank again. "My team against the Cobae. You other guys go sit down." The blacks who had been put out of the game were furious, but they followed my order. I heard a lot of language that the Cobae might not have understood. At least, I hope they didn't understand.

"*His* team. Huh," growled one of the men as he left the court.

"What we goin' to do with these blue bastards?" asked Foster.

"Play them loose," I said. "Maybe they just want to try it for a while.

Don't hit any of them."

"Just like my mama was playin'," said Bobby O. Brown.

"Yeah," I said. "Five blue monster mamas."

The scientists were busily talking into their recorders and videotaping what was happening. I gave the ball to Watkins. He took it out and tossed it in to me. I started dribbling, but there was a Coba guarding me. He played close. I glanced over at Watkins, who was running downcourt beside me. He had a Coba guard, too. The Cobae had started in a full-court press.

Where had they learned about a full-court press?

I passed over my Coba's head to Foster. A Coba nearly intercepted the ball. Foster put a good move on his Coba guard, twisted around, and spun back in the other direction. It would have worked against me and a lot of the others on the floor, but he ran into another Coba, who had anticipated Foster's move Foster hit the Coba hard, but he kept dribbling. The Coba reached out and swiped the ball away from Foster. "Goddamn it," said Foster.

The Coba threw a long pass to another alien downcourt. The second Coba was all alone, and made a nice layup for the first score of the game. The aliens were winning, two to nothing. I couldn't believe it.

The game went on for the entire hour. As it progressed, my team began to play harder and harder. We had to. The Cobae were quick, anticipating moves as if they had played basketball all their lives. Our shots were blocked or our men were prevented from getting near the basket, and we had to settle for long, low-percentage shots. The Cobae were playing with perfect teamwork, though. They had no difficulty finding one of their players open on offense. It didn't make any difference how we defensed them, one player was always maneuvering clear and the Coba with the ball always passed it to the open man (alien). After the first half hour, the Cobae were winning by a score of 48 to 20.

"Break," I called. "Take a rest." The black players walked off the court, muttering. All of them were glaring at me, at the aliens, at the scientists.

Monroe Parks passed near me. I could hear him say, "You can order me around all goddamn day, but don't mess with the game, you ofay son of a bitch." I said nothing.

I changed teams. The other men played the second half. I sat down and watched. The second half was about the same as the first. The Cobae were playing a tight game, perfect defense, amazing offense. They took no chances, but they were always in the right place. The final score was 106 to 52, in favor of the Cobae.

The scientists were just as confused as I was. I didn't care, though, right at the time. I went to the showers. The men showered, too, and none of us said a word. Not a sound. But there were some mean looks directed at me.

The following Thursday the five Cobae came to the gym for the game. The enlisted men started cursing loudly, and I had to order them to stop. Five black men played five Cobae. The Cobae won the game by 60 points.

The next Tuesday, the Cobae won by 48 points.

On Thursday, there wasn't a game, because only the Cobae and I showed up.

I wonder what would have happened if I had suggested to the speaker of the Cobae that I and two of his companions should play the remaining three Cobae.

Even though there were no more games with the Cobae, the scientific team that had come to study the aliens did not stop questioning me. It seemed to them that I was closer to the Cobae than anyone else on the base. I don't know. Against the Cobae, I averaged about 3 points a game. Maybe they should have talked to Foster, he got a pretty regular 10.

Colonel McNeill received regular reports from Washington about how the program to reveal the presence of the aliens on Earth was going. He showed me those reports. I read them, and I was at once amused and concerned Well, after all, maybe I did know the Cobae at least as well as anyone else, including the specialists who had assembled at our installation. The newspaper and television releases grew from hints and rumors to denials and finally a grudging, low-key statement that there were, in fact, a few intelligent visitors from another galaxy in seclusion somewhere in the United States.

The immediate response was not too violent, and the fellows in Washington did a good job regulating the subsequent reactions. The Soviet Union came forward with a claim that they, too, had visitors from beyond Earth. The ruler-for-life of an African nation tried to seize headlines with a related story that didn't make much sense to anyone, and I can't even remember exactly what he said. One of the scientists asked the Cobae if there were any more of them on Earth, in addition to the twelve in our compound. The speaker said no. So if the Soviet Union had their own aliens they were from somewhere else, and we never saw them in any case.

The Cobae showed a preference for remaining in their quarters, once it became evident that the basketball games were postponed indefinitely (read, "as long as the Cobae were around"). The researchers put their data together, argued, discussed, shouted, cursed, and generally behaved like children. Colonel McNeill and I ignored it all from that point on, because we still had a security installation to run. The scientists and researchers were doing their best to bend our regulations whenever it was comfortable for them to try. The colonel and I came down hard on them. I guess they didn't understand us, and we didn't understand them.

So which group of us was better qualified to understand the Cobae?

Nobody, that's who. Finally, though, about the middle of October the nominal head of the investigating team called a meeting, to which Colonel McNeill was invited. I came along, because I was indispensable or something. The meeting began as a series of reports, one by every single professor and investigator in the camp. I can't recall another time when I was so bored. Somehow they managed to make something as awesome as creatures from another world boring. It takes a good deal of skill, many years of training, constant practice, much self-denial to do a job that huge. But boring it was. The colonel was fidgeting before the first man had gone through half of his graphs. He had plotted something against something else, and I wonder where the guy got the information. He had a nice bunch of graphs, though, very impressive, very authoritative-looking. He spoke clearly, he enunciated very well, he was neatly dressed and well-groomed, and he rarely had to refer to his notes. Still, I was ready to scream myself before he finished. I don't remember a thing he was trying to say. In the weeks that he had to study the Cobae, he apparently didn't come across a single, solitary interesting fact.

Maybe that wasn't his department. I told myself. So I waited for the second researcher. He, too, had plenty of visual aids. He took a pointer and showed how his red line moved steadily down, while his blue line made a bell-shaped curve. I waited, but he was every bit as lacking in information as his predecessor.

That's the way that it went for most of the afternoon. I think that if I had been put in charge of those statisticians and, uh, alienographers, I might have done a better job. I might be fooling myself, of course, but I think I would have tried to learn why the Cobae had come to Earth in the first place. No one could give us a clue about that. Even with yes-and-no answers they should have been able to do that. Am I getting warm? Yes. No. Am I getting cold?

I think the idea is to start big and narrow down until you have the Cobae cornered, in an intellectual sense. Ask them if they came to Earth for a definite purpose. Yes or no. If the Coba answered no, well, they're all on vacation. If it said yes, start big again and whittle away until you learn something.

But evidently that's not the way our men and women of the study team worked. A large report was published eventually, excerpts appeared in newspapers and magazines, but not many people were satisfied. I'd still like to take my crack at the Cobae, my way. But I can't.

So, in any event, investigator after researcher after pedant after lecturer had his say. I got up after half an hour and went to the back of the room, where two enlisted men were setting up a film projector. Both men were black. One was a regular basketball player I knew, Kennedy Turner, and the other's I name I don't recall. I watched them threading the film; it was only slightly less boring than listening to the presentations. I noticed that right beside me was Colonel McNeill. He, too, was watching Turner thread film. After the film was wound into the machine, the two men turned to a slide projector.

"You want to kill the lights, please?" said the woman on the platform. Turner hastened to turn off the lights. "Roll that first reel, please," said the woman. The other enlisted man flicked a switch. I watched a few seconds of a basketball game. I saw myself embarrassed by the play of a short alien. "It seems to me, gentlemen," said the woman, "that these Cobae are governed by a single mind. I don't know how I can make the idea clearer. Perhaps the mind belongs to the Coba who always answers. But the visual input, *all* the sensory input, of the twelve Cobae is correlated and examined by the central mind. That was what made the Cobae so effective in this game, although we know through our questioning that they had never seen anything similar before."

"A single governing mind?" asked a man seated in the audience.

"Yes," said the woman, "capable of overseeing everything that is happening to all twelve units of the Cobae multi-personality. The basketball game here is a perfect example. Watch. See how every human move is anticipated, even by Cobae players on the opposite side of the court. One mind is observing everything, hovering above, so to speak, and decisions and commands are addressed to the individual Cobae to deal with any eventuality."

(I'm editing this from memory, of course. We didn't know they were called Cobae until much later. We just called them beings or creatures or aliens or blue men or something like that.)

"I'd like to ask a question, if I may—"

The man was interrupted by the lights going on again.

"Not yet, please," said the woman. She stopped speaking and gasped.

Everyone turned around. The twelve Cobae were in the back of the room.

The Coba speaker stepped forward. "Now you honkey chumps better dig what's going down," he said. "We got to tighten up around here, we got to get down to it. You dig where I'm coming from?"

I looked at Turner and his black companion. They were laughing so hard they could barely stand. Turner held out his hands, palms up, and the other man slapped them. Turner slapped his friend's hands. They were suddenly having a real good time.

I turned to Colonel McNeill. Everyone in the room was speechless. There was a long pause. Then the colonel whispered to me. "Uh, oh." was all he said.

New World in the Morning

Norman German

Somewhere on the outskirts
of a Southeast Texas town
where you burn your neighbor's house
for revenge
and then your own for insurance money
to leave the county,
the Zen Buddhist basketball team
is preparing for its next game.

Friday night on the court,
at peace with themselves,
the fans, the refs, the other players,
they make their baskets every time
and never trip their opponents on fast breaks
or pull their shorts down on jump shots.

Flowing to the rival end of the court
they politely step aside as the Cobras'
star player drives for a layup and,
having nothing to fight for, misses.

Waiting underneath, docile as a doe,
Sardria Char opens his hands
like a baby bird's mouth, open in praise.
Avoiding the karma-disturbing thuds of a dribble,
he takes the ball and hands off to Krishna
who passes to Gandhi sitting cross-legged

and sleepy-eyed under the home town hoop.
The ball rises in a perfect silent curve.
Never touching the rim, it swishes through the net
like a good soul coming into being.

Tonight they subdue with serenity.
Next year they take the title.

Basketball in the Year 2020

Therese Becker

"People will be able to fly.
Everybody will be above the rim."
Magic Johnson

The net will be raised to match
our newfound level of seeing;
everyone will play
and no one will win
until everyone's won: sweat,
one heart, one court
the only trophies.

Michael Jordan
will be all that remains
of the old system—
what shriveled and multiplied
before the year (which no one
remembers exactly, yet everyone
refers to like morning),
when time belted out
an international anthem,
did her uppity strut
and announced she would
no longer pose as the enemy:
leaving us, at last, to judge
our own game.

No one, who was there,
who had eyes for it,
who had ever been a fan,

been bred for it, weaved
a life of watching from it,
wishing for the ball, just once,
will ever forget what followed
as referees, everywhere,
shed their stripes, now sleek, un-
bridled animals, they picked
up the ball, began dribbling
up the stairs,
through the locker rooms,
out of the stadiums, down
the first open road enveloped
in light, as if they held
the sun or the moon in their hands
and were caught in a sudden,
collective rapture; seized
in an apocalypse of joy.

For it was then that the great crowd
rose from the stands and all
who had paid homage to the sound
of their breath beating against the night,
who had counted
their pale days mounting
before them like small heaps
of Midas gold, immediately
began to remove from their bodies
all obedience without belief.

A lightness followed lifting them
like a chorus of bright birds
to where each could recall a life
of jump shots, rebounds, goal tending,

fouls, fast breaks, free throws,
injuries (serious and imagined),
penetrations straight to the net,
last-second, direct hits
from center court.

Lifting us into a conspiracy
of the heart, of time, of flight
designed forever to free these feet
(we have finally earned), opening
us to each other, the game, and why
we are playing; enabling
the embrace in each fall we rose from,
each night we returned, alone,
to practice in the gym.
It's worth it now as we see
ourselves here, together, and finally
winning the game everyone
thought was impossible.

Breathing on the Third Stroke
Pete Fromm

From the pool where he swam during his lunch hour, Stewart could see the jet fighters from the base drop down for their touch-and-gos. They came in low and straight, following the river, then disappeared into the trees for a moment before shooting back into blue sky, noisier than they were before. The fighters glinted in the sun and sometimes, if their bank was right, Stewart could see the helmeted heads in the cockpits.

He would watch the fighters while he stood at the pool's edge. Then he would dive and begin stroking through the unnaturally clear, cool water and he would not be able to see the fighters anymore. The trains, which followed the track alongside the pool's southern edge, were much bigger and he could see them easily while he swam. He could even hear them sometimes, or smell their thick diesel breath.

Stewart always thought of travelling when he swam. As soon as he dove, and his momentum carried him for a few precious yards through the cool silence, Stewart felt the release he imagined travel would bring. And even when he began to swim, watching the bubbles slice away from his hands, it seemed that nothing could be as easy and soothing as travel. But then he had to breathe and he would lift his head and look down the length of the pool and travel would no longer seem effortless.

By the time he swam three lengths the pain would start and he'd have to start breathing every two strokes, instead of three, and nothing seemed easy anymore. Usually the pain did not get bad and was gone by five lengths, when he would settle into the day's stretch. But whenever he thought of travel it was the idea of that first rough spot that kept him from leaving. He had no way of knowing if the pain would lessen after that, and he had long since passed that painful stretch in Great Falls. He was into the grind now, and it did not hurt much. But he did wonder, every time he watched the jets and then dove, if he wasn't meant to have more of that first little bit, where there was momentum and the initial strokes made him feel strong enough to reach anything.

With the sun, the water in tile pool was brilliant and very blue, much more so than was possibly real. The sun sparkled in his goggles when he turned his head and in the first two lengths Stewart thought leaving would be nothing. Recently, the smell of chlorine, anywhere he ran across it, made Stewart think of things that were not quite trustworthy.

After swimming, in the showers, Stewart would try to wash away the chlorine. But it seemed to smell even stronger in the shower and he thought of his wife in the clean, quiet hallways of the hospital where she worked.

Not that she was untrustworthy, not in the typical marital sense. But with the cold water drumming over his head and running down his naked body, Stewart thought he knew so little about his wife that he might well be ignorant of another man. He felt that was untrustworthy —that he could discover after three years of marriage that he knew so little about his wife.

Her name was Kathy and she had red hair—red the color of the darkest kind of maple leaves—that she braided and tied the braids around her head for work. For play she left the hair loose and she had skin like cream, that burned too easily in the sun. Somehow, even with that hair and that skin, she had avoided freckles, and Stewart was grateful for that. She had grown up in Chickasha, Oklahoma, but didn't talk like it. Her voice was low, nearly husky, and she had pretty, tapering fingers. She was long and thin, without much in the way of voluptuous curves. In Chickasha, and then in Great Falls, at the Catholic college, she had been something of a basketball star. There were trophies on the mantle at home.

She laughed, when she did, from the toes, and her eyes squinted nearly shut and her mouth opened wide and she was embarrassed about it, although it was one of the things Stewart had first loved about her.

For work she wore a uniform that was as white as the water in the pool was clear and bright.

Stewart let the cold water cover him and he wondered if he knew anything else about his wife. When they had first met and started doing things together and then accepted that they were headed for marriage, Stewart had given her the ring with the diamond, and her hair had been long enough that, when she let it out for play, it would brush against his chest when she was on top of him, if she bent forward just a little. The first time that had happened had been beside the Missouri River, in broad daylight. It was the first time too, that it had been light enough to see all that he could feel and Stewart remembered being stunned and a little intimidated by her nakedness, and he had shut his eyes to feel the ends of all those deep red hairs dancing against his chest.

Afterwards they had lain side by side in the tall grass. She had jumped up much too soon and started to dress. "I can't help it," she'd said. "It's this damn peaches and cream. I'll burn the little I've got right off." She had touched her breasts playfully then, waving them at him and then she'd pulled her shirt over her head.

Stewart had smiled and said, "You're the most beautiful thing I've ever seen." And he'd meant it.

But she had tipped her head back and laughed hard. "I'm a carrot-topped, gangly geek," she'd said.

He had been surprised by that, and almost offended, because it was obvious she wasn't simply being modest. She believed that about herself. The most beautiful thing he had ever imagined. Then she'd said, "And I laugh like a mule, but I can't help it."

"I like the way you laugh," he had answered, and that was true too, though it was the first time he had realized it. "I love it." Then he had looked right at her and said, "I love you too. I love everything about you."

That had still been something new to say, and she said the same thing to him. Stewart remembered how the diamond on her finger had caught the light the same way the river had and he turned off the shower and picked up his towel. He was covered with goose bumps. As he drove back to work he realized Kathy's hair was shorter now. It no longer brushed against his chest. He didn't know when she'd cut it.

Kathy was on the day shift that month, and though their hours were identical, Stewart was the first one home after work. He walked around the silent house, looking for clues to find who he might be married to. He was reading the engravings on the flat brass name tags of her trophies when Kathy came in.

He turned quickly to the door and she said, "Hi, honey." Then she stuck out her bottom lip and blew a stream of air up over her face. That didn't push the few loose hairs off her forehead and she wiped them away with the back of her hand. She moved back to the bedroom saying, "Can you believe how hot it is?"

Stewart followed her back. It was the kind of thing they talked about now, the weather, as if they were strangers groping for some way to start at a party.

He sat down beside her on the bed and unzipped the back of her uniform. She kicked off her shoes, heel to toe without untying them. Then she stepped on the toe of her sock and drew her fool out of it, repeating the process on the other fool. She never wore nylons when it was this hot and she said, "I can't believe you haven't changed already."

"I just got in too," Stewart answered. Her back was just less than white, as dark a tan as she ever took. She stood up and let her white uniform dress fall to the floor. She unstrapped the white bra and let it drop on top of her uniform. Then she dropped back onto the bed, on her back, wearing nothing but her panties. "Whew," she said, wiping again at the hair on her forehead. "This, in Chickasha, is what we call a scorcher."

Stewart undid his tie and hung it on the rack in the closet. He took off his shirt and threw it into the laundry basket. Then he hung his pants over a hanger, and pushed his shoes into the closet with his toe. His socks and briefs followed his shirt into the basket. He lay down beside his wife but their bodies did not touch, because of the temperature.

"How long is this going to last?" Kathy said, and though Stewart doubted she really wanted an answer he said, "What?"

"The heat."

Stewart was on his stomach and he reached out and began to tickle his fingers over the length of her torso, from the protrusion of her hip bone, over the rise of her ribs and the smaller rise of her breast to the line of her collar bone and neck. It was quite a way on her body. She hummed the way she did to let him know that felt nice, and Stewart said that he had no idea how long it would last.

She sat up abruptly and said, "I can't stand this. I'm going to jump in the shower, hon'." She stepped out of her panties as she walked toward the bathroom and Stewart watched as she walked. She was only twenty-six and the muscles in her legs and buttocks flexed when she moved. They had undoubtedly been built up from her running and jumping and shooting. Stewart had met her after her last basketball season and, not being a fan, had never seen her play.

Stewart rolled onto his side and listened to the shower's water running over her. She always stood with her front to the water and she was the only person he had ever seen do that. He pictured the water spraying back away from her body and running down it, coiling around the curves and forming clear lines travelling down her legs. Stewart stood up and followed her path to the bathroom.

He slid the door open noiselessly and though her eyes had been closed she turned to him and smiled. He stepped in and stood behind her, wrapping his arms around her where they were pelted by the cool water.

"Didn't you swim today?" she asked. She tilted her head back so it rested alongside his on his shoulder. They were the same height and she hummed again, to let him know how she felt.

"Yes," Stewart said.

"You're a regular water bug," she said. They began to rock together and then more and they stayed in the big shower until even the little bit of hot ran out and the shower turned icily cold.

Kathy turned the water off and stepped a little shakily from the shower. Stewart sat on the tile floor. "That was nice," Kathy said. She shook her hair, which was still fairly long, and bent so it hung down from the top of her head. She wrapped a towel around it and stood straight again. "How are you, Turban-head?" Stewart said from the shower. He had almost said, "Who are you?"

"I'm wonderful. You?"

"What do you like about me?"

Kathy turned away from the shower and began to dry off with a second towel. "Everything," she said.

"What don't you like about me?"

"Nothing."

The questions had become a ritual. He desperately wanted answers, but her responses were rote and he didn't know any way to change that. He thought he would try hard to answer truthfully if she asked the questions, but she never did. Kathy dropped her towel over the bar and walked out of the room.

Now, he knew, the next thing they would discuss was dinner. As hot as it was they would have only salad, and maybe some bread. They might even settle for slices of watermelon. They would eat on the couch, in front of the TV, watching whatever came on next. Their only contact of the day was making love in the shower at six o'clock and even that had not been face to face. And then she had said, "That was nice," before walking to wherever she had walked.

When she poked her head into the bathroom she was wearing a short, filmy summer dress that she said was the only thing that was cool enough to wear. Stewart was still on the floor of the shower and she looked at him oddly. "What do you want to do for dinner?" she asked.

Stewart watched her for a moment. The dress billowing away from her torso and just touching against her upper thighs was a pale green print of stringing, leafy vines. The cut beneath the tiny sleeves extended halfway to the waist. Stewart didn't think she had ever been prettier and he said salad would be fine. She agreed, saying that it was too hot to eat anything else and she disappeared from the door.

Stewart walked to the bedroom and slipped on a pair of shorts without drying off. He sat on the bed, facing their dresser and he suddenly opened

one of his wife's drawers and stared at her clothes. He wasn't surprised
to find them there, he was simply curious to see what they looked like.

When Stewart came into the kitchen Kathy was pouring dressing on
the pair of salads. She smiled and gave him a bowl and said, "Forks're in
the drawer," as if he wouldn't know that. He followed her to the couch
and gave her a fork and tried not to listen to the answers and questions
on "Jeopardy."

After they were done eating they shared a glass of wine and he asked
if she'd like to go for a walk. She smiled and brushed the hair on his
head and said it was just too hot. He nodded his head under her hand
and left the couch.

Stewart walked to the bedroom and lay down on the bed and picked
a book from the nightstand. He perched on his elbows over the white
and black pages, but he did not read. They were done talking for the
night. There was absolutely nothing wrong, this is just what they had
come to. He didn't even know how it had happened. He was twenty-six
years old too, just like his wife.

Stewart began two-a-day workouts, swimming early with the high
school kids from the team as well as by himself over the lunch hour. He
had to get up at six, and he left Kathy in bed every morning. After she
went back to night shifts she wasn't home before he left in the morning. They only met in the evenings then, and they watched TV together
or he read, and she would kiss him goodnight as he went to bed and she
went to work.

He swam harder with the high school kids, and the onset of the
pain, when he had to breathe every second stroke or burst, dropped
from three lengths to five. It was a milestone, and when he told Kathy
she smiled and said that was great. She said she ought to start swimming with him too, when her shift changed again, but when it did she
did not start swimming.

Instead she pumped up her basketball and began to dribble around their
driveway, twisting and ducking and going behind her back and between

her legs and shooting from every point of the drive. She was rusty at first, but she polished quickly and it was amazing to Stewart how well she handled the ball for a tall girl. He had spent all his athletic time in pools, since he was six years old, and had never picked up basketball.

She braided her hair for basketball, as if it were work. It would glint coppery when the sun hit it right. The basketball, more and more often, went through the netting with a slick whish without having touched anything else. When she got up early to practice before work Stewart would watch from the window as he rolled his suit into his towel. One morning, instead of getting directly into his car, he leapt from the garage as she drove for the basket and he jumped, arms reaching up to block her shot.

She was in the air already and the way she traded hands on the ball and twisted her long body away from him left Stewart hanging above the ground with nothing to do but listen to the swish of the basketball through the netting. When he landed she was already dribbling back out toward the street and he heard the flat, repetitive slaps of the ball and her breathing which was hard and fast. She hadn't said anything, or done anything to acknowledge he was there other than twisting away from him and sinking the ball. Stewart watched her, muscles flexing as she reached the street, and he stepped back into the garage and into his car before she had a chance to turn around.

He seemed to hurt as soon as he hit the water that morning, and he didn't finish a lap before he started breathing every two strokes. He gave up after five hundred yards, and drove to work early, having to unlock the office himself. He made the coffee and waited for it to brew, picturing how she had turned away and what he had done to make it so easy. It was a noisy coffee machine and the water trickled into the pot like a tiny waterfall.

The next morning, as Stewart dressed, he listened to the dribbling in his driveway, and the interruptions that he knew were her shots. He couldn't hear if she scored or not, not from inside. When he stepped through the kitchen and into the garage he heard a swish immediately, then the hard breathing and the screech of a dragged basketball shoe and then the slapping of the ball.

Stewart opened his car door and dropped in his towel and suit. She was turning now at the end of the driveway and starting her drive for the basket. Stewart realized she had done this every day, beginning her drive when he opened his door, not just the day before when he had tried to block her shot.

She did not look at him but at the basket as she charged. She faded left around an imaginary defender and Stewart bolted from the garage before he knew what he was doing. As he left his feet he remembered how he had analyzed her shot all the previous morning and he was ready for the change of hands.

But she only faked the change of hands then hooked the ball in with her right as she floated across the front of the hoop. They came close to touching as they were both stretched out in the air, and Stewart flailed his arms too late behind her. Then she was dribbling away from him and he went back to his car and drove to the pool. She dodged around the car as he backed out, then pulled up and sank a shot off the board.

Every morning after that Kathy would begin her drive to the basket as soon as Stewart dropped his towel into his car. He failed to touch the ball, or her, for seven consecutive mornings. On the eighth morning he leapt, more at her than anything else. He had dissected every move she made until it was nearly all he thought about at work. Even at the pool he thought more of her moves than of travelling. The way she soared up reminded him of the jets coming out of the trees, putting on the power.

On the eighth morning he was using his size, getting in her way, challenging her with his superior weight. But somehow she began that beguiling twist and she was nearly behind him before he knew it and he saw her arms extend with the ball and he could already picture that feathery touch and he hacked at her lean white arms with his hard tan one. The ball sank to the asphalt without her arms there to guide it and she screamed, "Foul!" as if he had actually tried to injure her. They landed together and she glared at him, and he could not meet her eyes. He hadn't meant to hit her, he had just been so helpless he couldn't stand it. "I'm sorry," he said, very softly.

"Two shots," she hissed and she bounced the ball noisily to a place on the driveway he was sure was regulation distance. She stood motion-less for a second, then, with a light pump of her legs, she arced the ball up and Stewart, looking at her legs, heard it swish through the net without touching anything else. He didn't know why he stayed, but after she sank the second shot she dribbled away from him and he got into his car and drove to the pool. He sat in the stands in his business clothes, watching the high school swimmers churn the clean water back and forth. For some reason there were no jets that morning, but a train did go by, slowing to cross the river on its way out of town.

She went back to night shift the next day and she was not there to dribble the basketball in the morning. When he drove home she would be in the driveway, bouncing and shooting, and she would dodge around his car as he put it in the garage. He didn't challenge her anymore but walked straight through the side door and into the kitchen. She just kept at it out there though, and Stewart switched on the stereo and turned it up until it drowned the slap, slap, slap of the ball.

When she didn't come in to eat he fixed his own salad and started to the living room but stopped at the window in the back door and watched his wife out in the driveway. Stewart was breathing hard sud-denly, and his sweat smelled of chlorine. He stayed at the window until she was finished and he had to step away from the door to let her in.

Kathy was breathing hard too, and her sweat made dark patches on her shirt. Stewart was still in her way and without speaking she waited for him to move.

"We don't even talk to each other anymore," he said.

Kathy looked at him for a moment. She held her basketball against her stomach and Stewart thought how odd she would look pregnant, with that hump in the middle of her long, willowy body. Then Kathy dropped the ball into the corner and said, "I'm going to jump into the shower. I sweat like a mule."

She loosened her hair as she went and Stewart watched it fall wet and flat down her back as she walked away from him without saying anything more than that. "No," he said, "you laugh like a mule." She didn't turn or do anything but Stewart could see a tiny hitch in her walk, maybe just a second of a different tension in the muscles of her legs and he wondered why he had ever said that. He loved the way she laughed.

The bathroom door didn't slam shut and Stewart heard the water turn on and heard it change pitch when she stepped into it, face first. He kicked her basketball so hard it left a dent in the wall and his fingers trembled as he looked through the phonebook for the name of someone who could fix it.

After she left for work that night, neither one of them speaking, although he said Goodbye after she had shut the door, Stewart turned off all the lights in the house then turned on the flood light over the driveway. It was time for him to be in bed but he groped through the dark house until he found her basketball. He did not dribble it, but held it tightly between his hands as he walked into the garage and then out into the bright light on the driveway. His first shot missed even the backboard.

He didn't stop shooting and dribbling until his elderly neighbor walked out onto his lawn and said, "I figure midnight's late enough for anybody to play basketball." He took the ball from Stewart and took a shot with his crinkly old arms and missed. "Besides," he said, "your wife is so much better at it." When he was walking across his lawn again, he added, "And more fun to watch."

Stewart dropped his morning swims after that night. Instead he waited for Kathy to leave for the night shift before taking her basketball and shooting in the driveway. He always stopped just before midnight and he never had another complaint from his neighbors. When he carried the ball back in he wondered if there was a way Kathy could tell he had been using it, new scuffs or something. He almost wished she could. Every evening, when he came home from work, she would be out in the drive, firing away.

The last day of her night shift, after which she would have four days off, a vacation they had not even mentioned, Stewart overslept a few minutes and they passed each other in their cars as he drove to work. They didn't wave, but her window was down and he saw her smile. At work he thought of her sleeping at home in their bed and of her smile. She often smiled in her sleep, but he no longer thought he knew why.

At noon, when he drove quickly to the pool, the sky was heavy with clouds, the first for a month, and the wind had picked up in fitful gusts, seeming to shift direction with every new burst.

He changed and stood at the end of the pool. There were two fighters today, flying upon each other's wing tips. They didn't dip into the trees that way, but bellied low then arced into a hard, climbing turn, never looking as if there were more than inches between them. The wind made Stewart shiver and he dove.

The water was actually warmer than the air, and Stewart couldn't remember the last time he had felt that. His arms were cooled on every recovery stroke. It made him last longer, and he didn't drop back to breathing every two strokes until he had swum three hundred yards, a personal record.

When the rain started Stewart could smell it before he felt it. Even over the pervasive reek of chlorine, the clean, muddy smell of imminent rain came into his head and he couldn't have been more surprised at that. It carried the change kind of smell rain has in August, as if everything will be new once it is gone. Then Stewart felt the tiny cold pings on his arms and upper back, and when he turned his head for breaths he could catch glimpses of the drops pocking the surface of the pool. He started breathing on the third stroke again.

When Stewart finished his swim he stood again on the edge. The sky was covered in solid gray and there were whitecaps on the pool. For the first time that summer Stewart took a hot shower.

When he drove home from work that night the rain was coming down so hard people turned on their headlights. He left his off and when he turned the corner to his block he could see Kathy out in the driveway, dropping in a fade-away jumper.

With the rain her old high school basketball uniform was like a sec-

ond skin, a green one so dark it was nearly black, and Stewart could see
every part of his wife's hard, thin body and he loved her. Her hair was
down for once. Maybe the rain had pulled it out of the braid. All wet,
in the gloomy light of the storm, it was the color of blood that had
long since clotted.

Stewart parked his car in the street and sat in it a moment, with the
wipers on, so he could watch her move. Then he left the protection of
his car and in his business clothes he stood at the grassy edge of the
drive and kept watching her. She acted as if he wasn't there, as if he
could have been on one of those jets that turned and in seconds disappeared into the distance. The ball, each time it slapped down, made cir-
cular splashes that were immediately covered by the rain. More drops
flew from the ends of her fingers every time she sent the ball toward
the basket, but they too disappeared in the driving of the rain.

When Stewart cut in from the side he stole the ball as easily as if she
had let him and he hardly knew what to do with it. He dribbled some
but that was a mistake and she had it back before it hit the asphalt a
third time. His clothes stuck to him, but he felt light on his feet and he
chased after her, but she got around him near the street and drove in for
an undefended lay-up.

She retrieved the ball under the basket and looked right at him
before throwing a hard chest pass. Then she stood, slightly bent, weight
on the balls of her feet, the muscles in her thighs visible in three
groups, waiting.

Stewart came in and just as she reached to swat away his clumsy
dribble, he pulled up and shot. The ball banged once on the back of the
rim and once on the front and then went through the net and bounced
on the driveway.

Kathy stared at him, still bent, arm out to destroy his dribble. Then
she laughed. It came from her toes and she did not stop right away.
Stewart started to laugh too, though it brought tears to his eyes. The
rain covered that too.

He took one step forward and hugged Kathy, hugged her so tightly that if she wasn't so lean and so hard she might have broken. She hugged back, even harder, and she kept on laughing. "I knew you were practicing," she said. "I could tell." And that made her laugh even harder. "And you're right, I laugh like a mule. I can't help it."

"I love the way you laugh," Stewart said. "I always have."

"I know."

"I've been thinking of leaving here," Stewart said, without planning to. "I've been thinking about leaving you." They were still hugging each other. If anything, her grip tightened. "Every day when I swim, it's practically the only thing I think about."

"I know," she said. "I could tell."

Then she looked straight at him. "You couldn't ever do that though. You'd miss me until you died from it."

He looked back and their hugs finally began to wear away. "I know. I don't know what I was thinking." Their arms fell to their sides. "Lately all I've done is wonder how I could ever block one of your shots."

"You'll never be able to." Kathy smiled then without laughing. "You're no good at basketball."

"I know that too."

They stood in the driveway with their hands at their sides, looking at each other while the basketball rolled into the street, where the rain was beginning to make rivers in the gutters. Kathy said, "I'm exactly as tall as you are." She said it as a child would, proud of herself for something she couldn't help anyway.

The Jump Shooter
Dennis Trudell

The way the ball
hung there
against the blue or purple

one night last week
across town
at the playground where

I had gone to spare
my wife
from the mood I'd swallowed

and saw in the dusk
a stranger
shooting baskets a few

years older maybe
thirty-five
and overweight a little

beer belly saw him
shooting there
and joined him didn't

ask or anything simply
went over
picked off a rebound

and hooked it back up
while he
smiled I nodded and for

ten minutes or so we
took turns
taking shots and the thing

is neither of us said
a word
and this fellow who's

too heavy now and slow
to play
for any team still had

the old touch seldom
ever missed
kept moving farther out

and finally his T-shirt
a gray
and fuzzy blur I stood

under the rim could
almost hear
a high school cheer

begin and fill a gym
while wooden
bleachers rocked he made

three in a row from
twenty feet
moved back two steps

faked out a patch
of darkness
arched another one and

the way the ball
hung there
against the blue or purple

then suddenly filled
the net
made me wave goodbye

breathe deeply and begin
to whistle
as I walked back home.

Playing Basketball with the Viet Cong

Kevin Bowen

for Nguyễn Quang Sáng

You never thought it would come to this,
that afternoon in the war
when you leaned so hard into the controls
you almost became part of the landscape:
just you, the old man, old woman
and their buffalo.
You never thought then
that this grey-haired man in sandals
smoking Gauloises on your back porch,
drinking your beer, his rough cough
punctuating tales of how he fooled
the French in '54,
would arrive at your back door
to call you out to shoot some baskets, friend.
If at first he seems awkward,
before long he's got it down.
His left leg lifts from the ground,
his arms arch back then forward
from the waist to release the ball
arcing to the hoop, one, two, . . .
ten straight times. You stare at him
in his tee shirt, sandals, and shorts.
Yes, he smiles. It's a gift,
good for bringing gunships down
as he did in the Delta
and in other places where, he whispers,
there may be other scores to settle.

The All-American's Wife

Ernest J. Finney

I waited behind the gym. It was hot, the sun sending down flashes of light that bounced off the blacktop road and made me clinch my eyes almost closed. They were late. I could already hear the sounds of shoes on the wooden floor and the clank of folding chairs as a few of the kids set up for the assembly. In forty-five minutes the students would be going in, looking for a place to sit, waiting for the last hour of school on Friday.

I heard the car before I saw it, the squeaking of the unlubricated frame and the beating of the out-of-time tappets. It had to be them, but I couldn't be sure because the sun reflected off the windshield and turned it into a mirror. I'd only seen a photo of Stretch Jones, former All-American basketball star, but I knew I would recognize him. A half-hour before, I'd got a phone call; it was a woman asking for me by name: "Ronald Beason? This is Lorna Jones."

"Who?" I said.

"I'm the wife of Stretch Jones."

I felt relieved when she said that. I had already considered asking Mr. Cochran if we should call off the program. They were lost, she said, and I gave her directions to the school. This wasn't the way it was supposed to be; they were to be here at least two hours before the assembly; it was all in the contract.

As vice-president of assemblies, I was responsible for having a speaker once every three months. The student adviser had gone over my selec-

tions from the catalogue and approved them all. "A nice balance," he'd
said. The speaker for the first assembly was a politician who had spent
forty years in the state house before losing his seat. The second was a
retired prostitute who had turned into an evangelist; she was the most
interesting. There were complaints from some parents, but, as Mr.
Cochran said, you can't satisfy everyone. I don't think we satisfied anyone with the politician: he was nearly a hundred and probably senile.
When I led him to the microphone, he refused to speak into it and kept
pacing up and down. I tried a few times to put the microphone in front
of him, but he always moved. Luckily, there was a game after the assembly, and it was cold outside, so most of the kids stayed until it was over.

The motor turned off, and the car stopped. The windshield was covered with the splattered bodies of thousands of bugs, and I couldn't see
anyone through the dirty glass. I didn't want anyone I had to talk to
coming out of that wreck of a car. But I heard the window roll down
and then my name. "Are you Ronald Beason?" I nodded. "I'm Lorna,"
she said. I tried to see inside the car, bending down lower at the knees. I
saw the coffee cup first, a big white enamel pint-size with DADDY written in green letters across the bottom. A glass coffee warmer with a
cord going into the cigarette lighter was on the seat between them. His
knees were up high, angled, almost touching the gear shift on the steering column. I had to take four steps, then lean forward, almost touching Lorna's nose with my right ear, before I could see up to where his
face was. He looked pure, untouched.

But he didn't look like the photo in the book, slumped there. I wondered if he ever had. He changed the cup to his left hand and put out
his right to shake. I gripped his hand under his wife's chin. "Just call
me Stretch," he said. I tried to remember if the catalogue had said how
long ago he'd been on the All-American team. He looked as old as my
father. I said something like, "The whole high school welcomes you,"
while they both sat there, Stretch sipping from his coffee cup, Lorna
putting on lipstick, using a little hand mirror. The back of the station
wagon was jammed with boxes, and there was a rack with a lot of

clothes. A couple of unrolled sleeping bags were weighed down with a portable television set. The whole interior was covered with a fine coat of dust. I could hear more voices from the window of the gymnasium, and I hoped the air conditioning worked because it was going to be hot inside. They finally got out of the car. She carried a large chrome coffee pot and a small suitcase. He took a uniform in a plastic bag from the rack in the back, and a canvas sack that sagged with the weight of three basketballs. I opened the locker room door and then followed them inside.

I don't really know what I expected, but not this: Stretch slumped on a bench and Lorna going up and down the aisle between the lockers, the two-pronged plug at the end of her short arm, looking for an outlet to plug in a coffee pot. Even the senator had looked all right until he started speaking. "Do you know where I can plug this in?" Lorna called. I rushed after her, glad to get away from watching Stretch, who now held his face in his hands and didn't answer when I asked, "As a basketball star I'll bet you've been in a lot of locker rooms, huh?"

There wasn't an outlet. She asked, "What about the office?" It was locked because of theft and vandalism. I tried to get the window up where they gave out the equipment, but one of the teachers had hooked it closed. There was no way to get in there. I told that to Lorna and she groaned. "I have to plug this in," she said, holding up the plug to my face as if she were going to try to put it in my nostrils.

I stepped back. "Maybe I can get a key from somebody upstairs."

She sighed and walked back toward Stretch. I went up the stairs two at a time and saw Mr. Cochran at the door of the gymnasium, yelling "Knock it off, do it right," at the kids who were sliding the folded metal chairs across the floor. One of them looked over to where Mr. Cochran was yelling and laughed. "Did you hear?" Mr. Cochran started to yell again, and then he noticed me. Looking over his shoulder he snapped, "That's better," and we walked away from the door so we could hear each other, his hand on my shoulder. "Change in the weather; they're edgy today," he said. "Did they come yet?"

"They're downstairs now. Do you have the key to the office in the locker room?"

"What for?"

"They want to plug in their coffee pot."

"We have coffee over in the teachers' lounge, or in the snack bar. Did you tell them that?" I shook my head. "Well, you go tell them I don't know where a key is."

I went back down the three flights of stairs and then hurried to the locker room. Stretch was still sitting there, his face in his hands. I made as much noise as I could, coming up, clicking my fingers and whistling, then said, "How's it going, Stretch?" He mumbled something through his hands, and I said, "That's good." I felt more apprehensive than before. "Tired from the drive, huh, Stretch? Hope you don't mind me calling you Stretch. Driving in this heat is hard on anyone. We never had such a hot spring before, not that I can remember, anyway." He never said anything. I stood there watching him and felt glad I had only a little over two months left. It made me feel better that it was going to be over with. My father still thought he could change my mind about college: "You said you'd think about it last time. It's all arranged; you're in; you've got the grades. You said you might try it."

No more waxed corridors. No more. No more.

Lorna came out of the bathroom door with a quart thermos in her hand. "Did you get the key?" I shook my head no. "Well, the teachers must have a coffee pot somewhere." She handed me the thermos. "Here, get as much as you can, and make it hot and strong."

I went back through the locker room again, past Stretch and then up the stairs. The snack bar was closed. I turned toward the lounge. I found myself running and thought what's the rush and made myself slow down. Walk, damn it, I told myself, be cool. But after a few steps I was running again.

When I got to the lounge I went straight to the coffee urn and started filling the thermos. The coffee steamed as it came out, and watching it made me feel relieved. "Hey, don't take it all," Mr. Cochran said. He was sitting at the end of a table with two women teachers. He kept watching me so I had to turn it off. Through the steam coming out I could see that the brown greasy liquid was almost all the way up. "How is everything going with our entertainers?" he asked. I just looked at him, wondering if a basketball player could be considered an entertainer. "Well, I'll be down after I finish my coffee." He raised his cup in the air.

I hurried back down the stairs wondering what he would say when he came down. As I walked up, Lorna was standing behind Stretch, kneading his neck, and he was groaning softly. When she saw me, she grabbed the thermos and poured some coffee into his big white cup and put it into his hands. He inhaled once and then drank it all down without taking the cup from his lips. She poured another full cup and he drank it off. Then another and another. It was somehow embarrassing to watch. He drank with his eyes closed, the steam coming out of his open mouth, little trickles of brown liquid running over his fingers. I walked away before he was finished, mumbling, "I'll see about some towels," knowing the towel room was locked, too.

When I came back, she was unlacing his shoes, and he was tipping the cup straight up to get the last drop. He smacked his lips when he saw me and said, "That's what I needed," and started unbuttoning his shirt. "I know you can get me more of that coffee," he said. I just nodded. He was watching my face as he reached down and undid his belt. I averted my eyes for a while but had to look back. He was standing naked and she was handing him a pair of white socks.

"Ronald," Lorna asked, "are you going to get me some more of that coffee?"

"There's none left up there," I answered, not wanting to run into Mr. Cochran again. Stretch abruptly sat down and put his head back into his hands and said "Lorna" twice.

"What do you mean there's none left," she shouted. "Don't they have anything in this school?"

There was some left in the teachers' lounge, but I wasn't going to tell her that. Not if she was going to yell. And part of me was beginning to sort of enjoy this, waiting to see what was going to happen next. "Both the cafeteria and the snack bar are closed, and there's none left in the lounge," I said to Lorna.

"Get me the key so I can plug my coffee pot in," she yelled, slapping his supporter against the locker wall.

"I don't know who has it," I said back.

"Oh, Lorna, my head hurts."

She opened her mouth wide to yell again but then snapped it closed. She sounded like she was pleading with me when she asked, "Can't you get someone, a janitor?"

"I'll look," I said as indifferently as I could, and shuffled off.

"Now contain yourself, Stretch, we're going to have some soon," I heard her say as I started up the stairs.

My legs started pumping as if I were being chased. At the top I slowed down, almost out of breath. What's going on now, I asked myself. I knew I should never have run for vice-president. I knew it was a waste of time. Everyone said it was good to be well rounded. I went out for track and swimming, neither of which I enjoyed, for the same reason. Another thing, no one bothered the sports, no one pushed them against the wall or cornered them in the lavatories and said hey, loan me a dollar, kid. Self-defense wasn't the only reason, either; my parents wanted me to; the teachers did, too. They wanted someone like themselves to be up there. I went ahead and did what they told me. I always do.

When the evangelist had come, there was a long distance phone call for her, and I went and got her in the lounge. The operator said she would call back, and we waited in the adviser's office. The call was all the way from the South, where she had her home. Her secretary held both her hands as they sat in wooden chairs knee to knee, saying things like I hope it isn't Mamma. She looked all right when we left. Oh, she did, she waved at us until we got on the road. It couldn't have been Mamma. She's never phoned before. "Let's pray," the evangelist said, and they bowed their heads and I bent mine over, too. "When the phone rings, you answer it," she said, "and tell us who it is and what they want." I was telling myself, get up and walk out of here. You don't have to do this. Instead I broke into a sweat and sat there. When the phone finally rang, they slid off their chairs onto their knees on the floor. Then one of them took me by the arm. I kept my eyes closed. I was beside them. All three of us were on the floor, shoulder to shoulder. They were crying and rocking on their knees. The phone rang again and again. I knew someone would come in and see us. I opened my eyes to find the phone and lifted the receiver. It was her mother, who wanted to know when they were coming back.

I couldn't find anyone in the administration offices; they had all gone. The janitors were all hiding somewhere, and I didn't ask the secretaries because they never knew anything. I wandered around and finally ran into a maintenance man who was painting over obscene words on the east wall of the administration building. He didn't have the key and didn't know where I could find one. "We changed all the locks when the science wing was robbed," he said. "Takes time for them to spread the keys around again—cuts down on the stealing for a while, though." I found a coach and a gardener, but neither had the key.

I gave that up and went back to the lounge, but the coffee urn was empty. That made me feel better, anyway. I went back down the stairs. Whatever was wrong with Stretch was probably still wrong.

I knew the voice before I actually saw who it was in the locker room. Mr. Cochran and Lorna faced each other; Stretch sat in the same place with only his socks on. He had his face in his hands but wasn't moaning.

"Well, Mrs. Jones, we certainly can't present him to the entire student body this way."

"I told you he's tired; it was a long drive up here. He's just tired. If you could just open the office so I can plug in my coffee pot."

"We went through that," Mr. Cochran started out, and I interrupted, "I couldn't find one. I went all over. There's no key. I couldn't find one anywhere," I added when they ignored me.

"Wait a minute, let's be practical," Mr. Cochran said. "Can he even get up the stairs to the gym?"

"He was an All-American." Lorna said, holding up his blue and white uniform top. I could read the words ALL-AMERICAN in white lettering across the chest.

"Maybe he was an All-American, but can he get up the stairs today, now?"

"Why are you saying things like that? If you'll only get me the key so I can plug in my coffee pot!"

Mr. Cochran turned to me. "I think we should cancel the program."

"Now wait a minute, we have a contract."

"Okay, to collect the money, you might remember, you must be able to fulfill the contract, which means that he"—Mr. Cochran stopped and pointed his forefinger at Stretch—"has got to get up the stairs in about seventeen minutes and entertain those kids for one hour before we pay you."

Lorna looked down at Stretch for what seemed a long time, then said, still looking at Stretch, "We'll be upstairs in the seventeen minutes if you leave us alone."

"Leave you alone for what? Let me remind you this is school property. Adults as well as kids can be prosecuted for taking drugs."

From where I was standing I could see Lorna's face. He'd got to her. She said slowly, "He doesn't take drugs. If you'd . . ." she started out, but I knew what she was going to say and I said quickly, "Mrs. Jones, I'll break the small window and get in the office and open the door." She reached down for the coffee pot on the bench next to Stretch.

"Like hell you will," Mr. Cochran said. "That's school property." I almost laughed, thinking of all the smashing that went on in this school. The crashes as the typewriters fell from the second story and hit the parked cars below. Toilets torn out of the floor, firebombed lockers, the bullet holes in the windows. "Mrs. Jones, you'd better go. Send us a bill, and we'll reimburse you for your travel expenses."

"You can't do that," she said.

"Yes, I can. Or rather, our vice-president in charge of assemblies can. I'm just the adviser—I advise." He gave a little chuckle then. "The students run their own assemblies. They voted for Ronald here, who, I might add, selected you, and, I might add, can cancel you out."

I knew what he was going to say before he said it. It was as if I had heard it all before, as if we had been rehearsing it for years. Mr. Cochran said, "I'll leave it up to him."

"Now wait a minute, we didn't come up here all this way for our expenses. We're not your students that have to jump everytime you yell. You just can't say, Go now. We're going on, Stretch is going to go up there and show those kids what an All-American can do. He made All-American two years in a row. You don't see him at his best now, but there has never been a time that the kids who watched him didn't clap and say he was the best they ever saw. He played professional basketball for three seasons . . ."

"Excuse me, Mrs. Jones, I'm sure that's all very interesting, but the fact remains that he doesn't even look as if he can stand up, much less get upstairs. It's not my choice—this is a student body assembly organized for and by the students. It's Ronald's decision; he is the one who is going to be held responsible if all the kids go to the gym expecting an interesting program and your husband is either unable or unwilling to give them one. Kids this age are perceptive; they know when they've been had. It's Ronald's choice. All he has to do is ask me to announce that the assembly has been cancelled and the students can go home an hour early."

There was no more talking. I waited, I'm not sure what for. Then Lorna ran for the office and I heard a crash, then the window frame push up. I almost followed her, thinking, Can she climb through? But she could do anything. I went over and sat down in front of my locker, a couple of benches down from where Stretch was sitting. I tried not to hear or know if Mr. Cochran was there. I knew this wasn't important, if Stretch went upstairs or not. I wouldn't even remember this a week from now.

I smelled the aroma of coffee. It seemed to be pumping into the room, strong and pungent. I could hear the kids above me going into the gym. I wished I were up there with them. I just watched when Lorna brought in the first cup of coffee and saw Stretch sort of revive, shake himself with little jerks of his elbows. After the second cup he was standing up and Lorna was holding his jockstrap open so he could put his leg through. She started talking to both of us as she helped him dress. "There's plenty, there's plenty, take a deep breath, smell it, take it inside. He needs his coffee, without his coffee he has a hard time. He has to have a lot, and more has to be handy. I took him to doctors and they all said something different: metabolism, thyroid, allergy, all kinds of things." She turned to give me a look. "You know doctors. One said he was addicted to the caffeine in coffee, which may be true. But there's no law against it. He hasn't done anything wrong. He's always tried so hard. We went to the same school together; he was ahead of me three years, but I knew who he was. Everyone did; we all went to the games, the whole town, and yelled his name. That was even before he became an All-American. Out of all the girls he could have, he picked me. I didn't know what to say when he asked me to go out with him. I couldn't speak. He could have picked anyone, but it was me. When he wanted to marry me, I thought it was all a dream, that I would wake up and it would end. To this day it still seems a miracle I'm Stretch Jones's wife.

"He never got the big money the way they do now for playing, but we've always managed. After we were finished with pro ball, we went back to our old high school. That didn't work out. They wanted a winning team every year. People forget. They forget they have an obligation. They forget they yelled his name to make another two points. If everyone that ever saw Stretch play from grammar school on sent us a quarter, we wouldn't have to do this anymore."

He was lacing up his right shoe when she came back with the fourth cup of coffee. He drank holding the cup with both hands, doing deep knee bends. I looked at my watch when I heard the feet start stomping overhead. It was eight minutes past the time the assembly should have started. We went up the stairs together, Stretch carrying three basketballs and his coffee cup, Lorna carrying the coffee pot. I followed carrying a little metal table to put the pot on. As we went into the gym and started down the main aisle, the kids saw us and the stomping and yelling faded a little. It was cool in the gym, almost cold, and I shivered a little as I marched behind Lorna. I saw Mr. Cochran standing with a group of teachers, his arms folded over his chest, looking smug. I would never admit it, but I knew he was right. I should have paid Lorna off downstairs.

I introduced Stretch over the microphone, and as I spoke the kids quieted down a little more to listen and to watch Stretch, who was making the three basketballs travel around his body like some strange animals he had especially trained. I stopped talking and stepped aside. He put his coffee cup down on the table, the basketballs twirling on the tips of his fingers now, and began to speak. "Hi ya, gang," he started out. He went on to say where he had gone to school and how important school was if you wanted to get ahead. That high school was the most important time in our lives. That if we didn't understand that now, we would when we got to be his age. Now the three basketballs squirted around his back, between his legs, down one arm and up the other. I stood there by the microphone in a kind of trance, watching, listening to what he said. About 50 percent of the kids were watching with me. Stretch did some lay-ups, about a hundred, using all three balls from all the different approaches. It seemed as if there were a thousand balls in the air at the same time, dropping through the basket like magic. The kids started clapping and yelling after he made each basket. Then he took off his jacket and leaned down to the microphone. "I will now give you a demonstration of different kinds of shooting," he said.

He went over to the table and Lorna handed him another cup of coffee. He stood there, bouncing all three balls at once, drinking out of the big white cup in gulps. I watched Lorna, who was sitting next to the table. She had found an outlet I didn't know existed, the one the microphone was plugged into. Steam from the coffee pot spout puffed around her head. Her hands were folded over each other in her lap. When he finished, he held the cup toward her and she filled it to the top. The three balls kept bouncing and I could hear a few shouts: "Hey, pass it around, how about some for us." I felt so good watching him drink that coffee. I wanted to yell out, Go on, Stretch, go on, drink a million gallons if you want. This was by far the best assembly of the three.

He put the cup down when he finished, still bouncing the balls, and went to the free-throw line. He looked at the basket, the balls bouncing against the floor, shook his head, and went to the top of the key. He held his right arm straight up over his head, one ball in the palm of his hand, and just stood there, the other two balls still going up and down. All the sounds in the gym stopped except for the banging of the balls against the wooden floor. Then the ball left his hand; it seemed to go by itself, go straight up, then somehow come down and swish through the ring. The kids went wild, calling his name Stretch, Stretch, clapping, and stamping their feet. He shot the next one with his back turned from the basket, then shot the third so hard, throwing it like a baseball, that the backboard vibrated as if it were going to break loose and fly through the air. As the ball went through, it tore the net off. He went over for another cup of coffee as the crowd chanted "Do it again, do it again." Three kids ran out on the floor to retrieve the basketballs. Stretch shook their hands as he bounced the basketballs against the floor. A girl in my physics class had got the net. She brought that up to Stretch. He bent over the upper part of his body and she put the net over his head. It dangled down his chest as he kissed the top of her head. The clapping continued. He sipped his coffee. When he put the cup down, he signaled for quiet and started toward the center of the floor. Just then the last bell rang. I looked at the clock and it was time to go. No one moved. It was absolutely silent. He stood in the very center and looked around him, just moving his head, then turned himself slowly, his feet shuffling on the wooden floor. He was so tall out there. It seemed as if the minute held as he turned, then repeated itself as the balls went bam bam bam against the floor. He seemed to be grinning at something he saw. Then all three balls were in the air. He'd shot them from half court. They arched; the two in front revolved as they fell toward the basket. All three missed, the last rolling around the rim twice before falling away. There was a roar from the kids: "You missed, you missed!" Stretch feigned surprise and ran and got the balls and dribbled them back to half-court. He set two down by his feet and got ready to shoot the third. Everyone quieted down: the last sound before he shot was SSSHHH.

I glanced at Lorna. She sat relaxed, not even looking at Stretch or the basket but up and out the windows where the sun made the glass look like flame. He shot and missed and there was more yelling. He posed to shoot and everyone quieted down and he missed again. The shouts were even louder this time and the kids started throwing pennies onto the floor at his feet. Others ran out to try to pick them up. He missed again and someone threw a chair that slid across the floor past him.

Stretch went over and got another cup of coffee from Lorna and drank it unconcerned, watching the crowd yelling at him, throwing more pennies, a shoe, and some books. A lot of the kids were standing up on their chairs yelling. The teachers moved in but no one paid any attention to them. It seemed like more than three thousand kids were yelling, more like three million, mouths open, faces swollen with the effort. A group ran out onto the floor and grabbed the basketballs and threw them into the crowd. One was slashed and then thrown back at Stretch. It missed and hit the table and knocked over the coffee pot. Lorna was up and yelling into the microphone, "Now stop that," and the thing went dead. All the time the kids were going out; the noise got less and less until there were just Lorna, Stretch, and me standing there, watching each other.

We picked everything up and went back downstairs. Stretch stripped and went to take a shower. I could hear the water running while Lorna shook out his uniform and put it in her case. I had the check out, folded in a small square in the palm of my hand, waiting for the right time to hand it to her. She took the coffee pot into the office and filled it and then plugged it in. When she came out she was humming and she smiled at me. She was short and round and in her dark blue suit and white blouse she looked like a penguin. But it made me feel good when she smiled. I unfolded the check and handed it to her. She took it and said, "You don't have to pay for the ruined ball. It happens pretty often. He's got to try the hard ones; otherwise he doesn't think he's given his best." I thanked her. Stretch came back, and she dried him off while I went to the office to fill his cup. He dressed slowly, carefully, all the time taking sips of coffee, while Lorna handed him his clothes.

She filled the thermos with coffee and we carried everything out to the station wagon while Stretch combed his hair. The sun had gone behind the clouds and it seemed late now, almost dark. We had everything inside when he came out and shook my hand. Then Lorna took my hand in hers and rubbed the back of it with her fingers. I felt my eyes turn hot and then wet. I wanted to hug her, hold her there. She got in and started the motor. "If you need anyone, remember us," she said, and then the car moved off down the road.

In the Room of My Dying Father
Marie Henry

How perfectly we fit together,
my chin in the crook of your neck.
These long hugs so essential
to our routine. And with whatever
strength you have, you reach your arm around me,
rub my back,
then tell me of the faces from your past
that pass before you
as you lie there with nothing to do.
"I'm just fiddling around," you sigh,
"moving my butt from one side to the other
to keep from sticking to the bed."
Each evening
Mom and I join you, climb aboard
with our dinner plates, settle in for a
night of slow chewing.
It takes you forever
to get so little down.
One night Mom brings in a chocolate truffle,
asks if you'd like a bite.
"Let me smell it," you say.
When she pulls back her hand,
only the smallest bit of chocolate remains
and you lie there with an impish grin.
I stretch out alongside you and we watch the Suns go down
to the Chicago Bulls. All the while

your fingers stroke my arm
and I feel like a ringer, like a slam dunk,
like a jump shot, a three-point shot, feel like a
swish shot, the tickle of
perfection,
the quiet joy of sliding through.

Crisis on Toast

Sherman Alexie

We've been driving for hours
my father and I
through reservation farmland
talking the old stories:
Stubby Ford; Lana Turner
at the National Boy Scout Jamboree
my father pissing in a hole he dug
while his troop formed a circle
around him and Lana Turner drove by
breaking every boy's heart. He told me

old drunk stories
about the gallon of vodka a day
the DTs, snakes
falling out of the walls. We watched

two farm boys shooting baskets. Lean and hungry
they were "suicidally beautiful." *Jesus*
my father said. *I played ball like that.*
I looked into the sun and tears fell
without shame or honor. We got out of the car
in our basketball shoes. My father's belly
two hundred winter beers wide
and I've never been more afraid
of the fear in any man's eyes.

Top of the Game

John McCluskey, Jr.

They were standing at a snack shop in O'Hare, a midafternoon snack of jumbo hot dogs and colas on the counter in front of them, when Roberta Tolbert turned to her son and said, "Junior, this is the end of the line. That man better break Alvin's scoring record tonight, because I won't go another step further."

It was not the first time she had said something like this. Just four days earlier at Boston's Logan Airport she had turned to him as they neared the security check station. "We go from one arena to the next. Then they march us from one TV station to the next, just a-marching, just a-marching." She had smiled then, pumped her arms several times.

"No, son, I'm tired of all those grinning reporters asking about your daddy's scoring records and wanting to know about his appetite and habits and things." Alvin, Jr., remembered that a security guard, a balding Cape Verdean, had waited patiently for her to place her purse on the slow-moving belt.

"I simply don't need all those cameras up in my face while I'm trying to watch the game, especially when I can't give a kitty who wins. They don't give me time to blow my nose. And I don't—I mean, really don't—need to shake the hand of the first vice-president of this and the second vice-president of that. I need to be back home with my third graders." She had waved her hand then, shaken her head, and stepped through the security arch without a beep. Then they had flown on to Cleveland for a three-day stand and more interviews.

Now a group of arriving passengers was headed from a nearby gate. Tanned and in their wrinkled pastels or florals, they talked loudly to those meeting them. They must have landed from Florida, Alvin, Jr., guessed, the rush of waves and bright tropical light close to their memories. They would be ambushed by the Chicago cold, breaths stolen. He shook his head slowly, turned to his mother.

"Mama, I can't blame you one bit, you know that. Who could have guessed that the man would go into a slump right in the middle of the season with us following him from town to town? If anybody had told me that we'd be on this . . . this caravan so long, I would have called him crazy."

"Plus they're always asking silly questions," she said, using her straw to swirl the ice in her cup.

"What?"

"The reporters and the television folks. It's always, uh, 'Well, how do you feel now that Hurdie-Birdie is about to break your husband's record?' What do they expect me to say—I'm the happiest woman in the world to know my husband's name will be erased from the record books? What do they want me to say? It's silly is what it is. You got your good job with the city and me just one year from retirement. We don't need this, really." Then with two hands, she picked up her jumbo hot dog as if a sacred flute and turned it slowly to her lips.

Alvin, Jr., had seen it all coming. They had joined the Chicago Middies some ten days before. Alvin Tolbert's record as all-time American Basketball Federation scorer was to have been broken at Madison Square Garden, then Boston Garden before Cleveland Coliseum. Tonight the Middies were returning home to play the New Jersey Majors, and the Middies' aging forward, Clarence "Thunderin'" Hurd, was due again to smash the record that very night, if not tomorrow night or the next, before a wildly cheering crowd and a fleet of cameras. AFA officials thought it would be a good idea to have the Tolberts on hand for the occasion and practically begged them to join the team. "See it as a short vacation on us," someone had told them on a conference call. But they were losing patience.

Of course, the travel had its comforts and special pleasures. All their expenses were paid. They stayed in the best hotels with the team. Their steaks were most tender, their lobster tails most succulent. A limousine, usually off-white with smoked windows, maneuvered them soundlessly through traffic. A smiling front-office staff member, in obligatory gray pinstripes, sat with them at courtside, and their seats were just behind the Middies' bench, close enough for them to lean forward and tap one of the players on the shoulder, if they cared to. Thousands would gladly change spaces with them, and they knew it.

Chewing slowly, Roberta looked at her son and, raising her chin, tapped a corner of her mouth twice. As reflex he dabbed at the corners of his mustache, catching beads of mustard against his napkin. Then she started again, resolute, "I was doing just fine until all this came along. Just fine, thank you. Now they've brought us out here to all this cold weather and, Lord knows, I didn't bring along that many wool dresses." She sighed, glanced around quickly as if she had just discovered that they were among hundreds of strangers trading places.

"Let's go," she said after they had finished. "You can do all the talking this time, though. I'm talked out."

A machine from a dream, the limousine delivered them to a television station five blocks from the hotel. Passersby slowed to watch as they got out, the wind nearly taking Roberta's hat. They were whisked past cool-eyed secretaries to a studio set breezy in ferns and blond furniture. By now they no longer wondered about the small size of the sets. They knew well the quick movements of the staff, movements as precise as those of a surgery team. The lights, the tiny microphones, and the assured manner of a host with a ready smile—yes, they knew it all well.

For this taping, the Tolberts were seated on a low-backed couch. As their mikes were fitted on, Roberta leaned toward her son and whispered, "What's this show called again?"

"*Chicago Dateline*, I think."

He had been watching a young, richly brown woman in headphones working one of the cameras. She wore tight jeans and a bright-red over-sized sweater. Her headband matched her sweater. He smiled at her. She

smiled back. Stroking a corner of his mustache and bold with the energy of the newly famous, he winked. She winked back, then laughed
aloud, a warm and throaty laugh. He wanted to hear it closer, to lean
slowly against it.

What now? he wondered. Invite her to the game, to breakfast the next
morning? Or would she prefer the celebration party Hurd would plan
for after the game? Back in Dayton, his shyness would have stopped him
at the wink. He rubbed his hands together and wove feeble plots.

But they were already in the middle of the countdown, the host
(Fred, Dan, Jerry?) clearing his throat and straightening his tie. As the
final act, mouth closed, he slowly slid his tongue around his top row of
teeth. Roberta Tolbert fidgeted.

". . . four, three, two, one." The camera light blinked red and the
show began.

The man spoke easily, turning from the camera to the Tolberts and
back during the introduction. The questions were the expected ones,
the same ones asked in New York, Boston, Cleveland. They summoned
the familiar parade of memories that needed to be compressed into a
few sentences with no pauses, no stutters, and please look straight into
the camera.

WHAT WAS HE LIKE AS A FATHER?

*Late springs and early summers were his releases. The Baltimore Barons made it
to the playoffs only twice during his twelve years on the team. So, from early April
through mid-September he would be planted at home, cutting grass or painting or
standing out front swapping tales with other fathers. The youngest of three children,
Alvin, Jr., was the only son. The day after his twelfth birthday, he jogged with his
father to a nearby cinder track. There his father began to train him to be a world-
class sprinter. After every workout, Junior would return home exhausted, slumped
and straining for air, while his father fingered a stopwatch and talked about the feats
of Jesse Owens. ("They tell me ol' Jesse could have outrun Man o' War, if he had a
mind to.") It was not until Junior had made the junior high sprint relay team and
was in the care of a coach his father respected that he stopped the training sessions
with his son.*

But you should have been there the time I told him I was going to try out for the high school swim team and maybe rest through the track season. He just fell on the couch and laughed.

"A swimmer? My son, the swimmer?" he was asking the ceiling. My father had grown up in Detroit where there had been few pools available for blacks, and he had never learned to swim.

"A black man swimming in the Olympics. Now ain't this a blip? You'll be the first." Everything had to be Olympics, world class. Baltimore was too small; America was too small, you see. I said it over and over again, getting used to it like the notion was a new candy.

And why not swimming? It was all in the learning or, as his father always taught him, in the breathing and the balance, the concentration and the love. Besides, had his father been born shooting hook shots from fifteen feet from the basket? Though Junior did make the swim team at Howard University, he never got to the Olympic trials. Still, it was hard for him even now to pass up any water without plunging in—serene lakes, rivers, whole oceans invited him. As late as five years ago, at the age of twenty-seven, he thought briefly about starting training to swim the English Channel. You didn't need to be fast, just strong, steady.

To the invisible thousands watching, Roberta remembered him as the children's ally. Until they were teenagers, it seemed, he could carry two of his children, especially the daughters who curled like kittens, in a single arm. He soothed them after she had taken a switch or leather strap to their behinds. He would discipline them only rarely and, even then, more out of disappointment than anything else. Like the time Junior took $5 from the kitchen table and lied about never having seen it.

Once we drove out to California and stopped in Columbus. Alvin thought it would be fun to show the kids where he played college basketball. There was a summer camp for high school players or something like that going on at the Arena. Anyway, we got in and were walking the hallways of the gym, when we saw the old team pictures, the same ones we had at home. Junior found Alvin in three of them, asking before each one, "Daddy, is that you?"

He did look different in all three—mustache, no mustache and with goatee, then clean-faced. Seeing those pictures in that strange place, miles from Baltimore, thrilled the kids. They must have thought he had simply imagined those years or that his past was in a world they would never see. They might as well have seen his baby shoes.

WHAT WAS IT LIKE LIVING WITH A SUPERSTAR?

She glanced off, then back to the camera. She spoke proudly of the fact that he was recognized everywhere—the bank, the post office, the hardware store. Grown men pushed their way to him for autographs. She suggested how women batted their eyes and touched the ends of their hair while they talked—oh, he was a handsome man, my Alvin. Then she spoke of other things.

First, there's the phone, the calls of congratulations after the victories, and can you speak to the thus-and-so group next week, and could you please talk to my boy who's down on himself for missing that last-second shot against Douglas High. When the team lost and you had a bad night, the phones would be dead and you'd drag around the house. Oh, maybe one or two might call and say that the referees had the eyes of their twice-widowed aunts who were going in for cataract surgery that very day. Erskine was good for coming up with something like that, baldheaded Erskine who stuck by you through those years in Baltimore even after you retired. You can't buy a good friend like that. And you could be so cranky after you retired, even hurting people like Erskine. You found most things so dull and maybe they were, but it was Erskine who found you collapsed on the sidewalk and ran to get me, him already crying, you already dying.

Junior shifted on the couch as his mother spoke. Her thick gray hair, one thin spot at the crown, seemed to glow with a bluish tint. He was glad to have talked her out of the hair piece. It would have fooled no one. It was better this way. Her skin smooth and unblemished, she looked beautiful.

By the time he began his next answer, Junior was relaxed, the tightness easing across his stomach. For the audience, he could recall the awe which first stretched the eyes of his childhood friends. During his father's best seasons, Junior was always among the first ones picked for games during school recess period. When the professional playoffs approached, his buddies gathered shyly in one corner of his backyard, their questions given to them by curious parents and sprinkled at his feet during their football games. His imagined prowess had to be genetic like the color of his eyes, even if not handed down like a halo. It took them several seasons to realize that his jump shot was only average, that in touch football games he dropped long passes with calm regularity.

WHAT DOES IT FEEL LIKE TO WATCH THIS GREAT PLAYER MAKE THE FINAL ASSAULT ON THE RECORD WHICH YOU, THE LEAGUE, AND THE NATION HOLD SO DEAR?

Like watching a man on the last climb to the top of a great mountain who must look down to smile over the distance he has covered. Then he looks up and you watch the terror spread over his face like a shadow. The end is near. A finger slips, then a foot.

The answers given, the memories churned up, the interview ended. They shook hands with the host again and with the director who strode onto the set. Alvin, Jr., did manage to say hello to the woman handling the camera. He wanted to say something more but felt clumsy.

"Both of you were very good," she said, winding cord.

"Thank you," he said. "We've had a lot of practice lately."

"I hope the tired turkey doesn't break the record."

He blinked, trying to smile. "Records are made to be broken."

"I don't believe that," she said. "I bet you don't either." Her smile was dazzling. He rocked. Then someone tapped him on the shoulder and reminded him that the limousine was waiting. He handed her a business card.

Outside a cold rain had started, a rain they stared through over dinner, a rain the limousine purred through en route to the fieldhouse. At stops, other drivers and riders would rub out a circle on their own fogged windows and try to peer through the smoked windows of the limousine. Roberta looked straight ahead, but Junior would smile and wave, hoping someone could see. And he thought suddenly of the admiring glances he was sure to get back home from women who had seen him on national television, women who otherwise smiled only faintly when he greeted them each morning at the office. The men would ask for descriptions of the behind-the-scene personalities of wildly popular interviewers and

players. On the first morning back at the office, he might take an hour
to talk it all out before getting them back to work.

At the fieldhouse, they were met by a smiling, stocky man who held
an umbrella for them. Junior took him for an aging outside linebacker,
free-lancing with the Middie organization, a friend of a friend of a
friend. The Tolberts had forgotten his name and his title by the time
they settled inside.

Roberta sat between Junior and the front-office man. "Looks like a
good crowd tonight," the man said. "You win three in a row, and you
get a good crowd. You lose three in a row and, unless you got a superstar, people claim the weather is too bad and they stay home. Winning
brings good business and good weather. By the way, Hurd's going to do
all right tonight. We got him in with a sports psychologist this afternoon. Guy's the best, does wonders with some of the Bears players all
the time. The prima-donna types, you know."

He tapped his forehead. "We figure Hurd got a little problem, you
know, these last couple of weeks. The pressure and all is making him
blow the record out of proportion. There's gotta be a name for it, but I
can't remember it now. Anyway, the doc says he's over it. I bet the two
of you ready to take that walk to center court."

Roberta Tolbert nodded and sat back with her son. They turned
their attention to the warm-ups and Clarence "Thunderin'" Hurd. At
forty-two, he was the oldest player on the court. "Thunderin'" was a
high school coach's idea. Rookies flattered him by calling him "Too
Smooth." Players who knew him longer called him "Old 'n' Easy." Now
he was loose and laughing, taking passes and gliding in for lay-ups. His
shots banked softly off the glass. As he waited his turn for a rebound,
he bounced lightly on his toes. He let his arms go limber at his sides.
He would lean forward and say something to the player in line in front
of him. They would slap palms and laugh the laugh of conspirators.

With a different club representative, the Tolberts had had dinner
with Hurd that first cold night when they had arrived in New York.
Hurd had spoken cautiously, sitting stiffly, as if answering a question

put to him by Howard Cosell.

"Mr. Tolbert was a hero of mine, and he will always be the greatest for me. I'm fortunate to have learned so much from him on and off the court. For the two years I knew him before he retired, he was the perfect gentleman, taught plenty of us how to carry ourselves. I try to carry myself the way he did." Like a child ending his first recitation, he breathed deeply and leaned back. The executive smiled, stroked at an imaginary beard.

During that dinner, Roberta was cordial. She took Hurd's measure with a stern eye. Several times, during other less guarded moments, she started to interrupt and correct his grammar, but Junior had nudged her. Roberta softened only when he showed them pictures of his family, bragged about his daughter's grades. Junior had even thought about taking Hurd up on the early invitation to join some of the players for their afternoon bid-whist games. And he wanted to know whether there was any truth to the rumor that Hurd had planned to retire at the end of the last season, only to be talked out of it by club management. ("Think of the record, think of the crowds!" the front office must have begged.)

Tonight the stooped and jovial forward needed just 21 points, three fewer than his career game average, to break the all-time scorer's record. When the Tolberts had joined the team in New York, he had needed 36 points. An average night tonight and they could all go back to their normal lives. But only after the record-setting shot. There would be a break in the game and they would all go down to center court for the presentation of the game ball and a plaque to Hurd. He and Roberta would smile and shake Hurd's hand. Spotlights would race across the ceiling; a band would play. The cheers would be thunderous. A flock of balloons would float to the ceiling, and the President might call. Junior knew it all by heart.

Now, as if he himself were about to compete, Junior's stomach churned during the "Star-Spangled Banner" and through the introductions. Then he held his breath.

"Well, Mama, here we go."

"Yeah, I guess so," she said.

After the tip-off, Junior exhaled long and slow. When Hurd scored his first points just two minutes in, a jump shot banked in softly from six feet out, the crowd stomped and cheered. Behind them a man chanted, "Hurd, Hurd, Hurd." Junior turned, saw him slap palms with a man sitting next to him. "Tonight is the night, ba-bee! "

His mother frowned. "Your daddy didn't even bother with the backboard on a shot like that."

Hurd missed three shots in a row before he scored near the end of the quarter, a lazy hook with the defensive man well off him. In the second quarter he managed one tip-in before missing four shots in a row, four shots that hit the inside of the rim and bounced high outside or skimmed around the rim and fell off. When he came out of the game with six minutes left before half time, there was a smattering of applause and, like cruel slaps, two short boos from the seats far behind the bench. He waved to the Tolberts without smiling and took a seat on the bench. He shook his head as he toweled off his forehead, the back of his head. One or two teammates slapped him on the back. There was no gesture or posture of bright triumph. It was his antics—the waving of an arm high overhead like swinging a lasso (after a score), the jamming of an imagined spike through the floor (after blocking a shot), and the quick shimmy as if stepping into a cold shower (after a dunk)—that were copied on every playground in America. In his heyday this was the man who talked confusion into the men guarding him. He would whisper to them to get more sleep, eat extra bowls of cereal, forgo sex for months in order to have enough stamina to control him. When he guarded others, they would swear the rim would rise a foot, its circumference shrink. Junior knew all these stories. Hurd must be proud to know that ten or twenty years from now old and young would gather on park benches, street corners, barbershops to compare his exploits to Alvin's, then to the most recent record holder's. But now he sat as the second quarter wound down, and when the horn finally sounded, he jogged slowly off the court. His team was winning by six points.

Junior and Roberta sipped beer through the half-time show, neither of them looking for long at the high school drill team performing on the court. The front-office man had excused himself.

"What do you think is wrong with Hurd, Junior? Too much pressure?"

He shrugged. "It can't be nerves. You don't play sixteen years, make all the records that he's made, and suddenly act nervous. No, it's just a little bad luck, just a slump. We all have those."

"I guess it's better to blame luck than nerves," she said. She drew a small printed schedule from her purse. "At this rate, he won't get his record until . . ." She paused to count down the schedule. "Until Portland." She sighed and shook her head.

A man was making his way toward them from across the court. He wore a snap-brim hat, a pencil-thin mustache, and, closer in, they could see that he chewed a toothpick in a corner of his mouth. Junior could have shaved in the glassy shine off the man's knob-toed shoes. The man introduced himself as an old fan of Alvin's and politely asked to take their picture. They agreed and smiled weakly for him, their faces frozen in the flash. They also autographed his program.

"Thank you so very much, and God bless you. I got autographs of all the famous colored folks who ever came to Chicago. Got Muhammad Ali's, Lena Horne's, Count Basie's, Martin Luther King's . . . everybody's." He smiled proudly and tapped his camera. "Got most of them on camera, too, so thank you very much, you hear?"

"Well, thank you," Roberta said, touching the ends of her hair.

The man was backing away, but stopped. "You know, the first time I saw Alvin Tolbert play I said to myself, said 'He's going to be something special. Nothing tricky, just steady, until one day everybody will look up and he will have more points than anybody.' Yep, sure did, from the very start." He slapped his chest twice. "And a regular dude, too. Remember the Barons clinched the title here in '64, and they went over to Pancho's on 56th Street and we was sipping on scotch and milk—"

"My husband didn't drink" Roberta said.

The man scratched his chin. "Must got him confused then. Yeah, yeah. Probably one of them boxers I'm thinking about. Anyway, he was my man, my main man. Y'all enjoy what's left to enjoy." He turned to

Alvin, Jr. "Hurd can't do half of what your daddy could do on the court, I'm here to tell you." Then he left.

"Be patient with your public," Junior said, as if quoting from a rule book.

On the court someone was receiving a plaque and applause was starting up.

"How's the house?" Junior asked, startling himself. They had covered everything else on the trip—health, his prospects for marriage, why his sisters wrote or called so seldom. But he kept imagining his mother alone during the evenings. And wondered.

"Oh, it's fine," she said. "I got somebody to repaint the whole inside. Now, if the tulips and rosebushes act right in the spring, the house will look all right."

He had helped her move from Baltimore to Silver Spring six years ago. It was a smaller house that Roberta decorated well.

"You were thinking about a cleaning woman once a week. . . ."

"I thought better about it," Roberta said. "I can save the money and go on another sea cruise. This time to Mexico."

"Think you'll miss these bright lights back in Maryland?" Junior teased.

"Not me. But I can see it is going to your head. Grinning back at all these fast young women." She could not hide her smile. And it was true. The shapely producer in the peach knit dress in Boston, the petite flight attendant who touched his elbow and told him how much she enjoyed his last movie, the woman from the Cleveland front office whose soft hoarse laughs kept him joking all game, the one behind the camera this after-noon—he was growing irresistible.

"You do need to settle down," Roberta said. "One or two more grand-children I wouldn't mind."

He was relieved when the teams came back on the floor. Relieved, too, when the front-office man resumed with hot dogs and colas—a diet one for his mother. The man talked about inevitabilities.

"The balloons are ready, the spot man is waiting, the plaque is all shiny and under wraps. It's just up to Hurd."

When the third quarter began Junior sat forward to watch but soon the watching grew painful. Hurd missed his first eight shots and ran up and down the court with a bewildered expression. Once he arched a shot from the corner a shot fans called his "money shot." Junior knew from the arc that the ball would miss the basket by four feet. On the first bounce it landed in the lap of a startled woman in the second row. A minute later Hurd came in hard for a dunk knocking over a defender—were the referees pulling for him too?—before missing the shot. The crowd was poised to scream at the beauty of the soaring the power of the stroke the rattle of the rim. They groaned when the ball bounced out behind the foul line and the Majors started a fast break in the other direction. When he tried to compensate for too much power the ball fell short of the rim.

His movements grew stiff. He was called for traveling twice, a rarity for "Too Smooth." He must be thinking the mechanics of his motions Junior guessed. One could grow weary and confused just walking as if it depended upon the conscious command of each muscle and bone. Thinking can be an enemy in such moments.

He scored nothing in the third and each time he missed he looked not to the bench but to the crowd as if a child ashamed. But his team was still ahead. A boo or two could be heard as the team walked back out for the last quarter.

"I guess they figure they can do that for the price of the ticket," Roberta said.

Junior nodded. "They would faint if they had to run up and down the court six times. Most of them can barely get up the steps with their hot dogs and beer."

Hurd was soon at the foul line for two shots. Junior sweated with him. Could feel the pebbly grain of the ball and ran a finger along one of the seams. He took two deep breaths blew the air out relaxed the chest and stomach muscles before he shot. Missed.

"You bum, you shoulda quit already!"

Roberta turned and stared then pointed a finger at the man standing three rows behind them. The man sat and refused to meet her look.

Junior put his arm around his mother to turn her around. "Alvin would have been climbing these seats if he heard him say something like that," she said.

Hurd made the second shot. And that would be the extent of his scoring for the night. He came out their lead safe with four minutes left in the game.

"I'm beginning to feel sorry for him" Roberta said. "I don't remember your daddy going through all this. If he did he never told me."

"Don't feel sorry for him. He's got the rest of the season to score fourteen points. He endorses tennis shoes, has a street named after him in Birmingham, and, according to *Jet* magazine, will be in a spy movie next summer. He's all right."

"Well, you know what I mean."

"I don't think I do."

"The embarrassment, son. He got to have a certain amount of pride no matter how much money he makes. This is probably the only thing he knows how to do."

"The money will help ease his pain," Junior said. "Even if he never scored another basket, he's had a good career. Wish I could retire at forty-two."

"People will remember him for messing up when he could have had the record days ago."

"Why did you change your mind on him? A while ago you thought he was the boogieman, now you feeling for him."

She chuckled. She had called him "Hurdle-Birdie" and thought him as country as navy beans and cornbread, it was true. "I was just holding on to the past like a fool. Alvin was more than a record in some book or"—nodding behind her to the fan who had shouted at Hurd—"some legend for somebody like that."

Junior thought for a moment. "Yeah, this caravan's got nothing to do with us. It'll roll whether we're here or not. Nobody will miss us. They won't even miss Hurd this time next year. We've all been invented."

Junior thought to the shot his father had taken to break the old record. It was an ordinary follow-up. A guard, Smith, had missed a long and arching shot from just behind and to the right of the key. The ball hit high off the glass and to the left where Alvin was charging in. He took it waist high on one bounce and put it back up lightly as if placing a feather on the rim. Any school-aged player, after mastering the contradiction of hard charge and sudden soft release of the ball, could have made it. The record had been set by no high arching shot from the corner, no switch-handed jump shot in the faces of two charging defenders, but by a simple "bunny" shot.

Months later, he had tiptoed down from his bedroom to watch his father playing the video tape of the shot. The tape reversed, his father watched it again and again. Then he yawned and saw Junior.

"Son, you have just seen me watch this for the last time. See how easy these things happen? It's just as easy and natural as breathing. It's always that way. You just do it the way you always done it. People forget your sweat anyway." Then he turned off the recorder, not even waiting for the part where he received the game ball, waved to the crowd, and grinned. "Then you have to know when to get out. Same go for preachers and politicians, even the best of them. You got to know when you've reached your peak and when it's downhill You got to go before you start falling. Only Jimmy Brown and Wilt Chamberlain understood that. I may not be the smartest man in the world, but I got common sense." That's when he told him that he would retire after one more season. He was true to his word, and, as far as Junior knew, he never watched that tape again.

Junior stood as the crowd counted off the last seconds. When the buzzer sounded, the Middies charged off the court in triumph. Hurd trotted off last.

The front-office man was standing and muttering, "Damn." Junior shook his hand and told him better luck tomorrow night.

"Wait here for me, Mama. I'm going to the locker room."

"What for?" she asked.

"I'll be right back. Just five minutes."

"Well, hurry up. These folk got all that beer in them and can act crazy." She waited with the dazed man.

Junior walked across center court, pausing to look at each basket, then around the arena at the highest rows. For a moment he imagined, had there been the celebration, how faces would flush in the racing lights, how balloons would touch the ceiling just above their heads. Then he waited outside the locker room for a minute or two. There was a crowd of autograph seekers, mostly young boys, pulling their fathers, or loud-laughing men in tight bright blazers, or two or three women in expensive furs and glittering high-heeled shoes. Showing their press badges, sportswriters walked right past him. He followed one in, then identified himself to a short bald man just inside the door.

"Come on in," he was told.

The writers were finishing with the head coach and the team's high scorer. Only one interviewed Hurd at his locker.

He saw Junior and smiled. Waved him over. He quickly put an end to the interview. "We didn't look too bad, hunh?"

"No, not at all. Congratulations. You keep it up and y'all will sail right into the playoffs."

"You right." Junior noticed the specks of gray and the thinning hair at the top of Hurd's head as though for the first time. As Hurd pulled off his socks, he groaned.

"I'm getting too old for this, youngblood." It was a line, half serious, that he used a lot. "One of these days I'll retire and the hardest work you'll catch me doing is sitting up in the broadcast booth spinning yarns." Then he looked around. "Just between the two of us and my shoes over yonder, I'll probably hang it up after this season. Your daddy was smart. He got out at the top of his game. I don't want to hang around. Get called a bunch of bad names."

"Mr. Hurd, we're heading back tomorrow morning."

"Come on with that 'mister' jive. The name's Clarence. But, hey, you got to stay around. We ain't even played that little game of Tonk we was supposed to play."

"Sure would like to, but I got to get back to my job. A couple more days away and the office might just float on away without me there."

"Heh-heh, boss-man, huh?" Hurd chuckled. In his voice played the various sounds of workers in large, sweltering fields far from the cities, though he claimed Birmingham as home. "Well, I guess you got to get on home. But tomorrow night's gone be the night, you know."

They shook hands. "Good luck," Junior said. "We'll read about it in the papers." He hesitated, then said, "Just remember to take it easy. You already got what you need."

Hurd looked off. "You sure got that right. I been pressing too hard, forgetting everything I know even at my age. Yeah, I'll take it easy. It's the only way to take it."

Near the door Junior smiled and kept walking past two reporters who asked him to comment on the game.

The next morning on a plane soaring through eight thousand feet and banking east, he noticed a boat, most likely a cabin cruiser challenging sudden winter storms, skimming the surface of Lake Michigan. He imagined himself even smaller in, say, August on that same surface stroking toward Canada. It would be for something simple—a late brunch in Ontario where he'd rest for a spell before starting back. There would be no ceremony, no crowds, no interviews—just the quiet doing of the thing.

But it was February, and he was flying home. His mother had left two hours earlier. By the time his plane would land and he drove the twenty minutes of expressway to his apartment, he guessed that his mother would have already aired out the den in Silver Spring and lingered to dust Alvin's trophies. And, for sure, Clarence "Thunderin'" Hurd, in the middle of a card game, would be boasting, unchastened, that the scoring record, the record that had withstood assaults for eleven years, would fall that very night—second quarter, y'all just watch up—with a thunderous slam dunk.

Ex-Basketball Player
John Updike

Pearl Avenue runs past the high-school lot,
Bends with the trolley tracks, and stops, cut off
Before it has a chance to go two blocks,
At Colonel McComsky Plaza. Berth's Garage
Is on the corner facing west, and there,
Most days, you'll find Flick Webb, who helps Berth out.

Flick stands tall among the idiot pumps—
Five on a side, the old bubble-head style,
Their rubber elbows hanging loose and low.
One's nostrils are two S's, and his eyes
An E and O. And one is squat, without
A head at all—more of a football type.

Once Flick played for the high-school team, the Wizards.
He was good: in fact, the best. In '46
He bucketed three hundred ninety points,
A county record still. The ball loved Flick.
I saw him rack up thirty-eight or forty
In one home game. His hands were like wild birds.

He never learned a trade, he just sells gas,
Checks oil, and changes flats. Once in a while,
As a gag, he dribbles an inner tube,
But most of us remember anyway.
His hands are fine and nervous on the lug wrench.
It makes no difference to the lug wrench, though.

Off work, he hangs around Mae's luncheonette.
Grease-gray and kind of coiled, he plays pinball,
Smokes those thin cigars, nurses lemon phosphates.
Flick seldom says a word to Mae, just nods
Beyond her face toward bright applauding tiers
Of Necco Wafers, Nibs, and Juju Beads.

Night Gym

Jack Ridl

The gym is closed, locked
for the night. Through
the windows, a quiet
beam from the streetlights
lies across center court.
The darkness wraps itself
around the trophies, lies
softly on the coach's desk,
settles in the corners.
A few mice scratch
under the stands, at
the door of the concession booth.
The night wind rattles
the glass in the front doors.
The furnace, reliable
as grace, sends its steady
warmth through the rafters,
under the bleachers, down
the halls, into the offices
and locker rooms. Outside,
the snow falls, swirls, piles
up against the entrance.

Doc's Story
John Edgar Wideman

He thinks of her small, white hands, blue veined, gaunt, awkwardly knuckled. He'd teased her about the smallness of her hands, hers lost in the shadow of his when they pressed them together palm to palm to measure. The heavy drops of color on her nails barely reached the middle joints of his fingers. He'd teased her about her dwarf's hands but he'd also said to her one night when the wind was rattling the windows of the apartment on Cedar and they lay listening and shivering though it was summer on the brass bed she'd found in a junk store on Haverford Avenue, near the Woolworth's five-and-dime they'd picketed for two years, that God made little things closer to perfect than he ever made big things. Small, compact women like her could be perfectly formed, proportioned, and he'd smiled out loud running his hand up and down the just-right fine lines of her body, celebrating how good she felt to him.

She'd left him in May, when the shadows and green of the park had started to deepen. Hanging out, becoming a regular at the basketball court across the street in Regent Park was how he'd coped. No questions asked. Just the circle of stories. If you didn't want to miss anything good you came early and stayed late. He learned to wait, be patient. Long hours waiting were not time lost but time doing nothing because there was nothing better to do. Basking in sunshine on a stone bench, too beat to play any longer, nowhere to go but an empty apartment, he'd watch the afternoon traffic in Regent Park, dog strollers, baby carriages, wings, kids, gays, students with blankets they'd spread out on the grassy banks of the hollow and books they'd pretend to read, the black men from the neighborhood who'd search the park for braless young mothers and white girls on blankets who didn't care or didn't know any better than to sit with their crotches exposed. When he'd sit for hours like that, cooking like that, he'd feel himself empty out, see himself seep away and hover in the air, a fine mist, a little, flattened-out gray cloud of something wavering in the heat, a presence as visible as the steam on the window as he stares for hours at winter.

He's waiting for summer. For the guys to begin gathering on the court again. They'll sit in the shade with their backs against the Cyclone fencing or lean on cars parked at the roller-coaster curb or lounge in the sun on low, stone benches catty-corner from the basketball court. Some older ones still drink wine, but most everybody cools out on reefer, when there's reefer passed along, while they bullshit and wait for winners. He collects the stories they tell. He needs a story now. The right one now to get him through this long winter because she's gone and won't leave him alone.

In summer fine grit hangs in the air. Five minutes on the court and you're coughing. City dirt and park dust blowing off bald patches from which green is long gone, and deadly ash blowing over from New Jersey. You can taste it some days, bitter in your spit. Chunks pepper your skin, burn your eyes. Early fall while it's still warm enough to run outdoors the worst time of all. Leaves pile up against the fence, higher and higher, piles that explode and jitterbug across the court in the middle of a game, then sweep up again, slamming back where they blew from. After a while the leaves are ground into coarse, choking powder. You eat leaf trying to get in a little hoop before the weather turns, before those days when nobody's home from work yet but it's dark already and too cold to run again till spring. Fall's the only time sweet syrupy wine beats reefer. Ripple, Manischewitz, Taylor's Tawny Port coat your throat. He takes a hit when the jug comes round. He licks the sweetness from his lips, listens for his favorite stories one more time before everybody gives it up till next season.

His favorite stories made him giggle and laugh and hug the others, like they hugged him when a story got so good nobody's legs could hold them up. Some stories got under his skin in peculiar ways. Some he liked to hear because they made the one performing them do crazy stuff with his voice and body. He learned to be patient, learned his favorites would be repeated, get a turn just like he got a turn on the joints and wine bottles circulating the edges of the court.

Of all the stories, the one about Doc had bothered him most. Its orbit was unpredictable. Twice in one week, then only once more last summer. He'd only heard Doc's story three times, but that was enough to establish Doc behind and between the words of all the other stories. In a strange way Doc presided over the court. You didn't need to mention him. He was just there. Regent Park stories began with Doc and ended with Doc and everything in between was preparation, proof the circle was unbroken.

They say Doc lived on Regent Square, one of the streets like Cedar, dead-ending at the park. On the hottest afternoons the guys from the court would head for Doc's stoop. Jars of ice water, the good feeling and good talk they'd share in the shade of Doc's little front yard was what drew them. Sometimes they'd spray Doc's hose on one another. Get drenched like when they were kids and the city would turn on fire hydrants in the summer. Some of Doc's neighbors would give them dirty looks. Didn't like a whole bunch of loud, sweaty, half-naked niggers backed up in their nice street where Doc was the only colored on the block. They say Doc didn't care. He was just out there like everybody else having a good time.

Doc had played at the University. Same one where Doc taught for a while. They say Doc used to laugh when white people asked him if he was in the Athletic Department. No reason for niggers to be at the University if they weren't playing ball or coaching ball. At least that's what white people thought, and since they thought that way, that's the way it was. Never more than a sprinkle of black faces in the white sea of the University. Doc used to laugh until the joke got old. People freedom-marching and freedom-dying, Doc said, but some dumb stuff never changed.

He first heard Doc's story late one day, after the yellow streetlights had popped on. Pooner was finishing the one about gang warring in North Philly: Yeah. They sure nuff lynched this dude they caught on their turf. Hung him up on the goddamn poles behind the backboard. Little kids found the sucker the next morning with his tongue all black and shit down his legs, and the cops had to come cut him down. Worst part is them little kids finding a dead body swinging up there. Kids don't be needing to find nothing like that. But those North Philly gangs don't play. They don't even let the dead rest in peace. Run in a funeral parlor and fuck up the funeral. Dumping over the casket and tearing up the flowers. Scaring people and turning the joint out. It's some mean shit. But them gangs don't play. They kill you they ain't finished yet. Mess with your people, your house, your sorry-ass dead body to get even. Pooner finished telling it and he looked round at the fellows and people were shaking their heads and then there was a chorus of You got that right, man. It's a bitch out there, man. Them niggers crazy, boy, and Pooner holds out his hand and somebody passes the joint. Pooner pinches it in two fingers and takes a deep drag. Everybody knows he's finished, it's somebody else's turn.

One of the fellows says, I wonder what happened to old Doc. I always be thinking about Doc, wondering where the cat is, what he be doing now . . .

Don't nobody know why Doc's eyes start to going bad. It just happen. Doc never even wore glasses. Eyes good as anybody's far as anybody knew till one day he come round he got goggles on. Like Kareem. And people kinda joking, you know. Doc got him some goggles. Watch out, youall. Doc be skyhooking youall to death today. Punning, you know. Cause Doc like to joke and play. Doc one the fellas like I said, so when he come round in goggles he subject to some teasing and one another thing like that cause nobody thought nothing serious wrong. Doc's eyes just as good as yours or mine, far as anybody knew.

Doc been playing all his life. That's why you could stand him on the foul line and point him at the hoop and more times than not, Doc could sink it. See he be remembering. His muscles know just what to do. You get his feet aimed right, line him up so he's on target, and Doc would swish one for you. Was a game kinda. Sometimes you get a sucker and Doc win you some money. Swish. Then the cat lost the dough start crying. He ain't blind. Can't no blind man shoot no pill. Is you really blind, brother? You niggers trying to steal my money, trying to play me for a fool. When a dude start crying the blues like that Doc wouldn't like it. He'd walk away. Wouldn't answer.

Leave the man lone. You lost fair and square. Doc made the basket so shut up and pay up, chump.

Doc practiced. Remember how you'd hear him out here at night when people sleeping. It's dark but what dark mean to Doc? Blacker than the rentman's heart but don't make no nevermind to Doc, he be steady shooting fouls. Always be somebody out there to chase the ball and throw it back. But shit, man. When Doc into his rhythm, didn't need nobody chase the ball. Ball be swishing with that good backspin, that good arch bring it back blip, blip, blip, three bounces and it's coming right back to Doc's hands like he got a string on the pill. Spooky if you didn't know Doc or know about foul shooting and understand when you got your shit together don't matter if you blindfolded. You put the motherfucker up and you know it's spozed to come running back just like a dog with a stick in his mouth.

Doc always be hanging at the court. Blind as wood but you couldn't fool Doc. Eyes in his ears. Know you by your walk. He could tell if you wearing new sneaks, tell you if your old ones is laced or not. Know you by your breath. The holes you make in the air when you jump. Doc was hip to who fucking who and who was getting fucked. Who could play ball and who was jiving. Doc use to be out here every weekend, steady rapping with the fellows and doing his foul-shot thing between games. Every once in a while somebody tease him, Hey, Doc. You want to run winners next go? Doc laugh and say, No, Dupree . . . I'm tired today,

Dupree. Besides which you ain't been on a winning team in a week have you, Du? And everybody laugh. You know, just funning cause Doc one the fellas.

But one Sunday the shit got stone serious. Sunday I'm telling youall about, the action was real nice. If you wasn't ready, get back cause the brothers was cooking. Sixteen points, rise and fly. Next. Who got next? . . . Come on out here and take your ass kicking. One them good days when it's hot and everybody's juices is high and you feel you could play till next week. One them kind of days and a run's just over. Doc gets up and he goes with Billy Moon to the foul line. Fellas hanging under the basket for the rebound. Ain't hardly gon be a rebound Doc get hisself lined up right. But see, when the ball drop through the net you want to be the one grab it and throw it back to Billy. You want to be out there part of Doc shooting fouls just like you want to run when the running's good.

Doc bounce the ball, one, two, three times like he does. Then he raise it. Sift it in his fingers. You know he's a ballplayer, a shooter already way the ball spin in them long fingers way he raises it and cocks his wrist. You know Doc can't see a damn thing through his sunglasses but swear to God you'd think he was looking at the hoop way he study and measure. Then he shoots and ain't a sound in whole Johnson. Seems like everybody's heart stops. Everybody's breath behind that ball pushing it and steadying it so it drops through clean as new money.

But that Sunday something went wrong. Couldna been wind cause wasn't no wind. I was there. I know. Maybe Doc had playing on his mind. Couldn't help have playing on his mind cause it was one those days wasn't nothing better to do in the world than play. Whatever it was, soon as the ball left his hands, you could see Doc was missing, missing real bad. Way short and way off to the left. Might hit the backboard if everybody blew on it real hard.

A young boy, one them skinny, jumpingjack young boys got pogo sticks for legs, one them kids go up and don't come back down till they ready, he was standing on the left side the lane and leap up all the sudden catch the pill out the air and jams it through. Blam. A monster dunk and everybody break out in Goddamn. Do it, Sky, and Did you see that nigger get up? People slapping five and all that mess. Then Sky, the young boy they call Sky, grinning like a Chessy cat and strutting out with the ball squeezed in one hand to give it to Doc. In his glory. Grinning and strutting.

Gave you a little help, Doc.

Didn't ask for no help, Sky. Why'd you fuck with my shot, Sky?

Well, up jumped the Devil. The joint gets real quiet again real quick. Doc ain't cracked smile the first. He ain't playing.

Sorry, Doc. Didn't mean no harm, Doc.

You must think I'm some kind of chump fucking with my shot that way.

People start to feeling bad. Doc is steady getting on Sky's case. Sky just a young, light-in-the-ass kid. Jump to the moon but he's just a silly kid. Don't mean no harm. He just out there like everybody else trying to do his thing. No harm in Sky but Doc ain't playing and nobody else says shit. It's quiet like when Doc's shooting. Quiet as death and Sky don't know what to do. Can't wipe that lame look off his face and can't back off and can't hand the pill to Doc neither. He just stands there with his arm stretched out and his rusty fingers wrapped round the ball. Can't hold it much longer, can't let it go.

Seems like I coulda strolled over to Doc's stoop for a drinka water and strolled back and those two still be standing there. Doc and Sky. Billy Moon off to one side so it's just Doc and Sky.

Everybody holding they breath. Everybody want it over with and finally Doc says, Forget it, Sky. Just don't play with my shots anymore. And then Doc say, Who has next winners?

If Doc was joking nobody took it for no joke. His voice still hard. Doc ain't kidding around.

Who's next? I want to run.

Now Doc knows who's next. Leroy got next winners and Doc knows Leroy always saves a spot so he can pick up a big man from the losers.

Leroy tell you to your face, I got my five, man, but everybody know Leroy saving a place so he can build him a winner and stay on the court. Leroy's a cold dude that way, been that way since he first started coming round and ain't never gon change and Doc knows that, everybody knows that but even Leroy ain't cold enough to say no to Doc.

I got it, Doc.

You got your five yet?

You know you got a spot with me, Doc. Always did.

Then I'ma run.

Say to myself, Shit . . . Good God Almighty. Great Googa-Mooga. What is happening here? Doc can't see shit. Doc blind as this bench I'm sitting on. What Doc gon do out there?

Well, it ain't my game. If it was, I'd a lied and said I had five. Or maybe not. Don't know what I'da done, to tell the truth. But Leroy didn't have no choice. Doc caught him good. Course Doc knew all that before he asked.

Did Doc play? What kinda question is that? What you think I been talking about all this time, man? Course he played. Why the fuck he be asking for winners less he was gon play? Hellova run as I remember. Overtime and shit. Don't remember who won. Somebody did, sure nuff. Leroy had him a strong unit. You know how he is. And Doc? Doc ain't been out on the court for a while but Doc is Doc, you know. Held his own . . .

If he had tried to tell her about Doc, would it have made a difference? Would the idea of a blind man playing basketball get her attention or would she have listened the way she listened when he told her stories he'd read about slavery days when Africans could fly, change themselves to cats and hummingbirds, when black hoodoo priests and conjure queens were feared by powerful whites even though ordinary black lives weren't worth a penny. To her it was folklore, superstition. Interesting because it revealed the psychology, the pathology of the oppressed. She listened intently, not because she thought she'd hear truth. For her, belief in magic was like belief in God. Nice work if you could get it. Her skepticism, her hardheaded practicality, like the smallness of her hands, appealed to him. Opposites attracting. But more and more as the years went by, he'd wanted her with him, wanted them to be together . . .

They were walking in Regent Park. It was clear to both of them that things weren't going to work out. He'd never seen her so beautiful, perfect.

There should have been stars. Stars at least, and perhaps a sickle moon. Instead the edge of the world was on fire. They were walking in Regent Park and dusk had turned the tree trunks black. Beyond them in the distance, below the fading blue of sky, the colors of sunset were pinched into a narrow, radiant band. Perhaps he had listened too long. Perhaps he had listened too intently for his own voice to fill the emptiness. When he turned back to her, his eyes were glazed, stinging. Grit, chemicals, whatever it was coloring, poisoning the sky, blurred his vision. Before he could blink her into focus, before he could speak, she was gone.

If he'd known Doc's story he would have said: *There's still a chance. There's always a chance. I mean this guy, Doc. Christ. He was stone blind. But he got out on the court and played. Over there. Right over there. On that very court across the hollow from us. It happened. I've talked to people about it many times. If Doc could do that, then anything's possible. We're possible* . . .

If a blind man could play basketball, surely we . . . If he had known Doc's story, would it have saved them? He hears himself saying the words. The ball arches from Doc's fingertips, the miracle of it sinking. Would she have believed any of it?

Contributors

SHERMAN ALEXIE of Spokane, Washington, has recently published the story collection *The Lone Ranger and Tonto Fistfight in Heaven*, the novel *Reservation Blues*, and the poetry collection *The First Indian on the Moon*.

JONATHAN BAUMBACH teaches at Brooklyn College; his books of fiction include *Separate Hours*, *The Life and Times of Major Fiction*, and *My Father More or Less*.

GEOFFREY BECKER of Iowa City published within the last year a story collection, *Dangerous Men*, and a novel, *Bluestown*.

THERESE BECKER lives in Lake Orion, Michigan, and is looking for a publisher for her recently completed poetry collection, *All That We Cannot Name*.

RICHARD BLESSING taught at the University of Washington, Seattle; his books include the poetry collection *A Closed Book* and *Poems & Stories*.

NANCY BOUTILIER of San Francisco published a poetry and prose volume, *According to Her Contours*, from Black Sparrow Press.

KEVIN BOWEN's recent poetry volume, *Playing Basketball with the Viet Cong*, was published by Curbstone Press.

SHARON BRYAN lives in Salt Lake City and has published two poetry collections, *Salt Air* and *Objects of Affection*, from Wesleyan University Press.

SEAN THOMAS DOUGHERTY of DeWitt, New York, is the author of a recent poetry collection, *Love Song of the Young Couple, The Dumb Job*, and an earlier basketball chapbook, *Beyond The Chain-Link Fence*.

CLIFF DWELLER, also known as Cliff Saunders, lives in Murrells Inlet, South Carolina, and has published three "headline poem" chapbooks, most recently *This Candescent World*.

GEORGE ALEC EFFINGER of New Orleans is an acclaimed author of science fiction novels and story collections, including *The Exile Kiss, What Entropy Means to Me*, and *When Gravity Fails*.

ERNEST J. FINNEY lives in California and has published four books of fiction, including *Lady with the Alligator Purse* and the story collection *Flights in the Heavenlies*.

PETE FROMM of Great Falls, Montana, has published three books since 1992, including the story collection *The Tall Uncut*.

NORMAN GERMAN teaches at Southeastern Louisiana University in Hammond; he has published many poems and stories, plus two novels, including *No Other World*.

CHRIS GILBERT lives in Providence, Rhode Island, and published a poetry collection with Graywolf Press, *Across the Mutual Landscape*.

GARY GILDNER taught at Drake University before retiring to Idaho; his books include *Blue Like the Heavens: New & Selected Poems* and a nonfiction book about managing baseball in Poland, *The Warsaw Sparks*.

TONY GLOEGGLER manages a home for developmentally disabled young men in Brooklyn, NY, where he writes poems and can still hit an open jump shot.

STEPHANIE GRANT lives in Brooklyn, NY; her story "Posting-Up" in this anthology also appeared in *Tasting Life Twice: Literary Lesbian Fiction.*

MARIE HENRY is a native San Francisco poet; she has published in numerous literary journals and anthologies.

DAVID HILTON of Severna Park, Maryland, has two poetry collections, *Huladance* and *No Relation to the Hotel.*

EDWARD HIRSCH teaches at the University of Houston; his poetry volumes from Knopf include *Wild Gratitude* and the recent *Earthly Measures.*

LOUIS JENKINS of Duluth, Minnesota, is the author of two prose poem collections, *An Almost Human Gesture* and *Nice Fish: New and Selected Poems.*

YUSEF KOMUNYAKAA teaches at Indiana University; author of several poetry volumes, his *Neon Vernacular: New and Selected Poems* won the 1994 Pulitzer Prize.

BOB LEVIN of Berkeley, California, has published a basketball novel, *The Best Ride to New York*, and the nonfiction *Fully Armed: The Story of Jimmy Don Polk.*

CARL LINDNER teaches at the University of Wisconsin-Parkside in Kenosha and has published a poetry collection, *Shooting Baskets in a Dark Gymnasium.*

JOHN McCLUSKEY, Jr., teaches African-American Studies at Indiana University; his published fiction includes the novel *Mr. America's Last Season Blues.*

BOBBIE ANN MASON's acclaimed fiction includes the story collections *Shiloh and Other Stories* and *Love Life*, plus the novels *In Country* and *Feather Crowns.*

WILLIAM MATTHEWS lives in Manhattan and has published several poetry books, including *Selected Poems and Translations* and 1995 National Book Critics Circle winner, *Time & Money.*

TOM MESCHERY is a former NBA player and has published a collection of poems about the experience, *Over the Rim.*

COREY MESLER lives in Memphis, Tennessee, and has published poems in numerous literary magazines; he has edited fiction for Ion Books.

LEONARD MICHAELS teaches at the University of California, Berkeley, and is well-known for his prose works *Going Places, I Would Have Saved Them If I Could, The Men's Club*, and *Shuffle.*

JUSTIN MITCHAM's poem "The Touch" is from his University of Missouri Press collection *Somewhere in Ecclesiastes.*

WILLIE MORRIS's many prose volumes include the memoirs *North Toward Home* and *New York Days*, plus a collection of fiction and memoirs about sports, *After All, It's Only a Game.*

BARBARA MURPHY of Shelburne, Vermont, has poems in several journals; her poem in this book was published by Vermont Public Radio.

ANN PACKER lives in Eugene, Oregon, and is the author of *Mendocino and Other Stories* from Chronicle Books.

JONATHAN PENNER of Tucson, Arizona, has published a book of stories,

Private Parties, and a novel, *Natural Order.*

JACK RIDL teaches at Hope College, Holland, Michigan; he is the son of former basketball coach, "Buzz" Ridl, and author of *Poems From the Same Ghost and Between* and a basketball chapbook.

JOHN SAYLES lives in New Jersey when not making striking films such as *The Secret of Roan Inish* and *Matewan*; his fiction includes the novels *Los Gusanos* and *Union Dues* plus the story collection *The Anarchists' Convention.*

TIM SEIBLES teaches at Old Dominion University in Norfolk, Virginia, and has published three poetry collections, including *Hurdy-Gurdy* and *Kerosene.*

ALEDA SHIRLEY lives in Jackson, Mississippi, and is the author of two volumes, *Chinese Architecture*, a Poetry Society of America award winner, and the forthcoming *Long Distance.*

ROBERT T. SORRELLS of Rochester, Minnesota, has published a book of stories, *The Blacktop Champion of Ickey Honey*; its title piece appears in Breakaway Books' anthology *Tennis and the Meaning of Life.*

RODNEY TORRESON lives in Grand Rapids, Michigan, and has a forthcoming collection of New York Yankee poems, *The Ripening of Pinstripes.*

QUINCY TROUPE of LaJolla, California, has published several books, including one on James Baldwin and a co-authored autobiography of Miles Davis, plus *Weather Reports: New and Selected Poems.*

JOHN UPDIKE is the author of over 40 books, including the celebrated Rabbit Angstrom novels recently reprinted in one volume and *Collected Poems: 1953-1993*; his most recent novel is *In the Beauty of the Lilies.*

JON VEINBERG lives in Fresno, California, and has a poetry collection from Vanderbilt University Press, *An Owl's Landscape.*

STEPHEN VINCENT of San Francisco has published poetry collections including *White Lights and Whale Hearts*, *African Cycle*, and most recently, *Walking.*

RONALD WALLACE teaches at the University of Wisconsin, Madison; his four poetry volumes from the University of Pittsburgh Press include *The Makings of Happiness* and *Time's Fancy.*

THEODORE WEESNER teaches at Emerson College, Boston; his books include the novels *The Car Thief* and *Novemberfest*, and the story collection *Children's Hearts.*

JOHN EDGAR WIDEMAN of Amherst, Massachusetts, has published many books, including the memoir *Brothers and Keepers*, the novel *Philadelphia Fire*, and *The Stories of John Edgar Wideman.*

HERBERT WILNER, 1925-1977, is remembered for his novels *All the Little Heroes* and his collection of stories, *Dovisch in the Wilderness*, which includes "Whistle and the Heroes."

DICK WIMMER teaches at Pierce College, California; his publications include *Irish Wine*; *Baseball Fathers, Baseball Sons*; and the basketball anthology *The Schoolyard Game.*

ERNEST WATSON lives in Greensboro, NC; his paintings of American life, such as "Piedmont Court" on this anthology's cover, celebrate people's art and vitality. He is represented by The Collector's Art Gallery, 2044 Carolina Circle Mall, Greensboro, NC 27405, (910) 621-5551.

DENNIS TRUDELL teaches at the University of Wisconsin-Whitewater; his *Fragments in Us: Recent and Earlier Poems* is a 1996 Pollak Poetry Prize volume from the University of Wisconsin Press. He has a basketball story in a recent O. Henry Prize collection.

Permissions Acknowledgements

Sherman Alexie: "The Only Traffic Signal on the Reservation Doesn't Flash Red Anymore" from *The Lone Ranger and Tonto Fistfight in Heaven*, © 1993 by Sherman Alexie. Reprinted by permission of Grove/Atlantic, Inc. "Crisis on Toast" from *Old Shirts & New Skins,* © 1993 by Sherman Alexie. Reprinted by permission of the author. **Jonathan Baumbach**: "Familiar Games" from *The Life and Times of Major Fiction*, © 1986 by Jonathan Baumbach. Reprinted by permission of the author. **Geoffrey Becker**: "El Diablo de la Cienega" from Desperate Men, © 1995 by Geoffrey Becker. Reprinted by permission of University of Pittsburgh Press. **Therese Becker**: "Basketball in the Year 2020" printed by permission of the author. © 1996 by Therese Becker. **Richard Blessing**: "The Poet's Dream the Night After His Son Scores 36 in a Little Dribbler's Game" from *A Closed Book*, © 1981 by Richard Blessing (University of Washington Press). Reprinted by permission of Marlene Blessing. **Nancy Boutilier**: "To Throw Like a Boy" from *According to Her Contours*, © 1992 by Nancy Boutilier. Reprinted by permission of Black Sparrow Press. **Kevin Bowen**: "Playing Basketball With the Viet Cong" from *Playing Basketball With the Viet Cong*, © 1994 by Kevin Bowen. Reprinted by permission of Curbstone Press. **Sharon Bryan**: "Cheap Seats in the Kingdome" from *Objects of Affection,* © 1987 by Sharon Bryan. Reprinted by permission of Wesleyan University Press. **Sean Thomas Dougherty**: "Beyond the Chain-Link Fence" from *Beyond the Chain-Link Fence*, © 1993 by Sean Thomas Dougherty (Red Dancefloor Press). Reprinted by permission of the author. **"Cliff Dweller"**: "The Leap" printed by permission of Cliff Saunders. © 1996 by Cliff Saunders. **George Alec Effinger**: "From Downtown at the Buzzer" originally published in *Magazine of Fantasy & Science Fiction*, © 1977 by Mercury Press, Inc. Reprinted by permission of the author. **Ernest J. Finney**: "The All-American's Wife" from *Birds Landing*, © 1986 by Ernest J. Finney. Reprinted by permission of University of Illinois Press. **Pete Fromm**: "Breathing on the Third Stroke" from *The Tall Uncut,* ©1992 by Pete Fromm. Reprinted by permission of John Daniel & Co., Santa Barbara, California. **Norman German**: "New World in the Morning" reprinted by permission of the author. © 1986 by Norman German. Originally appeared in *The Worcester Review*. **Chris Gilbert**: "Charge" from *Across the Mutual Landscape,* © 1984 by Christopher Gilbert (Graywolf Press). Reprinted by permission of the author. **Gary Gildner**: "Fingers" from *The Runner*, © 1978 by Gary Gildner (University of Pittsburgh Press). Reprinted by permission of the author. **Tony Gloeggler**: "One on One" © by Tony Gloeggler. Reprinted by permission of the author. Originally published in *Urbanus.* **Stephanie Grant**: "Posting-Up" © 1990 by Stephanie Grant. Reprinted by permission of the author. Originally published in *AGOG.* **Marie Henry**: "In the Room of My Dying Father" printed by permission of the author. © 1996 by Marie Henry. **David Hilton**: "The Poet Tries to Turn in His Jock" from *Huladance,* © 1976 by David Hilton (Crossing Press). Reprinted by permission of the author. **Edward Hirsch**: "Fast Break" from *Wild Gratitude*, © 1985 by Edward Hirsch. Reprinted by permission of Alfred A. Knopf, Inc. **Louis Jenkins**: "Basketball" from *An Almost Human Gesture*, © 1987 by Louis Jenkins (Eighties Press & Ally Press). Reprinted by permission of the author. **Yusef Komunyakaa**: "Slam, Dunk, & Hook" from *Magic City*, © 1992 by Yusef Komunyakaa. Reprinted by permission of Wesleyan University Press. **Bob Levin**: "Open Man" © 1976 by Bob Levin. Reprinted by permission of the author. Originally published in *Carolina Quarterly.* **Carl Lindner**: "The Only Game" from *Shooting Baskets in an Empty Gymnasium*, © 1983 by Carl Lindner (Linwood Publishers). Reprinted by permission of the author. **John McCluskey, Jr.**: "Top of the Game" © 1989 by John McCluskey Jr. Reprinted by permission of the author. Originally published in *Black American Literature Forum.* **William Matthews**: "In Memory of the Utah Stars" from